PIGGIES ON TI

Smita Jain is the author of the bestselling *Kkrishnaa's Konfessions*. She has scripted numerous screenplays for television and film.

Smita is also an avid mountaineer and long-distance runner. She lives in Mumbai with her husband.

PIGGIES ON THE RAILWAY

A Kasthuri Kumar Mystery

Smita Jain

TRANQUEBAR

westland ltd
Venkat Towers, 165, P. H. Road, Opp. Maduravoyal Municipal office, Chennai 600 095
No. 38/10 (New No. 5), Raghava Nagar, New Timber Yard Layout, Bangalore 560 026
Survey No. A-9, II Floor, Moula Ali Industrial Area, Moula Ali, Hyderabad 500 040
Plot No. 102, Marol Coop Ind Estate, Marol, Andheri East, Mumbai 400 059
47, Brij Mohan Road, Daryaganj, New Delhi 110 002

First published by westland ltd 2010

10 9 8 7 6 5 4 3 2 1

ISBN: 978-93-80283-74-6

Typeset in Adobe Jenson Pro by SÚRYA, New Delhi
Printed at Replika Press Pvt Ltd

This is a work of fiction. Names, characters, places and incidents are either the product of the author's imagination or are used fictitiously, and any resemblance to any actual persons, living or dead, events or locales is entirely coincidental.

Preface

〜≈〜

My name is Kasthuri Kumar and I am twenty-eight years old—or thereabouts anyway. For reasons that many Thirumalas, Tilotammas and Bisheshwaris will understand, I like to be addressed either by my surname or my self-shortened moniker, Katie.

Contrary to what my first name might suggest, my ancestry is north Indian. My parents were both sensible, middle-class bureaucrats, the choice of my name being their one rash act. When they were posted in Kerala, my mother had patronised a local eponymous artist and recklessly promised her that she would name her daughter after her. And she did.

I recently (voluntarily) resigned my commission from the Indian Police Service (IPS) following some (minor) medical problems. After my retirement I came to Bombay with a vague but strong desire to do something creative, exciting even. Not as in adrenaline-pumping-dodging-Maoists'-bullets exciting, but something stimulating. And if it involved a bit of fame and glamour, well, so much the better.

In Bombay, I camped out with my best friend, Marie Banerjee, while I figured out what to do with my life. It was Marie who inadvertently got me started on my present career. While I was shacked up with her, one of her uncles had some procedural problems renewing his arms licence. I, having wielded a weapon all my professional life, and having routinely dealt with such issues, was able to help him out.

Which gave Marie the idea that that's what I could do with my life—and incidentally put my experience in the police to good use—private detecting.

Now, that's not exactly what I had in mind, but it would have to do till I figured out what it was that I actually wanted to do. Actually, I think I wanted to be a famous doctor, or a scientist. Although it is probably too late for either, I still have fantasies about receiving the Nobel Prize. I'm not sure what the breakthrough discovery is, other than the hazy notion that it might be in the field of astrophysics. Perhaps some advanced work on string theory? What I *am* pretty sure about is that I'm wearing a shimmering red gown by Valentino with black Fendi peep toes.

Chapter One

❧❧

It was seven forty-five on the evening of 18 September 2009. It had been a slow day to begin with and I had no real hopes of the action picking up anytime soon. Still, I had to clock in the minutes till it was eight and a respectable enough time to shut shop. I picked up the current issue of *Femina* from the unholy mess that was my desk and flipped it open.

The magazine opened on the trends page, featuring dresses by prominent Indian designers. Some of them were truly appalling—for instance, one actually had a live bird perched on the model's left shoulder! Some were quite good though, particularly an aquamarine gown by Sabyasachi.

I turned to an article about alternate careers. A young author, someone who had three chicklit titles under her belt, was talking about writing as a viable career option. That got me thinking. I could be an author, couldn't I? I could write a best-seller based on my experiences as a police officer. Of course, the author was talking about writing chicklit; but fluff, while being hugely entertaining, was hardly going to win me a Booker now, was it?

Already I could see myself at the podium, receiving a Booker for my best-selling novel, *Salwa Judum*. I was in the aquamarine Sabyasachi number and had blonde highlights in my hair. The current red highlights would have to go. Red with aqua was such a fashion faux pas. Blonde was so much better. Perhaps purple?

And as I stood, with the trophy in my arms (or do they just hand you a cheque?), the awed I've-won-the-Miss-Universe-contest smile on my face, people in the audience gushed, 'Oh so talented. And beautiful too.'

I was savouring the feel of flashbulbs exploding in my face when he walked in. And boy, was he cute! He had a good six inches over my own five feet six inches and, I bet, under the crisp, white linen shirt and khaki chinos, his slender body was hard. Not six-pack abs hard, just fit. He had a smooth olive complexion, big brown eyes and an aquiline nose. His thick, straight black hair was neatly and expensively trimmed. He was well-heeled too. Literally. His elegant brown loafers looked like they cost more than my monthly rent. And I live in Bombay.

He looked taken aback to see me. 'Katie Kumar?' he asked uncertainly in a pleasantly resonant voice.

I wanted to say something witty, outrageous even. Marie had told me that if you treated the arrogant ones with disdain, they became your willing minions. I would never have believed it, if I hadn't, myself, seen her in action a number of times. Besides, he looked like he should be taken down a notch or two.

But, nothing clever came to mind. 'Yes,' I said breathlessly. Immediately a voice in my head perversely whispered, *Gee, I wonder if the nameplate gave it away?*, *No, I'm an alien impersonator. The real Katie Kumar has been abducted for reproductive experimentation.* Now why couldn't I have thought of either earlier? Oh well, I wouldn't have been able to pull it off anyway. The diva act only worked if it was accompanied with the natural conceit that is the exclusive domain of the beau monde.

My visitor smiled, revealing a perfect set of pearlies. The hand he extended was slender and slim-fingered. 'I'm Kaustav Kapoor.'

I stared at him. 'Kaustav Kapoor? As in Blazar Films?'

He laughed. 'The same.'

Intriguing. Why was the notoriously publicity-shy head honcho of India's premier movie production house and the scion of the first family of Bollywood here? Most people of his standing didn't come to a private detective's office. They either summoned the PIs to theirs, or contacted them through their lawyers.

I tore my eyes away from his yummylicious dimples and gathered myself together. 'What can I do for you?'

Apart from the obvious, sprang to mind. He smiled sardonically, like he could actually see the graphic images in my head. I blushed.

'I'm sorry. Please have a seat. What can I do for you?'

Apparently the only thing required of me was credulity, because he told me a story so absurd, no self-respecting PI—actually, make that just PI (I was ready to forgo my self-respect for him)—would believe it.

According to him, there had been a crisis on the sets of his latest production, *Ransom*, starring top-line actors Sameer Khan and Urvashi. The film unit had been shooting at an outdoor location near Mulshi, Pune. There had been trouble with this schedule right from the start: the locals regarded the forest as sacred, and felt it would be desecrated if the film unit shot there. They had threatened the unit and often disrupted proceedings with morchas and picketing, forcing the unit to retreat frequently to their hotel.

Finally *Ransom* was able to finish the schedule yesterday; the rest of the unit had left for Mumbai in the morning, but Urvashi had stayed back in the hotel as she had been shooting till late the night before and was catching up on her sleep. She'd woken up at around four in the afternoon, ordered room service and left for Mumbai shortly afterwards. Then somewhere along the way, she had disappeared. According to Kaustav, he last had a conversation with her just before she reached the Khandala exit on the Mumbai–

Pune Expressway. There had been no contact with her after that and she hadn't reached her home in Mumbai either. He had tried to call her repeatedly but her cellphone was switched off.

I nodded, pretending to listen carefully. In reality, my mind was elsewhere. Why had Kaustav *really* come to my office? This story about Urvashi missing was obviously too ridiculous to be true. Perhaps . . . perhaps all this was just an excuse to observe me at work! Study my surroundings, you know. He was really here because he wanted to cast me in a detective flick.

Omigod! I was going to be in a Blazar film. I was going to be on Page 3. I was going to be on the cover of *Filmfare* and *Stardust*. Journalists were going to write stories about my alleged affair with John Abraham. People were going to queue up for my autograph. I was going to be mobbed wherever I went. I was going to have my own personal trainer and make-up person. I would get to wear all those lovely clothes. And, best of all, all this was going to be paid for by someone else.

Of course, in my fantasies, when I'd seen my pictures in publications, it was as a celebrity in a different, more cerebral field. But hey, celebrity was celebrity. And I could always pretend to be one of those grave, well-read, thinking actors. Only in my case it would be true, too. Maybe I could invest in a pair of tortoise-shell-frame glasses with no power?

I silently cursed myself for not having put up a mirror in office—I had no idea what state my hair and face were in. Thank god I had on my new white fitted Tahliani blouse. Now the only thing I could do was present Kaustav with my best profile and dazzle him with my smile. Accordingly, I half-turned my face and beamed at him.

He frowned. 'Is something the matter?'

'Sorry?'

'You looked like . . . well, you were sort of grimacing.'

I blinked stupidly. 'Oh no, no. There was ... my jaw's been bothering me today,' I said, thinking furiously. Just to make good my point I tilted my head this way and that and wagged my chin a bit. *Oh, that's attractive*, I thought with an actual grimace.

'You were saying?' I said.

He leaned forward and his tone assumed urgency. 'Urvashi's disappeared. Without a trace. We checked the entire hotel. We even traced her route from Pune all the way to Mumbai. There was no sign of her. It's like she's vanished into thin air. One moment I was talking to her and the next moment she was gone. Just like that!' he said, snapping his fingers. I followed the movement of his perfectly manicured fingers, fascinated. To be honest, I've never met a guy who gets manicures.

I sighed, having gained some control over my wayward thoughts. 'Look Mr Kapoor ...'

'Please call me Kaustav.'

'Kaustav ...' I said and paused, trying to choose my words carefully.

'You don't believe me,' he stated flatly, with what I thought was an angry flare in his eyes. But when I looked again, it was gone. Maybe I had imagined it.

Urvashi was very conveniently the last one to depart for Bombay; her cellphone is conveniently switched off; and she very considerately vanishes on the last day of the schedule, *after* finishing the shoot— what was there not to believe? The only thing missing was the ransom note-slash-call.

'I don't know how to convince you.'

'The truth usually works.'

'The truth?' he repeated stupidly.

He stared at me. I stared back. Truth be told, I was a little offended. The business about casting me in a picture aside, if he thought he was dealing with a brainless twit, he had another thought coming. It was on the tip of my tongue to tell him about my excellent, eighty-per cent-plus-all-the-way academic record, just to underscore the fact.

He laughed suddenly. 'Oh I see. You think it is a publicity stunt?'

Actually, that hadn't occurred to me, but now that he'd mentioned it—'Can you blame me?'

'I suppose you're right. The film industry and even Blazar have pulled some outrageous stunts in the past,' he admitted. 'But I assure you, this is no stunt.'

I studied him, trying to make up my mind. The strain in his eyes seemed genuine enough. But that was no indicator. It is a known fact that the film fraternity, even those behind the scenes, are skilled liars. Not that I can say this with any authority, having had virtually no experience in dealing with them. Tejas Deshpande is the PI who handles the film industry.

Actually, calling Deshpande a PI is a misnomer. He has a high-end security business that caters to most of the film industry. Come to think of it, that is not all he does either. It is believed that he has a high-end realty business, a matka business, that he secretly owns the 621 bidi label and a television programming company. It is also rumoured that he is one of the big stock market operators dealing in penny stocks. Hell, he even writes for one of the papers. Maybe he owns it.

He has so many businesses going that it is rumoured god must have given him an extra arm just so he could put the extra fingers in as many pies. Not that you will ever read about him. Most of his businesses are strictly the fringes-of-the-law variety. Almost none of them are carried on in his name. But people who should, know him. They reverently call him by all kinds of names. The troubleshooter. The crisis manager. In my opinion, they tax their imaginations too much considering there are other, rather more fitting, plain vanilla labels available. Gangster and money launderer come readily to mind.

Our paths have crossed on more than a couple of occasions and each time he has been with some high flying lowlife. When he's not in the company of some glamorous girl, that is.

If his story were true, why hadn't Kaustav Kapoor gone to Tejas Deshpande? And that threw up another interesting question. How had Kaustav Kapoor, media mogul, learnt about li'l ol' me?

When I put the question across, Kaustav answered unhesitatingly, 'The yellow pages.'

Aha! So the investment had finally paid off. As asserted confidently by the pesky salesman three months ago when he tried to put the bite on me for a few extra rupees for a 3" x 3" box advertisement instead of the usual two-line listing. But I'd had more serious concerns than 'extra visibility' at that time. Like how I was going to pay my rent. And the utilities bills. But the persistent guy just wouldn't leave. Perhaps the export-surplus FCUK shirt-vest I had on at the time made him think I could afford it. In the end I bought the box advertisement just to get rid of him and prepared myself for a month of strict dieting. I could lose the extra cushioning on my backside anyway.

I hated to do it, but it had to be said. 'Mr . . . Kaustav, touched as I am by your faith in me, the police are better equipped to handle a case like this.' Already I could see greenbacks flying away.

'The police must not enter the picture!'

I was taken aback by the vehemence in his voice. Maybe it wasn't a publicity stunt after all. More disappointingly, maybe it wasn't about casting me.

'Ms Kumar . . .' he said, regaining his composure.

'Katie.'

'Katie,' he said, starting a flutter in the pit of my stomach, 'if the police find out, the media finds out. Do you know how much money I've sunk into the picture? How much borrowed money I've invested in *Ransom*? The moment they find out that the leading lady has disappeared, the creditors will be all over me.'

Wrong. They'd have to fight me first. Aloud I said, 'Was there any sign of foul play?'

He shook his head.

'Then perhaps she left on her own and doesn't want to be found?'

'No,' he said shaking his head decisively, 'we still have some patchwork left to do on the film and she knows that. She would never do anything to disrupt the schedule. She's a professional.'

Yeah, right. The producer, Pawan Somani, would certainly like to differ, I thought with a giggle. Just recently I'd read his gripe about how Urvashi's incessant tantrums on his set had set his schedule back by ten days.

But perhaps she behaved herself on Kaustav's sets. It was no secret that the two were an item. The media and the film fraternity had speculated about it at length even as Urvashi steadfastly toed the stoic 'we're just good friends' line. Kaustav hadn't bothered to dignify the allegations with any kind of response.

He had given Urvashi her first major break six years ago and after that she had rapidly ascended the A-star list. In the process, it was alleged, she'd climbed the rungs of the ladder to his heart as well. It was a typical Mills & Boon romance—he, the strong, silent hero, and she, the fragile flower—and many a girl must have fantasised about being in Urvashi's Jimmy Choos.

The only thing standing in the way of the fairy tale romance, like the evil stepmother, was Kaustav's wife, Vidisha. Well, if you cast Meg Ryan in the role of the evil stepmother. She was cute in a homely, girl-next-door kind of way. Really, what had made Kaustav marry Vidisha? It was evident to everybody that they were wrong for each other—he, ever stylish and elegant; she, a tomboy and a fashion flouter. Now if it were me . . . my mind at once conjured up an image of me walking the red carpet on Kaustav's arm at Cannes, draped in that stunning black Valentino gown I had seen in *Vogue* last month.

But it's not as if I had anything against Vidisha. In fact, public sympathy lay with her, the 'suffering wife', rather than Urvashi, who was hardly the shrinking violet. More like a Venus flytrap.

'Still,' I said, 'she could have got lost, had car trouble. She could've been forced to spend the night at some hotel. Maybe she decided to take a holiday. Anything's possible. It's only been two days!'

'But why is her cellphone switched off?'

'No network.'

He shook his head. 'Something's not right.'

'Have you got a reason to believe that?'

'It's just a feeling I have. A very strong feeling. Urvashi wouldn't just disappear like that. She would have tried to contact me . . . us. Look,' he said leaning forward, 'if it's a question of money, I'll make it worth your while.'

He reached into his pocket for his Mont Blanc and, pulling a notepad lying on the table close to him, scribbled on it a six-digit figure that made my head spin. Let's just say I could never hope to make that much in ten cases, not while shadowing errant spouses anyway. Finally, I'd be able to buy the MacBook Pro I'd been eyeing for a while. And give my wardrobe a makeover. And while I was at it, I'd also finally get rid of my cubby-hole of an apartment that put such a crimp in my lifestyle. Although it wasn't as much the apartment as my neighbours that I objected to. Already I could see myself lounging in a jacuzzi and sipping umbrella drinks. Well, maybe not a jacuzzi. Not that it was excessive—there just weren't that many flats in Mumbai with those kinds of fixtures. I bet his house had one, though.

When I came to, he was saying, 'Plus expenses, of course.'

'Kaustav,' I began.

'Isn't it enough?'

I frowned. Enough? Hell, he had me at the first four digits. And I was sure he knew that. Why then the anxiety? Still, it was no skin off my nose.

'If you'll give me an advance I'll start right away,' I said.

He took out a cheque book.

'Are you going to pay by cheque?'

'Why, is there a problem?'

'It's just that it will take three days to clear. Make that five—it's a weekend starting tomorrow. Do you really want to wait until Wednesday?'

'No, but . . . couldn't you start anyway?'

He was cute, so I considered it for precisely two seconds. 'I'm sorry. Company policy.'

'But it's only you!'

'Yes, but it's still a company. Katie Kumar Investigations. I'm in the process of setting up a board and going public,' I said.

My attempt at levity went unappreciated. Instead, he looked openly irritated. 'But my cheque is good! You can take my word on that.'

'Tell you what, it's late now anyway. I don't see what I could accomplish by starting now. Why don't we just start tomorrow, *after* I've collected my contract and *cash* advance?' I said, soothingly.

'Fine then,' he said a bit huffily. 'Eleven tomorrow? In my office?'

I nodded. 'Eleven.'

I followed him to the door. After the monetary courtesy he had shown me, the least I could do was see him off. Plus I wanted to see that firm tushy once more, up close.

At the doorway we shook hands and I practically orgasmed at the touch of his hand on mine. He must have sensed it, because he hastily pried his hand loose and left. I stood there for a while, trying to analyse my emotions. For god's sake, not only was he married, he was having an affair. With Urvashi, no less. Then I chided myself for chiding myself. I was free, right? If I wanted to make a fool of myself over a man I was free to do that, right? So where was the problem?

Moreover, he was probably used to creating such an impact. In fact, he would have been surprised, if not outright disappointed, if he had not got such a reaction. Having convinced myself that my 'involuntary' reaction was indeed based on good business sense (I hadn't entirely given up the theory that he wanted to cast me) and therefore 'studied', I spent a couple of minutes practising my smiles.

I was about to go back in when I noticed the lights were still on in Zara's office. So the phoney psychic was working late, no doubt putting the bite on some poor bereaved soul. On a whim I decided to drop in. I was too elated to be by myself anyway; I wanted to share the good news with someone. And the old lush was as good as anybody.

I peeped in cautiously, expecting to find Zara's major domo (or given her ultra-petite size, minor domo), Rajeshwari, holding the fort while the former conducted her 'session'. I was surprised to find Zara alone.

Zara, real name Inderjit Kaur, is big on appearances. And I'm not talking about her five-feet-eight, hundred-and-fifty-kilo frame. She takes being a psychic seriously. She is always dressed in flowing caftans and turbans. And as if that wasn't enough to indicate her ghostly connections, she lavishly slathers her face with white powder and paints sinister kohl lines under her eyes.

'Guess what,' I said.

She looked up and said in feverish tones, 'Just the person I wanted to see! Come in, come in. I have something major to tell you. I had a vision about you.'

I sauntered in and parked my behind on a chair. 'It wouldn't have anything to do with a movie producer, would it?' I said, straight-faced.

I have a healthy suspicion of Zara's psychic abilities. Shirley Bose, she's not. For example, just today Shirley had written in the *Mid-Day*: Career is going great and prestigious contracts fall into your lap. And she wrote this as a generalised Aries forecast. *And she wrote it in the morning.*

Zara's jaw dropped. Then she pursed her lips which made the fine lines on her upper lip deepen. 'I didn't already tell you this morning, did I?' she asked suspiciously.

'How could you, when he arrived only just now?'

She scowled and her eyes narrowed. Her generous bosom quivered with pent-up emotion and she looked ready to explode. 'Are you calling me a fraud? Again. Let me tell you, *again*, I don't need to do that! I work with spirits,' she replied indignantly.

That, indeed, she had gotten right.

'Just kidding! Tell me, what else did your vision tell you?' I said in a mollifying tone. No point in upsetting her. For one, she is an incorrigible snoop and gossip and two, her network of informants is enviable. Plus she takes my messages and couriers in my absence. All in all, she was a very useful neighbour to have, as long as you kept an eye on her.

'Reveal. Visions reveal, not tell.' She got a sly look in her eyes. 'You wouldn't still happen to have that fine whisky?'

As if she didn't know. She had probably rifled through my office that very morning. I considered whether to waste my expensive bourbon on her. What the hell, I thought, I would probably be able to afford it on a regular basis from now on.

I went back into my office and opened the filing cabinet. I dug behind a heap of files and retrieved my half-empty bottle of Jack Daniels. I hide it there to keep it safe from free-loading policemen, municipal inspectors and others of that ilk, all looking to mooch off me in return for turning a blind eye to some transgression.

I took the whisky and two glasses back to Zara's office. After I had poured two generous measures and Zara had taken a huge gulp, she told me conversationally, 'You know, that DCP came in today.'

'Chodu? What did he want now?' I asked grouchily. Chodu, or Rajesh Chodankar as he was christened, is the divisional head of zone nine of Greater Mumbai.

'Nothing from you. He came in for a reading. But he did say something about some Sinha case. He said he'd be back,' the old sponge answered absently, draining her glass and training her gaze hungrily upon the bottle.

Just as I suspected. The case was long closed. Of course, there was still the trifling matter of my breaking and entering the accused, Akash Sinha's, pad to look for evidence of embezzlement. Chodankar had agreed to look the other way at that time but I had no doubt that he would collect, sooner or later. It was sooner was all. I swirled the golden liquid in my glass.

Zara's eyes followed the sloshing movement. 'About the vision,' she began, looking troubled.

'Hmmm?'

'It also revealed that there's great danger ahead.'

'No kidding,' I said with a lopsided smile.

'Wait, I haven't finished. I saw a place . . . it was all green . . . you were alone there. Suddenly someone grabbed you from behind.'

'Hmmm,' I muttered noncommittally. It wasn't the first time she had pronounced doom in my future, and it wouldn't be the last.

I finished the contents of my glass in one gulp and got up.

'Leaving? So soon?' Zara asked, disappointed. 'At least have another drink,' she cajoled.

'No can do. Here,' I added as an afterthought, pushing the bottle towards her, 'you keep the bottle.'

'In that case, go,' Zara said, grabbing the bottle greedily. 'At your age you need your beauty sleep. You look old when you haven't slept.'

I subjected her to my narrow-eyed, Damien look and left.

Chapter Two

꘏꘎

I grabbed my laptop, locked my office and made for the stairway. It was very dark in the stairwell, and the rickety stairs groaned in protest under my weight as I gingerly made my way down. I made a fresh mental note to look for alternate office space. We may have succeeded in buying (literally) time from the municipal corporator—ours is a condemned chawl—but I doubted our money would hold much weight with gravity. Not when pitted against the weight of the sagging chawl.

Gravity obliged that night and I emerged unscathed from the decrepit building. The road in front of my office leads to Andheri station and is normally a traffic nightmare at most times. But at this late hour, even the busy road was practically deserted save the usual suspects—drug addicts-slash-pushers and whores plying their trade. They ignored me and I ignored them. That is how it usually worked unless they wanted something from me (money), or I of them (information).

I walked to my bike parked a short distance away. I ride a 1991 Royal Enfield, a.k.a. the Bullet, in part because I got it as legacy, and in part because I can't afford a car. A little ahead on the pavement, I heard voices—a deep male voice and a thinner soprano—raised in heated argument. Recognising the latter, I quickened my step.

'Yoo hoo! Katie!' my transvestite friend, Sanjay, called out. Sanjay is of medium height and slender, with legs and a butt that any woman would kill for. He is also blessed with a smooth complexion and beautiful, large doe eyes. Tonight he was wearing a fitted dress and matching shoes so high they made my calves cramp just looking at them. And I, in three-inch heels, was no slouch. The ensemble looked vaguely familiar. Now where had I seen it? Of course! I started in surprise. The Promod store display window at the Atria Mall. Now how did he afford that? You see, Sanjay hopes to make a career for himself in Bollywood. As an actress. So far he hasn't had any luck—all the offers he gets are to play a chhakka or a drag dancer, which Sanjay refuses to do. Meanwhile, to supplement his income and gather enough money for a sex change operation, he services homosexuals.

So, how did he . . .? Unless . . . I looked closely. Yup, it was a knock-off. A good one, but a copy nevertheless.

'Omigod! Sanj, where did you get this killer outfit?'

He pirouetted. 'Eat your heart out.'

'I swear, if you don't tell me right now!'

He waved his hand effeminately. 'Okay, okay, baba, I'll tell you. You know that little gali next to Mac-Doe-naald on Linking Road. You take that gali and walk all the way down. Just before it meets S.V. Road, there's another gali going left. You take that and just a few feet ahead there's this shop, Funky Town.'

While Sanj prattled on about the designer rip-offs available at Funky Town, I peered in the dark to see who he had been arguing with. My eyes adjusted to the dark and I saw it was none other than the recently talked about Chodu, leaning against his jeep.

DCP Rajesh Chodankar is also of medium height but thickset, with a complexion and eyes the colour of dark chocolate. He has thick wavy hair and a neatly cropped moustache. Other than that his face is nothing to write home about, unless it is to say that he can look menacing with frightening ease.

In a twisted way, my relationship with Chodu is the only truly working one in my life, based as it is on mutual dislike bordering on hostility. Our relationship works because we know either can't wish the other away and therefore we have to make it work. Cross that. I know I can't wish him away. He can probably trump up some charges against me and have me locked up in some smelly and overcrowded dungeon where my youth will wither away under the combined and unremitting assault of a high carb diet, khatmals and harsh prison soap. So, yet again, I find myself giving more in a relationship.

'Well, well, if it isn't our dear friend Chodankar!' I drawled, walking closer. 'Don't you guys ever pay for anything?'

'Jealous?' Chodu responded.

That was probably true. I changed the subject. 'At least extract your freebies later, na. Not when Sanjay is on the clock.'

'Sanjana!' my friend corrected me, sulkily. Then, before Chodu could reply, added, 'Who was that in your office just now?'

'Kaustav Kapoor,' I replied absently and could've bitten my tongue the very next moment.

'Kaustav Kapoor? As in Blazar's Kaustav Kapoor? Really?' Sanj said excitedly. And then, 'What did he want with you?' I was thinking of a suitably cutting reply when he said, 'Ae, introduce me to him, na.'

'Is it true?' Chodu asked, pulling out a pack of cigarettes from his pocket and proffering it to me.

I shook my head. An eyebrow rose quizzically.

'I'm trying to quit.'

'Good luck with that,' he shrugged and extracted one for himself.

I presented him with my suffering-from-withdrawal-symptoms-bitch Gollum look.

As Chodu was lighting the ciggie, Sanj moved to snatch it from his mouth. 'It's disgusting! Kissing a smoker is like licking an ashtray.'

Chodu easily swatted his hand away. 'You'll lick the ashtray and like it.'

'Ae Katty,' Sanj complained, 'tell him, na.'

Ignoring him, I said, 'Zara mentioned you dropped by.'

He took a drag on his cigarette and looked into the distance vacantly. God, I hated when he did that, putting on an impassive face and forcing me to go into a conversation blind.

'Something about Akash Sinha?' I prompted.

He waved his hand dismissively. Then he playfully swatted Sanj's bottom and told him to bugger off for a while.

After Sanj left he asked, 'Why didn't Kaustav Kapoor call you to his office?'

I shrugged. 'You'll have to ask him.'

'I will. It won't, by any chance, have anything to do with Urvashi's disappearance?'

I could write reams of pages on the thoughts that ran through my mind. *How did he know? Has Kaustav told the police?* popped up surreally in front of my eyes like dialogue boxes in comic strips. But I also knew there was no point denying it. 'You know I can't tell you that.'

'You don't have to. Word travels. It's just that . . .' he paused.

'What?'

'It didn't look fishy to you that they are shooting a film called *Ransom* and Urvashi conveniently disappears?'

Of course it did, but Kaustav's greens persuaded me otherwise. 'Are you saying it is a publicity stunt?'

'If you want to earn some easy money, who am I to stop you?'

Who indeed? After all, it meant that much more he could mooch off me.

He got into his jeep and hollered for Sanj. After they'd left, I wasted no time in calling Marie.

'Em, guess who I just met?' I trilled excitedly into the phone. 'Kaustav Kapoor!'

'Non!' Em yelled. Em speaks with a strange fake French-Bengali accent that's calculated to drive men crazy. Hell, it drives me crazy too—but only because I find it irritating. I was in too good a mood to object, though.

'Yes!'

'Where? 'ow?'

'He came to my office.'

'Your offeece!' she gasped. 'What did 'e want weez you? Oh I know, 'e wants to cast you een a moobhie! Oh Kay, you're going to be een a Blezer film!'

'Hey!'

'Mon dieu! You're going to be a faamoos movie stir! You snik! Why deedn't you tell me you'd got your portfolio daan? What're you weareeng? Please taill me, eet eesn't that shapeless, darty grey tee shirt you like so much.'

'Em!' I practically yelled into the phone. 'Calm down. It's nothing of the sort.'

I regretted calling her now. What could I possibly say about why I'd met Kaustav Kapoor?

'He just wanted a routine background check done on someone he's planning on doing business with.'

Silence. Then, 'You're sheetteeng me, right? Eet wouldn't 'aiv anything to do weez Urboshi's deesappearance, would eet?'

Was there anyone who didn't know?

"Cos eef eet ees, you can forget about eet. She's een re'ab. Urboshi's suppliar mentioned to a client of a client of mine zat 'e 'adn't 'eard from 'er after ze long outdoor.'

We'd gossiped about this any number of times so the fact that Urvashi did drugs wasn't a shocker. 'And that's strange?'

'Duh! She mast've been running low after ze long sched, right? So 'e figured eef she 'asn't called 'im she must 'ave checked into re'ab.'

'Or. Or she could have gotten another supplier.'

'You don't do zat.'

'Why? It's a relationship sealed with a blood oath, and the penalty for breaking it is punishable by death?'

'Probably,' she giggled. 'A client–supplier relationsheep een thees business ees as sacred as a cosmetique surgeon–patient relationsheep. And you would not want to peess off your cosmetique surgeon, would you?'

I would not. Could it be that Urvashi was in rehab and an elaborate tale was being spun around her disappearance to deflect the attention from the real story?

'Taill me, does 'e look just as dreamy in real life?' she asked excitedly.

I sighed. 'Better.'

'Oooh,' she squealed. 'You are so laakee! When do you beegeen?'

'Well, I'm going to his office tomorrow at eleven . . .'

'No, no, no,' she screeched, in a perfect Indian accent. Usually she has to be bullied into dropping her pseudo accent, but sometimes, when she's excited or agitated, it slips on its own. 'Not eleven! We have an appointment at the beauty parlour tomorrow at ten.'

I groaned. 'I'd forgotten about that. What am I going to do?'

'You must postpone Kaustav's appointment.'

'Or I could just cancel Rosie's,' I suggested half-heartedly.

'You can't! You're going to meet Kaustav Kapoor!' She made it sound like he was . . . well, Kaustav Kapoor.

'So? It's not as though I'm going for an audition.'

'Steel, eet can't 'urt to look your best,' she pointed out defensively.

'You're hoping I'll be "discovered"!' I said with a laugh. 'Discovered in air quotes by the way.'

'"Ood zat be so bad?' she said defensively.

'No. Just nuts.' But reassuring nonetheless, to know that it wasn't just me who was immediately gripped with wild fantasies the moment I had the briefest encounter with a big ticket movie producer. 'Oh shit! In any case I can't make it to Rosie's at ten. Ani is coming to pick up his stuff at ten.'

'Aani? Aaniruddh? Your ex-boyfriend Aaniruddh? Aaniruddh Nair? Liar Nair?' Em fired out in staccato. 'Oh 'aaney! 'ow could you? Sweety, that's just break-aap sex waiting to happen.'

She was wrong. It already did. Twice. 'You're way off, Em. He's just coming to pick up his stuff.'

"Allooo! Ze two of you? Alone togezaar? Surrounded by all those romantique memories? Memories of deeleecious laavemaking? Break-aap sex! Break-aap sex!'

'Fine, I'll ask him to meet me somewhere else.'

'Good zinking. And figaar out about Rosie's.'

'I will.'

I kick-started my RE, already performing furious scheduling acrobatics in my head. If I got Ani to advance his nine o'clock appointment by an hour, he could, in turn, advance our meeting by an hour. And then if I were to postpone Kaustav's meeting by an hour, I could comfortably do Rosie's. Of course, my determination to keep Rosie's appointment had nothing to do with Kaustav Kapoor. It made good business sense to look presentable, was all. Didn't they say good-looking people were twice as likely to get promoted than ugly people?

My apartment building is like any other cooperative housing society in Mumbai. It's bang on the road with a little patch of overgrown weeds in the front that passes for a garden; it's rundown with the paint peeling in most places; it's uncomfortably close to the next one; and it comes with the added bonus of flooding in the monsoon. The society is inhabited predominantly by Gujaratis and even so much as cracking open an egg is grounds for eviction. But the rent is reasonable (for Mumbai) and, more importantly, I have a twenty-two month lease.

Shyam, the watchman, was missing from his post as usual, no doubt having a quick romp with Parvati, his latest girlfriend. He did that a lot, with a variety of girlfriends, but no one really minded because he always thoughtfully left the gates open so that the residents didn't have to stop and get out of their cars to do so.

I parked my bike and, dispensing with the elevator, decided to walk up the paan-stained stairwell to my fourth floor apartment. My weight issue was still preoccupying me. Of course, that didn't have anything to do with Kaustav either. It was just that now was as good a time as any to get started on Mission Buns-of-Steel.

As I approached the last flight of stairs leading up to my apartment, I slowed down. The door to my apartment was open. Ever so slightly, but it was ajar. My first instinct was to reach into my bag for my .38 Webley Scott. But then I realised the gun was in my apartment. I didn't carry it around anymore. In fact, I hadn't carried it since my days on active duty in Chhattisgarh. I wasn't a police officer in a Naxalite-infested region anymore. An incident had taken care of my career there. A situation had arisen which had triggered off a, let's say, rather 'disproportionate' response from me. Boy, you should have seen the higher-ups go ballistic. Undue use of force, like using a sledgehammer to squash a bug and conduct unseemly of a police officer were the terms, I believe, used to describe my actions. And they called *my* response excessive!

In their appraisal, they emphasised that they understood that pressures of serving in a constantly hostile environment led to the lapse in judgement. Nevertheless, they suspended me from active duty and recommended several hours of counselling post which, depending on the doctor's evaluation, they would reconsider their decision to reinstate me. I signed up for counselling but didn't wait for the board's verdict, electing to voluntarily resign instead.

Now I was just a small-time detective handling divorce work and the occasional theft and embezzlement. Nobody wanted to kill a crummy PI like me. Even the guys who lost out as a result of my investigations usually ended up feeling sorry for me, which was fortuitous since my license for the .38 prohibited bore hadn't been renewed.

Still, someone wanted me now. And it wasn't Jamila, my ditzy teenaged maid, because she had, just two days ago, rather inconsiderately upped and left for her village to get married. I looked around for a suitable weapon. There was an old tray table in the corner of the stairwell. I picked it up and advanced. I gave the door a cautionary poke. It swung open and an eerie greenish light filtered through and lit the floor at my feet. I tightened my grip on the tray table, kicked the door open with my foot and charged inside, weapon raised. I only had a split second to notice the presence of an alien lamp on my side table before someone grabbed me from behind.

'Caught 'cha!'

Ani!

I went still with shock. The tray table dropped on the floor with a clatter. Taking advantage of my immobility, Ani nuzzled my neck.

My heart still hammering, I struggled to break free.

'Ani!' I gasped. 'What are you doing here? And what's with the lamp and the ghoulish light?'

'Like it? I just picked it up. The light is supposed to be relaxing.'

'It had better be, after the heart attack you just gave me.'

'If that's what responsible for your beautiful heaving breasts, it's worth it,' he drawled, holding me firmly.

All that nuzzling was sending tingles up my spine and I sagged against him. 'What are you doing here?'

'I came to pick up my stuff, remember?' Yeah? More like pick up the pieces, if you know what I mean. I knew I should have resisted but it felt so good. Ani's hands had worked their way up to my breasts where his fingers were doing delicious stuff to my nipples. He turned me around and kissed me full on the lips.

Through all this another thought worked its way up in my brain. I don't know how she'd done it, but Zara was right. The apartment was bathed in green, Ani did grab me from behind and I was in real danger. Of falling back on old habits.

His lips were looking to fix on mine and I turned my head away. But, I knew I was weakening. He certainly did. I couldn't understand it. I couldn't understand this insane sexual attraction to a man who had lied to me. I told myself that I hadn't had much sex in the last few days. Or maybe it was unfulfilled desire for Kaustav. Or maybe it was just my hormones. I was approaching that time of the month. These were the same excuses I'd used the last two times.

'You were supposed to come tomorrow,' I said by way of a token protest.

'I felt like coming today,' he said, reclaiming my lips.

I gave in. I'd break up with him tomorrow. Again.

Chapter Three

The next morning, a couple of things happened as a result of which I was about half an hour late in reaching Rosie's. First, Ani jumped me in the shower and we ended up making love again. And then I couldn't decide what to wear. I dithered endlessly between a shirt dress and a slim skirt-and-blouse combo, finally abandoning both as being too wannabe.

But, I did also ditch my usual attire of jeans and a tee in favour of a fitted shirt and tailored pants that Em claimed (and I agreed) made my butt look smaller. I, rather gleefully, accessorised the outfit with a pair of stilettos. I don't usually get to wear stilettos because I'm on par with most Indian men without them. And let's face it, high heels are hardly expedient in my profession. Though that hasn't stopped me from fantasising about kicking some bad ass shod in six-inch stilettos à la Charlie's Angels. Of course, in those fantasies I'm also wearing a leather bustier and hot pants. Which just goes to show how impractical the whole thing is—everyone knows how inappropriate leather is for the hot Indian climate.

Em was waiting for me outside Rosie's, and as soon as she saw me, all of her petite five-feet-two-plus-five-inch-heels frame puffed up with indignation. Em is the happy result of a French-Bengali interracial union. As the progeny of such potent cocktails are wont to be, she is beautiful. She has a flawless golden complexion and currently sports a glossy bob. Her cheekbones are impossibly high and enhance her already slanting jade green eyes. She also has a wonderfully delicate bone structure and a small straight nose. In fact, she looks so exotic that you want to drape her in a sarong and put her on a Tahitian beach.

She was looking amazing in a breathtakingly beautiful shift dress that made me turn green. And it wasn't a reflection of the fresh pistachio shade of her dress either. Never, in a million years, would I be able to carry off that dress with my square-shouldered frame.

'You're late!' she accused, her translucent skin already a little flushed from the September sun.

'I . . . um . . . I woke up late,' I hedged guiltily as I parked the RE and removed my helmet.

She gasped. 'You've 'ad sex!'

'I haven't!' I lied.

'Don't lie to me, Katie! I know an aftar-sex glow when I see un!'

And she should. In her business she must see plenty of it. She manages a classy Madame Kitty type of saloon, Ego. Although, as she never tires of telling me, 'It's a nightclub.' *Yeah, whatever.*

Murmuring soothingly, I linked my arm through hers and we went in. Rosie was putting finishing touches on a woman and signalled us to wait.

As the many 'cover-girl' pictures of her adorning the salon walls reminded her visitors, in her heyday Rosie used to be a model. She's now fifty-something, with a bird's nest hairdo that looks rigid enough to stop a bullet.

We settled down and picked up reading material. Em picked up a glossy while I went for *Mid-Day*, opening it to the horoscopes page. Shirley wrote: Determination, independence and going your way will prove fruitful. A temporary trip out of town is on the cards. A gift at the beginning of the day marks the beginning of the cycle of receiving. Be careful of people whose interests are contradictory to yours.

Well, she was right about the gift at the beginning of the day. God, she was the best.

'I zought you agreed that meeting Ani at your aapartment was a bad idea,' Em said.

'I did!' Which was true.

'Zen why deed you let 'eem caam over zees morning?'

'I didn't!' Also true.

'Okay, so 'e came over on 'ees own. And why wouldn't he if you keep 'aving sex weez 'eem?'

'I didn't!' Which wasn't.

Em grimaced. 'At least ze one good zeeng ees that you can save some time. Weez a glow like that 'oo needs a facial?'

Rosie, who had finished with the client, materialised in front of us. She, unfortunately, heard the last part and indignantly faced us, arms akimbo. 'Marie Banerjee, are you trying to ruin my business?' Next, she peered at me over her bifocals perched precariously on the tip of her nose and said, 'Katie Kumar! Have you had sex?'

Customers started turning around to look at me.

'That's right! Go on, say it louder,' I hissed, burying my face in the magazine.

'Are you back wid dat scum of a boyfriend of yours, dhikra?'

'Mais oui, she ees!'

'I'm not!' I said hotly. 'And would you drop that irritating accent already?'

"Ow . . . how do you keep falling for his lies time and time again? What did he say this time? "You're the one"? "I love you"? "I just need some time"?'

He had, in fact, said all those things. And yes, they were all probably lies. But I'd had enough. I know Em meant well, but right now I needed her to be my friend, not my critic. I flung down the newspaper in a fine show of temper. 'Would you both stop it? I haven't had sex with Ani! And even if I have, so what? It's not like I can pick and choose. I take it where I can!'

Shit! That sounded pathetic. Desperate even.

Em stared at me. 'So deed you?'

I gave up and allowed myself to be subjected to Rosie's attentions. Rosie had received a limited number of trial kits for a new miracle facial that had recently been developed by Luminous Cosmetics and she was itching to try them out.

'It combines de anti-ageing and de whiteness formula and for you two, it's free. Are you interested?'

Was she kidding? It was touted to miraculously take ten years off your face. And it was free. Of course we were interested.

'But not today. I don't have the time for anything else besides hair and a bit of make-up,' I said as Rosie loosened my braid and prepared to wash and blow dry my hair.

I genuinely believe that my wavy, waist-length hair is my best feature, and I usually wear it in a French plait when I'm working. It makes me feel like Lara Croft. Kind of. It's a different matter that by the end of the day several tendrils have escaped from the plait in an unruly mess, giving me the appearance of Medusa. Which was how Kaustav probably saw me last night. Eeeks!

An hour and a half later, I confidently strode out of Rosie's, secure in the knowledge that I looked my best, my hair cascading down my back, a gleaming red-black keratinous waterfall, just like in romance novels. Just goes to show there's nothing quite like a good hair job to elevate your mood.

Since I wasn't about to spoil my new hairdo and subtle, professionally applied make-up under a helmet, I ditched the bike and hailed a taxi. A twenty-minute ride later, at the dot of twelve, the taxi deposited me outside Blazar. There are two gates leading into the Blazar Films' compound: gate one leads to the shooting floors and gate two opens into the driveway that leads to the corporate office. It was at gate two that I had my cab drop me. As instructed by Kaustav when I called him to postpone the appointment, I had telephoned five minutes before I reached.

As soon as the taxi turned into the road, I understood the need for calling in advance. Media thronged the hallowed gates, clamouring to be let in. Probably a routine occurrence, I thought at first, trying to cut my way through the crowd; but above the chaotic din I made out stray comments indicating that Urvashi's disappearance was now fairly well known.

I had not quite reached the gates and was wondering how I was supposed to get in when the small side-gate used by walk-in visitors opened and out came a slender young woman of medium height. *Straight from a designer office-wear photo-shoot for* Vogue, I thought in admiration and envy. She was dressed in an expertly cut skirt-blouse affair. Her lustrous hair, pulled back in a severe bun, only accentuated her impossibly high cheekbones. She wasn't conventionally beautiful, but she was certainly striking. Now who did she remind me of? Uma Thurman in *Gattaca?* Not quite, but the parallel was apt for the moment.

As soon as they saw her, the media were upon her like a pack of wild dogs. 'Is it true about Urvashi?' 'Has she really disappeared?' 'What happens to *Ransom?*' 'Is the shoot complete?'

'Please remain calm. Blazar Films will issue a statement soon,' Uma Thurman said. Immediately more questions were fired at her. Ignoring them, she scanned the crowd, her trained eye immediately spotting the one non-journalist. 'Ms Kumar?' she shouted. In response to my nod, she said, 'Come with me please.'

I pushed my way through and joined her in the driveway, aware of and thrilled with the resentful glares that I was sure were being directed at my back.

I noticed a beautifully landscaped lawn across the driveway. Beyond the lawn was another huge building, which I assumed housed the shooting floors. I'd heard gaining admission into any of those floors without an entrance pass was supposedly next to impossible. Well, so it was for a size six woman to squeeze into size four pants. And yet, I was in one, wasn't I?

'Phew!' I said, once the gates had shut firmly behind me. Although spruced up, I still felt positively dowdy next to the twiggy young woman. Not to mention gripped by a fierce determination to never eat again.

No sooner had I entered, Uma Thurman turned on her Manolo Blahniks and started striding ahead, her slim behind swaying with practiced seductiveness. 'Follow me please. I'm Neena Pundir, by the way. EA to Kaustav.'

'Nice to meet you,' I said, running a little to keep up with her. 'Quite a crowd out there.'

She grimaced.

'Is it usually like this?' I asked, a little breathless from the struggle to keep up with her.

'Like what? A pack of wolves?' She nodded. 'But they snap and snarl only when they smell a story,' she added, without breaking her trot.

Just then, gate one opened and admitted a black Porsche Cayenne. The car pulled to a stop in front of the studio building and out stepped Sameer Khan. *I had to get over there!*

Neena said something which I didn't quite catch. 'I'm sorry, what?'

Neena waved her nicely manicured hand. 'I said, in spite of our best efforts to keep it under wraps, they smell a story.'

'Uh-uh.' Maybe after my meeting I could sneak over to the studio side.

'But don't worry, Kaustav has everything under control,' she said confidently. It didn't look that way to me but I supposed he must know what he was doing.

'It's just that it's so irksome having to deal with this. As if Kaustav doesn't have enough to do,' she said as we walked past the reception area towards the staircase.

Uh-oh, so that's the way the wind blew! I've seen it before—when the secretary gets all proprietary about her boss it usually means she's sweet on him. The question was, was the . . . affection . . . returned? Or unrequited?

'Imagine, just taking off like that! And leaving Kaustav to deal with it!' she said on the stairway.

'You mean you think she took off on her own?'

'You don't?'

'Kaustav is convinced something bad has happened to her.'

'Oh,' she said, pausing on the staircase for a brief moment. 'Then that's what must have happened,' she said starting up once again. After a few seconds, she continued, 'Still, I don't see why he had to hire a private dick.' She made it sound like he had hired a sweeper to do an engineer's job! I bristled at the implied insult in her voice.

We reached the first floor and started down a long passage. Neena's heels click-clicked assuredly on the highly polished floor while mine clattered raucously as I attempted to stop myself from slithering all the way to Kaustav's office. Damn, I had to get more practice wearing stilts.

'But you're not convinced?' I pressed.

'Let's just say it's not the first time she's pulled a stunt like this. Forget I said anything.'

That's what people usually say when they don't want something forgotten. I filed it away in my mind for future reference.

The corridor led into a square sitting area. There was a door at the far end which read Kaustav Kapoor, MD. Neena indicated an overstuffed sofa and asked me to wait. 'Kaustav will be with you in a moment. He's just wrapping up something else.'

Neena disappeared into Kaustav's office and I sat down and idly picked up a glossy from the coffee table. Hrithik Roshan's bare-chested photograph graced the cover. In one corner was a smaller inset of a two-bit star, Desiree, along with a suitably salacious quote—'I do not have a drug problem.' Which, of course, meant that she did.

I took a moment to admire the sculpted, oiled torso and then flipped open the rag. I skimmed through Desiree's interview, where she denied that she had a cocaine habit, and settled on another story about an alleged tiff between Kaustav Kapoor and Sameer Khan over a contract.

According to the story, Sameer Khan had an offer to act in a Hollywood film. It was a lucrative offer and his ticket to international stardom. But he was bound to Blazar Films for their next two films and Kaustav Kapoor refused to release him from the contract. Kapoor felt that Blazar had identified Khan when he was a nobody and had invested huge amounts of money in him. And now that he was a star, it was only fair that Blazar reap the harvest. Meanwhile, Khan's window of opportunity was fast closing as the Hollywood film was scheduled to go on the floors by mid-October so it could be completed in time for a summer release in the US.

Both Khan and Kaustav had refused to comment, so in lieu of their versions of the story, the journalist had gone on to talk about Kaustav's alleged megalomania and hard-nosed business practices. She'd gathered quotes from various industry people who, on condition of anonymity, called him a 'poor loser' and someone 'in love with his own reputation as a star-maker'. One wise ass had even said, 'He pays a good day's wage . . . after he has extracted a week's work.'

I glanced up. Standing in Kaustav's open doorway was a veritable galaxy of stars: Shah Rukh Khan, Saif Ali Khan, Abhishek Bachchan, Katrina Kaif, Kareena Kapoor and Priyanka Chopra! I couldn't believe it! I instinctively knew I had stumbled upon the closely-guarded cast list for Blazar Films' next venture, also being kept a secret.

I found myself wondering what it would be like to be a famous actor. (And if my instinct about the real reason for Kaustav's visit to my office last night was right, it could happen! I could be one of the stars in Blazar's hallway, nattering with SRK about the party at Mannat last night while a star-struck somebody gawked at us, much like I was gawking at them.) I imagined spending my winters in St. Moritz, skiing and sipping Napoleon brandy just like in the song, *Where do you go to my lovely*. I was dressed in Prada breeches and boots, riding the Arabian horse the Aga Khan had sent me for Christmas when the magazine slipped from my suddenly lifeless fingers and dropped onto the floor with a loud snap. The sound alerted the celestial group in the doorway who all turned and looked at me. I hastily hinged my jaw shut, hoping they hadn't seen the vacuous, adoring expression on my face.

They spared me a scornful glance and went back to their polite chit-chat. Pretending that I hadn't been caught staring at them, and that I wasn't now blushing a deep red, I casually bent down and picked up the magazine, but not before I caught the expressions on Kaustav's and Neena's faces (impatient and sneering, respectively).

I buried my burning face behind the magazine, wishing I could bury the rest of me as well. I didn't dare look up until I heard soft muah-muahs and the click-click of departing heels. Even so I gave it a moment, just to be sure.

Only when Kaustav called out, 'Katie?' did I shut the magazine and look up. Out of the corner of my eye, I saw Neena walking away with the stars. I shifted my gaze to Kaustav. God, he looked good. My heart beat faster. I ran my fingers through my hair, fixed a smile on my face and stood up.

He was waiting for me at the doorway, all traces of his earlier impatience gone. 'Sorry to keep you waiting,' he said, with an apologetic smile.

Looking at his dazzling white teeth, I was instantly reminded of Ross in *Friends*, when he has that unfortunate dental treatment that makes his teeth glow eerily in the dark. I wondered if the same had happened to Kaustav. And were those brownish-orangeish glints in his hair? I found it a bit weird. For some reason, the thought of a man spending so much effort on his appearance bothered me.

I was at once irritated with myself. What's wrong with a man spending some time on looking good? Especially in this looks-obsessed industry? And even more especially, when the result was so yummy? Feeling slightly better I moved forward. Still, I couldn't rid myself of the suspicion that his bathroom closet probably contained way more chemicals than mine.

If his preoccupation with his personal grooming disturbed me, he wasn't indifferent to mine either. He took one look at me and said, 'Wow! You look . . . different.'

If a male eye, albeit a professional eye like Kaustav's, can spot the difference, you've done too much. I was mortified. I also wanted to kill Em and Rosie who had waved aside my complaint that I looked like a geisha with the amount of pancake they'd smeared on me. I frantically searched my brain for something smart and dismissive to say. Once again, nothing came to mind.

And then it got worse. I mistook his outstretched hand as an invitation to step closer for a bit of air-kissing. Kaustav reared back his head in surprise and, instead of my cheek brushing the air around his cheek, my puckered lips found his surprised—and rather unresponsive mouth—in a full-on lip lock!

All Kaustav's sporting, 'Women usually wait until after the first date to do that,' did was show him up as a sparkling wit and me as half a one. It did nothing to alleviate my embarrassment.

Meanwhile, Neena, having dispensed with her charges, materialised behind me. Her mocking look told me she'd sized me up much like I had sized her up earlier. I trailed Kaustav and Neena inside, taking unobtrusive stabs at my face with a tissue.

Complete with controlled lighting, original masterpieces and Blazar Films' posters on the walls, overstuffed leather furniture and thick carpeting, Kaustav's office was swish and cosy. Plus it had an elevator that opened into it directly. I've seen some plush offices but Kaustav's office gave a whole new meaning to the word.

I stumbled as my heels sank into the plush carpet. I stole an embarrassed look from under my lashes, but fortunately no one was looking.

Kaustav indicated that I should sit on one of the chairs across his desk. After I had done so, he perched on the edge of his desk, one leg dangling freely. He regarded me with a mixture of amusement and curiosity.

I squirmed under the scrutiny and pinned my eyes on one of the film posters on the wall. The poster was of *Shararatein*, a film about a middle-aged man's cruel sexual games with a young girl in the sunset years of his life. A desi version of *Last Tango in Paris*. Kaustav followed my gaze. 'What did you think of it?'

At once the image of a middle-aged actor's naked fleshy back flashed before my eyes. But the film was directed by Kaustav himself a few years ago. What was I going to say? That I thought it was appalling and had me cringing all through? 'I . . . it was interesting.'

'Kaustav,' Neena said impatiently.

He waved his hand dismissively at her and continued, 'Interesting? Interesting as in good?'

The actor's fat, greasy face, contorted in orgasm, swam in front of my eyes. I suppressed a shudder. 'Of course. It was a fascinating character study.'

He looked at me quizzically. 'Bull shit! You hated it.'

I started to protest but he cut me off. 'As well you should. It was a terrible film. A voyeur's delight.'

Was I expected to agree with him? Or was he fishing for compliments? You know, like where a person deliberately runs down his project so that you sportingly step up and defend it? I tried to read his face but it was expressionless. *Why was he doing this to me?* And shouldn't we be talking about Urvashi rather than a film that really should never have been made? I was all too aware that the silence was stretching. I panicked. *What was I supposed to say?*

'Then why did you make it?' I blurted.

He was taken aback for a moment. Then he laughed out loud in genuine amusement, shaking his head in wonder. 'Why did I make it?' Now, what had I said that was so funny? 'Did you hear that, Neena?' To further mystify me, Neena was also looking at me interestedly.

She tried to intervene once more. 'Kaustav, we really should—'

'God, woman, don't run my life. Why don't you try Rocky once more?'

Neena inclined her head and retreated.

'Now where were we? Ah yes, *Shararatein*. Would you believe I liked the script? Only, as we now know, painfully, Raghav Rai is no Marlon Brando.'

I dutifully murmured that he wasn't.

'Kaustav,' Neena said, 'Rocky's assistant answered the phone. Says Rocky is in the middle of a shot and that he'll call us back as soon as the shot's over.'

Kaustav's face darkened. 'Tell him, there's no need.'

Neena tried to reason with him. 'But Kaustav, he's in the middle of a shot. It's not as though he's throwing starry—'

'And then call Majid and sign him on,' Kaustav said, cutting her off. Ouch! Poor Rocky was going to be one unhappy actor.

Neena's phone rang again. She spoke briefly and then turned to Kaustav and said, 'Chandan just called. They entered the premises through the back gate; they're on their way up.'

'Right!' he said, straightening and turning towards the elevator.

A couple of moments later the elevator doors opened and ejected two occupants, a man and a woman. It was the first one, the woman, that left me momentarily confused. Urvashi!

Chapter Four

꧁꧂

S o, she was back. Then why had Kaustav still kept our appointment?

Looking at her then, several words jumped to mind. Beautiful. Ethereal. Waiflike. Fragile. In fact, her movies didn't do her justice, making her look older and fuller than she really was. She looked much more petite and pretty in real life, like a China doll. And just as remote. Still, I could understand why men went crazy over her. Vulnerability combined with the ice-queen vibe, I suppose.

If she was striking, the man with her was more so. But for the wrong reasons. He was tall and burly with a ruddy complexion. As if the network of fine blue veins running across his face wasn't bad enough, his beauty was further marred by angry red welts all over his face, neck and hands.

'Chandan! What happened?' Kaustav asked the florid-faced man.

Chandan grimaced and waved his hand dismissively. 'Allergic reaction. Prawnsh.'

Kaustav frowned. 'Really? You're allergic to prawns? I didn't know that.'

'That makes two of us.'

'God, man, do something about it. Go see a doctor or something.'

'I plan to. Just as soon as this is o'er,' Chandan slurred again.

Kaustav grimaced and turned to the woman who had arrived with the unfortunate Chandan. 'Falguni,' Kaustav said, extending his arms to greet her warmly. 'So glad you could come.'

Falguni! I looked at her in amazement. She looked so like Urvashi she could be her twin.

Falguni stared at Kaustav's arms, clearly taken aback by his friendliness. But she recovered fast enough and placed her hands in his. 'The playzer is all mine, Kostavji,' she returned in Gujarati-accented English.

Involuntarily my eyes swivelled to Neena who was looking at Kaustav as a woman looks at a man she adores. I thought I saw her looking at me from the corner of her eyes. She made me uneasy. I had a feeling that with her, all was not on the level. Instead, it was a skilfully orchestrated performance. I glanced at Chandan and caught him studying me with interest. He winked and smiled at me.

'You've understood what you have to do?' Kaustav asked Falguni.

Falguni nodded. 'I go out of your oafis, through the main resayp-sun area, get into Urvasiji's car and drive to her home. I stay there in her house till I hear from you.'

So that was the plan! And it was a good one. If I could be fooled by the double, even momentarily, the media could definitely be fooled. And they had the disadvantage of being further away.

'Don't take a chansh even if you feel the repor'ers are gone. There might be some lurking around,' Chandan said. 'We'll have someone keep wash and tell you when it's safe to leave her house.'

Was he sloshed? I glanced unobtrusively at my watch and noted that it was only half past noon.

Neena looked around. 'Ready?'

Falguni nodded, clamping oversized sunglasses firmly on her nose.

'Let's roll,' Neena said, opening the door.

Feeling superfluous and ignored, I did the only thing I could do. I followed them. Judging by the reactions within Blazar Films, I knew the plan was a success. People stopped doing whatever they were doing and stared. Now these people were used to seeing Urvashi so her presence didn't warrant such a reaction. Which left me with the only possible conclusion: that rumours about Urvashi's disappearance must have spread and this performance was putting those fears to rest.

At the reception Kaustav and Chandan ostensibly said their goodbyes and retreated to their respective offices, leaving Neena to escort Falguni to Urvashi's Lexus which had pulled up outside. I hung back inside.

The massive gates opened to let Urvashi's car out. As soon as they saw Urvashi's car and the occupant inside, the reporters fell upon it. They rapped on the tinted windows and hammered on the hatch, the hood and the roof. I felt sorry for Urvashi's auto insurer. After this onslaught Urvashi's car was going to need some serious body work.

Cries of, 'Urvashiji, what was the basis of the rumour about you going missing?', 'Urvashiji, where were you?' and 'Urvashiji, one photograph please' rent the air.

A regular driver may have been intimidated by the media onslaught, but Urvashi's driver was a pro. And even though the going was slow, he managed to navigate the car through the reporters without knocking anyone down and zoomed off.

Neena turned and our eyes met. I could see a replay of my thoughts mirrored in her eyes. The Blazar leg of the plan had gone off without a hitch; how it would go at Urvashi's house remained to be seen. 'Follow me please,' she said, walking past me towards the elevator.

'Where are we going?' I asked as she punched 2 on the elevator panel.

'To get your contract and advance,' she said.

The elevator arrived with a faint 'ting' and the doors slid open. We stepped out. Fortunately, the HR department was close to the elevator and I was spared the torture of having to walk on tiptoe. We collected my contract, according to which I was a writer.

'Kaustav and I agreed that your contract should say that. It's just better for the general staff. Not that it will stay secret for very long, but for the time being, it's just better. Won't alarm anyone unduly. I hope that's okay with you?' Neena said.

I nodded in agreement. I found it kind of funny since, lately, my writing had been limited to writing rent cheques. And even they were infrequent. I saw the HR guy look at me appraisingly and I wondered what he was so suspicious about—my remuneration as a writer or my capabilities as one.

The next stop was the adjoining room—the accounts office.

'Kadam, is the cheque ready?' Neena addressed the thin, dodgy rat of a guy with a long-suffering look about him.

Looking a tad shifty, Kadam said, 'No madam.'

Neena tapped her foot impatiently. 'Why not?'

'I haven't received any such order from EP,' he blurted out nervously.

'I'll speak to Elly. Put it under the general PR category for now.'

'But I'll need Chandan Sir's authorisation for that,' he protested.

'What is this, a government office?' Neena yelled, exasperated.

'Is there a problem?' I asked.

'Elly is the EP, the executive producer on *Ransom* and this baboon won't give us the cheque without her signature on the voucher,' she fumed.

I had to hand it to Kadam. He quailed, but he stood his ground and Neena had no option but to comply with his demand. She charged out of the office leaving me to console poor Kadam. So I said the first thing that came to my head: 'Keep up the balancing act,' I said and quickly exited after Neena. He may be an expert at balancing books, but he didn't know diddlysquat about balancing authority.

A few moments later, when Neena breezed into Chandan's office, all traces of her ill-humour were gone. Without so much as a knock, she walked in, trilling, 'Chandan, darling, I want you to meet someone—I don't think introductions were made.'

Chandan looked up from his laptop screen. For the briefest of moments I thought I saw dislike flit across his face as his eyes rested on Neena, but he quickly masked it with hearty cheeriness.

'Katie, meet Chandan Baweja, head of marketing and publicity. Chandan, this is Katie Kumar,' Neena said. 'She . . .'

He jumped to his feet and came around the table. 'Kayrie Kumar!' he boomed, slurring, 'Welcome. We jush love you. Don't we?' he asked of Neena.

With a huge smile, Chandan came forward and embraced me. This time there were no accidents and we managed the touchy-feely greeting. Maybe I was getting the hang of it after all.

Up close, further signs of dissipation were plainly visible on his face. His puffed-up skin was bad, and where unscathed by welts, marked by huge pores.

'We jush love your work. Simply love it.' Yup, that was alcohol vapour misting my face. I struggled not to recoil.

'Oh,' I said, 'are you familiar with my work?'

Chandan scratched the back of his neck and said enthusiastically. 'Are we famiriar! Neena, tell her. We jush love it. Simply love it.'

'Really? Which one? Akash Sinha? Kirti Rao?'

'Akashinha, Kirirao, everysing,' he said expansively. 'It rocks! Mind-blowing! Lemme tell you somesing,' he leaned forward, 'we're going to do some rocking work together, aren't we Neena?'

He was talking about MY MOVIE. He had to be. Why else would they look up all my cases if it wasn't research for a movie?

And why would he say, 'we're going to do some rocking work together' if he didn't mean my movie?

Omigod! I was right to think Kaustav wanted to cast me in a flick. This was just one more hint. My heart started beating faster. And suddenly a camera was pinned on me as I stood in the middle of a shooting floor, all pancaked up, and dressed in short shorts and a vest with 38 D padding underneath, showing off a generous quantity of toned, shimmering flesh.

'You,' he pointed at me, 'are going to write rocking heart-wrenching dramas . . . blockbusters. I'm thinking millions—no, *billions*—of rupees.'

And then the director yelled, 'Action!' and I withdrew a gun from the impressive arsenal fastened on me—Wait a minute. *Write?* Surely he meant *act* in? Unless . . . unless Neena had told him I was a writer? Of course, that had to be it. He didn't know the whole story.

'Save it. Katie is a private investigator,' Neena said tightly.

'I know!' he said with dignity. 'I was talking thrirrers . . . sushpense . . . you know . . . rocking stuff.'

'Yeah, yeah,' Neena said in a bored voice. 'Chandan I need a favour. Kadam won't issue Katie's cheque 'cos I forgot to get Elly's signature on the voucher. Could you . . .?'

He held up his large hand. 'Say n'more.' And he went behind his desk and started scribbling on a voucher. He signed it with a flourish and handed it to Neena, adding, with a wink at me, 'If only to get a prerry face around here.' He was a PR guy all right.

Neena's phone rang. She took it out and looked at the display. She looked up and some kind of silent communication passed between them.

'Talk to me,' she breathed into the phone. She listened for a moment and exploded, 'Are you fucking kidding me?' She walked out of the room, still talking, but now in a fierce whisper. Chandan followed her with nervous eyes.

'Problems?' I asked.

'What?' he blinked. 'Oh, no, no. Somesing to do with the publicity strat ... stragey for our next production. 's pro'ably nothing.'

'Chandan, can I ask you something?' When he nodded, I continued, 'Do you think Urvashi disappeared on her own?'

'D'you sink she 'speared on her own?'

'I asked you,' I said.

'And I 'sked you!' he said brightly. 'Jinx!'

In spite of myself I smiled. It was really difficult to dislike him. 'Okay, what do you think happened?' I asked patiently.

'Wanna know what I think?'

I nodded.

'I sink somesing's happened t'her.'

'Something?'

He nodded enthusiastically. 'Somesing bad.'

'Something bad as in an OD?'

'OD?' He looked puzzled and then smiled indulgently. 'Oh, I see. Rocky ish gay, S'meer Khan ish a cross-dresser.'

Where did that come from? *Sameer Khan is a cross-dresser?* 'I beg your pardon?'

'Whasish with you people? Y'all think oh this person'sh from the filmustry, he has to be gay, she has to be doing drugs. We are normal people.'

Right. Because normal people get sloshed by noon.

He waved his hand dismissively. 'Urrshi doesn't do 'rugs.'

She was also probably naturally thin and didn't need to work out or diet. Aloud I asked, 'Then what do you mean?'

'I don't know. I jush can't help sinking all's not well with her. 's just a feeling. Can't esplain it.'

On that wonderfully illuminating note, Neena came back into the room. Her brow was creased and the skin around her mouth was stretched tight, adding years to her face. At that moment I decidedly liked her.

She handed me an envelope, saying, 'Katie, can you find your way back? Something's come up and I need to talk to Chandan.'

'Oh but—' I blurted.

Neena smiled thinly, uncannily figuring that I was disappointed about not seeing Kaustav again. 'But what?'

'I need to speak to Kaustav,' I said resolutely.

'Don't we all?' she said with a saccharine sweet smile. 'While we're on the topic, let me tell you something. You better watch how you speak to Kaustav. You may have him all interested by your frank talk now, but the novelty will pass. And in the long run it doesn't pay to be outspoken with him. I should know!'

Now what the hell was that all about? I glanced at Chandan for some clue but he studiously avoided my gaze. I idly wondered if Neena was who Shirley had in mind when she told me to beware of people whose interests were contradictory to mine. I nodded to show my agreeableness and retreated. But once I was outside, my instincts kicked in and I couldn't resist a little eavesdropping. I might learn something about their next venture and could sell the scoop to one of the journalists parked outside.

Making sure that the coast was clear, I tiptoed to the door, hoping Neena and Baweja would oblige by shouting out their conversation. They didn't. In fact, they contrarily chose to speak in hushed tones and I had to press my ear hard against the door.

'. . . she could be?' I eventually heard Neena say.

Unless all their heroines were in the habit of disappearing, it didn't take a rocket scientist to know who she talking about.

'Beatsh me.' I could hear the shrug in his voice. Shuffling of papers.

'For god's sake!' Neena exploded. 'Am I the only one who's concerned here?'

'What do you want me to do?'

'Haven't you done enough?' Neena bit out. Now what did she mean by that?

'Ish as mush your fault as mine,' Chandan whined.

Silence.

'Whadre we goantodo?' Chandan asked worriedly.

'What do you mean?'

'If anyone findsh out about . . .?'

'How will they? You were with me at Firangi Paani, remember?'

'I've a bad feeling about thish. We shou've left ish well alone.'

'. . . get away with it?'

'And wash with thish Katie Kumar?' Chandan asked.

'I don't know. Kaustav sprang it on me this morning.' There was a pause. 'Oh for god's sake, Chandan, must you scratch yourself like that?' Neena exploded.

'I can't help it,' he whined. And then he muttered an unintelligible curse.

A pause. Then, 'What are you doing?' Chandan asked.

'What do you think?' Neena said briefly.

I could hear the click-click of a phone number being dialled. Suddenly someone crept up close behind me and whispered, 'I thought I might find you here.'

Startled out of my wits, I jumped back as though the wooden door had hit me with a thousand volt charge. Tejas Deshpande!

'Get away from there!' I hissed.

'Why, what's going on?' he whispered and pressed his ear to the door.

'Never mind. Just get away from there,' I said urgently.

He gestured for silence while he listened and I glared at him.

If I were to describe him in a single term, I would have to say Indian (Native American). He's taller than the average Indian (the subcontinent variety) and has a whipcord lean, lithe body. He has a lustrous crop of poker-straight, black hair, which he wears slightly long. His skin looks kinda ... shiny. Like burnished bronze-gold. Women find that hot. I just find it sissy. I mean, even after you've been freshly waxed, the guy's skin is still smoother than yours. How creepy is that.

He's almost always dressed in snug jeans, which he combines with tees or shirts, sometimes both. They're always sans labels, which means one of two things: either they are extremely high-end designer or fake, Fashion Street variety. I'm guessing, the former.

His face is all angles and planes like it's been carved with a fine chisel. His eyes are coal black and can be bland or devious and it's difficult to tell which. Most women think he's drop-dead gorgeous. I agree. He would be gorgeous if he dropped dead.

A moment later his look of 'concentration' passed and he stepped away from the door.

'I don't hear anything, Coomaar,' he complained. Tejas has always had the irritating habit of anglicising my name, which really gets my goat. My mind is always immediately bombarded with images from 'Harold and Kumar' movies—pictures of Kal Penn in a whorehouse surrounded by buxom, bare-breasted beauties, or worse, him jerking off under the covers. Unfortunately, I let my annoyance show when he first employed the accent which, of course, resulted in his persisting with it. And now, even though I pretend to be unruffled by it, his habit has stuck.

'Just as well,' I said turning to walk towards the elevator. 'What did you mean by I thought I might find you here? Were you expecting to see me here?'

He nodded, falling into step beside me.

'Who told you?' I asked, jabbing at the elevator button.

'Word travels. You ought to know by now. By the way, what *were* you doing back there?'

'Why? What's it to you?'

'Wow, that's crabby. You're not usually that crabby. Are you PMS-ing?'

'That's a good line. Why don't you hang yourself with it?'

'It's worse than I thought. Is it menopause? Are you going through menopause?' he asked, holding my hand and adopting a concerned, avuncular tone. 'Talk to me.'

I pulled my hand from his grasp and looked him squarely in the eye. 'No, I just hate you.'

He looked at me in bewildered innocence. 'Why?'

I assaulted him with my blazing-eyeball Sauron look.

'Really? After all this time you still don't trust me?' he said, thrusting his hands into his hip pockets.

Trust was a contentious issue, considering the last time I did, it cost me a case. And earned me a very irate client. We were both on a stake-out, for opposing parties of a case. There was a husband–wife duo, both of whom suspected the other of cheating. It was a run-of-the-mill divorce case with the two parties scrounging for court evidence. The husband was a rich guy and, understandably, anxious to preserve his net worth. Equally understandable was the wife's eagerness to relieve him of half of it. The wife had hired me and Deshpande had stepped in to help the husband. He had to. The husband was his business associate and my client was threatening to blow the whistle on their financial dealings.

Sometime during the night, when we were parked outside the husband's love nest, Deshpande got out of his car and approached me. He took out his hip flask and said amicably, 'Looks like we're both stuck here for the night. Might as well make the most of it.' And he proceeded to make small talk.

I was still naïve then and didn't realise what he was doing. I took him at his word, swigging away merrily from the proffered flask; I only realised later that he hadn't had a sip. By then it was too late.

I woke up in my car the next morning with a note from Deshpande saying, 'Good morning. Enjoy your liquor mortis.'

To date I don't know what Deshpande did after I passed out. All I know is his 'associate' won the case. My client was left out in the cold with a settlement that could just about meet her monthly salon bills. If she skipped the weekly manicure, that is.

That I would have to forfeit my fee was a foregone conclusion, but my client was so furious she refused to even cover my expenses. I was still embarrassed about it.

'Now, now. You have to let it go. Hate is such a debilitating emotion. It's like drinking poison in the hope that it will kill your enemy. You have to let me make it up to you.'

I gasped like I'd been happily surprised. 'So you'll jump off a building?'

He shook his head mournfully. 'Oh well, I tried. Anyway, I just thought I'd help you with some info,' he said. 'But, since it is quite clear you don't my help . . .' He sighed exaggeratedly.

What did he mean? Did he know? Who told him? What help? What info? Was my cover blown already? Before I'd even started on the case? Before I could ask him anything, the elevator tinged and a harried looking Kaustav stepped out.

'Oh,' he said and stopped short. His body tensed. His eyes went from me to Deshpande, before slipping down, almost in a gesture of avoidance. Intriguing.

Deshpande said, 'Hey Kapoor, I was just coming to see you.'

Kaustav forced himself to relax. 'Of course. Why don't you wait in my office? I'll be there shortly.'

Deshpande gave a curt nod. 'And bring the books.'

'What books?' I blurted.

'Why, the reading kind.' On that smart-assed quip, the elevator doors shut on his face.

He didn't look like a devourer of classical literature. In fact, I doubted very much he could read at all. That meant he could only be talking about account books. Interesting.

'Kaustav, does Deshpande know about Urvashi?'

A wry smile. 'He should. He handles the security around here and Urvashi did go missing on his watch. And it was his people who went looking for her after she disappeared.'

'And does he know about me? That I'm working on the case?'

He shrugged. 'I haven't told him.'

Well, then, that one didn't stay secret for long at all. Before I could dwell on that further, Kaustav drew me towards Chandan's office. 'I want to speak to you,' he said urgently.

'What's wrong, Kaustav?'

He relaxed. 'Nothing. Why?' he asked causally.

'Nothing. It's just that you looked kind of tense so I thought maybe . . .'

'Maybe what?' he asked, his eyes twinkling.

'Maybe there has been some development.'

He grimaced and shook his head.

I hesitated. 'Kaustav, do you trust Neena and Chandan?'

He looked at me sharply. 'Why?'

I wondered if I should mention the exchange I'd overheard between Neena and Chandan. I might be jumping the gun if I did. After all, I'd only overheard snatches of conversation, which, frankly, could have been about anything. It wasn't as though they'd mentioned Urvashi's name.

'Katie!'

I chose to be evasive. 'It's just that if anything's happened to . . . if there's been foul play, the best place to look for suspects is usually home.'

'Well, I trust them as much as anybody I suppose. They've both worked here a long time.'

'And would they have a reason to harm Urvashi?'

He struggled with himself. 'No, I can't believe they'd harm her,' he said finally.

'But did they have a reason?' I persisted, although, in Neena's case, I already had an idea.

'As much as anybody. Petty jealousies and insecurities run very high in this industry.' Yes, I thought, especially if Urvashi happened to be the object of affection of your object of affection.

Just then Neena exited from Chandan's office, trilling, 'There you are! I was just coming to get you.'

'Well, I've got everything I need to get started here, so . . .' I said.

'Wait,' he said.

'Kaustav,' Neena said bossily, 'we have a lot to do.'

'I know what I have to do,' he said.

The quiet authority in Kaustav's voice and the accompanying icy stare did the trick and Neena retreated. 'Of course,' she said, swallowing.

He turned to me. 'What's the next step?'

'You mean the first step?' I said in an attempt to lighten the mood.

He frowned in puzzlement.

'The next step comes afterwards? You have to get onto the first step to get to the next step . . . never mind. It's a PJ,' I said lamely.

He didn't look amused. In fact, he looked impatient. I fully expected Neena to gloat but she was uncharacteristically subdued.

'Okay, let's go over the facts as we know them. Your team was shooting near Pune where they were being harassed by the locals. They were staying at a hotel . . .'

'Princeton,' Kaustav said.

'They were staying at Hotel Princeton on the outskirts of Pune, near Mulshi. Day before yesterday, that is, on 17th September, your team wrapped up the shoot and left for Mumbai. Urvashi was the last one to leave. At around four, she woke up, ordered room service and left. All was well till just before the Khandala exit, after which there was no communication with her, right?'

'Broadly.'

'And you sent people up and down the entire expressway, searching for her?'

He nodded.

'Well then, let's assume that she turned off somewhere near Khandala.'

'But there are so many turn-offs!'

'True, but Urvashi's car would have been expensive, conspicuous. Someone, in some village, will surely remember it.'

Kaustav and Neena exchanged uncomfortable looks.

'What?' I asked.

'You see, Urvashi's Merc developed a snag the previous morning and was sent back to Mumbai. She was travelling in a hired car.'

'You've got to be kidding me!'

Kaustav shook his head. 'It was an Accent.'

How conveniently anonymous.

'What about the driver?'

Again, the exchange of uncomfortable looks. This was beginning to smell and how.

'Urvashi lost her temper with him and threw him out. In fact, that's what her last call to me just before Khandala was about.'

I must look simpler than I thought. 'And what about Deshpande?'

'What about him?'

'What is his role in all this? You said it was his watch.'

'Oh. That's right. His firm provided the security on the outdoor as well. In fact, it was largely thanks to them that we could get any work done at all. But, they, like the rest of the unit, packed up and left earlier on. I called him in again only when Urvashi failed to reach Mumbai.'

I sighed. 'Look Kaustav, just tell me the truth. I'll even play along for appearances if you want.' For the amount written on the cheque in my hand, I'd do more than play along. I would invent stuff. *And not just at work.*

He shrugged helplessly. 'I know how it looks but I said it once and I'll say it again: it's no publicity stunt.'

'At least not on our part,' Neena added enigmatically.

'What's that supposed to mean?' he demanded.

'Nothing! I . . .'

I don't know why I did it but I saved her sorry ass by interjecting, 'Well, she could have taken off on her own.' To be fair she hadn't suggested anything that wasn't already on my mind. I stole a sideways glance at Neena, but she was looking down demurely.

'Kaustav, it *is* a possibility,' I interrupted.

'No,' he barked, irritably. I looked at him, aghast, and then at Neena. She had a look in her eye that said, 'I told you so.' Kaustav checked himself and said more evenly, 'She would never do something like that. Neena, tell her . . .'

'Tell me honestly, is this the first time something like this has happened?'

He looked uncomfortable. 'No,' he admitted, hesitating, 'but it's different this time.'

'How?'

'The last few times she was under tremendous strain.'

'And she wasn't, this time?'

He glanced at Neena and exhaled. 'I might as well tell her. She'll find out anyway.'

Neena's expression was unreadable.

Kaustav didn't tell me anything that anyone who read the papers, or watched news channels, or surfed the Internet, didn't know. In fact, he didn't tell me anything anyone even vaguely of Indian descent didn't know.

'Urvashi and I have been . . . more than friends for quite some time. Initially we kept it under wraps for obvious reasons. But, as usually happens sooner or later, word gets out. Vidisha, that's my wife, found out. Needless to say, she wasn't happy about it and demanded that we stop. This led to a few arguments between us. At that time Urvashi and I, we, didn't realise the depth of our feelings. It was only later that we realised that we wanted to get married.

'I had to tread carefully, you understand? I didn't want to hurt Vidisha any more than necessary. But Urvashi was unhappy. She wanted to get married right away and wanted me to ask for a divorce. I told her it wasn't that simple. I couldn't just ask for a divorce straight out. I had to work my way around Vidisha. To be fair to Urvashi, I did procrastinate. I just couldn't summon up the nerve to ask Vidisha. It was during this phase that Urvashi took off, to force my hand. It worked.

'I broached the topic of divorce with Vidisha. Of course, this didn't go down well with her, as she had thought our ... the situation would sort itself out. She refused. I tried, in various ways, to get her to agree but she wouldn't relent. I decided to let the matter rest for the time being and then try again. That's when Urvashi took off again.'

'So what's different this time?' I asked. *Besides the zillion carat Bulgari ring that you presented her with recently?*

He looked reluctant and I couldn't really blame him. If there were any sensational developments he couldn't risk the news leaking to the media.

'If it's the press you're worried about, your secret's safe with me. I am a professional. And I am bound by client confidentiality,' I said.

'Vidisha has agreed to a divorce,' he said quietly. 'So you see Urvashi has no need to punish me anymore.'

'So where did Urvashi go those two times?' I asked.

He shrugged. 'Beats me. Whenever I asked her she smiled mysteriously and said, "It's my secret."'

'Still, where do you think she went? Did she go over to a friend's? Or a hotel? Or does she have any property nearby?'

Both professed ignorance on the first two counts, but, Kaustav told me, Urvashi did own considerable farm land near Pune. The farmhouse there was very basic though, he said, and it was unlikely that she would choose to stay there. He added that he'd called the farmhouse number, but there hadn't been any response. Deshpande had even sent someone over to check it out personally. She wasn't there. And from the signs of it, she hadn't been there in a while.

Kaustav then asked me if I needed anything else and much as I tried, I couldn't think of anything. I shook my head. 'No.'

'Fine. I'll run along then.' And he left.

I glanced at my watch and turned to Neena. 'I'd better be going too if I want anything done today. Before I go, I need some information. I need Urvashi's contact details. And then I need you to call Urvashi's mother and fix an appointment for me. I'll have to meet her and get Urvashi's financial details. Bank accounts, credit cards, that sort of thing.'

'I can save you the bother. Her fee is directly credited into her various accounts. As for credit cards, you didn't think she'd pay for anything when she can bill it to Blazar?' Neena said bitchily. She got on the phone with Kadam and asked him to bring the information down to the reception area.

I was standing by the elevator, waiting for Neena to finish instructing Kadam, when I noticed a small notebook lying on the ground. It was not more than four inches long and three inches wide, the kind you can easily slip into your pocket. Curious, I picked it up and flipped it open.

Omigod! Unless he was in the habit of defacing other peoples' books by doodling his name all over—and this was not impossible given the immense egotism of the guy—it was Deshpande's notebook. It was relatively new and only the first few pages were written on—names, phone numbers, addresses and broken phrases. I looked around to see if anyone had noticed and quickly shoved it in my bag.

Chapter Five

Neena offered to escort me down to the reception. I insisted that it wasn't necessary, but she insisted more. I would have appreciated the courtesy except I didn't think it was mere etiquette on her part. She was keeping an eye on me.

'Oh by the way, do you think we can go across to the *Ransom* set?' I asked casually.

'I don't know about that. We have a strict closed-door policy on our sets.'

'But I would like to talk to the EP,' I argued. 'You know, just in case someone saw anything that might help. I'll be discreet, of course.'

'No, it's too risky. I'll have Elly give you a call.'

We were in the reception area now, waiting for Kadam. I was eyeing the studio area, wondering how I was going to go across with Neena tailing me like a watchdog, when Vidisha walked in! Vidisha was about thirty years old. Tall and athletic, she had short hair and small, even features. Even though she was totally devoid of make-up, her skin was smooth and healthy and her lips full and pink. She wore her usual attire of low-waisted blue jeans and a full-sleeved white shirt. Her feet were shod in sneakers.

She spotted us and stopped short. 'Oh! Hi, Neena.' She shot me a swift glance and then looked at Neena sharply.

Neena made the introductions. 'Vidisha, Katie Kumar. Katie, this is Vidisha. Vidisha is the supervising producer for Blazar's films.'

'Hello,' I said.

She ignored me. 'Neena, there's a hiccup on *Taaron ki Baaraat*. *Ransom* is eating into all my dates with Sameer Khan. I need to talk to Kaustav. Is he here?'

'He is, but he's rather busy. Perhaps I could help?' Neena offered sweetly, although even an idiot could sense the implied dissuasion in her voice.

Clearly Vidisha was no idiot. She looked at Neena with narrowed eyes. 'No, thanks, I'd rather speak to him myself. Unless there's a problem?'

In the face of Vidisha's not-so-subtle challenge, Neena considered her response. She pasted a polite smile on her face. 'No, of course not,' she said, retreating. She was good at that. She knew when to push and when to let go. She would go far, I thought.

'Good.' And Vidisha left without so much as a goodbye. I guess a 'nice meeting you' was too much to ask for.

After she had left, I said, 'That must be awkward.'

'What?'

'The fact that Vidisha is the supervising producer. I mean, the two *are* getting divorced, right?'

'So?'

'What are you saying? That the two are getting divorced but will continue to work together professionally?'

Neena didn't answer.

Wow! Leaving company finances in the hands of your bitter ex. So, apparently Kaustav was not content with just personal bankruptcy. He was gunning for total ruin!

'Oh, Neena, one more thing. Do you know something more about this whole thing? Something you may have forgotten to tell me earlier?'

I'm sure my tone told her I knew she knew more. But she didn't miss a beat. She looked me straight in the eye. 'I don't think so.'

Kadam arrived then and Neena handed me the information I had asked for. While leaving, I hunched my shoulders, trying to be as inconspicuous as possible. Knowing Deshpande, he would be loitering around somewhere, just waiting to pounce on me. Luckily he wasn't.

I hailed an auto and gave him directions to Rosie's where my bike was parked. Once the auto was on its way I settled back and checked my voicemail messages. There was a suicide note from a client I had refused to help and a death threat from an errant spouse whose marriage, and net worth, I had helped dissolve. Apart from that there was no evidence that any human being had missed me much.

I picked up my bike and decided to pay my friend, Hardik Dikshit, a visit. Dikshit is a computer prodigy who helps me out with my information needs. He started out in life as a nimble-fingered hacker. He finally caught the authorities' attention when he broke into the Indian Army's server. The authorities then decided to enrol his services in securing data. Government agencies were soon followed by banks, stock exchanges, phone companies and anyone with any information to guard. He and his cronies handled pretty much all sensitive data now.

I had met him while I was still in the police, following the Naxal money trail. The Mumbai police had recommended him highly to me. During that operation, there was a raid on the police headquarters and I was instrumental in saving Dikshit's ass. Since then he's felt obligated to me. Not that I ever remind him of it. Then again, I don't discourage him either.

I rang Dikshit's doorbell and waited for him to open the door. 'Katie!' he said with genuine pleasure.

'Hey, Dick-shit!' I said and stepped in.

Despite the piles of cash credited in his name in various banks, Dikshit lives in a small apartment. I use the term apartment in the loosest sense. It is actually a crummy one room-kitchen affair. The room, all of two hundred square feet, is packed to overflowing with all kinds of stuff—servers, monitor screens, a television, a stereo, a scanner-printer and even a ham radio. Not to mention a limp mattress and a shoe rack that passes for a wardrobe.

'I need some information,' I said.

'I figured.'

Somewhat guiltily, I made a note to visit him more often. He was a sweet kid, really.

I gave him Urvashi's number and asked him to find out which cell tower Urvashi's phone was locked into. I was working on the off chance that Urvashi had switched on her phone and if she had, there must be a cell tower it was beaming signals into. Luckily, Dikshit didn't ask questions. I guess, compared to the kind of data I'd asked for on previous occasions, this was tame.

Unfortunately, Dikshit's data only confirmed what Kaustav had told me. Urvashi had made a call two days ago from just before Khandala. Then she'd received a call from a local Mumbai number at around five-seventeen p.m. Thereafter her phone had been switched off and had remained off.

Next, I gave him Urvashi's credit card details and asked him to find out when and where they had been last swiped. There also I faced a roadblock. Urvashi's card hadn't been used in a week.

I was intrigued, because Urvashi had covered her tracks so well. (I couldn't quite let go of the notion that she had wilfully disappeared like a truculent child.) Usually people who want to disappear overlook small details.

But I was a lot more upset because I had been quite confident that I would get a definite lead from Dikshit which would narrow down my search area. As it was, I would now have to look for the proverbial needle in the haystack.

If Kaustav was to be believed, and Urvashi had not gone to her property near Poona, the reasonable thing to do next would be to go to Hotel Princeton and find out if anyone there had seen anything of note. And while I was there, I might as well go to Khandala and enquire at real estate agents about any high-end property that had been leased recently. If Urvashi was indeed in voluntary hiding, she must have rented a place.

Of course, it was equally possible that she was holed up at a friend's place. Lots of people from the film community had weekend homes in and around Khandala. But, somehow, I didn't think she would have risked anyone's help, just in case they got publicity hungry and spilled all to the media. Either way, the only way to find out was to go to Pune.

'Some tea?' Dikshit asked.

'No thanks. I've got to leave for Poona.'

'Good luck with that!'

'What do you mean?'

'Haven't you heard? There's been a major landslide and the expressway is closed.'

'So? I'll take the old highway.'

'You and the rest of Mumbai. The traffic there is backed up till Panvel.'

I glanced at my watch. It was only six p.m. I called Neena.

'You're still here?' she asked.

'I need you to speak with Urvashi's mother and tell her I'll be visiting sometime today.'

'So what, you're just going to hang around there chit-chatting with Geeta?'

'Not just chit-chatting. I'll get some tips on acting from the legendary actress as well.'

The quip was lost on her. She complained that there was no point since Geeta was equally clueless about Urvashi, not to mention worried. I hadn't had lunch and hunger always makes me a little cranky. So I told Neena where she could get off (and not on Kaustav either) and killed the line before she could retort.

I figured if Urvashi had leased a property, someone must have paid for it. And that meant accounts needed to be looked into. Of course, Urvashi's financial details could turn out to be of little use as she might have paid cash. But Blazar Films' account books and expense vouchers may reveal something.

Turning to Dikshit I handed him Urvashi's account numbers. 'Can you get me details of Urvashi's bank accounts? Deposits, withdrawals, recent transactions, you know, those kind of details.'

He nodded. 'These banks are my clients.'

Moments later he had the relevant data for me. Interestingly, all of Urvashi's accounts were joint accounts with her mother. As I had speculated, they were singularly useless. That is, aside from revealing that Urvashi deposited obscene amounts of money and withdrew miniscule amounts in comparison.

Even the regular donations to a Nirmala Nari Niketan didn't fool me. They weren't done out of largesse. At least, not out of any great concern for underprivileged women. The taxman was another matter.

It was criminal to let all that money rot in the bank in the form of savings when one could be shopping. But then, as Neena had suggested earlier, Kaustav was there to take care of that, wasn't he?

Thinking of whom, I asked Dikshit to hack into Blazar Films' server and elicit financial details of a film called *Ransom*. I was particularly interested in any payment made for a house. I didn't hold out much hope against this either. They might have paid cash or the expense might be listed under some other category.

Dikshit complied but it was a secure server and he said it would take some time. Meanwhile, Neena called back saying she had spoken with Geeta and I was free to visit her anytime. So, leaving

Dikshit to hack at it, I left. On the street across Dikshit's apartment were a couple of street-food vendors. Ignoring the relatively healthier option of bhel puri, I made straight for the pav bhaji guy and grabbed a plate. Then I hit the road for Versova, which was where Urvashi lived with her mother.

Urvashi's luxury high-rise building, Manas Canãs, was situated on a piece of reclaimed land, surrounded by slums and kolis. Heeding the ferocious warning on the gate, 'Visitors' vehicles not allowed inside. Tyres will be deflated', I parked my bike by the compound wall outside and walked in. I didn't have to battle media as I'd been expecting to; it made me wonder if perhaps Kaustav's subterfuge had been successful and the media, losing interest, had departed. Getting past the security guard was another matter, however. Geeta had neglected to inform him of my arrival and he was reluctant to let me through. It was only when I flashed my police ID, long since expired, did he allow me in. He escorted me into the elevator and all the way to the penthouse floor.

I rang the bell to the penthouse. While waiting for the door to open, I walked up to the window in the landing, which overlooked shabby shanties and, beyond them, majestic mangroves. I noticed a couple of tapori-type youths eyeing my bike speculatively from the slum across the road. Then, not content to admire it from afar, they crossed the road!

Alarmed, I rushed to the elevator just as the penthouse door opened and I found myself face-to-face with Geeta. I crossed my fingers, hoping that the taporis would stop at admiring the bike and not steal it or strip it for parts, and turned my attention to her.

I must admit that the idea of meeting yesteryear siren Geeta was thrilling. And for the most part, I wasn't disappointed. Her complexion was still creamy and all the other adjectives that are used to describe sublime skin. But, boy, had she piled on the pounds! Let's just say that she once had a splendid hourglass figure. Obviously the sands of time had run it down—all to the bottom. If I wasn't careful that could be me in twenty years. Maybe ten. Omigod!

'Good evening. I'm Katie Kumar. Neena may have told you about me?'

Geeta looked dismayed. 'Ah yes, yes. But I didn't think you'd be here so soon. Can you come back later? Now is not a good time.'

'Oh?' I looked at her curiously. Now, what could be more important than finding her daughter? Unless, of course, she wasn't missing in the first place.

Aware of how she must have sounded given the circumstances, she changed her mind and unlocked the door. 'It can wait. I suppose you had better come in,' she said grudgingly, walking in and waving me towards a sofa.

I took a moment to study the large photographs of Urvashi that lined the walls before replying, 'Thank you. This won't take long.'

'What do you want to know?' she asked, sitting down on the plush sofa. I swear I thought I heard the sofa go *oomph* in protest as Geeta's considerable weight sank in. I wondered if that's why they used to call her 'the oomph girl'. I bit back a giggle.

'Ms Geeta . . .'

'Call me Mummyji,' she invited. 'Everyone does.'

Right. 'Can you tell me what happened?'

'Haven't they told you already?'

I nodded. 'I'd like to know what you think.'

Though, outwardly, she didn't display any signs of stress, she clasped her hands together tight. 'Why?' She noticed my gaze on her hands and relaxed.

'Let's just say I'm looking for another perspective.'

And then it was like a dam had burst. 'I don't know what to think. Here I was, expecting my daughter back after a long schedule and the next moment I'm told she's disappeared.'

'You were told?'

'Yes. You see, she called me just before leaving, asking me to make tinda for dinner. She was telling me how much she was looking forward to coming back home. That's it. That's the last time I heard from her. At around seven that evening I tried her number again to ask her where she'd reached. But her cellphone was switched off. I thought nothing of it then, thinking her battery must've died, or she was in a bad network area. But when seven became eight and eight became nine, I started getting worried. That's when I called Kaustav. He was also worried. Even he had not heard from Uru.'

'Then what happened?'

'Kaustav told me to relax, saying he had sent somebody to check along the expressway. But that person could not find Uru,' she said, with a catch in her voice.

'You didn't inform the police?'

'Kaustav told me not to, saying it was too soon to panic and that it was probably nothing. And in any case, if the news leaked to the media it would be disastrous. He said he had people working on it.'

'What did you do then?'

'What can I do? I've just been sitting by the phone, waiting for it to ring, for Uru to call me. For anyone to call me and tell me they've found my little girl.' She broke down then and started crying with great heaving sobs. 'I couldn't bear it if something happened to Uru.'

'Ms Gee . . . Ma'am,' I paused awkwardly. Two years in the business and I still hadn't mastered the art of consoling weeping women. I sidled close to her and put my arm around her shoulders. 'Please . . . Mummyji.' She responded by clutching my hand, crying even more passionately. Yikes. 'Please don't cry. We don't know yet if anything has happened to Urvashi. For all we know she's taken off on her own again and is having the time of her life right now.'

She calmed down after a couple of minutes, and then delicately dabbed at her eyes with her pallu. When she looked at me, there was no puffiness, nor any red in her eyes. She looked as though she'd just had a cucumber slice treatment on her eyes, not cried them out. Amazing.

She sniffled. 'Kaustav told you about that?'

I nodded. 'Actually it was Neena.'

Geeta's eyes narrowed. 'I wouldn't go by what she says. She hates my baby.'

'That aside, it is a possibility that Urvashi took off on her own just like the previous two times.'

'But she always called me! Why hasn't she called?'

Oh?

'How did she sound when you spoke to her?'

'What do you mean?'

'I mean did she sound happy, sad, anxious, angry—anything out of the ordinary?'

Geeta fell silent, thinking. 'No. At least I don't think so. She sounded normal. She was looking forward to coming home.'

'What do you think happened? Do you think the Mulshi locals had something to do with it? You know, as revenge for desecrating their forest?'

'Anything's possible, I suppose.' She became agitated. 'You will find her? You'll find my baby?' she asked anxiously.

Knowing the folly of promising her that, I resisted. 'I'll do my best,' I said. I gave her my card and asked her to inform me in case she thought of anything else I should know.

Mounting my RE—I was grateful to find it intact and still there by the wall where I'd left it—I decided to head home. At the entrance to my apartment building, Shyam handed me two couriers that had arrived for me. They were the latest issues of *Vogue* and *Cosmopolitan*, encased in transparent cellophane. Cool—so that took care of my evening. I was relieved to find Ani wasn't home (as evidenced by a still locked door) and also kind of wished he were.

My plants looked sulky at being ignored the entire day, but cheered up on being watered. Next, I dialled the local pizza joint and was about to order a large cheese pizza when I caught my profile in the mirror. I switched the order to a large salad and then decided to tackle some long-pending chores while I waited for the greens.

I was loading the washing machine when the doorbell rang. Thinking it was the salad, I unsuspectingly went to the door. As soon as I opened the door a woman screamed, 'Bitch!' and lunged at me!

Chapter Six

≈•≈

She launched her full weight on me and we both went down with a crash. Winded, I lay there, having taken the brunt of her fall as well. She quickly propped herself on her knees and grabbed my hair, screaming, 'Bitch! You fucking bitch!'

It was mandatory for everyone posted in Naxalite areas to take some classes in self-defence. I didn't quite see the point of karate-chopping air and screaming haiii-yaaaah! when a dozen guns were pointed at you, but I dutifully underwent the training that was a cocktail of the best moves from karate, judo and jujitsu. And although I hadn't had much occasion to employ it earlier, I found good use for it just then. I twisted my body and in one heave managed to dislodge her. I planted myself atop her, grabbed her hands and pinned them above her head. The woman kept shouting profanities all through.

'Are you crazy?' I panted. 'Who are you? What do you want?'

I could hear cries of 'What's all that noise?', 'What's going on?', as my next-door neighbours came to see what the fuss was all about. I looked up to see the shrivelled-up prune, Miss Poonawala, and the lecherous old uncle, Mr Hiten Gandhi, watching the shenanigans from the open doorway.

Miss Poonawala is, by the most conservative estimate, eighty-five years old and hopelessly addicted to soap operas. She is also notoriously tight-fisted and tries to pinch a free tea whenever she can under the guise of neighbourly camaraderie. Initially, when I had just moved in, I had fallen prey to her machinations till I realised that, one, she was always chummy towards the end of the month, and two, the arrangement only worked one-way—into my apartment.

Gandhi is a middle-aged equities broker who lives alone. His family lives in Baroda where his wife runs a papad-making business while their daughter pursues an undergraduate degree in mass communication at the local university. They have some kind of arrangement where, every other weekend, either Mrs Gandhi comes down to Mumbai, or he goes up to Baroda. Gandhi is also a pot-bellied, lascivious prat of a man who is always trying to sell me stock ideas and cop a feel, usually at the same time.

At the moment, Miss Poonawala looked disapproving while Gandhi looked like his wildest fantasies had come true.

The young woman realised she had an audience and yelled, 'Husband stealer!'

Uh-oh. Sweety. And a very sour one too.

I instinctively loosened my grip on her. She rewarded me by trying to scratch my eyes out. I had no choice but to pin her arms back above her head.

Miss Poonawala started to look interested. Obviously this made up for the soap we had interrupted.

'Kasthuri!' she tut-tutted, evincing shock, but clearly enjoying herself.

'Look,' I said to Miss Poonawala, 'there's been a mistake.' Then, realising that I didn't need to explain myself to her, I turned to Sweety, 'You've obviously made a mistake. I don't know what you're talking about.'

'Really? I can spell it out if you want,' she said, trying to break free.

'There's no need for that,' I said. 'I don't know your husband.'

'Is she talking about dat boyfriend of yours?' Miss Poonawala chirped helpfully.

'No,' I denied quickly. 'I don't have a boyfriend.'

'You know that boy wid de curly hair and glasses?' Miss Poonawala persisted.

'You bitch!' Sweety shouted, stabbing me with her accusing eyes and desperately trying to wriggle free.

'Calm down. He's not my boyfriend. He's just the cable guy.'

'What was he doing here at night?'

'Umm, my cable's been on the blink and he came to fix it.'

'Really? Why were you moaning yes, yes, yes last night?' Gandhi said, almost moaning himself. A small frisson ripped through his body at the memory. I guess there was no mystery to what he was doing at the time!

'I . . . I . . . was just really happy I could watch *Grey's Anatomy* again.'

'No, I'm pretty sure you said, oh yes, do that again, Ani.'

'Are you both still here?' I exclaimed in exasperation. To Sweety, I explained, 'He's mistaken. I didn't say Ani. I said honey.'

'How many men are you sleeping with?' she asked.

Both Miss Poonawala and Gandhi looked more interested in my answer than she did.

I got up and slammed the door in their faces. When I turned back, Sweety was on her feet and looking ready to spring once again.

'Look,' I said reasonably, 'we can do this all night, or we can try and sort this out.'

Silence. But at least she didn't attack.

I regarded her. Ever since I'd learned about her, I had tried several times to picture what she looked like. And each time she was various shades of ugly. Unfortunately for me, while not quite pretty, she was nowhere near unattractive. A slick mushroom cut, a pixie-face and a pert nose—she was kinda cute.

'So are we going to keep staring at each other? Or are you going to admit it?' she said scornfully.

'Okay, fine,' I said. 'I admit I was seeing him. But you have to believe me, as soon as I found out he was married, I broke it off.'

It was true too. Ani had lied to me about his marital status, although he was of the view that when you hold something back, it's technically not lying. But from the moment I had found out, I had been trying to break it off. It's a different matter that Ani kept coming up with winning arguments that persuaded me otherwise.

Sweety's face became ugly and she started to resemble the monster I had imagined her to be. 'Really?' she snapped and flung a sheaf of photographs in my face. All of them of a couple, *in flagrante delicto*.

'How did you . . .?'

'I hired an investigator.'

'You *what*?'

'That's right.'

Who was it? Was it that scrawny guy who was always hanging around our society gate, ostensibly chatting with Shyam? *He* showed an undue interest in my comings and goings. Or was it that huge thakur-type guy with the impressive moustache who hung around the corner paanwala?

Sweety broke into my thoughts, 'He's been keeping watch on you for the past one month.'

A month! Fine detective I was. I'd been shadowed every day for a month and hadn't even realised.

I peered at the pictures and something caught my eye. 'Hey! That isn't me!' True, her face couldn't be seen but the slim derriere wasn't mine. I wished it was, but it wasn't.

Sweety grabbed the pictures from my hand. 'What? Let me see.'

'That woman isn't me,' I said. But my triumph quickly dissolved when I realised what a sucker that made me. He had cheated on me! 'The bastard!'

'Really?' she asked suspiciously.

'That isn't my ass.'

To add insult to injury she glanced lingeringly at my heiny and said, 'True.' Then, 'How do I know the detective didn't airbrush this?'

'Yeah, right. 'Cos it was important to him that I looked good?'

Her objection didn't have any real conviction to begin with and she bought my denial without argument. 'But ... but I don't understand,' Sweety stammered. 'The detective specifically said it was you.'

'This is what probably happened. Ani cheated on you with me and he cheated on me with her. The detective just got his pictures and names mixed up.'

Sweety burst into tears. If she expected me to console her she had another thought coming. I had my own miseries to contend with. But after a while her sniffling got to me.

'Look, Sweety,' I began, grimacing at her name, 'he's not worth it.'

'It's easy for you to say,' she blubbered. 'He's my husband. What am I supposed to do?'

'Leave him!' I said suddenly. 'Let's both of us dump him.'

She stopped crying and looked at me in wonder. 'You think?'

'Remember I said I broke it off with him? Well, it's true, and I think you should do the same. That'll show him.'

'But I love him,' she wailed.

'Well, honey, a leopard doesn't change his spots. It's up to you now. Keep him and put up with his cheating or keep your pride and walk out.'

At that point I felt she needed a little Dutch courage, so I got up and fetched a bottle of vodka and two glasses. Sweety grabbed the bottle and I thought that she wanted to do the honours. But she obviously thought that pouring the vodka into glasses was an unnecessary waste of time and started swigging straight from the bottle. I found myself wishing for a cigarette and then remembered I wasn't supposed to do that. It was something to do with breaking the dependency pattern.

A half-litre of vodka later, Sweety left. But I had lost my appetite—for the salad and the mags.

Feeling low, I called Em and started to tell her about what had happened. She made all the right noises but I could tell she was not really listening.

'Can I come over?' I asked.

'What, now?' she asked, startled.

'No, next year. Yes now!'

'Um . . . I'm really beesy.'

'But it's your night off!'

'I 'ave uzer zeengs to do, you know.'

'Like what?'

'Like . . . like pay beells.'

In the middle of the night? But it was clear that she was blowing me off. I spent a few minutes wallowing in pleasurable self-pity, put my phone on silent, and called it a night.

The next morning I woke up at nine to find several missed calls from Ani. I decided not to return them. To celebrate my new-found independence, I briefly considered sweeping my apartment to 'get rid of the physical clutter' and, just as soon, ditched it as being too much hard work. Really, there was not much difference between an inch and an inch-and-a-half layer of dust. I decided to risk cooking a scrambled eggs and bacon breakfast instead.

Over breakfast I pondered my next course of action. Should I go to Poona first or make a stopover at Blazar? I hadn't received any missive from Dikshit, which meant he hadn't had any luck hacking into the Blazar server. Which meant I'd have to do it the old-fashioned way. I knew that going through the Blazar Films' books, especially the *Ransom* job sheets, might turn out to be as fruitless as going through Urvashi's financial statements. In all probability, the payment would have been made in cash and would be listed under various sundry expenses. Even so, it had to be done. I was debating who would be easier to manipulate into revealing information, Kadam or Baweja, when the doorbell rang.

'Kay? You there?' Ani called out.

'No,' I shouted back.

'Come on Kay, open up. It's urgent!'

'Go away.'

'It's about Sweety. She's gone.'

I heard Miss Poonawala's door open with that characteristic scrape that set my teeth on edge.

'I said, go away!'

'Open up! I want to talk to you. I know she was here.'

'Serves you right, you lafanga!' Miss Poonawala said, before I could voice the same thought. 'Treating your sweet little wife dat way. And for who? Dat Kasthuri who's sleeping . . .'

In a trice I was at the door. I flung it open and dragged Ani inside just as Miss Poonawala was saying, '. . . God knows how many . . .'

Ani looked puzzled. 'What is she talking about?'

'Never mind. How did you know she was here?' I asked.

Ani agitatedly ran his hands through his hair. 'After I left your place yesterday, I had to rush to Delhi for a last minute meeting. When I came back early this morning, she was gone. She'd left me a note saying she knew about you and had met you. And that she was leaving me.'

'I know.'

Ani stared at me. 'You do? It wasn't you, was it, on the phone this morning, asking for her?'

'What?'

'Never mind. It wasn't your voice anyway. How did you know?'

'She told me last night she was going to.'

'She told you? And you couldn't give me a little heads up?'

'Gee, I don't know. I thought I would, but when Sweety gave me these I figured it might be a bad time.' I shoved the incriminating pictures Sweety had considerately left behind in his nerveless hands, 'You might've been busy.'

Ani stared at the pictures and sank down heavily on the sofa. He seemed to be in shock.

'How . . .?' he started to say.

'Sweety gave them to me. She suspected you were having an affair with me and hired a detective. Imagine her surprise—and mine—when these came up instead.'

'I can explain.'

'How? That your dick got lost and mysteriously found its way into her vagina?'

He winced but didn't object. The consequences of his multiple cheating seemed to have dawned on him. 'Dear god, I'm ruined,' he said miserably, covering his face with his hands.

Let's see. So his wife had left him and his mistress (me, yegad!) was about to do the same. In addition, he risked losing half his net worth in an expensive divorce. Yeah, he was pretty much screwed.

'It was just that one time,' he said rocking back and forth.

'And a good one at that, it seems,' I said, twisting the knife in deeper, although it was debatable who I was hurting more, him or me.

'You don't understand. She was a client. An investor. She made it clear that she would invest in our company if I . . . if I . . .'

'. . . made the proper pitch?'

The corner of his mouth quirked up in a wry smile. 'You could say that. What was I gonna do? We needed the money. I'm sorry. I'm so sorry.'

All of a sudden I felt drained. Deflated. I couldn't summon the energy to be angry. 'Is that all it was? A one-time thing?'

He hesitated and then shook his head. 'No. It went on for about three months.'

Much as it hurt, at least he was being honest.

'At first I felt horribly guilty. I even thought of telling you, but then I figured it was just a one-time thing, and there was no point in hurting you. But then it happened again. And again. And somewhere along the line the guilt vanished. I only wish . . . But it's over, I swear.' He fell silent.

'Is it?' I asked cuttingly.

He nodded emphatically. 'I don't blame you if you don't believe me.' I looked at him closely and decided that he was telling the truth. 'I only wish I'd told you earlier. And now . . . I knew this would happen. I knew she would react like this. I told you I needed time!' He jumped up in agitation.

'I didn't tell her, Ani,' I pointed out hotly.

He rubbed his eyes wearily. 'I know. I'm sorry.'

He had such a forlorn expression on his handsome face that even I felt a momentary pang.

'What are you going to do now?'

'I dunno. Find Sweety, I guess.'

'Oh, so it's all Sweety now? What happened to "I love you, Kay, I want to be with you"?'

'I can't leave it like this! *She's my wife!*'

I was cut to the quick. 'No need to remind me.'

He moved towards me. 'Oh god, I'm sorry. I didn't mean it like that.'

I dodged his attempted embrace. Only then did I notice that he looked terrible. His clothes were crumpled and there were lines of tension visible on his face. He looked like he hadn't slept the entire night. Which made me feel good. I like it when men who are purportedly contrite (let's face it, it's mostly a put-on show) at least look the part. Plus he was pretty much wiped out. I could afford to be generous.

'Go home, Ani. You looked tired,' I said.

'About us . . .'

'There's no us.'

'But . . . at least talk about it! Yell, shout, give me hell, but do something!'

'Oh, I will. But I'm going to wait until after you've rested first,' I said, moving towards the door.

Ani's mouth widened slightly in a weary, lopsided smile. 'She's taken my Beemer too.'

I stopped. 'She was driving?'

I considered telling him that Sweety had been drinking last night. And then I saw his haggard face and decided against it. No point in worrying him now, I thought. Besides, she hadn't drunk *all* that much.

As I unlocked the door, I heard sounds of scurrying feet. I had no doubt who those feet belonged to and had a good mind to tell them off, but before I could fling the door open, Ani shut the door from behind me. Surprised, I turned around.

With a 'God, I'm going to miss you,' he brought his lips down on mine.

I was right. The remorse *was* a put-on show to get me back into bed. The cad!

'Wha . . . mmmmphf,' I tried to protest, unsuccessfully. Ani took advantage of my open mouth and forced his tongue inside. Out of sheer habit, but more because of the delicious sensations coursing through my body, my mouth slackened. Ani deepened the kiss.

I resisted. At my fourth attempt I succeeded in breaking the kiss and turning my head away. 'What are you doing? No, Ani . . . I said no!'

'Oh come on, don't be like this. Don't do this to me now.'

I knew I shouldn't give in. Just like I'd known the previous few times. Only this time there was a difference. I had met Sweety. She was no longer an unseen, formless being, but a real flesh and blood person. A person who, under normal circumstances, I'd have liked and even been friends with. This knowledge made the betrayal more reprehensible.

Ani's hands started exploring. They ran up along the length of my leg and massaged my hips. Then they found the hem of my nightshirt and off came the garment. He planted a series of soft kisses all along my face and neck. 'I need you,' he pleaded between kisses.

He needed me. What kind of a heartless bitch holds out when her man needs her? I struggled with myself, though, in all honesty, I was only looking for excuses to give in. *Don't! Think of all the guilt, all the self-loathing that will surely follow!* But the sensations he was arousing! Dammit, why did my conscience have to be the only part that felt bad when all the other parts felt so good?

Then his mouth found my nipple. That was it. My resistance was squashed. 'This doesn't mean it's back on between us,' I said and surrendered. It was only a pity fuck. And everyone knows that doesn't count.

Ani whisked me off to the bed. He might be a heel but he sure was good in the sack and had me worked up within no time. He kissed, bit, licked and sucked as he travelled leisurely down my body. He was at my navel, making his way lower when the doorbell rang.

'Ignore it,' Ani whispered.

The bell rang again.

'Coomaar, you there?' Deshpande called out.

Jolted out of my pleasure trip, I went still. 'Deshpande?' I asked incredulously.

'Yeah. Open up.'

'Um . . . now is not a good time.'

'This won't take long.'

'Ignore him,' Ani said, burying his face between my legs.

I couldn't. Ani's tongue flicked in and out and where I should have been seeing exploding stars, I only saw Deshpande's face. With a muffled curse, I got out of bed and struggled into my robe.

'How do you know where I live?' I bawled, opening the door.

'You mean, after all the evasive action you took, disguising yourself, shaking off shadows and never staying in the same place for more than a day?' he wise-cracked. 'Neena gave me your office address. That big, delightful lady next door, what's her name, Zara, gave me your home address.'

'Why?'

'Why? I guess she wanted to be helpful.'

'Why are you looking for me?'

'You didn't, by any chance, find my notebook? I think I dropped it at Blazar.'

'No,' I lied. Fuck! The notebook.

Deshpande looked suspicious. 'Sure? 'Cos it was in my hip pocket and I figured I must've dropped it near the elevators at Blazar,' he said, craning to look inside.

I shifted slightly, barring his view. 'Quite sure.'

'All the same, can I come in and look? You may have put it in your purse and forgotten all about it.'

'Well, then, you'll never know, will you? You'll just have to buy a new one, huh?' And I started to shut the door.

Deshpande quickly wedged his face in. 'Why the hurry to get rid of me? You got somebody inside?'

'So what if I have?'

'Anyone I know?'

As if on cue, Ani padded across to the door and materialised behind me. 'What's taking so long?'

I was torn between wanting to kill him and wanting to kill him. 'Get back! I'm coming,' I said.

With a desultory mumble, he padded off.

Deshpande looked at me keenly and then looked pointedly at his watch. He whistled. 'At ten in the morning? What are you, a rabbit?'

'Better a rabbit than a louse.'

'Hurry,' Ani called out. 'Mr Big isn't going to wait all day.'

'Mr Big?' Deshpande mouthed incredulously.

Mr Big was just a nickname we had come up with for Ani. It wasn't particularly imaginative—or even accurate. It was just something we'd started after watching *Sex and the City*. Writhing with embarrassment, I pushed his face out and slammed the door shut. In a way, I should have thanked Deshpande. Had he not showed up when he did, I would have succumbed to Ani's charms. But his arrival had driven all erotic thoughts out of my mind. And not only because his was such an obnoxious presence. I had forgotten all about his notebook. I had meant to look at it last night, but then the encounter with Sweety happened.

I walked to my bag and took out Deshpande's notebook.

'Are you coming?' Ani complained.

'Not today. And neither are you. So up and leave. I have work to do,' I said firmly.

Ani pouted but did as he was told. The good thing with Ani was that he knew when my no meant a definitive no and when it meant I could be cajoled. How many women can say that about their men? Perhaps I was being hasty in dumping him. Maybe I should give him another chance. After all, he hadn't said he wanted to get back with Sweety. Only that he couldn't leave it like this.

The sound of water running in the bathroom snapped me out of my deleterious thoughts. While Ani was in the shower, I quickly took out Deshpande's notebook and scanned it. More than half the pages that had actually been used were full of doodles; that left only five pages full of worthwhile information.

There were telephone numbers, but there were no names next to them; just single alphabets. One entry—U, followed by a mobile number—caught my eye. I compared it with the number Neena had given me. It was indeed Urvashi's.

Then there were abbreviated entries such as HP Pune, eleven a.m., LR followed by a mobile number. These I assumed were details of appointments—venue, time and the initials of the person followed by his/her telephone number.

And then I struck pay dirt. On the last page was a rough map, at the edge of which was scrawled Mulshi. There were lots of arrows along a thin road on the map. The road itself wound southwest and led to a spot labelled Talyarkhan Cottage. The cottage was marked over with a huge X and a question mark. The X was circled several times over as though Deshpande had run his pen over and over around it. Was it possible that the locals had had something to do with Urvashi's disappearance after all? Or was it indeed a publicity stunt which Deshpande was in on? Was Talyarkhan Cottage where she was?

Chapter Seven

❧

I was already copying the map when Ani, showered and dressed, said that he was leaving. I grunted absently. Almost on the heels of Ani's departure there was a loud rap on the door. I opened the door only to find Deshpande on my doorstep. Again.

'That was quick. Either he suffers from premature ejaculation, or you're remarkably easy to please,' Deshpande said, eyeing me speculatively.

'Don't tell me you were waiting outside all this time!'

'Well, the only other option was to wait here, but I didn't think it was polite. Besides it wasn't all that long.' He glanced at his watch. 'No, not long at all. Only about fifteen minutes. So which is it?'

'Excuse me?'

'Premature ejaculation or . . .'

'None of your business. What do you want Deshpande?'

'That,' he said, crooking his neck in the direction of my desk.

The notebook! And my own copy of the information!

'See, I knew you'd find it,' he said, walking to my desk.

Not knowing what else to do, I quickly ran around ahead of him and flattened my backside against the desk, effectively shielding it from him. In my desperate lunge to reach the desk before he did, my robe fell open, offering everything on display.

Deshpande's step faltered momentarily. Leaving the desk unguarded for the merest moment, I made a desperate effort to pull the runaway ends of my robe together. That split second was all he needed and, dodging around me, he grabbed the notebook. Which was, a quick glance over my shoulder told me, fine. At least, my own copy was safe.

'Fine,' I said sulkily, 'you've got what you wanted. Now how about giving me what I want?'

'And what is it you want?'

'What's your deal in this whole Urvashi thing?'

'Who says there has to be a deal?'

'Then why are you so interested in this case? And don't say you're not interested. I read your notebook.'

'My interest is simple. I tend to take it personally when people I'm hired to protect disappear on my watch.'

'About that. It was very convenient how your people packed up with the rest of the unit and left Urvashi behind. Alone.'

His eyes narrowed. 'I would take that up with Kapoor if I were you. He insisted on it.'

'And you didn't think that was suspicious?'

'What exactly are you implying?'

Good question.

His face smoothed over and became expressionless. 'Is there anything else?'

I shook my head.

After Deshpande had left, I quickly dressed. Before leaving for Mulshi, I decided to try Urvashi's number one more time. Expectedly, the mobile was unavailable. As I was leaving, I noticed the elderly men in my building cast speculative-bordering-on-lustful looks my way, as though mentally undressing me. On the other side stood their frumpy wives, looking all the more severe for the disapproving frowns they wore on their foreheads. Okay, so my exploits with Ani were well known by now.

Seeking refuge behind my fake Gucci sunglasses, I kick-started my bike. En route I decided to stop by my office to pick up my camera and binoculars. Outside my office, I encountered the diminutive Rajeshwari standing on a stool, hammering something into the wall.

Rajeshwari is quick-witted and devoted to Zara. She is a born coquette and has all the watchmen, delivery boys and assorted riff-raff eating out of her hands. This makes her extremely resourceful. She is also given to wearing sarees so vibrant a colour therapist could use any of them to cure a variety of ailments.

Curious, I crept up behind her. She was putting up a plaque that read, 'Don't waste time on a private eye, come to Zara, the all-seeing eye'.

I couldn't believe it. My gasp startled Rajeshwari and she wobbled on the stool. For the longest moment we both observed her desperate fight for control. She lost and went down with a loud crash, the plaque still in her hands.

'Some idiot put this up! I was just taking it down,' she said.

Enraged, I grabbed the plaque and marched into Zara's office. One look at my face and Zara's unfocussed eyes rolled into alertness.

I threw the plaque on her desk. 'What's the meaning of this?'

Zara peered at the offending object and slurred, 'Whash's thish?'

'Spare me the act,' I said, 'Rajeshwari told me everything.'

Zara hastened to mollify me. 'Now, there'sh no need to be ushpet.'

'No need? NO NEED! What were you trying to pull?'

'In my defensh you were not shupposhed to find out. And I'm jushh trying to get shome clientsh,' she whined. 'Businessh is slow. Can't even buy decent whishky.'

Which was probably a good thing.

'Listen, you old hag, try and pull that one again and you've had it,' I said and stomped out in a fine show of temper.

Behind me I heard a desk rattle and a chair scrape as Zara extricated her considerable bulk. Something fell to the floor with a terrific crash.

She ran after me into my office. 'It washn't to steal your clientsh. I jusht figured there wash no point in both of us losing out.' Zara brightened and added ingratiatingly, 'I read your cardsh today.'

I refused to be enticed.

She continued, 'You want to know what I drew?'

I kept quiet, looking uninterested, which is what I was, of course.

Zara looked hurt. 'Hermit. Upright. It meansh there'sh need for dishcretion, prudensh . . .'

'I know what it means,' I interrupted. 'And I'm not interested.'

'Could have been Hermit ill-dignified,' she added sourly, under her alcohol-saturated breath.

'Whatever,' I said and left after picking up the stuff I needed.

I was soon zipping along the expressway. Just before Poona, I took the turn-off for Mulshi. I found the village easily and, thanks to Deshpande's detailed map, Talyarkhan Cottage without difficulty.

I don't know what I expected but the dilapidated bungalow standing in front of me wasn't it. I guess I had secretly been hoping that I'd find Urvashi holed up there, but looking at the ramshackle building in front of me, I figured the only thing holed up inside would be termites and rodents.

I gingerly opened the rickety wooden gate which obliged me by falling away at my touch. I walked across the overrun remains of what must have once been a garden. At the front door I stopped short. There, I saw something I least expected to see. Sitting on the steps was a young man with a headful of impressive Rastafarian dreadlocks, nonchalantly chewing gum.

Upon seeing me, he jumped to his feet. 'Oh there you are. You took your own sweet time coming. What did you do? Walk?'

I blinked. 'Excuse me?'

'Are you Katie Kumar?'

'Yes,' I answered, surprised. 'How did you know?'

He fished out a slim envelope from his satchel and passed it over to me. The envelope had my name written on it. I flipped it over but there was no information about the sender anywhere.

He thrust a blank sheet of paper at me. 'Would you sign for this please?'

With a sinking feeling in the pit of my stomach I complied. 'Who is this from?'

'You'll find out,' he said and left.

I tore open the envelope and looked inside. There was only a single sheet of paper on which a neatly printed line read, 'I can't believe it. You fell for it again!' Below this were drawn some duck-like figures which, I assumed, were geese considering the now apparent nature of my chase.

Rage, white hot rage took over. Deshpande had done it one too many times. Suddenly I couldn't bear to be there another second. Blindly, I hopped on my bike and rode off.

I have often fantasised about what I'd do if a genie granted me three wishes. And no asking for three extra wishes either. I'd wish to be rich enough to never have to worry about money again. I'd wish to be young and beautiful for the rest of my life. As for the third wish, it has always been a toss-up between being able to eat everything and still be reed thin, and finding true love, depending on my mood. Right then, I knew what I'd wish for. I would ask for Deshpande to be removed, immediately, from the face of the Earth. I figured my last wish was worth expending if it meant being rid of him forever. I could always run if I wanted to be skinny.

I was so angry and consumed with vengeful thoughts that it was only after I had ridden for about half an hour that I realised that nothing on the road looked familiar. Distracted, I hadn't paid any attention to the turnings I'd taken, and was now hopelessly lost. (Technically, though, if you didn't care where you were going, were you still lost?)

I stopped at the first paanwala and, flashing a hundred, asked for a packet of smokes. He handed me a packet of cigarettes, a matchbox, and the only thing he had worth five bucks, a box of slim Diwali crackers, by way of change. I looked askance at the crackers, trying to figure out if he was abysmally late or impetuously early on his inventory control.

I lit a cigarette and puffed on it furiously, thinking about the many ways in which I would kill Deshpande and mutilate his body. The stick was too small to keep up with the extensive scenarios my mind was conjuring up, and before I knew it, I had smoked four. At which point I was angry with him all over again for making me relapse into a habit I had kicked with so much difficulty.

I decided to salvage the rest of the day by retracing my steps to Mulshi and visiting Hotel Princeton. I was about to start my bike again when my eye fell on a signboard which read: For Sale, Purchais and Ranting of Luxry Private Villa / Bangalowe, contact Honey Tuteja.

On an impulse I followed the directions on the signboard and found myself outside Honey Tuteja's office. As I walked in, he shot to his feet, patted his hair and said jovially, 'Walcome, walcome ji. Myself Hunnee Tuteja.'

At a guess, Honey Tuteja must have measured at least six-feet on the tape. And that was just sideways. Height-wise he was even taller. And he had weird hair on his head—kind of straight and stiff like a badly trimmed hedge.

I looked askance at the meaty hand he'd extended towards me and, suppressing a shudder, quickly folded my hands in a namaste.

He hastily did the same saying, "'maste, 'maste ji,' and waved me into a chair.

'Well, Mr Tuteja —' I began.

'—Call me Hunnee,' he interrupted.

Sure. 'Uh . . . as I was saying, I'm looking for a bungalow . . .'

'Of course, of course ji. You have come to the right place. I have two badroom, three badroom, four badroom, five badroom . . .'

'I get the picture. But . . .'

Unmindful of my interjection he continued, '. . . bangalowe with swimming pool, tannis court . . .'

'Yes, yes, all that is fine,' I said hastily, 'but, you see, what I'm looking for is complete privacy. Not a soul in sight for miles around. You know, the kind of place where one can simply disappear and no one would ever know.'

He brightened. 'O yas ji, I have exactly what you want.' He took out a bulky catalogue, went back and forth till he'd found what he wanted, and then pushed it towards me.

He jabbed his pudgy finger at a picture. 'Now this is what you want—two badrooms, two bathrooms, fully equipped kitchen, fridge, ACs . . .'

'Yeah, but what about that?' I said, pointing to another cottage visible in the background.

'That is not included.'

'I meant what about privacy?'

'There is two hundred metres between you and that cottage!'

His outrage was valid. For a Bombayite, that was almost like being on an island.

'Still, these are not what I am looking for. Maybe I should try another estate agent.'

'No point ji. You will find the same properties only listed with other brokers. You see all lugzry properties are syndicated among all brokers.'

'But . . .'

'Latt us drive out there ji,' he suggested, getting up. 'Once you see the property, you will change your mind. And if you don't, no problem.'

Perhaps I should impress upon him that I was an investigator. 'You see I'm not looking for . . .'

'Oh ji there is no charge for looking. So why not look?'

Why not indeed? I followed him outside.

Tuteja was perched on a scooter which was groaning under his weight. As soon as he saw me, he patted the seat behind him. 'Come on ji.'

'Um, I have my bike . . .'

'Why didn't you mantion before?' he said cheerfully and jumped off the scooter with an alacrity that should have been impossible given his size.

Alarm bells went off in my mind when he started to park it. 'I meant why don't I just follow you?' I said hastily.

'Why waste costly patrol on two veehcals?'

Tuteja displayed none of the reactions most men tend to have when asked to ride pillion behind a girl on a motorcycle. Disbelief, macho posturing, nervous laughter. If Tuteja had any such qualms, considerations of thrift undermined them.

I couldn't think of a way to rebut so I shrugged my acquiescence, mentally apologising to my trusty RE, which almost did a wild wheely in protest as soon as Tuteja parked his generous proportions on the seat. It was all I could do to control the bike. 'Hold on to your hair,' I said.

'I plan to,' he said and clutched his head.

Soon we were wobbling along the scenic country roads. He took me to several properties, all of which, besides being pretty and fantastically unaffordable, weren't quite what I was looking for. After about three hours of house-hunting, Tuteja was beginning to develop a pout and I was ready to accept defeat.

However, he had to make one last attempt and cajoled me into riding back to the office along another route. The road that Tuteja took me on passed through a small village—Indapur. Just beyond Indapur, the road cut between a picturesque lake on one side and a hill on the other.

'That is Pavana Lake,' he said.

I glanced at it and then at the isolated low hill on the other side. The hill was richly forested and looked like the beginning of a range, presumably a section of the Western Ghats. There was a barbed wire fence running all around it. Out of curiosity I asked Tuteja about it.

'That's Hermit Hill,' Tuteja said dismissively.

I almost stood on the brakes which made Tuteja crash into me. I thought I heard a crack from the region of my twenty-sixth vertebra moments before I fell forward on the handle bar. The bike wobbled dangerously but I managed to plant my feet on the ground and steadied it.

'I have to see that place,' I declared, stopping dead in the centre of the road.

I don't believe in coincidences. I believe that everything in the world happens for a reason. Of course, till now it only applied to the bad stuff. I figured it was about time I got some breaks. There had to be a reason Zara had drawn that particular card that morning.

'But it's private property!' Tuteja said. 'And it's not avalabel.'

'I don't care,' I said, engaging gear once again.

I rode along the road which wound sharply, almost like a blind turn, around the hill. I took the turn at a speed of sixty and almost banged into a bullock cart coming from the opposite side, eliciting a high-pitched 'Eoww!' from Tuteja and an angry snort from the bull. I barely avoided collision by veering sharply to the other side.

I parked my bike on the mud shoulder off the road and walked up to the wooden gate. A narrow cobbled driveway, lined with lush trees on either side, led up the hill.

I gave the gate an experimental tug. It swung open. 'Come on.'

Tuteja pointed nervously to a set of tyre tracks in the short mud trail just before it merged into the cobbled driveway. 'I don't think we should go in ji.'

'Come on, we don't know if anyone's home. These tracks could be leading out. And if there are people there, we'll just say we got lost.'

'There could be dogs.'

'You can either wait here or come along. Either way, I'm going in.'

I started off at a brisk pace. The hill sloped up steeply and the post-monsoon September heat had caused the densely populated tall trees to trap the humidity. As a result I was perspiring in no time. The property was huge and there didn't seem to be another soul in sight. As I worked my way to the top (it took ten minutes), I noticed, with a little interest, that the foliage was not native to Maharashtra.

Presently, and rather abruptly, I came upon a little clearing with a quaint stone cottage sitting bang in the middle. I hung back to study the layout. The cottage was surrounded by small patches of gardens on all sides, ringed by tall trees. A black Mercedes was parked out front in the porch! *Urvashi's?* It couldn't be. She was travelling in an Accent.

Nevertheless, my pulse quickened and my mind jumped several guns, as usual. And suddenly I was back in Bombay, Urvashi in tow, her face sheltered behind oversized Prada shades, while I warded off the paparazzi. And then it was a succession of interviews and photo shoots. I was a hero for finding Urvashi when everyone had failed, and the media couldn't get enough of me. They wanted to know what I liked to eat, what my favourite poison was, what fragrance I wore, who my dream date was and where I shopped. I was on the cover of every magazine . . .

Tuteja's laboured breathing announced his arrival. He was sweating profusely and wheezing alarmingly, displaying all signs of an imminent coronary. I had a good mind to tell him to go back. If he did die, I would have the devil's own time taking him down.

I waited for about five minutes but there were no signs of any human or canine activity, which was a relief. For all my earlier bravado, I have a healthy fear of dogs, especially the large Rottweiler variety.

As I drew closer to the cottage, I noticed a set of tyre tracks in the clearing beside the Merc. The imprint was different from the tread on the Merc's tyres. It was broader, with a unique and distinct pattern, usually seen on those fat tyres fitted on foreign SUVs.

I walked up to the cottage while Tuteja lingered behind. I skirted around the car and climbed the two wooden steps onto the veranda. I rapped on the door two times and called out tentatively, 'Urvashi?' When there was no response, I poked at the door. It opened without protest. I walked in, calling her name.

The cottage opened into a small foyer which housed a small sideboard and an umbrella stand. A wooden staircase led upstairs and a small passage on the right eased into a spacious living-cum-dining room. Looking into the living room from the foyer, I noticed a line in the middle of the marble floor. It was like someone had half-heartedly run a mop through the passage. Other than the shoddy cleaning job, the room was rather nice. It was done up in stone, with a fireplace, large French windows, colonial-style furniture and exquisite durries.

A door at the far end led to a kitchen. If the living room bore no signs of recent occupancy, the kitchen was a different matter. The sink was piled up with dirty crockery and cutlery. The refrigerator was stacked with leftover dishes, vegetables, fruits and opened cartons of milk and juice. Interestingly, stacks of packaged food and beverages were lined on the kitchen counter—enough to sustain one person for a month!

Again, I noticed a streak on the floor leading from the sink, through the kitchen and into the living room. The impression was that of someone having cleaned up a major spill that had run all the way from the kitchen into the living room.

When I came out of the kitchen, I saw that Tuteja had followed me inside and was studying his surroundings with interest. Leaving him to wander around downstairs, I climbed up the stairs to the first floor. The staircase opened straight into a cosy den, lined with bookcases. There was a comfortable sofa and a coffee table in the centre. A passage from the den led to two bedrooms. I walked into the first one. And boy, was it a mess!

The room had a queen-sized bed, a wooden dressing table, a wooden writing desk and a cupboard. The bed, covered in black satin sheets, was rumpled. Pillows, also in black satin, lay askew on the bed. The dressing table had a couple of bottles of perfume, a hairbrush and some cosmetics on it. Everything was out of kilter, in disarray. A perfume bottle lay smashed on the floor near the dressing table, and while the perfume had long since evaporated, the air was still saturated with a flowery fragrance. A MAC foundation bottle was open and there were huge beige globs everywhere, even on the mirror. A bottle of lotion lay on its side, its cap unscrewed and its contents pooled underneath in a viscous puddle. There was a huge open suitcase lying by the wall, with clothes and shoes heaped inside in a chaotic jumble. All in all, someone sure had done a thorough job of ransacking the room.

As per standard procedure, I reached into my bag for my camera. I photographed the room as it was and moved to take a closer look at an awesome sweater lying atop everything in the suitcase. I was sorely tempted to bag it.

'Katieji?' Tuteja said from behind me. 'What are you doing?'

Startled, I looked back and saw him, aghast, watching me reverently nuzzling the soft-as-a-baby's-bottom cashmere sweater.

'Are you stealing that sweater?' he asked.

Embarrassed at being caught with my hand in the cookie jar, I hastily dumped it in the suitcase and dropped the lid. 'Of course not! I was just admiring it,' I said, but I could see he wasn't buying any of it.

With exaggerated nonchalance, I flounced out of the room. I climbed down the stairs and was on my way out when a metallic door under the stairs caught my eye. The door hung open, slightly ajar.

I pulled it open and entered. There was a concrete staircase leading down into a dark basement. I climbed down gingerly and was at once enveloped in noisome air. An unpleasant smell, redolent of rot and decay, assailed my nostrils, and I started to get a sinking feeling in the pit of my stomach. As I climbed down, it became darker and I couldn't see anything at all. I fumbled along the wall for a switch, found it, and turned it on. Nothing. I took out my matchbox and struck one.

I held the match a little further. And then I saw her. At the far end of the basement was Urvashi, sitting rigidly against the wall, in what looked like a pool of congealed blood. Her T-shirt was soaked in blood, and she was staring sightlessly ahead of her, her legs thrust out and a knife sticking out of her stomach.

Chapter Eight

❧❧

People consider queasiness in police personnel strange. They expect that the police, especially the experienced cadres, would have seen and done their fair share of killing. Not true. While I had seen my fair share of corpses while I was in the police, I'd never actually shot anyone. Well, except for that one time. And even with corpses, I'd never stumbled upon one accidentally. When there were bodies to be examined after a night of Naxal carousing, I'd usually been pre-warned and had time to steel myself. Besides, the bodies were always covered with shrouds. Coming upon one unexpectedly, therefore, and in such gruesome circumstances, was quite another thing.

My lungs squeezed shut and my vision swam. I felt bile rise up in my throat. I started backing out of there carefully and walked straight into someone. Stifling a scream, I turned around sharply and saw that it was Tuteja.

He had followed me in and was, at the moment, looking extremely pale. It was a toss-up between whose eyes were the more lifeless—Urvashi's or Tuteja's. I watched in alarm as Tuteja started swaying gently and then more dangerously. He fell forward on me, taking me down with a terrific crash that shook the entire cottage. Something rolled off his head. *So it was a wig,* I thought somewhat incongruously.

I lay there, pinned under Tuteja's four-hundred-plus pounds, unable to move. I tried to shake him off, wriggle out from under him, but all I could manage was to free one arm. So I did the only thing I could. With my only mobile arm, I reached into my hip pocket and retrieved my cellphone. Not knowing who else to call for help, I dialled Chodu. As humiliating as it was for him to see me like this, it was better than being asphyxiated to death under Tuteja.

'Urvashi's dead,' I blurted hoarsely as soon as he answered.

'What?' he yelled. 'Are you sure?'

'Considering that I am staring at her dead body, I'd have to say yes.'

'You're not having me on?'

I assured him I wasn't. He wanted to know the details and briefly, I told him. Thankfully he didn't grill me on what I was doing there. I gave him directions to Hermit Hill and hung up. He didn't have to tell me not to touch anything.

Presently, Tuteja moaned and his eyelashes fluttered. I shook him hopefully, but he only sighed deeply and sank deeper into his swoon. Resignedly, I figured I just had to lie like that for however long it would take Chodu to get here.

I turned my head. It turned out to be a big mistake because my gaze fell on Urvashi. I couldn't breathe, and my vision swam again. I panicked. What if I didn't survive? Perhaps I'd better do something to revive Tuteja. I was considering the rousing effects of saliva, since there was no way I could reach any water, but how was I to spit on his face with him lying face down on top of me?

I don't know how long I lay there, but I was near passing out when I heard the sounds of cars pulling up. There seemed to be three. I heard doors opening and slamming shut, followed by human voices.

'What are you doing here?'

'Why, is there a law against being here?'

The first, barking voice was definitely Chodu's. I couldn't place the other man as he was speaking in lower tones.

'We can discuss that in the lock-up, if you wish,' Chodu said.

'You would like that.'

'Yeah, it'll be a regular party.'

'Can I bring my lawyer?' the other one wise-cracked.

Great. They were discussing the finer points of proper arrest procedure while I was dying a slow death. With one burst of energy, I sucked in as much air as I could and yelled, 'In here!'

The effort made me see spots. 'In here!' I cried again, hoarsely.

The voice I couldn't place said, 'Did you hear that?'

'As a matter of fact, I did. Who do you think that is?'

They would find out if they looked, instead of standing around discussing it, I cursed.

I heard footsteps mount the stairs to the porch. The cottage door creaked. And then silence.

'I'm here! In the basement,' I yelled before they went elsewhere.

I saw two shadows reflected on the basement staircase wall and then Chodu appeared with another man. Deshpande. How mortifying.

The two men stopped short and looked at one another. I saw various expressions flit across their faces. Shock on seeing Urvashi, disbelief on seeing me pinned under a giant. They stood there hesitating, not knowing what to do, who to go to first.

'Dear god!' Deshpande exclaimed.

Chodu unfroze and barked into his walkie-talkie, 'Get the forensics guys down in the basement. Now!'

He disconnected and made a move towards Urvashi.

'Great. Attend to the dead first while the living die.'

Chodu and Deshpande shifted focus. They stood and looked down at me, considering how to move the mountain.

'You take the arms, I'll take the legs,' Chodu said.

Deshpande took one look at Tuteja, perspiring even more profusely in the fetid air, and shuddered. 'Why should I take the arms? You take the arms.'

'Listen,' Chodu said, 'it's my crime scene. You have no business being here.'

Faced with eviction, Deshpande reconsidered his options. Seizing Tuteja's wrists, he said, 'Ready when you are.'

Chodu grabbed Tuteja's legs and said, 'One, two, three, heave!'

Tuteja refused to budge.

'Again!' Chodu said.

Tuteja stubbornly stayed where he was.

Deshpande and Chodu sat back panting.

'Guys, get him off me!' I croaked.

Deshpande shook his head. 'Babe, we need more hands.'

More footsteps clattered down the basement steps. Havaldars, followed by a forensic doctor! My humiliation was complete. Tuteja was finally moved with the help of four men and I was brought to my feet. I was sure that my muscles would've atrophied after having lain under Tuteja for three hours and was surprised, and more than a little relieved, to be able to totter outside.

Chodu asked Deshpande and me to wait while he went off to oversee his team casing the crime scene. Honey Tuteja had been revived, his statement recorded, and he was sent on his way with a dire warning not to talk to anybody. As Chodu spelled out, in graphic detail, all the manners in which he would suffer if he opened his mouth, Tuteja looked ready for a second bout of fainting.

But everyone knew it was a futile warning. Chodu's ferocious cop posturing didn't fool me and it wouldn't fool Tuteja for long. It was only a matter of time before Tuteja croaked and morbid curiosity drove hordes of people to the crime scene. Hermit Hill was a huge property and there were only so many guards you could post. Ergo, the hurry to gather evidence before it got contaminated.

I sat down on the porch steps and lit a cigarette. I found that once I'd started smoking again, I couldn't stop. But on the flip side, I hadn't once felt hungry or had the urge to eat vada-pav since morning.

Deshpande was leaning against his Jeep Cherokee, talking on his phone. Once his conversation was over, he detached himself from his car and sat down next to me. 'You smell terrible,' he said, crinkling his nose.

I looked at him sideways. 'That's my new perfume. To keep you away.'

The corner of his mouth lifted in a lopsided smile. 'It's working. May I now ask how you happened to know about this place and how you happened to be buried under the giant?'

'You may,' I said, leisurely taking a drag on the cigarette.

'And?'

I had planned on smiling at him enigmatically, grinding out the cigarette underfoot and sauntering off unhurriedly like all those femme fatales in noir films, but Chodu arrived, ruining my stylish exit. One hand holding his cellphone to his ear, he put his other hand on my shoulder and forcibly sat me down.

'Ho . . . ho . . . and find out who the property belongs to.' He disconnected and turned to us. 'Now. What were you two doing here?'

I was looking for a place to perform a pagan initiation ritual and this place seemed perfect. Several such witty answers came to mind but I chickened out when I saw suspicion lurking in his eyes. I told him the straightforward version of events ending with, 'You can check with Honey Tuteja's statement.'

He looked disinclined to believe me, but obviously decided to reserve judgement till he had indeed tallied the two stories in minute detail. 'And it was exactly like this when you arrived?'

'Of course. Why wouldn't it be?'

He casually reached for my bag and flipped it open.

'What do you think you're doing?' I said.

'Just making sure no piece of evidence accidentally fell into your bag.' Chodu poked his head inside my bag and jiggled it. Boy, was I glad Tuteja had interrupted me when he did!

I noticed Deshpande taking an undue interest in the contents of my bag. 'What are you looking at?'

He shrugged.

Apparently satisfied, Chodu chucked the bag back at me and turned to Deshpande. 'What about you?'

'I was scouting for property nearby when I saw your entourage tearing past. I figured it was something important and followed you.'

'That's all it was, eh?'

'That's right. Just idle curiosity.'

'Then you wouldn't mind telling me which property you were looking at?'

Deshpande didn't bat an eyelid. 'Farm property in Bhushi, just off Lonavala. You can check with the sarpanch.'

Chodu nodded. 'Mind telling me where you were last night?'

'Sure. I was at Ego, entertaining some clients.'

He turned to me. 'What about you?'

'I was home. You can check with the neighbours.'

'Is that when it happened?' Deshpande asked.

'For idle curiosity, you're taking an undue interest,' Chodu said.

'It was idle curiosity,' Deshpande rejoined. 'But Blazar is my client. So that makes it my business.'

'The doctor thinks it happened between eleven and eleven-thirty last night. What do you make of it?'

'Wait a minute!' I interjected, offended. 'It's *my* crime scene. I discovered it. Why does he get to tell you what he thinks?'

'Blazar is his client,' Chodu explained patiently.

Deshpande shrugged. 'Murder.'

'Really? I was going to go with Seppuku.'

Deshpande pretended to consider it seriously. 'Me too. But two things held me back. One, I don't think Urvashi knew much about Japanese ritual suicide. If she did, she would know that women lodged the knife in their throats. It was the men who spilled their guts. And two, she wasn't suicidal.'

'Any substance to the Urvashi disappearance rumours?' Chodu said.

Deshpande shrugged. 'If we had any theories about her being abducted, I think we can discard them. If she had been kidnapped, the Accent would've been here. Instead, her Merc's here. So, to me, it's quite clear that she came out here on her own. There are no signs that anybody else lived here, however temporarily. And there are no signs of a forced entry. Plus, there was no ransom demand. You'd hardly kill your hostage before making a demand, not that it looks like she was kept in captivity. It's obvious it was done by someone Urvashi knew and who had a reason to want her dead.'

I was determined not be left out. 'Wait a minute! How can you assume she knew the killer? People in the countryside often leave their doors unlocked. Some random guy could have crept up with the idea of robbing her and then something went wrong and he killed her.'

'There are no signs of struggle,' Deshpande said.

'Did you not see the room upstairs?'

'I'm not convinced. If all he wanted was to rob the place, why kill her? Even if she came upon him unexpectedly, it's a big property. He could just have hidden till she walked away.'

'Maybe he wanted what she had on her person. Don't forget, there was no jewellery found on her.'

'How do you know she was wearing jewellery in the first place?'

'Well, at least she must have been wearing the diamond solitaire ring that Kaustav gave her. Rumour has it, she never takes it off. Wears it like a prize.'

Deshpande looked at Chodu who was rubbing his chin thoughtfully. 'You can't be taking her seriously!'

'I have to. I always thought Bulgari presented her with that ring!'

'Please! That's just what she told the media. Besides, why would they? When she's not even their brand ambassador? It had to be Kaustav.'

Deshpande threw up his hands. 'Oh, come on!'

'Actually her theory does make sense,' Chodu said defensively.

'Really?' I was surprised since I didn't quite buy it myself; I'd only been playing devil's advocate.

'First of all, whoever killed her probably came on foot. There's only one set of tyre tracks up here. And they belong to the Merc.'

I frowned. What happened to the other set? And then I looked in the direction of the cottage. Police Jeeps were parked over them! On vital evidence! I cursed myself for not taking a photograph of the tracks earlier. I was about to tell them about it when Chodu continued.

'As of now, it looks like he came upon her in the kitchen and killed her there. Then he panicked and dragged the body down to the basement so it would be undiscovered for as long as possible. Then he cleaned all traces of blood from the kitchen and the living room. We found bloody mops in the kitchen store,' Chodu said.

Ah, that would explain the clean streaks on the floor.

Chodu continued, 'Moreover, whoever killed her didn't plan on doing so. He didn't come here with the weapon. There's an empty slot in the knife stand in the kitchen, so the cleaver was probably taken from there. Otherwise we could've traced it,' he said glumly.

'Yeah, right. A hundred and fifty kilos of RDX smuggled into the city and a terrorist plot involving scores of men you can't trace, but an innocuous knife, sure.'

'IT WAS AN OVERALL INTELLIGENCE LAPSE!'

'Whatever. Another thing. There was another set of tracks.'

They both stared at me.

'Right beside the Merc.'

Collective swivel in the direction of the cars.

'They're gone now!'

They both jumped up and ran before I could throw in the self-righteous, 'Perhaps if you'd been more careful?'

While they were crouching near the cars, I decided to stretch my legs. As I was wandering around, I happened to walk past Deshpande's Jeep. I glanced inside and noticed a folded piece of paper lying on the dashboard. I picked it up and was about to open it when I looked up and saw the two men approaching me. I crushed the paper in my fist and turned to face them.

'Nothing,' Chodu said.

'Anyway, the tracks looked like they belonged to one of those fat foreign SUV tyres,' I said to the sheepish-looking men.

'Fresh?' Chodu asked.

'The imprint wasn't smudged, so chances are it was fresh. But was it made post the 17th which is when Urvashi went missing?' I shrugged. 'It hasn't rained for sometime so it's impossible to tell really.'

I then told Chodu that I was going home. I had had enough for the day. I was tired and dirty and couldn't wait to wash Tuteja off me fast enough. But there was just one more thing I had to do before I left. And that was to call Kaustav and tell him to keep my cheque ready. I figured the case was closed. I had been hired to find Urvashi and found her I had. Nowhere in the contract did it mention that I was obliged to find her alive. Then, since I didn't have Kaustav's mobile number, I called the Blazar board line and asked the receptionist to connect me to him.

'I have some bad news. I found her. She's dead,' I said flatly as soon as he answered.

Silence.

'If this is a joke it's in very poor taste,' he said eventually.

'I wish it were a joke.' I told him that it appeared she had been stabbed and I'd found her at Hermit Hill. I knew he'd want more details, but I wasn't sure how much I could reveal. I didn't want to incur Chodu's wrath. Also, it occurred to me that this whole stunt might've been planned along with Blazar Films like I had suspected from the beginning, and then something had gone wrong.

For a moment I considered calling Kaustav's bluff, but then I decided not to give him a hard time till one, I had proof, and two, I had my cheque.

'Hermit Hill?' he said with just the right amount of surprise in it. He was good. I had to give him that.

'You sound surprised.'

'Of course, I'm surprised. What kind of thing is that to say?'

'No . . . actually . . . I was thinking of something else. It's just . . . well, it's nothing.'

'I'm coming there.' I supposed his intentions were noble but there was really no point in rushing up to Hermit Hill. It wasn't as though Urvashi was going anywhere except to the autopsy table.

'What's the point? The police have everything covered. Besides, the body would have been taken away already.'

As I was walking down the trail, I felt a familiar pressure build up in my bladder. I quickly scanned the area. Convinced that no one was around, I veered off the pathway and onto an existing trail. I was squatting, feeling a pleasurable sense of relief when I happened to glance to my front and right. There, in the foliage, I thought I saw what looked to be the remains of a small fire. That was odd.

I finished my business, pulled up my pants and walked across to inspect the remains of the fire. It looked fresh. It was fresh. I poked in the fire with a stick and found a partly charred piece of newspaper. It appeared to be a section from a Marathi edition and carried the headline, 'Mumbai Clears 21 Highwa . . .' Under the partially obliterated headline, the byline read, 'Our correspondent, Mumbai, 18 September'. That meant it was yesterday's paper, the 19th. Who had lit the fire? It was highly unlikely that it was Urvashi. And then I noticed another thing. A little distance away, on the underside of some shrubs, something bright yellow was peeping out. On closer inspection, the bright yellow turned out to be plastic gun from a veritable cache of boys' toys. There were three other guns and two home-made bows and several arrows.

Looking up, I detected what looked like the beginnings of another trail. Seeking a better vantage point, I zeroed in on a largish rock jutting out. Standing on the rock I saw that the trail led downhill, to the village Indapur in the distance. Well, that would have to wait for another day.

I started stripping as soon as I entered my apartment, leaving a trail of clothes from the living room to the bathroom. As I turned on the shower and let the hot water wash over me, lots of unanswered questions raced through my mind. Uppermost was, what was Urvashi doing at Hermit Hill? What happened to the Accent? And how did her Merc reach there? All signs indicated that she was not a captive and had occupied the bedroom upstairs. All the packaged food in the kitchen seemed to suggest that someone had planned on staying there for a long time. Was it Urvashi, planning on disappearing again? Or someone else, as suggested by the second set of tyres? If so, who was it and what had gone wrong? Why had she been murdered? And by whom? And then there was the inexplicable fire in the middle of the woods. Was it that I'd been accidentally right and she was indeed murdered by an intruder? From Indapur perhaps?

I turned off the shower and started soaping my body vigorously in the hope of jogging some theories along with my circulation. Unfortunately, I couldn't come up with anything that resolved all the contradictions.

Later, I was on the sofa, studiously avoiding looking at the packet of cigarettes lying on the table in front of me. I was telling myself all the reasons for not smoking and simultaneously looking for excuses to. I think I actually induced the growling sensation in my stomach. Oh well, I was hungry and there was only one way I knew how to cut appetite. I reached for my cigarettes.

Puffing away furiously, I dwelt on my achievements. Death, especially the death of a young person, always inspires this morbid self-examination in me. Urvashi had done enough in her short life to book her berth in the annals of history. She had starred in several blockbuster, albeit shitty, movies. In time, with the benevolence of nostalgia, they would become classics. If Yamraj landed on my doorstep tomorrow, what would I have to show for my lifetime?

Not much, I concluded. My personal life was a mess. And had it not been for Kaustav's contract, my professional life would have joined my personal life in the toilet. The little gratuity I had received from the government upon my discharge was long gone.

I had met Ani while on a case involving minor company espionage. Ani, along with a partner, owned a software services company and they were both concerned that one of their employees was stealing data. I had nabbed the thief and Ani's heart in the process. For a while I thought that he actually might be the one. We liked each other's company, the sex was great and he had no reservations about my un-ladylike job. In fact, he thought it was a huge turn-on. Plus he was smart, funny and good-looking. I should have known immediately that something was wrong.

Given my track record with men, it was nothing short of miraculous to have an uncomplicated relationship. Not that I have a track record or anything. I mean, I've only dated two men besides Ani. The first one, Jai Saxena, was a colleague during police training at Mussourie. He was all right except we had a serious difference of opinion. He was a great believer in the 'send women back to the home and hearth' movement. And I am not. And the other one, Vishal, was an IAS guy. There was nothing wrong there except that there was no spark in the bedroom. At the time I couldn't figure out what was wrong. I do now. Last I heard, he is a homosexual.

There were others during school and college, but nothing serious. It's not as though there was any sex involved. We did fool around a bit. Okay, a lot, but there was no actual penetration. And everyone knows those don't count. So, technically, I was a virgin till the age of twenty-three. Guess who could take home the good parenting award.

Sighing, I flipped on the telly and scanned news channels. I was surprised to learn that none were covering Urvashi's murder. Instead, all of them were talking about a sensational drug bust at a party in a popular Juhu disco the previous night. I switched to a movie channel and settled down to watch *Elizabeth—The Golden Age*. Clive Owen in tights was always worth a watch.

Midway through the movie, I suddenly remembered Sweety and wondered if she was back. I muted the telly and called Ani, feeling somewhat guilty. After all, I had encouraged her to leave.

He answered on the first ring. 'Kay! Have you heard from her?'

I guess that answered my question. 'No. I was calling to ask you the same.'

'She is not at her parents'. She's not at her best friend's. Her phone's off. No one's heard from her,' he sighed. 'I'm worried. I'll never forgive myself if something happens to her.'

He did sound upset. And when he was upset he rubbed his eyes and ran his hands through his wonderfully silky . . .

Stop it!

'What?' Ani asked incredulously, and I realised I'd spoken out aloud.

'Uh ... I meant stop worrying,' I hedged. 'I'm sure she's okay. She probably needs some alone time, you know, to think.'

He sighed. 'You're right.'

'Of course I am,' I said.

'Kay?'

'Um?'

'I really could use some TLC right now.'

I considered my position. Should I allow him to come over? His anxiety revealed that he had made his choice. More or less. On the other hand, Sweety might decide to dump him for good. In which case there really wasn't much point in both of us losing him.

Just then another number flashed on my screen. *Saved by the bell!* I told Ani I would call him back and switched calls. It was Kaustav, asking me if I would come over to his house. 'I know we agreed to meet tomorrow but I thought ... do you mind?'

I assured him that I wouldn't mind in the least. After hanging up, I rushed into my room, all thoughts of calling Ani back gone from my mind. I rummaged about in my cupboard for something to wear. I picked out a dress and immediately discarded it as being too fancy. Carefully casual was the way to go. The idea was to convey the 'I couldn't give a damn about what I wore' look, belying the extreme thought that had gone behind it.

In the end I decided on my faithful jeans and a T-shirt. Following Em's expert advice, I applied some tinted moisturiser all over my face, followed by a light rub of Vaseline on my cheeks and my eyelids. Next, I dabbed a bit of the highlighter at the corner of my eyes and gently merged it in. I followed it up with a light slick of kajal. I finished by slathering rose-coloured lip balm on my lips. The result was a radiant, wide-eyed, au naturel look. And it was so *easy*! I wondered why I'd never gone this route before. I stopped and considered my hair. I finally snapped on a scrunchy, figuring I could always take if off later.

Kaustav's residence was a huge, sea-facing bungalow. It was obstructed from general view by tall wire mesh squares mounted on the boundary walls. The walls and the mesh netting were attractively camouflaged by lush creepers.

There was a tall gate, but unlike bungalows belonging to stars, it wasn't flanked by a security cabin. There was just a small button under the nameplate which I pressed. While I was waiting to be let in, I removed my scrunchy and ran my fingers through my hair. While I was at it, I couldn't resist whipping out my compact. And this is how The Face saw me. While I was busy sprucing up my appearance, a small window had opened in the gate and an impassive rat-like face had peeked out.

I felt a little silly being caught like that, although I don't know why. It was a perfectly natural thing for a woman to do. 'I'm here to see Mr Kapoor,' I said tersely. I felt foolish all over again as I said that. Why would I be there if I wanted to meet the neighbour, who, a quick glance told me, was Hrithik Roshan!

The Face looked unimpressed, retreated and shut the window. I waited. When nothing happened for the next five minutes, I rang the bell again. Again, The Face peeked out. 'It's you. Again? Didn't you come by earlier? What do you want?'

Just then I heard a female voice behind The Face. They argued briefly and then the gate opened and a young maid appeared. She escorted me along a short driveway with well-kept gardens on either side. There was even a neat little swing, hanging from a hook on the underside of a terrace. To the left of the driveway was a garage that housed three cars—a black Merc E class Coupe, a silver Lexus and a midnight blue Beemer 7 series.

In the foyer, I glanced around idly. The bungalow itself was two storeys with a wooden staircase leading up to the first floor. To the left of the foyer was the dining area with an adjoining kitchen and to the right was a longish passage. Presumably, three rooms opened into it, judging by as many closed doors.

The bungalow was even more elegant inside than it was on the outside. Everything was very expensive, yet simple and tasteful. Lots of wood, cosy recesses made all the more intimate by muted lighting and everything done up in warm earthen colours.

The maid gestured towards the living room. 'Please wait. Saabji is in the shower.'

There was a painting on the living room wall portraying the scene of Sita's abduction at the hands of Ravana with Jatayu fluttering about in the background. The painting was rather kitschy, but it reminded me of all the uncomfortable Ram Leelas I had to take part in when I was younger. Of course, if you ask Em, she'll say they were a breeze. But then she always got to play the angelic Sita instead of Jatayu, with the scratchy stick-on feather costume.

I was still thinking about this when Kaustav's voice startled me. He had on a cool white tee and black drawstring pyjamas, both of which hung on his wiry frame with crumpled elegance. His cheeks, with just a hint of stubble on them, looked hollow. There were lines of tension visible on his face and his eyes were just a wee bit bloodshot. Altogether, he presented a very dignified appearance. I marvelled at his composure and wished I looked half as good on my off days. Actually I wished I looked half as good. Period.

'I was just admiring this painting,' I said.

'It's an original Raja Ravi Varma.' He said it like it was supposed to impress me.

'Really,' I murmured in awe. Who the hell was Raja Ravi Varma? Meanwhile Kaustav was waiting for me to say something more. 'Although, I personally prefer the work of . . .' I frantically tried to remember the name of the guy whose Nativity painting hung in the assembly hall in school. I willed my mind to recall the cheap plastic print with the painter's name printed at the bottom. '. . . Rembrandt?'

He frowned. Oh my god, I'd got the name wrong. Now why

couldn't I just have said something like 'It's fabulous!' and left it at that? Or just said Van Gogh? You can't go wrong with Van Gogh.

'Oh, but surely you can't compare the two?'

You can't? Why the fuck not? They were both painters, weren't they? Unless . . . oh my god, Rembrandt wasn't a painter at all. He was a sculptor. I should've said Van Gogh.

'I mean they're from completely different periods and styles. One is from the European late Renaissance period . . .'

Relief washed over me. This was manageable. 'That's what I meant. I prefer Renaissance art over . . . over this.'

He looked intrigued. 'Really. What Renaissance painters do you like?'

Fuck. Why couldn't he get off the subject? Or at least take it up later when I'd had time to read up on it?

'Oh, there are so many and I . . . right now we've got more important things to talk about.'

'Yes. Right. Shall we?' Kaustav said tiredly, gesturing towards a couple of chairs.

The young maid who'd escorted me inside appeared as if by magic and deposited two glasses of water on the table in front of me. 'Thank you, Asha,' he said and waved her away.

'Oh, by the way, did you know you have a crazy guard out there?'

He smiled. 'Zuari Mal? I'm sorry. Zuari Mal is a little old and difficult but he's devoted. He's been with us since Dad was a young man.'

He sprawled on a chair across me, all stylish repose. My heart went out to him and I wanted to console him. But I didn't know how. 'I'm sorry,' I began awkwardly.

Kaustav waved his hand dismissively and rubbed his eyes.

'If it's any consolation, I think it happened very quickly. I don't think she suffered . . . much,' I lied.

A wry smile. 'Thank you for saying that.' A beat. 'Tell me everything,' he said simply.

I related to him the sequence of events, ending with how I stumbled upon Hermit Hill.

'So, it was pure chance?' he asked incredulously.

I nodded. 'What do you think happened, Kaustav? How did she end up there? *In her own car.*'

'I don't know!' he said helplessly. He hesitated as though making up his mind about something. He reached a decision and leaned forward. 'I'm going to tell you something.'

I already had an idea of what was coming. Nevertheless, to humour him, I schooled my features to reflect eager anticipation.

'All right. You were right. It *was* a publicity stunt. A product is only as good as its marketing,' he said, shame-faced and a little defensive. 'We figured that if it appeared that Urvashi had actually been kidnapped during the making of the film, it would create a buzz and raise interest in the film. So we came up with a plan: Urvashi was to be the last one to leave the hotel on the 17th. She was supposed to drive to this spot where Chandan was going to meet her and escort her to an isolated villa in Khandala. Only a handful of us knew—Chandan, Neena, I, and of course, Urvashi's mother.'

Urvashi's mother too? I should've known, I thought, mentally kicking myself. All that elaborate tale about Urvashi calling her and demanding tinda for dinner—who likes tinda anyway?

'The idea was to use an innocuous car so it wouldn't be noticed. So, the day before, that is, on 16th September, Urvashi's Mercedes was sent home, ostensibly to have a problem checked up. In its place we arranged a nondescript car, a Hyundai Accent. So Urvashi drove out in that car. Chandan met her and drove her to Khandala to the villa where she was supposed to stay—'

I nodded intelligently. 'Hermit Hill.'

He frowned. 'No. Serenity Villa.'

Chapter Nine

❦

'*Serenity Villa*! But I thought . . .' I sputtered.

'Why do you think I was surprised when you mentioned Hermit Hill? Serenity Villa had been arranged by Chandan, after a careful recce. Chandan was to settle her in and leave for Mumbai in the Accent. Meanwhile there was to be no communication between Urvashi and the outside world. She was to switch off her phone at the Khandala exit itself. On the morning of the 18th, Omkar, a junior artiste who has worked with us for a while and is therefore trustworthy, was to reach Serenity Villa and pretend to be the kidnapper. In keeping with the role of the kidnapper, he was to make ransom demands and . . .'

'That's the most insane plan I've heard,' I blurted. 'The police would have been onto him in no time at all! The moment he made the first call he would've been traced.'

Kaustav looked briefly annoyed. 'It seemed like a good plan at the time. You see he wasn't going to make any calls. He was to communicate only through notes and those too were to be fabricated using words cut out from newspapers and magazines. We'd worked out an elaborate relay courier system.'

'Still, it seems risky. After the first note, the police would be watching the mailmen and the mailboxes too.'

'And they would have gotten nowhere fast. You see, Omkar was to send the notes to a PO box from where it would be picked up by another junior artiste and forwarded to yet another PO box from where it would be forwarded to Blazar.'

'Still . . .'

'Katie!' he said firmly. 'It would've worked. The police wouldn't have worked it out. Not before we'd had created sufficient media coverage. And even if they did, there are ways around that,' he added significantly.

'That's what you think,' I rejoined heatedly. I take all this talk of police simple-mindedness and corruption terribly personally. 'They are not idiots, you know. In fact, most of them are very good at their jobs.'

'Look, I didn't mean to . . .'

'I should know. I used to be in the police.'

'I know.'

I gaped at him. 'You do?'

'DCP Chodankar was just here,' Kaustav explained. 'Your name came up in conversation.'

'What . . .' I managed to choke out, 'what did he say?'

He smiled, tiny grooves appearing at the corners of his lips as he recollected the conversation. I could have died.

'He was quite complimentary. He said you were like a chocolate bar.' Then his brow crinkled and he said, 'Although, he did add, she's half nuts. Now, *that* doesn't sound very complimentary.'

'Did he . . . did he mention anything about . . .?'

'Chhattisgarh?' he nodded, eyeing me speculatively. 'Is it true? Did you really run out of your house naked, firing a gun?'

'I DID NOT!' I bawled, silently vowing to kill Chodu the next time I saw him.

And then I caught the expression on his face. It wasn't amused or derisive as I had expected it to be. It was . . . interested! He had a peculiar gleam in his eyes which I recognised. It was the look Ani always got just before he was about to jump me. So he found naked gunwomen a turn-on. Actually, come to think of it, it kinda was. Like Modesty Blaise. I felt a familiar tell-tale shiver of excitement in my lower abdomen. I was getting turned on by myself! *Was I sick?*

'So, tell me, what happened?' he said.

'Why?'

'I just want to know.'

Aha! So I was right about the movie thing. Didn't he just prove it by confessing to having approached me with a bogus case? And now he 'just wanted to know'?

'Didn't Chodankar tell you?'

'I want to know from you.'

Well, I'd give him a story to think about. But later. 'Maybe some other time. Right now we have more important stuff to talk about.'

Kaustav looked distressed, upset with himself for his momentary lapse. As though he'd suddenly been reminded about the inappropriateness of the exchange, given the circumstances.

Coming back to the matter at hand, I asked him, 'So what did Chodankar tell you about the murder?'

'Not much. Just that it was probably a thief who came in with the idea of robbing the place and panicked and killed her with the first thing that came to hand.' He shook his head. 'What a way to die. The pictures . . . they were—'

'He showed you pictures?'

He nodded. 'Imagine defiling a body like that. God, what a monster! What a senseless, meaningless tragedy,' he said, breaking down. After a while he composed himself and said, 'He also wanted to know where I was yesterday night.'

'Why . . . why would he ask you that?' I asked, agitated for some reason.

'Apparently the coroner thinks the murder took place sometime last night.'

'I know *why* he was asking. What I meant was he can't possibly . . . that there was . . . that you . . .'

'Katie,' he chided me gently, 'you're the police officer. You tell me.'

'What did you tell him?'

'The truth. That I was at home, in my room—my room doubles up as my study. I came home around seven and had a bite to eat. Then I went straight to my room and worked there till late. I told him that my mother and Vidisha could corroborate that.'

I still couldn't believe he was a suspect. After all, he loved Urvashi. They were going to get married. Who kills the woman he loves? And a voice in my head whispered, *Rajesh Khanna in Red Rose*. At once, I pictured Kaustav, his face painted white, his hand raised and holding a dagger, advancing upon Urvashi who, dressed in a virginal flimsy white gown, lay helplessly on a sofa, watching his advance with dread.

Stop it!

Kaustav looked shocked and I realised that I had again spoken out aloud. Blushing furiously I said, 'I wasn't talking to you. I was talking to my stomach . . . it was growling. You know, commanding it to stop.' Aware that Kaustav was looking more and more befuddled, I resisted the urge to explain about positive affirmations. 'Speaking of the others, where was Vidisha?'

'In her bedroom.'

'And your mother?'

'My mother usually takes a stroll in the garden after dinner. She was in her room afterwards.'

I nodded, and then asked, 'Kaustav, assuming for the moment that it wasn't a random burglar, who would want to kill her?'

He became agitated. 'I've been trying to figure that out. It could be anybody. It could be my competitors trying to ruin my project. It could be the underworld. *I just don't know!*'

'It could be someone in Blazar?'

'It's possible, I suppose. She's India's number one heroine. And the top spot is a lonely one.'

Besides, she hadn't helped her cause any. Urvashi was known to have had a foul temper and a mouth to match. From producers to co-stars to assistants, everyone had suffered at her hands. She wasn't known as the Naomi Campbell of Bollywood for nothing. I changed the subject. 'Kaustav, you mentioned earlier that Serenity Villa was where she was supposed to camp out. Any idea then how she reached Hermit Hill? And where did her Merc come from?'

'No,' he said helplessly.

'Well, I was just trying to put the pieces together. See if I can make sense of what happened. And I just had a crazy thought. You see, Hermit Hill was well stocked. Like someone was planning to camp out there for a long time. And you did say that Urvashi used to take off on her own, so I figured perhaps . . .'

'Urvashi might have gone there all those times she disappeared,' he finished for me. 'Yes, it does appear like she made other plans on the side, doesn't it?' He inhaled sharply. 'We'll never know now, will we?'

Maybe, maybe not. I wondered whether to mention anything about the mysterious tyre marks I'd found outside the cottage. I decided to keep the information to myself for the moment. Not that I thought he'd done it, but he might not have been totally ignorant about Hermit Hill either. He did, after all, have an SUV. The Lexus.

'Anyway, now that Urvashi is . . . you know, I guess your job is done. Of course, that doesn't affect your remuneration. We'll pay you the full amount,' he said, beginning to walk towards the front door.

That was that. The End of the Affair. I'd never see him again. Before my heart could plummet to the depths of despair, he said, 'But I hope to continue our association, perhaps on a more personal level?' He reached for a notepad lying around and scribbled a number on it. 'Here's my mobile phone number. I trust you not to share it with anybody.'

And my heart soared. His mobile number. I had Kaustav's mobile number. Golly.

I was already planning our first date by the time I exited the door. It would have to be an intimate candlelight dinner in a five-star hotel. There'd be champagne and musicians playing violins; we'd clink our glasses and take sips from our flutes, not taking our eyes off each other. He'd ask me for a dance and then, somewhere in between, kiss me lightly on the lips. And then more passionately. We'd be tearing off each other's . . . I stopped, appalled at myself. *I couldn't sleep with him on our first date!*

Okay, maybe that wouldn't be our first date. It was such a cliché anyway. Let's see, what would be more offbeat and yet romantic? A yacht! Yes, that's where we'd have our first date. The trappings would be the same—champagne and musicians. After a while I'd walk across and lean over the rails, enjoying the sea breeze. He'd come up from behind, embrace me. I'd turn around in his arms and he would pull me closer and kiss me, like Clark Gable did Scarlet O'Hara. And then he'd whisk me up in his arms and carry me into the cabin. We'd barely be inside when he'd put me down, flatten me against the door and kiss me passionately. I'd feel his arousal against my pelvis. We'd tear off each other's clothes . . . *What was wrong with me? Why was I such a slut?*

A voice called out to me. I peered into the dimly-lit gardens and saw two women gently rocking back and forth on the swing. One was a smartly dressed older woman whom I didn't recognise, but the younger one was Vidisha. She nimbly jumped off the swing and walked across to me. 'You're the private detective, aren't you? Making romantic plans with my husband?' she asked mockingly and I realised she had overheard our conversation at the door. 'Dream on!' she said lightly.

'Why? You think he didn't mean it?' I blurted out.

She gave me a strange look, an 'are you for real?' kinda look. 'Oh don't worry. You have my blessings. You're not the first one I've had to give them to. And you won't be the last. Just one word of advice though, considering you're not from the industry and all,' she said kindly. 'Just don't give your heart to him. He has what you call ... what's the term ...'

'Commitment issues?' I blurted.

'No, that's not it. It's more like ... a rush addiction.'

I'd read about that. It was a condition in which those afflicted were forever chasing adrenaline. Some people did bungee jumping, some paragliding, and some chased the heady feeling that comes with the first flush of love.

'But what about Urvashi?'

'What about her? Just between you and me,' she added conspiratorially, 'that was never going to happen.'

I looked at her pityingly. Denial was one thing. But she took it to a whole new level. Delusion.

'Don't look at me like that. You think that's wishful thinking on my part? Let me tell you, Kaustav is never going to leave me. In his own way he loves me. And I'm convenient to have around in case some woman starts demanding more. Think about it.'

'That's not what he told me,' I said boldly.

'Oh yeah? What exactly did he tell you?'

'He told me that it was over between him and you. That he had asked you for a divorce. And you agreed.'

Her face turned ugly. 'He did, did he?'

I nodded.

'It's not true,' she said without any real conviction, and turned to go back inside.

'By the way, where were you last night, say, between eight and ten?'

She stopped and walked back, laughing amusedly. 'Why? You think I'm the burglar who crept up on Urvashi and killed her?' In a gesture that was openly patronising, she tucked a wayward lock of my hair behind my ear.

'If you're not, you'd have no problem telling me where you were.'

She continued fiddling with my hair. 'Not doing creative art with Urvashi's precious MAC foundation anyway, which, by the way, is at least three shades lighter than her skin tone.'

I stepped back out of her reach. 'How did you know about that?'

'Duh! Everyone knows she's really not fair. What you see on the screen is an expert make-up job. She has a real complex about her dusky complexion.'

'Fascinating.' And it really was. 'But I meant how did you know her make-up was messed with?'

She gave me an odd look. 'Didn't anyone show you the pictures?'

Right. Chodu. 'That still doesn't answer the question. Where were you?'

Her lips slowly parted in a mean smile. 'I was home. With Ma out in the garden and then in my bedroom. There.' She pointed towards the left side of the house, to a darkened room on the first floor. Still smiling mysteriously, she pointed to a room adjoining the terrace at the other end. 'And that's where Kaustav says he was.'

And she went inside, leaving me alone, staring after her. What did this mean? Was Vidisha deliberately trying to screw his happiness by implying she didn't actually know if he was home, in his room? There certainly was no love lost between the two. Or was there? And what was all that about the divorce? Had Kaustav really asked her for one? Or had Urvashi become a liability? No, the distress on Vidisha's face had been plain to see when I had confronted her with the fact that I knew about Kaustav asking her for a divorce. And there was no real conviction in her denial subsequently. No, it had to be that she was lying.

I eyed the Lexus in the garage briefly, but with so many people around there was no way I was getting a look at the tyres tonight. As I turned to go, I saw the older woman get off the swing and march briskly towards me. She was tall, slender and uber elegant. She wore expensive riding breeches, a fitted silk blouse and riding boots with spurs and all. Her hair, coiffed in a short, wispy kinda style, must have cost her at least five grand to colour. I knew because the particular shade, raven black with a midnight hue, was not available as a standalone colour under any label. It had to have been a blend of several expertly-applied layers.

Her Chanel No. 5 wafted up to me long before she reached me. 'Hello,' she said pleasantly in a deep, husky voice. 'I'm Meher Kapoor.' Kaustav's mother. Of course. I remember wondering where Kaustav got his good looks and sense of style from, because his father, the late Rajinder Kapoor, while being a canny businessman, was no Adonis. He'd been an earthy son of the Punjab soil and ugly in a good-natured sort of way.

'Hello,' I said shyly. In this instance, I had to bite my tongue to stop myself from adding Mummyji.

'Please excuse my daughter-in-law's behaviour. She's just a little . . . overwrought.'

'Oh?'

'You think she doesn't realise how it affects her? She didn't have anything to do with it, of course.'

'Oh?'

She shook her head. 'She had nothing to gain by Urvashi's death. Kaustav was never going to divorce her.'

'So she told me.'

'Well, it's true.'

'Why? Because in his own way he loves her?'

'Because it doesn't make good business sense!'

'You mean like division of assets and stuff?'

She didn't answer me. 'Moreover, Vidisha was home last night. All the time. I know because we were out in the garden, walking between eight and nine. Then we went inside, to our rooms.'

'So she could have left afterwards,' I pointed out.

She shook her head. 'I would have known about it. My room is on the ground floor, right next to the main door. It overlooks the driveway. I would have heard something. Some movement in the hall, a car revving up, something.'

Well, she was certainly going out of her way to defend Vidisha. I wondered if she'd feel the same way if she found out her darling daughter-in-law was trying to screw over her son.

'What about Kaustav?'

'Why? You don't think he did it?'

'I'll tell you how Chodankar's mind will work. If what you say is true, and Kaustav was never going to divorce Vidisha, Urvashi could have become a liability,' I pointed out. 'Especially if she was putting pressure on him to marry her.'

She laughed. 'If that were the case, Kaustav would be a serial killer by now.'

Was he? Again, Rajesh Khanna's face loomed large in my imagination. I pushed it out of my head with some effort.

'What about you? Did anyone see you after you both went indoors?'

'Well, I was in my room. Ask the servants. Ask Zuari Mal.'

'What are your thoughts on this whole thing? Do you think it was a random act? Or was she done in by someone deliberately?'

I had a feeling she wanted to say something, but she checked herself. In the end she chose to go with the ambiguous but safe, 'Her room was ransacked, her suitcases rummaged through, her jewellery was missing . . . you tell me.'

'Assuming for the moment it wasn't a burglar?'

She sighed. 'She wasn't popular.'

'How did you feel about her?'

'She was a wonderful talent. A real asset to Blazar.'

'But personally?'

She hesitated. 'Look, I'm fond of Vidisha. I feel for Vidisha. I really do. But my son is a young man. A handsome, powerful, virile young man. These things happen. If it wasn't Urvashi, it would've been someone else. Besides, as I mentioned before, he wasn't going to divorce Vidisha.'

When I turned to go, The Face, a.k.a. Zuari Mal, was holding the gate open for me. I thought he was looking at me mockingly.

On an impulse I stopped and asked him, 'Were you here last night?'

'Who wants to know?' he said impassively.

Was he crazy? Who else was there other than me? 'Me!'

'Who's me?'

I peered at his face. Was he high on some hallucinogenic substance?

I waved my arms. 'Hello! Here. I'm a detective.'

'Are you with the police?'

'Yes,' I lied, fumbling in my bag for my long-expired identity card.

He opened the gates wider and stood aside.

'Wait! I'm not the police.'

'Ram, Ram,' he said coldly and shut the gate in my face.

Outside, I figured it would be a waste to have come to the neighbourhood and not try and catch a glimpse of Hrithik Roshan. So I sat on my bike and waited.

My phone rang, startling me. I glanced at the number, an international code, and scowled. Like I needed more stress. I briefly considered not answering it. But I knew that was only postponing the inevitable. Besides, all was quiet on the Roshan front, so I had the time. I decided to get the unpleasantness out of the way.

'Hello?' I said into the phone.

'Baby?' Mom said.

'Hi, Mom, how's the cruise going?' I monotoned.

'Oh, it's fabulous. All the gorgeous food and the exciting places. And I made some nice friends. Anne and Elena. Anne is from England and Elena is from Russia . . . or is it Armenia . . .'

'Mom, it doesn't matter.'

'Anyway, it doesn't matter. Oh, and I've joined aerobics. That handsome young instructor says I've got a forty-five-year-old's body.'

Mom, you're fifty! 'That's nice.'

'Isn't he nice?'

'Good to know you're having fun.'

'Fun? Where's the fun?' she groused. 'It would have been fun if your father had considered spending some time with me. He's met some old friends here and all these old fogies do is drink and gossip like old women all day . . . it's not reminiscing, Sunil, it's gossiping. And he's gorging on all that food. He has dessert morning, noon and night. God knows he's going to have a heart attack right here on the ship . . . I'm not exaggerating, Sunil. You had three scoops of ice cream after lunch today!'

'Mom!'

'Stop lying. I saw you, Sunil . . . If that's not a recipe for a cardiac arrest, Baby, I don't know what is . . . So, now I'll be the cause of your death?

'Mom!'

'It's impossible to reason with him. Here, you talk to him, Baby. It might be your only chance before he dies on us.'

'Wait, Mom ...'

But she'd already handed the phone over to Dad. 'Baby? Listen, I met an old friend of mine on the ship. He has a stock broking firm and says he can get you a job in sales. Here take down this number and contact a man named Srinivas ...'

Christ! 'Papa,' I said, summoning all the patience at my disposal, 'I have a job.'

'You're still persisting with that detective nonsense? When are you going to get a real job?'

'It *is* a real job, Papa. I get paid for it.'

'Stop arguing with me, Baby. Now take down this number and give them a call.'

I sighed. 'Okay, Papa.'

I was still pretending to take down the number when Mom grabbed the phone again. 'Baby, this call is very costly so I have to disconnect soon. We'll be back in Delhi on the 30th. Will you call Manju and ask her to come and clean the house?'

I agreed, heaved a sigh of relief and disconnected. And then, since the Roshan house remained stubbornly, deathly still, I decided to give up my vigil for the night. I lit a cigarette and dialled Em's number. I was close to her nightclub and figured I'd drop in. But once again, she blew me off before I could even begin. What was going on?

Just then the gates of the Kapoor residence opened and evicted the young maid who had earlier served me water. What had Kaustav called her? Thinking quickly, I approached her.

'Just a minute. Asha, right?'

She looked at me suspiciously for a moment, then her face cleared. 'Oh, you were with Saabji earlier.'

'Yes. I was wondering if I could ask you some questions.'

'I don't know,' she said uncertainly. 'I have to get back quick. Memsaab is waiting for her inhaler.'

'This won't take long.'

'What kind of questions?'

This time around I decided to play safe and flashed my identity card. 'I'm with the police, you see.'

If she looked hesitant earlier, she looked plain terrified now. 'Is this about the burglary last night?'

'I just want . . . oh?'

'I told Saabji also, I had nothing to do with it,' she whined. 'I told him it must be the workmen. Why would I steal documents anyway?'

'What workmen?'

'There was some repair work going on around the house during the day. I told Saabji, they must have come back and robbed the place later.'

'What was stolen?'

'I don't know. This morning Saabji said some papers were missing from the cupboard in his room. He was very angry. He said that he'd seen those papers yesterday and how could they have just vanished.'

'When did this happen?'

'I don't know. I suppose sometime last night.'

'Why do you say that? Did you see anything?'

'Nothing! I told Saabji also. I was in the kitchen the whole time, grinding dosa batter and coconut chutney for the next day's breakfast. And then I went off to my room to sleep. I didn't see or hear anything.'

With the blender going on? No kidding!

'Where were your Saabji and Memsaab?'

'They were all home, in their rooms. The workmen must've returned after everybody went to sleep.'

'What about the security guard?' I said gesturing towards The Face.

'Him? He was there but it's as good as not being there,' she said dismissively.

'And why is that?'

'When Saabji asked him if he saw anyone, he said he saw his wife.'

'So?'

'His wife has been dead for twenty years. Then he also said he saw Bhagwan Ram. He's crazy. Especially after he has . . .' And she pretended to smoke up.

So he *was* on a hallucinogenic substance.

My cellphone display flashed an unknown mobile number. 'What?' I bawled into the phone.

'It's . . . er . . . Geeta,' a voice said nervously. 'Urvashi's mother.'

'Oh! I'm . . . I'm so sorry for your loss, Ms Geeta . . . I . . .' I gestured to Asha indicating the interview was over. 'Is there anything I can do for you?'

'I heard that you were the one who found . . . found,' Geeta fumbled. 'I was wondering if you would be so kind as to come by. I . . . I wanted to talk to you.'

Actually, I wanted to talk to her too, if only to satisfy my curiosity. I had many unanswered questions. Like what Urvashi was doing at Hermit Hill. But I thought it best to wait till the next morning, till she'd had time for the news to sink in. I wasn't great with displays of emotion, particularly distress. So I tried to put it off, but she insisted and, ultimately, I had to agree. I fired the RE and took off.

Before ringing the bell at Urvashi's penthouse, I paused and studied my appearance in the huge mirror adorning the landing. I realised, to my dismay, that I looked wholly too sanguine. Totally inappropriate for the occasion.

I crinkled my eyes in the hope of inducing a tear or two. No go. I tightened my throat till it hurt and thought of all the sad things that had happened to me. Still the lachrymal glands refused to oblige. I shrugged. Urvashi was no one of mine. I rang the bell.

Geeta opened the door and stared at me through swollen, red eyes. 'Thank you for coming,' she said, opening the door wider.

'I'm so sorry for your loss,' I said once again, stepping in. The very next moment I could have bitten my tongue as I saw her eyes start to fill.

'Thank you,' she said huskily. 'Come in, won't you? Have a seat.'

The sofa protested once more as Geeta eased into it. Once seated, we regarded each other wordlessly. The oppressive silence stretched only for about thirty seconds or so but it felt much longer, and I thought I would scream if she didn't speak soon.

'Did she . . .?' Geeta began and stopped. 'Do you think my baby suffered a lot?'

Okay, the silence was better.

Let's see. She'd been stabbed. The death wasn't instantaneous. In all probability, she had writhed in pain, slowly bleeding to death. For quite a while. I don't know what prompts families of victims of violent deaths to torture themselves by asking for details. Is it to alleviate their guilt over being alive and relatively pain free while a loved one died painfully? Is it morbid fascination?

'Didn't you see . . .?' I hedged.

She nodded. 'I had to. For identification purposes.' She shuddered as her mind remembered the pictures. 'But I would like to know your opinion also. After all you found her.'

'Well, I think it was relatively painless. I don't think she suffered much at all,' I said.

She nodded solemnly. 'Thank you.'

'My pleasure.' And when I realised how callous that probably sounded, I blabbed, 'I mean it was my pleasure to give you the good news,' I added hastily. 'I mean it is good news to be told that your loved one didn't suffer. In that sense it was my pleasure to reassure you ...' I trailed off lamely, wishing the ground would open and swallow me.

She stared at me for a moment. 'I want you to find out who did it.'

'What?'

'I want you to find out who did it,' she repeated.

'But the police can do that much better,' I protested.

'Come on, we all know what's going to happen. They are going to catch some innocent guy and torture him into confessing while the real culprit goes scot free.'

That was twice in a span of less than two hours that I'd heard the Indian police abused! It was too much. 'Oh?' I said, wondering what was behind her distrust of the police. 'Why? What did Chodankar say?'

Geeta scowled. 'Please. He said that they're investigating. That so far, it appears that she was killed by a person or persons unknown.'

Not an unreasonable statement given the circumstances. So what had prompted her ire?

'Why would strangers want to kill her? Kill Urvashi! Urvashi is a star. Everyone loves her.'

The statement, while being a sterling show of doting motherhood, was not strictly true. For instance, if the gossip columns were to be believed, there was no love lost between Colleen Bandukwala and Urvashi. The latter's repeated physical assaults on the scribe were legendary. And Razia, Urvashi's former personal assistant, had had so many stitches from having stuff chucked at her over the years, she was a veritable patchwork quilt. And she had used her influence to get roles taken away from so many colleagues, they weren't exactly clamouring to join her fan club either. In fact, it was a wonder she hadn't been bumped off earlier.

'I think what Chodankar meant was, the motive was burglary and that the thief killed her in panic.'

'So, why wasn't anything taken from her stuff?'

'Didn't Chodankar tell you? Her jewellery was taken.'

'Only what she had on her. The DCP showed me the pictures and an inventory of Urvashi's stuff found at Hermit Hill. There's nothing missing. For god's sake, her laptop was still there in her suitcase. Even a thief has to know it's valuable. Why didn't he take it?'

'Maybe he panicked and just grabbed whatever he could and ran.'

'Or the scene was set up to look like burglary.'

'So what are you saying?' I asked. 'Do you know who killed her?'

'I don't know for sure . . .'

'But you suspect someone?' I prompted.

'Look, you might as well know. This . . . Uru's disappearance, was all a publicity stunt planned by Kaustav.'

She stopped and waited for my reaction. And looked sorely disappointed when none was forthcoming. 'I see,' she said disgruntled, 'you know about it.'

'I've heard it mentioned in passing. But please continue. I'd like to know your version of it.'

'Only Chandan Baweja and Neena Pundir apart from Kaustav, Uru and I knew about it. According to the plan, Urvashi was to disappear en route to Mumbai. She was supposed to have been kidnapped. In reality, she was to be escorted by Chandan Baweja to a secluded house that he had arranged earlier, discreetly. He was to leave her there, make sure she was settled in and come back to Mumbai.

'Meanwhile Uru was supposed to stay hidden at that secluded house, Serenity Villa. Her phone was to be turned off and there was to be no contact between her and anyone else. Not even me.

I was worried about that, I tell you. But Kaustav assured me that it was like she was away at a retreat.

'The next day one junior artiste was to go to Serenity Villa and camp out there. Omkar ... he's the junior artiste ... was to pretend to be a kidnapper and make a ransom demand ...'

'That's the one thing I don't understand,' I interrupted. 'Why involve another person? If Omkar only had to pretend to be the kidnapper and send ransom notes, anyone—Chandan, Neena, Kaustav himself—could have done it, right?'

She shrugged. 'I don't know. Perhaps Kasutav felt it was safer not to involve any company personnel directly.'

'Okay. But why send Omkar to Serenity Villa? He could have sent the notes from anywhere, right?'

'Oh, that's because Uru was afraid to be alone. Besides what if she needed something? She couldn't very well get it herself, could she?'

I nodded. 'Continue please.'

'The news about the kidnapping was to be carefully leaked to the press. What with information about the progress of negotiations with the kidnappers, journalists' own speculations, etc., over the next few days, the media would have been full of Uru's kidnapping. After sufficient hype had been created, we were going to announce that a *Ransom* amount had been agreed on and paid, and Uru would return unharmed.'

After she had finished I asked her, 'I understand she was travelling in a hired car, an Accent. How did Urvashi get hold of her Merc? Because I was given to understand that it had been sent back to Mumbai?'

'Even I thought that the car was in the garage. But today, the driver confessed to me that Uru had asked him to park the car discreetly outside Serenity Villa. Apparently, she wasn't comfortable being stuck out there without her car. She wanted some transport handy, just in case, you understand?'

'The question still remains, how and why did she reach Hermit Hill? Did something upset her for her to take off again?'

'Maybe, maybe not. That's what I want you to find out. Maybe she was lured there by somebody.'

'Oh?'

She didn't answer directly. 'According to the plan, Chandan Baweja escorted her from her hotel all the way to Serenity Villa. He settled her in and returned to Mumbai. This was on 17th September. But something happened during the night. The next morning, when Omkar went to the house, she wasn't there,' she sobbed.

'So, if Omkar is to be believed, Urvashi left Serenity Villa sometime during the night of September 17th?'

'Or early 18th morning.'

'Do you think this Omkar is lying?'

'Why?'

'I don't know. Maybe he reached before he was supposed to, just as Urvashi was leaving. And then he followed her to Hermit Hill and killed her?'

'Why would he do that? He is a small-time junior artiste. What would he gain by killing her?'

'Then who? Chandan Baweja? Neena Pundir? You said she hated Urvashi.'

Geeta leaned forward. 'What would you say if I said it was Vidisha? Think about it. Who else stood to gain from Uru's ... Uru's ...' her voice caught.

From my earlier encounter with her, I could agree that Vidisha was keen to keep her husband. All the same, it seemed a rather drastic way to do it. Then again, murders have been committed for less. Moreover, she, being Kaustav's wife, could have known about the plan and decided to capitalise on it. But that still didn't explain how she knew about Hermit Hill.

'Besides, you see, I haven't told you the entire story. Urvashi did call me on the night of the 17th. She was most upset. She said that Vidisha had just been there and that they'd had the most frightful row. Vidisha threatened her to lay off Kaustav. She also taunted her saying he was never going to leave her.'

'But I checked Urvashi's cellphone records. She didn't make that call.'

'Oh but she did. From the landline.'

'So, according to Urvashi, Vidisha came to Serenity Villa, fought with her and left? That still doesn't explain how she knew about Hermit Hill.'

'Maybe she didn't leave. Maybe she waited and then followed Uru.'

'Okay, but why wait till the 19th? Why not kill her right then?'

Geeta had no answer to that.

'Look, you're not just saying this? I mean, why didn't you tell me this earlier? You had to have been worried.'

'I wanted to. Oh god, how I wanted to. But Kaustav convinced me there was nothing to worry about. And you don't cross Kaustav. Why do you think, even when she was so upset, Uru didn't dare use her cellphone? I should have told you. It's my fault my baby's dead,' she said, anguished.

'Okay, did you tell Chodankar this?' I asked.

Geeta dabbed at her eyes and nodded.

'And?'

'All he said was he'll look into it. But I could tell he didn't believe me. I don't think he's going to do anything about it.' And then she added rather cattily, 'Even if he does, we all know Meher Kapoor will never allow her beloved daughter-in-law to be taken to jail.'

That was certainly something to think about. And while my curiosity was piqued, I had no experience in solving homicide cases.

'I appreciate your faith in me but I have to ask, why me?'

'I don't know anyone else.'

Great! Chosen by default. Always a confidence booster.

'Plus you did find Urvashi when everyone else failed,' she amended.

Better. But dear god, if only she knew how.

Geeta paid me a modest retainer, that is, modest compared to the one paid by Kaustav, but way better than what I was used to. And in return I agreed to do my best, adding, 'You are not going to like it but I have to tell you, I'm not entirely convinced about Vidisha. I agree that the motivation existed, but I'm not sure about the opportunity. I mean look at it. Almost everyone else—hell, even the villagers at Mulshi—had more opportunity than Vidisha.'

Geeta snorted derisively. 'Please! That was just a publicity stunt. The "villagers" were paid junior artistees hired to create a nuisance. Just so Blazar would have something to tell reporters. And it would've served very well as a foundation for the kidnap part of the plan. The idea was to create the speculation that Uru had been kidnapped by the Mulshi locals as revenge for defiling their forest.'

Was anything for real? All at once I had a horrific thought. Maybe Urvashi wasn't dead at all! Maybe it was a life-sized, very real dummy that I'd found! Or maybe someone who looked like her. It could be Falguni!

Chapter Ten

On the way home, I decided to stop over at the Versova police station: for one, I could check if Urvashi's autopsy report had come in. And two, I had to have dinner and there's a thelawala next door which serves the meanest keema-pav in Bombay.

'Is Urvashi really dead?' I blurted as soon as I entered Chodu's room.

Chodu was sitting on his desk. He had an audience of two junior officers, neither of whom I knew. Judging from his crude hand gestures, and his audience's raucous laughter, he was regaling them with some bawdy anecdote.

He stared at me for a beat. Then turning to his colleagues, said, 'This is *Kasthuri Kumar*.'

I didn't like the way he enunciated my name. As though it had some special significance. The junior colleagues looked at me as though they were looking at a celebrity—with a mixture of awe, disbelief and a sense of privilege.

I turned to them and snarled, 'What?'

They cut their eyes to Chodu. I saw him shake his head warningly before he caught my eyes on him and checked himself. The junies hastily muttered, 'Nothing!' and ran.

I turned on Chodu. 'What's with them? Why did they run off like that?'

He shrugged as if to say he hadn't the faintest idea. But his act didn't fool me.

'Have you been telling them about Chhattisgarh?' I asked, outraged.

'I didn't have to! They knew. Everyone knows.'

So I was legend. How come I didn't feel like Will Smith?

'Now what is this about Urvashi?' he wanted to know.

'I just wanted to know if it was really Urvashi. That it wasn't a dummy or anything.'

Chodu jumped off his desk and, hitching up his pants, came up to me. 'I see what's going on. What has that bewdi been telling you now?'

'Zara? Nothing! I haven't even spoken to her.' Feeling totally foolish, I said, 'It's just that you never know with film people.'

'Aaah. So, you've learnt about the "publicity stunt".'

He assured me that Geeta and several others had identified the body. They had also carried out a DNA test, though they were still waiting for those results. Then, he asked, 'What is it to you anyway?'

'I've been hired to find out who the murderer is,' I told him, a little superciliously. It *was* my first murder case.

'You've been what?' he sputtered incredulously and burst into snorting laughter.

I tolerated his amusement with fortitude. When I found the murderer, well, who would be laughing then? I mustered as much dignity as I could and said, 'Geeta hired me. So I would greatly appreciate it if you would share your information with me.'

Chodu uttered some choice expletives. My Marathi isn't all that good but I think there were references to Geeta's behind and private detectives in that order. 'Does she know about your ... does *she* know about Chhattisgarh? She doesn't, does she? I bet if she knew she would think twice before hiring you.'

'Oh come on, Chodu. It was a long time ago. My . . .'

'Two years and sixty-one days today,' he said helpfully.

Okay, so he had a lot of idle time on his hands. Not to mention an undue interest in my career.

'As I was saying, my psychiatric evaluation has come back clean.' Chodu looked like he was enjoying my discomfort immensely. And just then I felt that I'd had enough. I was done grovelling. 'You know what, tell her. I don't care. I'm sure she'll understand these things happen under pressure. After all she's from the film industry. Hell, she might even think it fashionable.'

'But we think it's plain cuckoo!' he chortled.

'Think what you will but give me the info I need. You know you will eventually, 'cos I'll just haunt you till you do. I'll invoke the RTI act, if I have to.'

Like most public servants, he quailed at the mention of the RTI act. Glancing at his watch, he said, 'Fine. I'll tell Dogra to update you.'

'Not Prado!' I squealed. 'Not tonight!'

'I have to be somewhere else. So, unless you can wait till tomorrow, it's either Prado or no go.' He laughed gleefully once more.

'Fine, I'll talk to Prado,' I said ungraciously.

He exited the room, only to peek his head in a few moments later. 'He's waiting for you. But before you speak with him, we need your fingerprints for elimination purposes. They've recovered many fingerprints from the crime scene. Some were Urvashi's, of course, but there were many unidentified ones.'

I agreed and did as told.

ASP Prakash Dogra is all of twenty-five-years old. He is a tall, gangly fellow who has an enormous crush on me. He thinks I'm a hotshot private detective, on the same cerebral plane as Hercule Poirot and Sherlock Holmes. Obviously, I encourage this notion.

Sometimes, when I'm in the mood, I even allow him to take me out for a meal. You know, as a favour to him. These are the high points of his life. He talks about them for weeks. He practically gets a hard-on whenever I'm around and I wonder what would happen if I actually touched him. He might go into an involuntary orgasm or worse, die of an adrenaline rush.

Fortunately, although he hopes for reciprocity, he doesn't really expect it and is content to worship me from afar. Prado had once told me about an erotic dream he had about me. In his dream, he bent to kiss me, only to discover it wasn't him at all! *Even in his fantasies he is someone else.* In other words, a complete loser.

Dogra jumped up as soon as he saw me. 'Katie!'

He surreptitiously touched his hair and patted a few stray strands into place.

'Hey Prado,' I said sighing as I plonked myself heavily on the chair across his desk.

'Bad day?' he asked, pushing a glass of water towards me.

'Like you wouldn't believe.'

'Katie?'

'Ummm?'

His huge Adam's apple bobbed up and down as he swallowed. 'I . . . I spoke to my parents today. I told them I was ready. I was ready to get married,' he said and stopped for dramatic effect. 'And they agreed. They said yes,' he added when I failed to comply with a breathless, 'And?'

'That's great,' I said absently. 'When's the wedding?'

'Katie!' he pouted.

'Hey, has Urvashi's autopsy report come in?'

He nodded and pointed to a thick file in front of me. 'It's in here. So as I was saying . . .'

'Great! What's the cause of death?'

'One knife wound to the solar plexus. Extensive internal and external bleeding. Er . . . Katie?'

I nodded. 'Time of death?'

'Between eleven and eleven-thirty p.m. on 19th September, going by the body temperature and the state of rigor mortis.'

'What about preliminary forensics tests. Any traces of fabric or alien DNA? Fingerprint analysis?'

'We're still waiting for the full report. Katie?'

'What about Omkar? Did you guys speak to him yet? And did you find out who owns the Hermit Hill property?'

'Here, take the entire file,' he said, violently pushing it towards me.

'Thanks, I'll just photocopy it here,' I said, getting up.

'Katie! I said my parents have given me permission to marry. So what do you say?'

Why was he asking me? Unless he was asking me to marry him! Dear god! I stared at him in horror.

'But . . . but,' I stuttered.

To my surprise he came around the desk and before I could react, planted a wet, full-mouthed kiss on my lips! Ugh!

I wrenched my head away and yelled, 'What do you think you're doing?'

Dogra skittered back to the desk, knocked over my glass of water, set it upright and generally behaved like a goat in an abattoir. 'I'm sorry . . . I . . . I just spoke to sir and . . . and . . .'

'And *what*? Chodu told you to grab me?'

He swallowed. 'No! He told me to grab initiative. He said I suffer from low self-esteem.'

No kidding. And then I turned and saw Chodu looking in from the doorway, laughing helplessly. If he wasn't in the police I would have lunged at Chodu right there and then. But a charge of assaulting a police officer didn't exactly expedite my case. So I decided to risk ulcers and settled for simmering silence instead.

After photocopying the file, I walked across to the thelawala next door and, in spite of the raging acids in my stomach, had an extremely satisfying dinner. Then I picked up my bike and drove home. When I was within a hundred metres of my building I cut the engine and glided the rest of the way. To my surprise, Kaustav was outside, lounging against his Beemer. I slammed on the brakes. 'Kaustav! What are you doing here?'

'I'm sorry to barge in on you like this, but I was too restless to be by myself. I figured I'd come and talk to you. Besides, you said you'd tell me your story later.'

When I'd said that, I'd had days, not mere hours, in mind.

'I've brought some wine,' he said.

'Well, come on in then.'

He reached into his car and retrieved a dusty bottle of wine. Which, of course, meant that it was very old and very expensive. *Don't get caught out again. Admit you don't know much about wines.* But of course, the minute I opened my mouth, out came: 'What's that, Romanee Conti 1967?'

He lifted an eyebrow. 'You do know that Romanee Conti 1967 sells for upwards of 5,000 pounds per bottle?'

Of course I knew that. But I couldn't tell him it was the only fancy wine I knew about—and that was because it sat atop the pile of results of an accidental Google search. 'That was a joke. I meant . . .' under the pretext of fumbling for my keys, I stole a covert glimpse at the label, '. . . Chateau Latour Pauillac 2000?'

I was hopeless.

He looked pleased. 'You like it?'

'Oh yes! I love the . . . the smoky flavour?'

He frowned. 'But it's not smoky at all . . . it's actually quite silky. And fruity . . .'

Crap! Crap! Crap! '—Oh, I was talking about the 1990.'

'But—'

'—I'll get the glasses,' I said and rushed into the kitchen.

Meanwhile, Kaustav opened the bottle and left it on the coffee table in the centre of the room to 'let it breathe'. While the wine carried on its respiratory communion with the atmosphere, I said conversationally, 'I just had a meeting with Geeta.'

'Oh? What did she want?'

'She wants me to find the killer.'

'But aren't the police on it?'

'Sure. It's just her way of buying extra insurance.'

'So what did she say?'

'Well, pretty much what you told me. About how it started off as a publicity stunt. She was equally clueless about Hermit Hill. She did say, though, that the driver confessed to driving the Merc to Serenity Villa as per Urvashi's instructions. So it does seem like Urvashi was planning on disappearing once again. Kaustav, you said that Vidisha had agreed to a divorce—why do you think Urvashi wanted to take off?'

'I have no idea,' he said helplessly.

'Did Vidisha agree to the divorce? Really?'

'Why do you ask?'

'Because she went down to Serenity Villa and, like, really had it out with Urvashi. And tonight she told me you were never going to marry Urvashi. Makes me wonder if she was really reconciled to it.'

He hesitated. 'Look, I'll tell you something. Urvashi called me as well that night. She was near hysterical and kept ranting about Vidisha hounding her and how she'd had enough.'

'So what did you do?'

'What was I going to do? I was here and she was in Khandala. What could I do? I calmed her down as best I could. When you've been in showbiz as long as I have, you learn the best thing to do with hysterical heroines is to do nothing at all. So I told her to take a chill pill and that everything would be better in the morning.'

'That's it?!'

'What else was I going to do? It wasn't the first time she'd called me, ranting about real or imagined showdowns with Vidisha.'

'She was delusional? Paranoid?'

He hesitated. 'Or she was just trying to get my attention.'

'And did she?'

'What are you implying?'

'Did you know about Hermit Hill?'

'So now you think *I* killed her?'

'No . . . I don't know . . . it's just that there was another set of tyre imprints next to Urvashi's Merc. One of those fat SUV tyres. They looked fresh.'

'Is that so?' His next words took me completely by surprise. 'So now I know why she disappeared this time. She was cheating on me!'

'*What?*'

'She took off for no apparent reason. She didn't tell me where she was going. Then someone visited her there in an SUV. What does it look like?'

'We don't even know if it was a man. It could have been a woman.'

'Which makes it worse.'

'*What?*'

He smiled crookedly. 'Kidding. You're right. I am overreacting.'

He reached for the wine and poured a little bit into a glass. He picked up the glass, sniffed at the red liquid inside, swirled it around once, sniffed some more, sloshed it around a bit and held up the glass against the light to 'study the legs'. Only then did he proclaim his satisfaction with it. I lit a cigarette while he poured out a glass for me.

He frowned as he handed me my glass. 'You're going to smoke?'

'Er . . . I'm sorry. Are you allergic or something?'

'No, but I'm sure you know this wine has a very delicate flavour and smoke ruins it.'

'Yes, I did know and I'm sorry,' I said, doing a mental eye roll. One thing I've never been accused of is having a sensitive palate and chances were, if the wine were that delicate, I'd miss whatever it was I wasn't supposed to miss anyway. Nonetheless, I stubbed out the ciggie.

'Cheers,' I said and took a sip. 'Kaustav, can I ask you a personal question?'

'Sure.'

'Why did you marry Vidisha?'

'It's a long story. But, in a nutshell, Vidisha is the daughter of my mother's best friend. My mom and she were like sisters and my mother promised her that Vidisha would one day be her daughter-in-law. My father was equally fond of Vidisha and he, too, agreed. It was his dying wish to see me married to Vidisha.'

I started to laugh but I caught sight of his face. He was deadly serious! Which filmi world did these people live in? For god's sake, even movies today had abandoned that antiquated 'kya hua tera vada' theme.

I glanced at his face again and saw a smile sneak in.

'You're yanking my chain!'

The smile widened and he held up his hands. 'Guilty as charged. It was the usual story. Our parents were friends and when we grew up, we fell in love, or so we thought. But enough about me. Let's talk about you.'

He looked so eager, so expectant of being dazzled that it didn't seem right to let him down. Plus it was only fair that I returned the favour. So I told him an Oscar winning story of a girl child, unwanted at birth and unloved as a child. All because she was the wrong sex. The girl who had absolutely no breaks was, nevertheless, determined to make something of her life and created opportunities where none existed. Through sheer grit she prevailed and made a career for herself in the IPS.

One would've thought that at last her troubles had ended, but it wasn't to be. Here too, she faced discrimination and had to work twice as hard as her male counterparts to prove herself. But she didn't mind the hard work. She was used to carrying the extra burden. Her willing and uncomplaining attitude to work only made her male colleagues more insecure and they used every weapon in their arsenal to get rid of her. At first they tried petty pressure tactics in an effort to break her, but gradually they became bolder. She was subjected to sexual and psychological harassment. And when this too failed, they hatched a conspiracy so foul that even her remarkable fortitude wasn't able to weather it. The strain proved too much and she suffered a nervous breakdown. Her conspirators had won.

I'm not sure where I'd read it—I think I might've picked some of the themes from the film *North Country*—anyway, I told a story so poignant, so heart-rending that Kaustav's eyes misted over. Hell, I had myself sniffling. Damn, I was good.

'My god, is it true?' he asked huskily.

I glanced at his face. His expression was tender, admiring. 'Sure, why not?'

He sighed. 'Just goes to show the world's full of gutsy, talented, accomplished women. Usually, I only get to meet the beautiful, glamorous ones.'

'I'm sure it must get quite tedious.'

He laughed gleefully. 'See what I mean? No one, I mean, no one would dare talk to me like that.'

If the penalty for crossing him was similar to what had happened to Rocky earlier, I didn't blame them. 'So why are you such a hard ass?'

He sighed. 'It's good business. Give people an inch and they grab a yard. That's why I'm so glad I met you. I mean it. I know you don't want anything from me materially so I can be myself without any fear of getting exploited.'

If only it were true. I felt ashamed of harbouring ambitions for my own movie and looked away.

'Kaustav, there was a burglary at your house last night?'

He stilled. 'How do you know about that?'

'I . . . er . . . someone mentioned it in passing.'

His nostrils flared briefly. But if it was anger he felt, none of it was apparent when he spoke. 'It wasn't a burglary. Just a bunch of documents went missing which, as it happened, I found later on in my office. I'd just misplaced them.'

He was lying. I was sure about that. But why? Before I could dwell upon it, Kaustav set his glass down and gazed deeply into my eyes. My pulse quickened and I didn't quite know what to do. Meanwhile, ever so slowly, he brought his head closer.

Omigod! He was going to kiss me. My heart started thudding. And then, quite irrationally, I found myself thinking about Sanj and what he'd said about kissing a smoker. Shit, I must have the worst case of halitosis. Already I could see him cut off the kiss and discreetly grimace. Oh god, why did I have to smoke?

Meanwhile, his lips inexorably moved closer. Not knowing what else to do, I picked up my glass and jumped up. 'Wine! We need more wine.' Unfortunately, this happened to be at the same time that he extended his hand and brushed the corner of my mouth with his thumb. 'There's something there.'

A clash of hands, a bit back curse, and I found myself staring in horror at a large, and fast-spreading, dark red stain on his blue shirt and beige chinos.

'Oh god! Oh god, I'm so sorry!' I rushed into the kitchen, grabbed a clean towel and returned to the living room.

He surveyed the damage ruefully. 'It's all right.'

'No, it's not. Let me help you with that,' I said, frantically dabbing at his clothes.

'It's all right,' he said, squirming under my ministrations.

'No, it'll leave a stain,' I insisted.

Finally, he grabbed my hands. 'Really, it's all right,' he said firmly. 'It's late anyway. I'll just go home and change.'

Oh well, it was better to embarrass myself this way rather than puckering up for a kiss that was never coming.

After he left, I figured I'd better get started on the case. But, first things first, I needed index cards. Since I didn't have any and it was way too late even for the enterprising Baniya down the street, I decided to make do with the reverse side of old business cards.

I lit a cigarette and began to write. Half an hour later, all I had to show for my progress were three cigarette butts and the same questions. How had Urvashi landed up at Hermit Hill? Who would want to kill her? Who had killed her? There were so many things I didn't know. I didn't even know enough to build a premise on. All I knew was Urvashi had disappeared on 17th September and two days later, on 19th September, she had been killed.

I abandoned the exercise, picked up the file I had procured from Prado and stretched out comfortably on the sofa. I flipped through the pages till I found what I was looking for. The transcript of Omkar's interrogation. Omkar steadfastly maintained that when he had landed up at Serenity Villa on the morning of September 18th, Urvashi was gone. He looked for her but she wasn't around. He even waited for a while thinking that she may have stepped out but she didn't return.

On the page after that was the result of the polygraph test. Since it was a high profile case, the police had chargesheeted him in a hurry and run a lie detector test on him. It came out clean. To further support the case for his innocence, none of the fingerprints found at Hermit Hill matched his. It appeared that Omkar was indeed telling the truth.

The next page had pictures of the crime scene and listed an inventory of Urvashi's belongings found there. There was a suitcase, one vanity case and a handbag. In the suitcase had been her laptop, clothes, two pairs of shoes, a copy of the *Ransom* script and assorted female hygiene stuff. Her vanity case contained top-end cosmetics. It was the contents of the handbag that caught my interest. Apart from the usual—hairbrush, lipstick, compact, cheque book, cigarettes, lighter, mints—there was also a small sachet of cocaine! *So much for Urvashi not doing drugs.*

There was something bothering me about the file. Was it something Omkar said? Or was it the inventory list? I couldn't put my finger on it. I must have dozed off at some point. I was halfway between sleep and wakefulness when a sharp sound awoke me. Groggily, I opened one eye and saw that the file had slipped from my hands and hit the floor with a *phat*.

I reached out and picked up the file. As I was sleepily shoving it in my bag, my eyes caught a balled-up piece of paper inside, the one I'd pinched from Deshpande's car. I smoothed it out and discovered it was a delivery challan for a double bed. The address for delivery was a building on Juhu Tara Road.

I resolutely flipped onto my stomach and tried to go back to sleep. But something else started nagging me. After about fifteen minutes of restless tossing and turning, I opened one eye and stared down, unseeing. Again, my gaze fell upon the delivery challan lying on the table. And just like that I knew what was niggling at me.

Should I? I sat up and looked at the time on my cellphone. It was only eleven. *I should.* I got up, splashed some water on my face, ran a comb through my hair and left.

As I was cruising along Juhu Tara Road, it occurred to me that if I was visiting someone at eleven, the least I could do was take a little present along. The problem was there were precious few shops open at this late hour. I looked around and spotted a booze shop a little ahead to my right.

After a bit of deliberation, I made my purchase and hit the road once again. Within five minutes I was at my destination and was reassured by the sight of the plush high-rise. That looked about right. I parked the RE and walked in, past the sleeping security guard.

I stepped out of the elevator on the fourteenth floor, rang the bell of apartment 1401 and waited. I could hear sounds of laboured breathing, punctuated by grunts and gasps coming from inside. That sounded like ... *Omigod! Was he was having sex?*

I gleefully pressed the doorbell again, and then again. A muffled curse. The door opened a crack.

'Coomaar?' Deshpande asked incredulously.

'Hey, can we talk?'

'How did you find me?'

'You mean after all the evasive action you took?' I said and held up the delivery challan as explanation.

'Where did you get that?'

'Er ... it fell out of your pocket at Hermit Hill.'

'Oh.' And after a moment, again, 'Oh. Can't it wait till the morning?'

Of course it can. 'It's important. It won't take long. Besides, I'm not going to leave till we've talked.'

'Just a moment,' he said and shut the door.

I stuck my ear to the door in the hopes of listening in on something. But all I heard was silence. Then the door opened once again, wider this time. Deshpande stood on the doorstep clad in nothing but a pair of boxer shorts with an elephant print.

'Now, that's a treat,' I said and meant it, too. His shorts were riding low, way below his navel, displaying a tantalizing amount of smooth hairless chest and flat, rock-hard abs. His legs were sinewy and well-sculpted, like the legs of an athlete. I didn't need to look at his butt to know it was trim and taut. His skin glistened with a thin film of perspiration. 'Were you working out?'

'You can say that.'

I handed him the gift I'd bought on the way. 'Well, in that case you'll really appreciate this.'

He took out a bottle from the plastic bag. For a split second he stared at it speechlessly. 'Water. Wow. Thanks.'

'The only thing open was a dodgy liquor shop. And all he had besides alcohol and soda was water. I would've got you some alcohol but wasn't sure you drank. So . . .'

'It's fine, Coomaar. What do you want?'

'Aren't you even going to ask me in? Offer me a drink?'

He looked mulish. Then, acquiescing, he stepped aside. 'Have a seat,' he said and disappeared into the adjoining kitchen.

I looked around. To be perfectly honest I was a little taken aback by his bachelor studio. I had expected something more lavish. But his pad was surprisingly simple. It had a large living room area with a small sleeping loft above. The only thing that looked flashy was a huge flat-screen TV on the wall and a stereo system that looked distinctly cutting edge. And one corner of the studio, lined with a stack of dusty files, looked positively like a government office.

Curious, I walked across and picked up the topmost file and flipped it open. It seemed to be an exhaustive dossier on Chhota Rajan. Similarly, the next one was a dossier on Sushil Shetty, another gangster. They were all comprehensive records of famous and infamous personalities ranging from gangsters to film stars to politicians and industrialists.

'Here you go,' Deshpande said from behind me, making me jump. He had two glasses and a bottle of Jack Daniels in his hands. He handed me the glasses and poured a small measure of the bourbon into each.

I indicated the slush pile. 'What's that? A database of your clients?'

He shrugged. 'You know what they say. Keep your friends close and enemies closer. Anyway, what did you want?'

'My, you're in a hurry to get rid of me. Sure I didn't interrupt anything?' His eyes shot up to the loft. 'Is someone there? Dazzle?'

Dazzle Lyngdoh was Deshpande's most recent and imaginatively, if misleadingly, named girlfriend from Shillong. I'd met her once and she was as brainless as she was beautiful. She was also all of eighteen years old. Which, in my opinion, made him practically a paedophile.

'No.'

I shrugged to show I didn't care either way. 'So, why didn't you want Urvashi found?'

He raised an eyebrow. 'Excuse me?'

'You knew Urvashi was missing. You weren't surprised to see me at Blazar so I assume you knew Kaustav had hired me. It was in Blazar's best interests that I find her. And fast. And yet you sent me on a wild goose chase?'

'Did it occur to you that that might have just been a prank?'

'Because between running a security firm, a matka business, a newspaper and a real estate company, you were bored?' I shook my head.

He hesitated. 'Okay, fine. I admit it. But that's only because I wanted to find her. I was the one that lost her, I wanted to be the one to find her.'

I looked at him sceptically. 'There are several crores riding on *Ransom* and you were only concerned about proving a point? Unless . . . did you have anything to do with her murder?' I asked suddenly. After all, he, too, had a Jeep Cherokee.

He choked. '*What?*'

'There can only be two reasons for you not wanting her found.

Either you benefited in some way by her continued absence, or you knew she was dead, which makes you a probable murderer. So which is it?'

'Your powers of deduction astound me.'

'Oh yeah? Then prepare to be blown away. You have an SUV too.'

'How do I know you didn't invent that stuff about tyre imprints? We have only your word for it.'

'It makes sense,' I said defensively. 'First you lead me astray . . . and then you're there at Hermit Hill? Just like that? Happy coincidence?'

'As were you.'

'I already explained that this morning. I was driving by with Tuteja when he mentioned the name of the place. Since that was exactly the card Zara had drawn for me this morning, I just happened to check it out.'

He remained silent after I had finished.

'Well? Where were you last night?' I asked.

'I was home.'

'I'm sure someone can vouch for you?'

He nodded and was about to speak when he glanced up. Abruptly, he shook his head. 'I was alone.'

I followed his gaze. 'Is someone there?' I asked insistently.

He ignored my question. 'Before you go "Aha!", I had no reason to want Urvashi dead. Quite the opposite.'

'Why? Were you having an affair with her?'

'*What?*'

'Then why . . .?'

'For god's sake, because I've got money riding on *Ransom!*'

I kept quiet. Something just wasn't making sense.

He broke into my thoughts. 'Let it go.'

'Can't—I've been hired to find the murderer.'

'Geeta?'

I flashed him my Damien look. 'How do you know?'

That was silly. He knew everything. He probably had a dossier on me somewhere in that pile of files.

'I make it my business to know about people I'm doing business with.'

'Are we? Doing business together?'

'We could. I'll tell you what, I'll help you all I can if you keep your nose out of my business.'

'Of course. We wouldn't want to open Pandora's Box now, would we?'

'Do we have a deal?'

'Deal,' I lied and made a mental note to ask Dikshit to dig into his background a bit.

Deshpande gave me his phone number after which I finished my drink and got up to go.

As I was leaving, he said in a low voice, 'Your hair.'

My hand went up to my hair self-consciously. 'What about it?'

'It looks nice, loose like that. You should do it more often.'

And then he shut the door.

Talk about it raining men.

Chapter Eleven

I was in a good mood when I woke up the next morning. And then I picked up the newspaper. Urvashi's picture was splashed across the front page, under the grisly headline, 'Actress Urvashi Murdered'. I ditched the paper and switched on the telly. Predictably, all the news channels were also focussed on the topic. Ah well, it couldn't be helped. That the police had succeeded in containing the news yesterday was an achievement in itself. I switched off the telly and went in for a shower.

As I was leaving for Blazar, I met Mr Gandhi on the stairway, coming up.

'Katie!' he said. 'I wont to toke to you.'

'Not now, Mr Gandhi! I'm late,' I said, trying to dodge past him.

'This will note take longe,' he said, putting one arm on the banister and the other one on the wall. He likes to do this a lot too. He deliberately blocks my way up or down the narrow staircase, just to have me wriggle past him.

I knew I was effectively blockaded. So I did the sensible thing. I ducked under his arm and ran.

'Katie!' he shouted.

'This evening. I promise!' I yelled, pulling on my helmet as I did so.

Fifteen minutes later, I was at Blazar Films. As it turned out, Neena was late and I needn't have hurried. Such was the media presence outside the corporate office, that it was impossible to even approach the gates, let alone enter.

I was beginning to feel foolish, parked outside Blazar like some news-hungry journalist. Frankly, it was humiliating. Plus I had just seen a Maserati enter the compound through gate one, which meant it was Sanjay Dutt! Which meant they were shooting for *Achanak*. Which meant the rest of the cast, including Aishwarya Rai and Abhishek Bachchan, might be there. And I was standing outside twiddling my thumbs when I could be posing for pictures with them!

Thinking quickly I ran to the small side gate at the rear side of the complex. There was some media there, but not much, validating the phrase 'little known' that was usually prefixed to the description of that entrance.

I tried to gain admission but the security personnel flatly refused to let me enter. They couldn't let me in if I wasn't accompanied by a Blazar employee. Company policy, they said.

'No, you don't understand,' I argued. 'I'm not a journalist. I have an appointment with Neena Pundir.'

'I told him the same thing, but he wouldn't listen,' said a scruffy guy with a Nikon camera slung around his neck.

The security guy looked at me, challenging me to come up with another argument. I wondered if I should perhaps flash my outdated police ID and decided against it. I had a feeling they wouldn't even let the prime minister enter until they had carefully studied his credentials. Exasperated, I dialled Neena's number. Her phone was busy and understandably so. She must be swamped.

It was only ten-thirty in the morning but the temperature was already in the high thirties. I stood outside, adding Celsiuses to an already hot morning, when I heard a chuckle. I turned to look.

Deshpande was sitting on the hood of his Merc, eating the last of a banana.

'What happened to the Jeep?' I asked.

He looked puzzled. 'Nothing. Why?'

So he had a plethora of cars. Maybe even a car dealership. Why didn't that surprise me?

He jumped off and strolled over to me, nonchalantly chucking the banana skin into a bush by the side of the road.

My eyes followed the offending skin. 'Are you going to pick that up?'

'It's bio-degradable.'

'I suppose that makes it all right,' I said sarcastically.

'See, I knew you would understand,' he said. 'Want to go in?'

'No, I do this for fun in the mornings,' I bit out.

Deshpande's eyebrows shot up. He shrugged and started to go back to his car.

'Wait,' I said.

Deshpande stopped and said, 'Say please.'

I gritted my teeth. 'Please.'

'Why are you in such a hurry to go in anyway?' he asked.

'I've started chumming. I need to put in a tampon,' I said.

At least that would shut him up.

'So it *was* PMS!' he said, and walked over to the security guards.

A hushed conversation took place, along with a lot of gesticulating and a lot of suspicious peering at me. Wait a minute! They weren't looking at me. They were scrutinising my pants! *Surely he had not told them about my period!*

Finally he came back and said, 'You're clear. You can come and go as you please.'

'Did you tell them about my period?' I hissed.

Deshpande looked surprised. 'No. Should I?' And he made a move towards the security cabin.

I grabbed his arm. 'Very funny!'

'Don't burst your bladder.'

It was just the activation signal my hitherto dormant bladder was waiting for and I had an uncontrollable urge to pee. Consequently, once inside the corporate office building, the first stop I made was to the loo.

I emerged from the toilet to find Deshpande waiting for me outside. He detached himself from the pillar he was leaning against and came towards me. 'Just checking to see if you were okay.'

'Yeah? What did you think would happen to me there?'

'I don't know, but my girlfriend has these terrible cramps when she starts her period. In fact, sometimes they are so bad she passes out.'

'Awww! Aren't you sweet!' I said, clutching my heart and fluttering my eyelashes at him. 'But save your concern for Dazzle. I'm fine.'

'Dazzle's not my girlfriend anymore,' he said. 'Hasn't been for some time.'

'Really? What happened? Did she grow up?'

Deshpande smiled mysteriously. 'Get those hormone levels checked. Too much oestrogen can cause cervical cancer,' he said and left.

Outside the office doors, instead of walking on straight and exiting through gate two, Deshpande turned left. But that cut across to the studios!

'Wait!' I shouted and ran after him. He stopped and turned around. 'Where are you going?'

'To the studios. Why?' He took one look at my face and started backing away. 'No, no, don't even think about it.'

'Come on! Please, please, please, pretty please.'

'No way! I'm going to meet someone. It's work.'

'Is it someone to do with the Urvashi case?'

He didn't answer.

'Okay fine. Don't tell me. But let me come along. I'll stay out of your hair. I just want to look around. Please, please, please . . .'

'All right!' he said, exasperated. 'But you have to promise to behave.'

'I promise.'

There were six shooting floors spread over two storeys. At the time only three were in use. Floor one housed the set of *Achanak*, floor two was being used by a television producer shooting a game show and floor five was where *Ransom* was being shot. I know because I looked at the studio bookings listed on the soft board behind the receptionist.

As I'd expected, there were security personnel everywhere. But they let Deshpande, and by association me, through. As we walked towards the studios, I asked, 'Are you going to the *Achanak* set? Is Sanjay Dutt there? Is Aishwarya? Or are they shooting with the second lead, wazzername . . . Mohini?'

We walked past floor number one.

'*Ransom* then? But how are they shooting without Urvashi? Have they got her double to stand in for her?'

We arrived at a huge vanity van parked between floor numbers one and three.

'That's odd. Why a vanity van when there are en suite Green Rooms?'

He shrugged. 'Some stars are particular.'

'Like who?'

Deshpande smiled sardonically and opened the door of the van. 'Wait here,' he said laconically and disappeared inside.

'But—' I started to object but he was already gone.

I hung around, smoking and feeling foolish, like a groupie stalking a rock star. To add to the humiliation, a young man of about twenty, sporting the same hairdo as Shah Rukh Khan, arrived with two glasses of cutting chai. He saw me, shook his head and muttered something that sounded like, 'Not another one', and added loudly, 'Shoo! Shoo! Saab is busy!'

Shoo? What did he think I was? A bird? Who wants to see your Saab, I wanted to say indignantly. But I was also curious to know who was inside, so instead, I asked, 'Who is that? SRK?'

He gave me a look that said, right, like I'll tell you. 'Shoo!' he said once more, this time supplementing it with deterring claps.

'All right, all right! I'm going,' I said crossly and wandered off.

I stopped by the door to floor number one and looked around. No one paid me any heed. I pressed closer and stuck my ear to the door.

Silence.

Maybe there wasn't anything going on. I opened the door cautiously and slipped in just as someone yelled, 'Bahar koi hai!' and found myself pinned under a spotlight staring at a shocked Sanjay Dutt!

In the pin drop silence I head the whir of the camera as the film rolled. Dazed, I looked around. All eyes were on me. Then all hell broke loose as an unkempt, portly and bearded man, sitting by the video assist a little distance away, jumped up and waving his hands frantically, shouted, 'Cut! Cut!'

The paralysed cameraman hastily complied.

The director then threw down his cap and stomped on it. 'Behenchod!' he cursed loudly.

I stared at him. Was he for real? Did directors really do that anymore? Hell, even Sanjay Leela Bhansali had graduated to throwing slippers at people who offended him.

Feeling extremely awkward, I said the only thing I could think of. 'I was looking for Kaustav.'

The director advanced on me menacingly and hissed, 'Do I fucking look like fucking Kaustav?'

Not even if you lost thirty kilos and got your face lifted by a crane.
Hysteria and embarrassment bubbled inside me.

He yelled some more and some four-five young men converged
on him from all directions. The director yelled for some Babloo.
Immediately, the shout was picked up and relayed across the floor.
Although why that was required was beyond me—the director had
shouted loud enough for all the Babloos in Andheri to have heard.

I looked at Sanjay Dutt who now sat by the video assist, looking
vastly amused as his make-up man fell over himself dabbing his
face with a sponge.

A thin, young boy was produced in front of the director. The
latter subjected a shivering Babloo to the most wonderfully inventive
invective. I could only follow a few words of the rapid-fire speech
but it was enough to figure out that it was Babloo's job to guard
the doors while the shot was in progress and that he was guilty of
looping off. As a result the unit had wasted their last can of film.

Everyone turned on me accusingly and yet again I found myself
the subject of sullen, resentful gazes. So I did the only thing I
could. I ran.

While leaving I sneaked one last look at Sanjay Dutt. Our eyes
locked and then he smiled and *winked at me*! I nearly collided into
one of those heavy duty lights, forcing another expletive from the
director.

Outside, I considered what to do next. The Shah Rukh Khan
doppelganger still hovered around the van. I assumed that Saab,
whoever he was, and Deshpande were still inside. But as I stood
indecisive about what to do next, Deshpande emerged from the
van. Followed by Sameer Khan!

Quite irrationally, my first reaction was, how does he tolerate an
obvious SRKphile as a lackey? And then mixed emotions ran
through me. Disbelief, awe and disappointment, in that order.
Sameer Khan looked nothing like he did on screen. He was short,
just under five-and-a-half-feet-tall, judging by the way Deshpande

towered over him. He was thin, not buff like he looked in the movies. And his face was rather ordinary, ugly even, with a largish nose and fat lips. But he did have a nice complexion, smooth and fair.

By the time I shook myself out of my stupor, Deshpande and Khan were shaking hands. As soon as Deshpande moved away, a posse of six guards formed a protective circle around Khan and whisked him away towards floor five.

I wondered if Deshpande hadn't been talking to him about Urvashi's murder. They were, after all, co-stars in *Ransom*. And Sameer Khan did own a Porsche Cayenne. But by the time the thought worked itself into my addled brain, Deshpande was already at the studio exit. I was just about to give chase when I looked towards floor five. The door was open and there was a lot of traffic in and out of the floor. At least there was no shot in progress there. While I was debating who to follow, a curly-haired young woman emerged and proceeded to shout out directions to some men who were unloading stuff from a van. A young man came running towards her, shouting her name to get her attention—Elly!

That decided it. I followed Sameer Khan to floor five. Meanwhile, the young man caught up with Elly and together they went back inside.

Luckily, there was so much chaos at the door that I managed to slip in without a hitch. Inside I immediately wedged myself between a wall and a light cutter and studied the layout covertly from there. I noticed that while it was business as usual on the *Ransom* set, the mood was perceptibly sombre.

A little further to my left, on the wall behind me, was a door with a sign that read Green Rooms.

A group of two men and Vidisha stood in the middle of the floor discussing something intently. I recognised one of the men with Vidisha as Bhanu Khanna, the director. I figured the second man with Vidisha was the DOP or the cameraman. A gaffer stood beside them, one ear cocked to the discussion. Following the discussion, he periodically shouted out directions to light men who were perched on the beam above, securing lights there.

Towards the far end of the floor, some dancers were practising their moves along with a spry, effeminate choreographer who provided the beat by clapping his hands rhythmically. Every once in a while he would stop and rebuke a dancer and then demonstrate the correct step with remarkable grace. Vidisha walked up to the choreographer and said something. He looked upset and let off a verbal diatribe coupled with a lot of pronounced shrugging and gesticulating. He then haughtily stomped off, dance troupe in tow, towards me!

I looked around for some place to hide just as Kaustav's mother, Meher Kapoor, entered the room. She stood at the door for a moment, her eyes searching the floor. An assistant came and picked up the cutter from in front of me the same moment her eyes rested on me. Her brow creased in puzzlement. Shit! I looked around for something to shield me from her gaze. Another light cutter, a prop, anything would do. But there was nothing. Thinking quickly, I turned and fell in with the dance troupe.

We exited through the door leading into the Green Rooms. There was a longish passage inside with four doors. The first door announced that the room had been assigned to Sulekha Kamat and Anushree Mehra, two senior character artistes. Similarly, rooms two and three were allotted to other character artistes. The last one was reserved for the dance troupe. I figured that the stars' rooms were on the other side where a similar door led into another set of Green Rooms. I resolved to get there as soon as I could.

As I was about to follow the dancers into the room, the choreographer popped out. His eyes searched and found me.

'You!' he cried, pointing at me with a hand that sported a ring on each finger. 'You're late!'

I stared at him, speechless.

'What call time did Jojo give you?' he continued.

He thought I was a dancer! And he was wearing make-up!

'You're wearing lipstick!' I blurted.

'Ha ha, breaking news. Angel is gay,' he sing-songed. Then he straightened and snapped, 'Get into your costume!'

'But, I'm not a dancer!'

He looked at me, as one looks at a coveted but unaffordable objet d'art: with incredible yearning but not much hope. Like he was almost willing me to be his dancer but knew that it was impossible. He made up his mind and said, 'You're the right height. You'll have to do.'

'Do what?'

'Be my tenth dancer.'

'But I don't know the steps!'

'Don't worry. I'll give you the easy part. Now get into your costume.'

I thought of refusing. But then another thought crept into my brain and I figured, why not? I have always been fascinated by the many anonymous dancers who go *jhingalala hur jhingalala hur, hur hur* behind the hero. Of course, facing the camera as an extra isn't quite what I had in mind when I thought I was going to be in a movie, but what the hell. No one had to know. No one in the film business, that is. Friends, family, acquaintances and strangers in the cinema hall sitting next to me would be proudly informed, of course.

'Hurry! Sameer Khan is almost ready,' he said.

Sameer Khan! I had to dance with Sameer Khan? Oh boy. Wait till I told Em.

'Now!' he barked.

I scooted inside and someone handed me a tiny bikini!

I stared at the garment, feeling a mild sense of panic. I had not thought this through. I had completely forgotten about the state of my body. With the recent weight gain, I was nowhere near sending guys into a frenzy with a wiggle of my shapely hips. And my underarms weren't done! As for the bikini line, let's not even go there.

A bikini! Why? We were indoors! There wasn't even a pool, for god's sake!

Suddenly someone screamed, '*Ae* Katie!'

I turned to look. Sanj!

'Sanjay—' I started to say in surprise when he shot me a warning look, '—ana,' I hastily amended.

He took the teeny tiny bikini from my hands and frowned. 'You can't wear this *re*,' he declared.

'I *know!*' I noticed that he didn't have any problems with his costume, showing toned, smooth flesh. But then he had a short sequined skirt to go with the bra. 'Why the hell do you get to wear a skirt?'

'I'm the central dancer. The central dancer gets to wear a skirt. Besides, have you ever seen a transvestite in a bikini?'

'What are you doing here, anyway?' I said crossly. 'Didn't you say you'd never be a part of a dance troupe? That if you did it once you got labelled an extra for life?'

Sanj whisked me aside and whispered, his voice literally dripping with excitement, 'I'm here to meet Sameer Khan. After the take is over, I'll smuggle myself into his Green Room.'

I was appalled. 'He's going to have you thrown out!'

'He won't,' Sanj said confidently. He had a funny look in his eyes. Like he was privy to a secret.

'Okay, what's going on?'

'Fine,' he blurted, 'I'll tell you, but you've got to promise me you won't tell anybody.'

I nodded. 'I promise.'

'Night before last, I gave him a bj!'

Chapter Twelve

~≈~

I looked at him as though he had gone insane. 'Of course you didn't!' I blurted. At his hurt look, I hastily added, 'Sameer isn't gay!'

'He is! I'm telling you, he was driving past Santa Cruz police station in his Porsche Cayenne and stopped when he saw me. He was looking for a lay and I did him *re*.'

Sameer Khan did own a Porsche Cayenne. Could it be true? Somehow it was difficult to imagine the macho star as gay. Then again, Rock Hudson was gay.

'He doesn't look gay.'

Sanj looked at me as though I were simple. 'And how does one look gay?'

'You know . . . just . . .' I said vaguely. I could hardly tell him that my opinion was based solely on the fact that he didn't strut about like a peacock.

'You mean he doesn't talk like this?' he said, waving his hands about effeminately.

'Of course not!' I lied.

Just then, Angel walked in, clapping his hands.

'Quick,' Sanj said, thrusting the bikini back at me, 'tell him you can't wear this.'

Timidly I walked up to Angel. 'I can't wear this.'

He looked at me in exasperation. 'What is it now? Too tight? Too loose? Too fat?'

'That and this,' I said, holding up my arms mutely. Angel's face turned chalk-white and he stopped breathing. He looked like he was going to pass out.

'Dear god!' he managed to choke out.

The sum total of it was that Angel declared an emergency. On a scale of one to ten it made the plot-to-assassinate-the-president-has-been-uncovered grade, going by the way the room exploded into activity. A bottle of wax was brought out. Heating apparatus, cellophane strips, talcum powder and astringent followed.

Next, I was ceremoniously disrobed. In front of Angel too! I writhed in embarrassment. I knew it was silly, Angel being gay and all that, but he was a guy. And I was spreadeagled before him in all my hirsute glory! I saw him shudder.

And then everything was blanked out by excruciating pain. 'The wax is too hot!' I yelled. They paid no attention. Strip after strip of cellophane was slapped on, pressed down and yanked off without mercy. The same procedure was repeated on the other side till I thought I would pass out. And this was only the underarms. We hadn't even got to the bikini line yet.

Ten minutes of unbearable agony later, when I was weak and dizzy from the pain, they were done. I fully expected the maltreated areas to look like they had been exposed to high-intensity radiation, but when I looked, I saw the skin was shiny, silky and smooth (a combination of ice, astringent and aloe vera lotion)—and I was willing to go through the pain again, right there and then.

I squeezed myself into the bikini, slipped into impossibly high stilettos, hastily slapped on some make-up and trooped out with the rest of the dancers. Just before leaving I looked at Sanj for approval. If he had any reservations about my appearance, he hid them well and even gave me a muted thumbs up.

On the way to the floor, we passed Bhanu Khanna sitting by the video assist, nursing a glass of tea and shooting the breeze with a young man. Just then, the door to the far right opened and out sailed Desiree. She was dressed in a bra comprising two cones of wound metal tubes and a short shimmering sheath of a skirt which clung lovingly to her curvy hips and thighs.

She glided across to where Khanna was sitting, and I could hardly take my eyes off her. She was hot! All tanned and toned flesh, showing in generous proportions through the revealing costume (not that I was in any position to comment on that). Of course, a lot of it was because of make-up, but a lot of it was just her. She had high cheekbones and enormous hazel eyes. She was tall and voluptuous and walked with an easy, feline grace. The whole effect was electrifying. And not just on me. The entire unit stopped for a split second and watched her; I swear I heard a collective sigh when she reached Khanna and sat down beside him.

I was told we were to dance around Sameer Khan and Desiree, and the song we would be dancing to was the title song, the lyrics of which were: *Hey handsome, what's your ransom? Tujhe apna bana ke, rakh loon zindagi bhar, toh bol, what's your ransom?* This was followed by a woman breathing throatily, '*ransom, ransom, ransom*'. The song ended with one final explosion of the chorus '*oogamaga chicarica aiyyayiyayiyayiyaaahhhhh!*' The song was set to a catchy tune and was a guaranteed superhit. I just knew it.

There was a delay. Apparently, one wayward curl on Sameer Khan's head refused to fall in line. While his hairdresser wrestled with the recalcitrant lock, Angel decided to use the time for one more rehearsal. The dancers dutifully went through the complicated moves to Angel's rhythmic directive of, 'a one, a two, a three, and kick and kick and pirouette and kick.' I panicked then. *Which was the easy part?*

'Angel,' I wailed, 'I can't do this.'

'Don't worry. Just stand like this,' he said, standing by the pole and gripping it firmly with his right hand. 'And when the song starts, just twirl around it like so.' And he nimbly jumped up, grabbed the pole, wrapped his legs around it and slid down with fluid grace. 'Can you do that?'

That looked easy. 'I think so,' I said doubtfully.

My gaze skidded across to where Khanna and Desiree sat watching the proceedings with exaggerated boredom. Even as I looked, Desiree leaned towards Khanna and murmured something in his ear. Khanna shot a glance at her and then a slow smile split his face.

Desiree stood and sailed past him, swinging her hips coquettishly. After about five minutes, Khanna casually got up, stretched and followed her into her Green Room with exaggerated nonchalance. The dancers sniggered. What was that all about? What were they going to do? Bonk? Do coke? I bet they were going to do coke. I longed to be a fly on Desiree's Green Room wall.

Just then someone came to tell Angel that Sameer Khan was ready. He turned to us and said, 'Okay, ready everybody. Sameer Khan's coming to take his position.' Even as I was digesting this, fighting hysteria, Angel sidled up to me and hissed, 'You better not fuck this up!' Like there wasn't enough pressure already.

Desiree and Khanna, with much giggling, spilled out of the Green Room. They looked unnaturally bright-eyed and unsteady on their feet. It had to be coke. If it was sex, it had to be some pretty amazing, earth-shattering sex. Not to mention, quick.

We took our positions. I didn't know about the others, but my stomach was in knots. I felt like an athlete just before the race is about to start. Sanj was standing next to me and he squeezed my hand reassuringly.

And then it all started. Sameer Khan walked in with his entourage. He stopped to shake hands and greet people on the way to the sets. And then I saw what made him a superstar. His smile lit up his entire face and somehow managed to make every person he smiled at feel special—as though he were carrying on a private conversation with them, to the exclusion of everyone else. Maybe he *was* gay!

I snuck a glance at Sanj. Sanj was looking at Sameer with a mixture of perplexity and disappointment.

'What's wrong?' I hissed.

'I don't know . . . something. My gay-dar isn't picking up anything,' he complained.

'I knew it!' I said triumphantly. 'He isn't gay!'

'But how . . .' Sanj said, genuinely puzzled. 'I swear it was him. He picked me up in his car and we drove around for some time. Then he parked at a secluded spot and . . . I swear it was him, *re*.' He looked ready to burst into tears.

'Maybe he's gay and is hiding it. Maybe he's just a good actor,' I suggested.

'It's not something you can hide! A gay-dar to us is like BO to a dog!' he muttered tearfully.

'Even dogs can be fooled by pepper,' I said helpfully.

Khan stopped at the edge of the set where his make-up man fluffed him up once more. And he was ready.

Khan and Desiree took their positions on the floor. Angel, equipped with the microphone, yelled, 'Roll sound!' And the opening strains of the song filtered out. Angel started his beat, 'A one, a two . . .'

Things went well. And then it was my cue to strut my stuff. I grabbed the pole and jumped up. Unfortunately, my hands were so clammy that instead of slithering down the pole seductively like Angel had shown me, I came crashing down. I landed on one foot, but because my leg was wrapped around the pole, I landed awkwardly and twisted my ankle. My leg buckled and I smacked the ground with my ass, with my foot trapped underneath. It was all very ungainly, very embarrassing and unbearably painful.

The other dancers sniggered bitchily, Desiree looked impatient and Angel cringed with mortification, as though it had happened to him, not me. The only sympathetic reaction I got was from Sameer Khan.

Khan, rumoured to be the perfect gentleman, quickly came across and bent down beside me. Concern reflected on his face. 'Are you aw'ight?' he asked me in that strange Brit-American accent of his. Yup, he was perfect. Perfectly sloshed. 'Are you okay? Doan wowwy. Smeer Khan will look affer you.'

Sanj realised this was his one chance to get close to Khan and immediately hopped down beside me.

'You!' Khan said to Sanj.

Sanj looked at him eagerly, waiting for recognition, but Khan's face remained blank. Put-on job or real?

'You! Help her up!' was all Khan said.

With Sanj's help, I untangled my foot and felt my ankle. It was swollen, but nothing seemed broken. I tried to hobble across to a chair, but the pain made my vision swim and I staggered. Smeer Khan (I couldn't help it. I couldn't think of him as Sameer Khan anymore) insisted on carrying me in his arms. Much as I would have liked that, I declined. And not only for the sake of politeness. He *was* awfully small. And tanked up on the happy water. Leaning on Sanj and Smeer, I somehow limped across to the chairs where Khan parked himself next to me solicitously. He yelled for an ice pack which sent the production manager, the spot boys and assistant directors skittering all over the place. A cold compress was hastily fashioned.

I wanted to ask Smeer Khan what Deshpande and he were talking about but decided to wait a bit. For god's sake, he was administering the ice pack himself! Wait till I told Mom. She would never believe it. And Em, she would just die of envy.

All the while he tended to my ankle, he carried on a light conversation, saying, 'There, there, does it fill berrer? Don' wowwy, you'll fill berrer in no time at all.'

Just when I figured I'd basked enough in his attention and that it was time to get on with business, Sanj, who had been holding himself back admirably, blurted, 'How can you not remember me?'

Khan's hands stilled. He looked up at him coolly and said, 'What?'

'Here!' I said hurriedly, grabbing the ice pack and thrusting it at Sanj. 'You do it.'

Sanj ignored me. 'How can you not remember me after that night *re*?'

Khan looked furious. 'Who the fuck are you?' he said icily.

'Oh so you don't know. Maybe this will remind you!' And he started making fellatio gestures with his hands and mouth. 'Oh . . . oh . . . yes! Yes! . . . Do it some more . . . Oh yes, that's it . . .' he moaned.

Smeer Khan looked ready to pop a vein. 'Leave!' he said with barley controlled fury. He glanced at his security guards standing a little distance away and nodded ever so slightly.

'Fine, call security. But I know what happened between us two nights back, even if you deny it. I'll tell everybody. You picked me up in your car and we drove around,' Sanj managed defiantly before two beefy guards materialised behind him and grabbed his arms. 'It was you! I saw the tattoo on your groin . . . a snake around a dagger.'

Smeer turned white. 'Take him away. And please, don't neglect to give him some of your special tweatment.'

'*Ae*, leave me alone,' Sanj said as the guards tried to drag him away. When the guards refused to let go, Sanj said more reasonably, 'Okay baba! I'm coming, I'm coming!'

As soon as the guards relaxed their grip, Sanj wriggled out of their grasp, dodged past them and ran out. With a startled shout, the guards followed. I was horrified but not as horrified as Angel who, seeing another one of his dancers running away, looked like he was going to have a heart attack.

Presently Smeer Khan regained his good cheer. Turning to me, he asked with a smile, 'You're new at this, aren't you?'

'I'm not really a dancer,' I confessed in a rush.

He lost his smile and his manner became wary. 'Oh?' I saw him look towards his security guards.

'Oh no, no, no, it's not what you think,' I said in a rush. 'I . . .' The security guards sauntered across and grabbed me. I gave in and allowed myself to be led away.

There was some commotion at the door and Elly came running in, shouting, 'Was there an accident? I heard one of the dancers got hurt.' A young man said something and pointed towards us. Following his finger, Elly zoomed in on us. She ran up, stopped beside us and said breathlessly, 'I've called for a car to take you to the hospital. And don't worry, Blazar will take care of the bills.'

That was damn decent of them I thought, till I figured they probably didn't have insurance and were trying to prevent a lawsuit.

She saw the guards holding me and reckoned all was not all right. 'What's going on?'

And then, as I looked at her, I couldn't believe it. It was Lizzy! Elly was our Lizzy from college! The same mottled skin, the same frizzy hair which made her look like she was perpetually having a bad hair day.

'Lizzy!' I screamed excitedly.

Suddenly I was more than just an anonymous dancer. I was worth a closer look.

'Katie?' she asked doubtfully. Then, 'Oh my god! It *is* you! Katie!' We both hugged each other and hopped around in excitement. She turned to Sameer Khan and said, 'Oh, a DCP Chodankar is here. He wants to talk to you.'

Smeer made a disgusted sound and stomped off. First Deshpande and now Chodu. What was going on? I cursed myself for not seizing the opportunity when I'd had it.

Lizzy, or Elly as she was now called, looked at me. 'What are you doing here? Dressed like this? Don't tell me you're a dancer now.'

'Of course not!'

'Then why . . .?'

'It's a long story. I'll tell you some other time.'

She looked at me pitifully. Dear god! She didn't believe me. She thought I actually was a chorus dancer and lying about it.

'No, really. I'm not a dancer!' I insisted. 'I'm a PI.'

'Okay, whatever,' she said dubiously.

'No really. Okay, here's the deal,' I said lowering my voice. 'I'm investigating Urvashi's murder.'

Her eyes widened. 'Really? Who did it?'

Really. 'That's what I'm trying to find out.'

'Hey, do you think it was . . .?'

Just then someone called out to her urgently.

'Coming!' she said and looked at me apologetically. 'Listen, I gotta go. But hey, any news of Em?'

I nodded. 'She manages Ego.'

'She's here? No!' Elly gasped. 'How is she? Does she still talk in that weird accent? I have talk to her.'

She wanted me to call Em right away but I demurred. After the way she'd treated me the last two times I'd called her, I figured she didn't want to talk to me. And if that were the case, far be it from me to foist my unwanted company on her. 'My phone's in the Green Room,' I said.

'Here take mine.' Elly offered me her phone.

I didn't want to get into a long-winded explanation of why I was unwilling to call Em, so I took the phone and dialled the number.

"Allo?' she answered.

'Em, it's me,' I said unenthusiastically. 'I'm at Blazar and guess—'

'Ow ees ze eenvaisteegation . . .'

'Em!' I said warningly.

'How is the murder investigation coming along?' she said.

'How do you know about that?'

'Um . . . just a minute . . . there's someone at the door.' She came back after a few seconds. 'It was Louis. Where were we? Ah yes, how did I know? Well, I figured when you called from Kaustav Kapoor's bungalow last night. Why else would you be there? So? How's it going?'

'Tell her about me,' Elly stage whispered.

'Who's that?' Em asked.

Elly grabbed the phone and squealed, 'It's me, Lizzy!'

Some more squealing happened and then Elly started on an exaggerated narrative of my unfortunate and abbreviated dancing career. I lunged for the phone and managed to scream, 'It isn't true,' before Elly grabbed it from me once again. Finally, because there was so much grabbing and shouting that no one could hear anything, or indeed make any sense of the conversation, we put the phone on speaker.

'Well, well, my dancing queen! See I told you. The moment you told me about Kaustav coming to your office, I knew you were going to be in a Blazar movie!'

'He doesn't go to his heroines' houses to sign them, but a small-time dancer, yeah, that merits a personal visit,' I said.

Elly peered at me. 'What is this about Kaustav visiting you?'

After a moment's hesitation I said, 'I guess there's no harm in telling you guys now since Urvashi's dead,' I said and gave her an abbreviated version of the events.

When Elly heard about Kaustav hiring me to find his missing heroine, she frowned. 'But that doesn't make sense.'

'I know. I suspected all along that it was a publicity stunt. But hey, who am I to argue against a six-figure fee?' I said.

Em sounded hurt. 'And you couldn't tell me this earlier?'

'Em, there is something called client confidentiality.'

'How come you forget that when you ask me for gossip about my clients?' she asked waspishly.

'There's a difference. My clients' secrets include kidnapping and murder.'

'So? My clients' secrets involve fetishes and fantasies!'

At this point, Elly started to interject, 'Guys please, let's not . . . Oh?'

'Forget it. I'm not telling,' Em declared huffily.

Elly looked disappointed and threw accusing glances my way. Like somehow it was my fault she had missed out on so much all these years.

The upshot of the rest of the conversation was that we all agreed to meet later that evening at Ego. At which point I couldn't resist saying bitchily, 'That is, if you have some time for us lesser mortals.'

I was rewarded with a guilty, 'I'm so sorry, Kay. But I'll explain everything tonight. I promise.'

After that, since Elly was busy, she left. My ankle was much better so I took off to the Green Room to change out of the ridiculous costume. Angel was there and I bid him goodbye. And he assured me that he would manage with a formation of nine . . . eight dancers.

Chapter Thirteen

❧

When I was about thirty feet from the corporate office, I caught sight of Neena. I called out her name and jogged up to her.

She pushed her huge brown shades over her head and squinted at me. I thought I saw her briefly grimace, but nevertheless, she waited for me. As always, her clothes were expertly cut and flattering. Today she was dressed in a pale peach pant suit and brown shoes. On her arm was an oversized bottle-green Louis Vuitton bag that made me swoon with envy.

I caught up with her and we both walked into the office together. If the mood on the *Ransom* sets was solemn, it was positively subdued here. People spoke in low voices and laughs were swiftly and guiltily cut off. Which made me wonder about Neena's charged countenance. She positively crackled with energy. Either she wasn't too heartbroken about Urvashi's death or she was hiding her distress well. Which was it?

'I guess, everyone's heard,' I said conversationally while we were walking up to Kaustav's office.

'Yes,' Neena said. 'Everyone's very upset.'

'But not you?'

She looked a little surprised. 'Why? Because I'm not crying my eyes out? Of course it was upsetting. It was gruesome. The way she died would upset anyone.'

She continued, 'My god, who would kill her in such a bloody manner? And then steal jewellery off a dead woman and ransack her room?'

'Let me guess. Chodankar showed you the photos.' Really why didn't he just post the pictures on his Facebook profile?

She nodded. 'What kind of a monster would do that?'

'But you're not surprised that she was killed?'

Neena hesitated. 'No, can't say that I am. Urvashi certainly knew how to alienate people.'

We arrived outside Kaustav's office and Neena opened the door.

'Including you?' I asked.

Neena stared at me for a moment without moving. She shut the door and said, 'Are you suggesting I had something to do with it?'

'You could have. After all, you were one of the few people other than Urvashi who knew about the publicity plan.'

'Yes. *One of the few people*. And my motive?'

Hmmm, interesting question.

'Look, if you're suggesting that I killed her, you're wrong. I didn't even know about Hermit Hill. I thought she was at Serenity Villa. So how could I have killed her?'

'Then you won't mind answering where you were the night of 19th September?'

'I don't mind answering the question. But I do mind answering you.' She smiled thinly, opened the door to Kaustav's office and said, 'Kaustav will be here shortly.'

'Fine, don't answer me. But you *will* have to answer Chodankar,' I said walking in. 'If you haven't already. I'll just check with him.' Yeah, right. And I'd probably go out with Kaustav and we'd get married and live happily ever after.

She hesitated by the door. Then, finally making up her mind, she shut the door behind her and walked in. 'Look, I had nothing to do with Urvashi's death. I was home that night.'

'From what time to what time?'

'Let's see. I was working late so I must have got home at about ten-thirty? And then I was there till the next morning—till I left for work. This was around ten a.m.'

'Anybody who can verify that?'

She hesitated. 'Well, no, I was alone. But as I already told the police, I did receive a couple of phone calls on the landline that night. You can check it out.'

I nodded. 'Do you live alone?'

'No, actually. I have a flatmate.'

'So it could've been your flatmate who answered the phone?'

'Yes. If she were home.'

'Where was your flatmate?'

'I don't know. At a party maybe? We don't keep tabs on each other.'

'So she wasn't there the entire night?'

'No. When I came home her door was shut. I peeked in, just in case she was home. She wasn't. Her door was still shut when I left for work the next morning.'

'Uh-uh.' I took down her landline number and the details of her flatmate who happened to be a model and answered to the name of Yula Menezes. I then asked her to recount events from 17th September, just in case there were inconsistencies between the various accounts I'd heard.

Neena's version of the 'plan' was more or less the same as Kaustav's and Geeta's. 'I don't know much more beyond that as I was back here in office. But from what I've heard from Chandan, things went pretty much according to plan. Urvashi left Hotel Princeton at around four p.m. She was driving a white Hyundai Accent and was on her own. A little distance away, Chandan joined her and took over the wheel. The journey was uneventful and they reached Serenity Villa at around six. Chandan then settled her in and drove back to the office. We then spent the major part of the evening and night working on the promotion strategy of *Taaron ki Baaraat* at Firangi Paani.'

The mention of Firangi Paani reminded me of an earlier overheard conversation between Baweja and Neena. The way she'd said, 'You were with me, remember?' had, even then, smacked of a rehearsed story.

'You sure about that?'

'Sure about what?'

'About being at Firangi Paani?'

'I'm quite capable of remembering the name of the pub we regularly go to,' she said dryly.

'Uh-huh. Perhaps Chandan did something that wasn't according to plan? Something that you were a part of too? Something that went wrong? Something you don't want found out?'

She stiffened. 'What are you hinting at?'

Good question. 'Never mind.'

'No. This is the second time you've mentioned this. Do you know something?'

'I overheard a conversation between you and Chandan earlier. He was concerned about something. Something that he felt you two should have left alone and something that he felt was as much your fault. He was afraid of being found out. And then you said something about not wanting to let her get away with it. So the question is who and get away with what?'

She laughed. 'Is that it? Your big clue? First of all, we weren't even talking about Urvashi. Hell, we weren't even talking about *Ransom*. We were talking about *Taaron ki Baaraat*. The answer to your "who" is Mohini. She is giving us hell over dates and we didn't ... don't want her to hold us to ransom, talk about irony. Did you even once hear us mention Urvashi's name?'

I had to admit that I hadn't. But I was convinced she was lying. Why else had they also mentioned my name in the same conversation? I let it go for the moment.

'Fine. Chandan dropped her and came away. Then what?'

She shrugged. 'There's not much else to tell. Apparently something happened that night itself, because when Omkar went there the next morning, she was gone.'

'So, who in your opinion could have killed Urvashi?'

Neena shrugged. 'I don't know.'

'But just now you said that she wasn't liked,' I argued. 'There must be a name in your head, someone you were referring to?'

'There's a difference between not liking someone and taking a hatchet to her,' she argued back.

'Unless you stand to gain from her death.'

'Maybe. But no one knew about Hermit Hill.' Neena shot back.

'What if we assume for a moment that the person found out somehow?'

'I don't know. It could have been anybody.'

'Vidisha?' I said.

Neena stared at me. 'Why would she kill Urvashi? I mean, why now?' she corrected herself. 'Why not earlier?'

'Maybe she didn't get a chance earlier.'

Neena thought for a while then shook her head. 'I don't buy it. There's certainly no love lost between Vidisha and Kaustav. Plus . . .'

'Really? 'Cos I heard Kaustav had no intention of divorcing Vidisha.'

She shrugged. 'You're mistaken.'

'Are you sure? Heard anything about a tiff between Vidisha and Urvashi at Serenity Villa on the night of the 17th?'

'Vidisha went down to Serenity Villa?'

Although she injected the right amount of surprise into her voice, I got the distinct impression that this wasn't news to her.

'I don't know anything about that,' she said. 'As far as I know, Vidisha doesn't love Kaustav. If anybody had a motive it was Bhanu Khanna.'

Now that she mentioned it, I remembered reading in the gossip columns about Bhanu Khanna's unhappiness with Urvashi. According to a report in *Screen*, my bible for any facts filmi, Urvashi behaved like the queen bee at Blazar, interfering in everything from managerial to administrative to creative matters. The report suggested that Khanna would openly gripe to anybody who would listen about how Urvashi's meddling in directorial decisions was ruining *Ransom*. She would freely edit the script at the last moment if she felt the scene didn't do her justice, and openly override calls on lighting and camera placement.

Of course, when contacted, Khanna denied everything. But one source, on the condition of anonymity, had verified it. The source added that the rushes of *Ransom* were very bad and that Kaustav, while salvaging the film at the editing table, had been heard blaming the director for the fiasco.

Neena said, 'It's common knowledge that his career is finished. Blazar will never work with Bhanu Khanna again. Not on a meaningful project anyway. Which pretty much means that no one else will. And he holds Urvashi responsible.'

That certainly was something to think about. Of course, Neena was one of the five who knew about the plan so it was possible that she was lying. Presently, she excused herself to get my cheque.

No sooner had she left than the door opened again. Thinking that it was Neena, I started to say, 'That was quick', but when I turned I saw it was Chandan Baweja. His skin allergy had subsided considerably and he looked a lot better than he had when I'd met him last.

'Oh good, you're here!' he said, shutting the door and walking carefully across the room. 'I hear you found Urrrshi?' he asked slurring slightly. It was only noon but going by his drooping eyes, he already had a load on.

I nodded.

'Di' she . . . di' she look bad?'

'Didn't you see the photos?'

'I couldn't b'ing myself to.'

'Well, she didn't look pretty.'

He squeezed his eyes shut and opened them again. I wasn't sure if it was in pity, or to clear his vision. He shook his head as though he couldn't quite believe it. 'I could ne'er imagine . . . when I left her at Sener . . . Senerty Villa I could ne'er imagine thish would happen to her. She looked so calm and re'axed. She was really looking forward to some r'n'r.'

'So what do you think happened?'

He blinked. 'I haven't the foggiest. All I know is that everything was going beau'fully. We left Hotel Prinson at four in the afternoon, and reached Sererty Villa jush after shix. I put her stuff inside, made sure she was comfortable and drove back to Mumbai.'

'Think back. Did anyone follow you? Was there any incident?'

'No, in fact, everything was going accor'ing to plan. We made good time till Khandala where Urrshi took out her phone to call . . .' He stopped as if struck. 'Ulness!'

Good. I like unless. Especially when it is said as an exclamation. I waited for him to continue but he seemed lost in thought.

'Unless?' I prompted him.

He peered at me owlishly. 'Ulness what?'

'You were saying something about making good time till Khandala and then Urrshi, sorry, Urvashi took out her phone to call someone?'

He looked befuddled. 'She did? Y'know talking on the cell while driving is really dangerous. Y'know that mollel . . . wazzer name . . . Ka' Moss died tha' way,' he said sagely. 'Sad. She was hot.'

'Kate Moss isn't dead and I'll be sure to remember that,' I said. 'Now whom did Urvashi call?'

'Ah yes!' he said remembering. 'According to the plan we, thash ish, Urrshi and me, we were to leave Hotel Princeton in a hired car and drive to Sereny Villa. At Khandala, either Urrshi or I was supposed to call Kaushtav and check in. If it wash Urrshi, thash wash the last call she was supposed to make or receive from her phone. Thereafter she wash supposed to switch it off. I remember this happened jush before we hit Khandala. It must have been around five or just after. Urrshi checked in with Kaustav and started to put the phone away. But before she could do that, someone called her and I could see that she wash very disturbed by it. It was a very odd consersation. As soon as Urrshi answered she went "You!", ash though it were someone she least expected. And then she shaid something like, "You're not supposed to call me!" Then "No, no, I just washn't expecting to talk to you" and "I've told you o'er'no'er it washn't my fault" and "What do you want?" and "Fine, you know where to find me."'

That must've been the call Urvashi had received at five-seventeen p.m. 'That's it? Anything else?' I asked.

'Thash all. Then I settled her in at S'ren'y Villa and came back to Mumbai.' And then he gasped as though he'd just remembered something.

'Yes?'

He thought hard and finally shook his head. 'Nothing.'

I gritted my teeth. 'Was someone blackmailing her?'

He looked shocked. 'Blackmail!'

'Sounds like it from the conversation.'

He shrugged helplessly. 'Coul' be, I guesh.' After a moment he said, 'Say, if Ka' Moss din die, who did?'

I ignored him. What had Urvashi meant by 'Fine, you know where to find me'—had she meant in Bombay? Or at Serenity Villa? That would mean it was one of the five who knew about the plan. It was also possible that the blackmailer had found out about

Serenity Villa and followed her from there to Hermit Hill, if indeed Urvashi had gone voluntarily. Although why he or she would kill her was a mystery. A little bit like killing the goose that lays golden eggs. Unless the 'blackmailer' was Bhanu Khanna and the motive was revenge. But how did he know about Hermit Hill? And then there was the fact that Hermit Hill was fantastically stocked. If indeed Urvashi had been lured there or taken there by force, as Geeta seemed to think, then the killer had planned it in advance.

Of course, Baweja was also one of the five who knew about Serenity Villa, so it was equally possible that he was also lying. But I doubted that. He was a lush, not stupid. He would know that telephone calls can be verified.

All the same I had to ask him where he was on the night of September 19th. He said that he was out drinking at one of his regular watering holes, Myst. He added that he had been there from seven p.m. till well past midnight. Earlier on, from seven p.m. till eight-thirty he had had a friend—Ajay Mahajan—for company. Later, he had sat there alone. He had reached home well past midnight. When asked if someone could verify his claim, he said that the waiters probably could.

'Chandan, who in your opinion would have wanted to kill Urvashi?'

'Jorran!' he said triumphantly after a moment. 'Jorran wazza one that died. She was hot too.'

I gnashed my teeth. My dentist was going to be a horrified man by the time the case was over. 'How about Vidisha? You must've heard about her trip down to Serenity Villa on 17th night?'

He looked stunned. 'Who tol' you about that?'

'So it's true?'

'Was it Neena? 'Cos if I were you I wouldn't believe ever'thing she says where Vi'sha is concerned. She's . . . par'isan.' The moment he said it, I could tell he was annoyed with himself. 'I mean she . . . I think . . . well . . .'

I took pity on him. 'It's okay. I know how she feels about Kaustav.'

Relief washed over his face.

'And Bhanu Khanna? Could he have been the one who called Urvashi?' I said.

He shrugged. 'Coul' be. He hated her.'

Neena returned with my cheque then and I left soon after. Chandan Baweja, who wanted to step out for a smoke, accompanied me outside. He took out some strange brown cigarettes and offered me one. I declined. I wasn't about to smoke anywhere near where there was the remotest possibility of running into Kaustav.

After he'd finished, I took a stroll down to the studio area for the second time that day. The door to floor one was shut but Babloo was standing guard outside. He glared at me, daring me to come any closer. I quickly walked away from there. The vanity van was still there, parked between floors one and three. As was its young attendant. I steered clear of him too and made my way to the *Ransom* floor.

The *Ransom* set still exploded with activity, with caterers and light men milling about. To one side, a little away from the chaos, Bhanu Khanna and Desiree seemed to be having what appeared to be a heated discussion. As I watched, Desiree reached into her bag and took out a piece of paper. Khanna snatched it from her hands and tore it into a zillion pieces. He then surveyed the scene to see if he had been observed. I hastily looked away.

After they had both walked back inside, I looked around. No one seemed to have noticed. I quickly hopped across to where Khanna had chucked the pieces of paper. The wind had whipped up a little and some of the pieces had blown away. But most remained. I bent down to pick them up. I grabbed the pieces of paper and stuffed them into my bag and walked away quickly. I heard a startled shout behind me but I pretended not to have heard and walked even faster. Suddenly someone came up from behind and grabbed my arm. My heart pounding and my mouth completely dry, I turned. Bhanu Khanna! Had he seen me pick up the pieces of paper?

'Ms Kumar? Katie Kumar?'

I nodded, still unable to speak.

He practically grabbed and pumped my hand enthusiastically. 'I'm Bhanu Khanna. Elly told me it was you. It is so great to finally meet you.'

'It . . . it is?'

'You kidding? After the way Kaustav spoke about you?'

'Kaustav talked about me?' I said, trying not to sound too excited.

He nodded. 'In fact, he's talked of little else. May I say how excited I am about working with you?'

'Working with me?' I said in surprise and mounting excitement. Surely, he meant . . .? And all of a sudden, I found myself thinking of *Elizabeth—The Golden Age* and the rousing description Sir Walter Raleigh gives of a sailor's life. *Pure, naked, fragile hope when all your senses scream at you, lost! At first it's no more than a haze on the horizon, the ghost of a haze, the pure line corrupted. But clouds do that, and storms. So you watch, you watch.*

'Yes.' He held up his hands. 'Don't worry, I'll do all the work and you can fill in all the details. I've almost nailed the whole story anyway.'

Then it's a smudge, a shadow on the far water. For a day. For another day. The stain slowly spreads along the horizon and takes form—until on the third day you let yourself believe.

'Mr Khanna . . .'

'Bhanu.'

'Bhanu, what are you talking about?'

He blinked. 'About the film. On you.'

You dare to whisper the word—Land. 'What? He's making a film on me?'

He looked dismayed. 'You didn't know. Shit! I spoke out of turn. Please don't tell Kaustav I told you.'

'Actually I did know. Well, sort of. Tell me more.'

He started backing away. 'I've already said too much. Please . . .'

'I promise I won't tell him.'

'Promise?'

'I promise.'

'Okay,' he said reluctantly. 'The film is about this young girl. She's smart and funny, a little clumsy. Think Kajol in *Pyar To Hona Hi Tha.*'

'Go on,' I said, liking what I'd heard so far. Images of Kaustav and me in a red Ferrari, powering down an autobahn started unspooling in my mind. There were snow-capped mountain peaks on one side and lush green meadows on the other. Like in the song *Kyon Chalti Hai Pawan* from *Kaho Na Pyaar Hai.* Then we were in Mauritius, scuba diving. And then we were in France, crushing grapes with our feet. And then . . . I was so busy circling the English countryside in a hot air balloon that I almost missed what he said next.

'So she runs a detective agency. She's very vain. She thinks there's no one more beautiful or smarter than her. But the thing is she's not. She's not smart. In fact, whenever she gets a case, she mostly bungles it.'

A pinprick. The bulbous part of the balloon danced crazily as the air rushed out with a whoosh. The billowing cloth started to collapse and I plummeted down to Earth.

'Uh-huh?' I said sceptically. I had a growing suspicion that what he had in mind wasn't a Lara Croft, but a female Jacques Clouseau.

'Yeah. She ultimately solves it in the end but not because she's done anything right, but because the other guy screws up.'

'Uh-huh?' I was right. The romantic images in my mind were immediately replaced with pictures of Jamila karate-chopping me at the entrance to my apartment à la Cato.

'This part is not modelled on you, of course,' he added hastily. 'It's just a better character, screenplay-wise, you understand? People love a loveable buffoon. Then she gets a case to track down a missing husband.'

'That's it? That's the whole story?'

'I said I've almost got the whole story,' he said defensively. 'Anyway, I'm thinking, what starts off as a simple enough case soon turns complicated with corporate espionage, drug smuggling and terrorism.'

'Not assassination?' I said.

'Assassination, assassination,' he mulled it over, my sarcasm going completely over his head. 'You may have something there. Let me think about it,' he said, making a note in his book.

'Let me get this straight. Kaustav told you to write a story about such a character?'

'Well, he gave me the essentials and told me to work with it. He wanted to go with a grittier film, with a powerful character. Like Ashley Judd's in all those serial killer movies. But I thought, in these times of recession, a light-hearted comedy with a quirky character would work better. So what do you think?'

'I think you should leave the thinking to Kaustav,' I said. Perhaps Kaustav's mistrust of Bhanu's directorial abilities wasn't misplaced. He screwed up his eyes, unable to figure out if he was being insulted.

I was dying to ask him how Kaustav was letting him direct another film. What about the 'Blazar-will-never-work-with-him-again-his-career-is-over' business? But how did one come right out and ask something like that?

'Actually I wanted to speak to you too,' I said. 'About Urvashi.'

His face sobered up. 'It's a real tragedy. She was the best.'

'Really?'

'Really.

'But I thought you two didn't get along?'

He laughed. 'Didn't get along? Where did you hear that?'

'Here and there. Word gets around.'

'All rubbish. We got along famously.'

'What about her excessive interference?'

He waved his hand dismissively. 'All media speculation. As I said, rubbish. She is ... was a thorough professional. She was there to do a job which she did.'

'Uh-huh.' I changed the subject. 'Did you know about the publicity plan?'

'Well, I knew something was afoot. Everyone did. But not specifically about the plan, no. I'm hardly a part of the inner coterie.'

Aha! Possible motive, bitterness.

'What about Desiree? Did she know?'

'You'll have to speak to her of course, but I doubt it. As I said, we're hardly the blue-eyed boys.'

'She got along with Urvashi?'

'As well as any two heroines can get along, I suppose.' After a pause he said, 'About your inputs for the story, I'd love to hear about your cases ...'

'I'll get back to you on that,' I said and edged away.

Outside Blazar, I fought my way through the swarming reporters. As soon as they saw me they assumed I was a company spokesperson and pivoted towards me. A couple of them asked me hopefully, 'Who murdered Urvashi?' 'Why was she murdered? Was it an inside job?' One wanted me to describe the mood in Blazar. 'Is there a feeling of loss?' 'No comment,' I said. I've always wanted to say that.

I thought about what to do next. I took out my cellphone to call Dikshit and tell him to start investigating Deshpande when I noticed there was a message in my inbox. It was a bulk message from a beauty salon offering discount rates during the upcoming Navratri festival. Which reminded me of an equally pressing matter. I called Rosie and asked her if she still had any of those miracle facial kits left. She did, but only two. She urged me to come quickly as she couldn't guarantee their availability beyond the next ten minutes. Apparently, they were selling like hot dhansak.

'Fine. I'll be there in twenty. Lemme just grab a vada-pav.'

I heard her gasp in horror. 'Vada-pav! Why don't I just flush your facial down de toilet? How many times have I told you dhikra, to look good outside you have to look good inside. True beauty comes from widin.'

'But,' I sputtered, 'I thought that was just for ugly people.' I certainly wasn't ugly, I thought indignantly. Not a raving beauty like Em, but not ugly either. And when I put my mind to it, I could even give Em a run for her money. 'Besides, what has vada-pav got to do with inner beauty?'

'What I meant was, what you eat goes a long way in determining how good you look inside,' she huffed. 'But eat vada-pav. See if I care. And while you are at it, you might as well take medicine for sprouting pimples!'

I skipped the vada-pav and grabbed a plate of fruit chaat, hoping that all the flies buzzing around wouldn't give me a bout of cholera or worse. Then I'd really have something to worry about besides acne.

'I'm here!' I said, breathlessly rushing into Rosie's.

In my blind rush, I knocked against somebody who said, 'So I see.'

Startled, I looked up. Vidisha!

'Sorry.'

'You should be,' she said and sailed out.

What was that supposed to mean? I ran up to her. 'Wait a minute. I want to speak to you.'

She stopped. 'About what? Tips on how to seduce my husband?'

'No, but maybe you can explain what you were doing at Serenity Villa on the night of the 17th.'

'I can't.'

'You can't?'

'I can't, because I was never there,' she said.

Rosie harrumphed behind me. I turned to look. 'Are you planning on coming in sometime today?'

I allowed myself to be led inside. Rosie's parlour is a biggish place, done up in Japanese style with lots of rooms separated by sliding doors.

'Just a minute,' she said, stopping outside a room. 'I just need to check up on one facial client.'

She knocked softly on the door. No answer.

She knocked again. 'Ma'am?'

No answer.

'Must've fallen asleep,' Rosie said, sliding the door open and stepping inside.

A woman lay on a mattress on the floor, her face covered with a towel. Rosie walked up to the woman and gently shook her. No response. She removed the towel from the woman's face.

Next thing I knew, she was shrieking like a banshee. I frowned. Such reactions are commonplace in a beauty parlour, except it's usually the clients who do the shrieking, not the other way around. Just how bad was the facial?

Hearing the commotion, everybody started coming over. I went into the room and found myself staring at a face covered with a mud pack, and into a pair of eyes staring at the ceiling. Lifelessly. Telltale froth at the corner of her mouth drove all thoughts of a facial out of my mind.

I felt a momentary wave of blackness leaping out to envelop me. Fortunately, a sudden sugar rush, courtesy the recently consumed watermelon, ensured that it passed quickly.

'Okay, step away Rosie! Don't touch anything,' I said taking charge.

By now an audience had gathered outside the room and everybody wanted to know what had happened.

'Call the police!' I barked at the frightened receptionist who looked most reluctant to leave. 'I said, call the police!'

The poor girl left unwillingly, leaving restless murmurs in her wake.

'Her face must have got burnt,' someone said with malicious pleasure masquerading as horror. 'Which treatment was it?'

'Must be one of those new-fangled treatments. They promise you the heaven and you end up looking like hell.'

The receptionist returned saying the police were on their way.

'All right!' I said. 'Clear out. This woman's dead.'

That raised another furore with exclamations of, 'Was she allergic to something?' 'Was it ammonia? 'Cos I can't stand the stuff myself', 'Me too. I break out into a rash every time', and 'The stuff they put in these things! Even herbal ones. I believe they're highly toxic.'

Eventually Chodu arrived on the scene. His eyes scanned the room and came to rest on me. 'What are you doing here?'

Duh! What did he think I was doing there? 'I came in for a facial.'

'Really?' He peered suspiciously at my face. 'You don't look any different.'

'I haven't had one yet!'

A hysterical Rosie blabbed, 'I can't understand how it could've happened. I just can't! It's not our fault. She didn't tell us she was allergic to any chemicals.' Then realising what she'd just said, she hastily added, 'Not dat we use any chemicals. We use hundred per cent natural products.'

Sure. If you're willing to allow that lead is natural.

Chodu asked to her narrate everything from the beginning.

Rosie didn't need any encouragement and launched into her story. 'Dis woman came to us for a facial. She had just come back from out of station and was in urgent need of skin care she said. Her skin looked like hell so I recommended de Luminous facial. It's de best. You see as we grow older our skin loses elasticity. Dis new treatment comes wid a mixture of collagen and a deep hydrating cream which restores your skin's elasticity . . .'

Chodu made a deep, growling noise from the base of his throat. Rosie took one look at him and said quickly, 'Anyway, she said she wanted it and I did the facial myself. Dina, Maheen and Nancy here were wid me. You see, this facial needs a specialist to do it or it won't work. And here only I am qualified for it. So I was training the udders. Everything went well and I finished the facial. Den when I went to check on the face pack, she was . . . she was . . .' Rosie's chin wobbled.

'What was her name?' Chodu said hastily.

The receptionist came forward, holding the register, and said, 'Sweety Nair.'

Chapter Fourteen

❧

I felt another wave of blackness hit me. When my vision cleared I saw Chodu looking at me queerly. He was in the midst of taking down Sweety's details.

'Are you all right? You're not going to pass out on me again, are you?'

'No,' I said, trembling. 'I haven't eaten. That's all. A bit of air will sort it out.'

I stepped outside on shaky legs, my mind working furiously. I whipped out my cellphone to call Ani. I was about to dial his number when some instinct made me stop. I immediately switched it off instead. I looked around, spotted a public telephone booth and called him from there.

'Sweety's dead,' I said as soon as he answered.

It didn't seem to have registered because he asked after a moment's pause, 'Kay?'

'It's me.'

'Why are you calling from this number?' he asked.

'Did you hear what I said? Sweety's dead.'

'Is this a joke?' His voice had a distinct edge to it.

'No,' I insisted. 'She's really dead.'

'No, she isn't. I just saw her. She came back this morning.'

'Ani! Listen to me. I'm at Rosie's beauty parlour. Sweety is inside. Dead. Chodu . . . DCP Chodankar is here this very moment.'

In the silence that followed, the noises in the background seemed even louder.

'Are you there?' I asked.

'Just give me a moment. I need to sit down.' Then, 'Oh my god, you killed her!' he whispered.

'What? Of course not! What a ridiculous thing to say! And who said anything about murder? Anyway, where are you?'

'At the car workshop. Sweety . . . Sweety banged up my Beemer real bad . . .'

There was silence for a couple of seconds.

'Listen, I gotta go now. Remember, if DCP Chodankar calls, pretend to be surprised, okay?' I said.

On the whole, it was a very strange conversation. But then we were in shock. After I'd hung up, I walked back to Rosie's and stood outside. I lit a cigarette and inhaled shakily. I noticed that my hands were trembling. I may not have had much affection for Sweety and, on occasion, may have wished her ill as well. But I hadn't really meant it.

And there was the fact that Sweety was way too young to die of natural causes. Which left two options—suicide and murder. Actually three—it could very well have been an allergic reaction. Although I knew the chances of that were slim, I hoped that was it, because if it turned out to be foul play, shit would hit the fan. And no points for guessing where it would land.

Presently, Chodu stepped outside and stood beside me. I silently offered him a cigarette.

'Bad business,' he said conversationally, taking the proffered stick.

'Murder?' I said as nonchalantly as I could manage.

He nodded.

'How do you know?'

'It's just a hunch. Spoke to the husband.'

My heart stopped. That was quick. It had been what, five, ten minutes since I'd spoken with Ani? I glanced at my watch and realised with a start that it had been a good half hour. And I had smoked three cigarettes.

'He didn't seem all that surprised,' Chodu said.

In spite of warning him! I silently cursed Ani. Aloud I said, 'Maybe he was just in shock. Happens. Besides, he wasn't even here!'

He looked at me sharply. 'How do you know?'

Shit! 'Do you see a man around here?'

'He needn't have done it himself. He could have an accomplice, maybe a lover. Anyway, we'll know soon. The body has already been sent for post-mortem.'

'Speaking of murders, did Geeta tell you about Vidisha fighting with Urvashi on 17th night?'

'Yes. But Vidisha says she didn't go to Serenity Villa. Says she was with someone but she can't talk about it. Claims it's sensitive.'

'She's lying! It's a murder case. If she was with someone she would have given the name.' Unless she was getting plastic surgery done in which case it's better to risk jail time than divulge that you were getting a boob job done.

He shrugged. 'Could be. But I'm not sure why she would wait till the 19th to kill Urvashi. And don't forget, she has an alibi for the 19th.'

'Of course. Ma-in-law. In my opinion, the lady doth protest Vidisha's innocence too much.'

He reacted sharply to my tone of voice. 'You think Meher Kapoor knows something?'

'I got that feeling. But then, I'd bet my ass, almost everyone involved knows more.'

'Then what are you getting at? You think Meher Kapoor had something to do with it?'

'Anything's possible, I suppose. Especially if Urvashi was making her son's life miserable.'

'She has an alibi, too, for the 19th. The watchman corroborates her story,' he pointed out.

'He's a charasi! Besides, he's devoted to the family. He'll say anything they tell him to.'

'Yes, but so far we haven't been able to shake him. Till we do, or till we find evidence to the contrary, we've got to go along with Zuari Mal's story. And according to him, they were all where they say they were.'

'All?'

'You didn't think we forgot Kaustav Kapoor?'

'You can't think he has anything to do with it! He loved her.'

He nodded. 'Everyone seems to think he's innocent. Something to do with CQ, I suppose.'

'CQ?'

'Cuteness Quotient.'

'Wow, Cuteness Quotient,' I teased. 'You do know he's not . . .?'

He pulled a face. 'Chill. It's not what you think. That's just the term Solanki used.'

I was unable to hide my dismay. 'Ilina's on the case?'

ACP Ilina Solanki is Chodu's junior and a very bright police officer. She's also a total knockout.

Chodu smiled amusedly. 'No. She just gave her opinion in passing.'

I hid my relief. I didn't want another Xena vying for Kaustav's attention. 'Did you find out who owns Hermit Hill?'

'It may take some time. The land records don't show any recent sales. That means whoever owns it has had it for years. And the older records are fuzzy.'

'Meanwhile, any trace of that Bulgari ring?'

He shook his head, ground out his ciggie and went back inside. Sweety! I'd completely forgotten about her for a few minutes. My mind raced. They would soon swoop down on Ani. They would consider motives—money, jealousy, revenge, an affair. His financial details would be dredged up, his whereabouts investigated, his phone records checked. Dear god!

I kicked the RE into action and raced to Dikshit's.

'I need a huge favour,' I said as soon as he opened the door.

He shot me a dour look as if saying, 'When don't you?'

'I need you to change my phone number with someone else's in the phone company's records for a little while.' I figured he would need an explanation as to why I needed such an extraordinary thing done, but I couldn't tell him about Sweety. He just might get queasy about being an accessory to murder. *What was wrong with me? I hadn't murdered her!* 'I'm so sick and tired of being over-billed. I've complained and complained and all they've done is send me thank you notes for valuable feedback. Let someone else do the complaining for a while.'

With a few key strokes he opened the records of the phone company. He scrolled down to my name and frowned. 'But, the bill amount is only 2201.56!'

'It's still over-billing. I know I haven't talked that much,' I said lamely.

He shrugged and pointed his finger at the name just above mine and looked at me with a question mark in his eyes. The record read Malhar, Beena.

'No way!' I exclaimed. 'The governor's wife?'

He gave me a 'Come, now' look.

'What? Not the governor's wife? Who then? The chief secretary's?'

'Try again.'

God, this was infuriating. Why couldn't he just tell me instead of forcing me to play a guessing game that would reveal my shocking lack of general knowledge? Although, why I should know who the various public officers were was beyond me, I thought a bit defensively. It wasn't as though I was on their Z-plus security detail.

After a few misses, I was appalled to learn that she was the police commissioner's wife. But then, the more I thought about it, the more I liked it. Chodu would obviously have to tread carefully with that one.

'Why not,' I said, my heart beating fast. I dreaded to think what would happen when the whole thing unravelled, as I knew it would. Hopefully, by then they would have caught the actual culprit and this entire business would be shoved under the carpet.

After he had done the needful, I asked him to start looking into Deshpande's affairs.

'You can't ask me something like that!' he protested. 'Where do I even begin?'

'Begin with his involvement in Blazar Films' *Ransom* and work your way backwards. Find out who he spoke to in the past week, where he went, details of financial transactions, etc. And call me on my other cell if you have anything.'

Next, I decided to pay Prado a visit. I could easily have gotten the info at Dikshit's but I wanted to ease the awkward situation between Prado and me. Luckily, he was just as eager to do that, and that resulted in him being extra helpful.

I asked him about the call Urvashi had received at five-seventeen p.m. on 17th September.

Prado removed the topmost file from the pile on his desk and slapped it down in front of him. He leafed through the file and stopped at a page. He ran his eye down and confirmed that Urvashi had indeed received a call at five-seventeen p.m. from a local Mumbai number. He paused.

'For god's sake! Tell me already.'

'It is Chandan Baweja's direct number at Blazar. But that doesn't prove anything. Anyone could have slipped into his office and made the call. During his interrogation Baweja mentioned that he was in Khandala with Urvashi at the time the call was made. Plus we've spoken to people in Blazar and they confirm that he was out of office.'

Next, I asked him if Geeta had received a call from Serenity Villa on the night of the 17th. He scanned the file and confirmed that she had. 'Interestingly, Urvashi also made three other calls that night from the same number. The first one was to Kaustav Kapoor's cellphone and the next one to a number that belongs to a certain Mayuri. Mayuri is a small-time choreographer who mostly does low-budget and south Indian films. Apparently she's also Urvashi's latest best friend.'

'What does she say?'

'Nothing. Just what everyone's been telling us. That Urvashi was near hysterical when she called. She wasn't making much sense. She kept blabbing something about Vidisha and Kaustav. She called him a lying bastard and how she'd had it with the whole Kapoor lot. She also mentioned something about screwing him over.'

'What about the third number?'

'It's registered to an Abdulla, a broker.'

'Of what?'

'Anything. Everything.'

Basically, a euphemism for 'shady character'. 'But that doesn't make sense!'

'Tell me about it.'

'Did you speak to Abdulla?'

He nodded. 'Says he'd been negotiating with Urvashi about her dates for another project and that she called to confirm the dates.'

'Really. So he's a producer now?'

'No, but his client is—the one on whose behalf he was in touch with Urvashi.'

'Who is it?'

'He didn't say. But we can guess, considering where he was when the conversation happened. Dubai.'

'Are you thinking what I'm thinking?'

'Underworld? Extortion killing?' He shrugged. 'He got back only early yesterday morning. Immigration records verify his story. Besides his fingerprints weren't found at the crime scene.'

'That doesn't mean anything. He could have been wearing gloves. Or he could have hired someone to do it for him. Assuming Urvashi told him where she was, he could have sent someone.'

Prado nodded. 'We are looking into it.'

'Did you ask Geeta or Kaustav about this guy?'

'We did. They say they don't know anything about any Abdulla.'

I made a note of all the phone numbers and Abdulla's address. 'And that's all the conversations she had?'

'When you put it that way, no. She also received a call after speaking with Abdulla. From Kaustav Kapoor's cellphone.'

Abdulla's residence happened to be in a seedy neighbourhood near my apartment so I decided to make a stopover there on the way home. It was locked. Upon enquiring with the neighbours, I was told that Abdulla had, just about an hour ago, departed on what appeared to be a business trip. He had a large suitcase with him and was heard instructing the cab driver to take him to the airport. Great.

Next, I stopped at my bank. While I was filling out a deposit slip, it occurred to me that it might not be such a good idea to deposit the cheque. Just in case the police froze my accounts. They do that in murder investigations, you know, along with confiscating your passport. And if the money was already in the bank, it was as good as gone. On the other hand, if the cheque had not been deposited they couldn't touch it, could they? Of course, in its current state it was no good to me either, besides providing an illusion of money. In the end I deposited the cheque.

Back home, it was only five in the evening and I was exhausted. And scared. And in no mood to meet Elly and Em that night. Not knowing what was happening was driving me crazy and I longed to call Ani. But that wasn't wise. Restlessly, I prowled about my apartment, smoking incessantly, trying to figure out Urvashi's case. But my mind kept going back to Sweety. Had they found out what happened? One didn't need Toxicology 101 (although I took the course) to know that the froth near her mouth suggested poison. Was it suicide? An allergic reaction? Maybe it was food poisoning. Maybe she'd had lobsters for lunch not realising she was allergic to crustaceans ... *Stop it!* I silently screamed.

I needed something to take my mind off Sweety. Otherwise I was just going to drive myself crazy. And then, just like that, I knew what I would do. I would take a leisurely bath, get into a dress, put on some make-up ... In short, for the first time in a really long time, I would really get ready for tonight. And then I would go to Ego.

The warm water felt wonderful and I stepped out of the bathroom relaxed, ready to make the all-important decision of what to wear. I grabbed a knee-length, slinky black number that I had bought back in the days when I could fit into it and breathe at the same time. Now, although I've longed to be, I've never been a Twiggy. Even back in those days, when I was at my fittest best, I was solid, like Serena Williams. But you know how these shops seduce you into making senseless purchases by employing trick mirrors which make you look tall and slim? And then you come home and stand in front of your unforgiving mirror and realise you've made a horrible mistake? The dress was deemed such a mistake and relegated to the back of the cupboard.

I took it out now and decided I would wear it. I pulled the dress over my head and struggled to pull it down. Okay, maybe my ass wasn't the only place I'd added insulation on, I thought as I attempted to pull up the zipper . . . *Could Sweety have been threatening him with divorce and in a fit of rage Ani . . . No, no, no. How could I suspect Ani? Hadn't I been dating the guy?* An ominous chirr! I twisted around and saw that I had ripped the zipper right off the dress!

Oh screw it! I grabbed my favourite blue jeans and a clingy red tee. A light dab of make-up and I was all done. Battle-worn, but ready. Since there was some time before I had to leave for Ego, I took out my other cellphone and dialled Mayuri's number.

She answered on the fifth ring. 'He*n*llo*n*,' she sang nasally into the phone.

'Mayuri?'

'Tha*n*t's right,' she trilled, setting my teeth on edge.

'My name is Katie Kumar. I'm a private investigator and Ms Geeta has hired me to work on the Urvashi case. I was wondering if I could come by and see you.'

'Oh, but I ha*n*ve a show*n*. I'm leaving for Nasik tonight. I'll be ba*n*ck only day*n* a*n*fter tomorrow. Wou*n*ld that be o*n*kay?'

'Okay. I'll call you.'

The next call I made was to Dikshit. I gave him Abdulla's number and asked him to get the dope on him. 'Phone calls, financial transactions, business partners, you know the drill.'

As I was going over the events of the day, I remembered Bhanu Khanna. I retrieved the torn pieces of paper from my bag. Some of the pieces were scribbled on and some had sketches. I tried to assemble them into one whole. Even though some of the jigsaw pieces were missing, I had enough to tape together a lewd ode to Desiree's anatomy and the various things the writer of the note, presumably Bhanu Khanna, would like to do to them. *So, they were having sex*, I thought. That didn't preclude coke, though. Perhaps they were doing both?

That doesn't make sense, I thought, dragging my mind away from puerile ruminations. Why would they be arguing so heatedly about the nonsensical note? I flipped the paper over. And I knew what the bone of contention was. It wasn't the note at all. It was a rough, handmade map of the route from Serenity Villa to Hermit Hill!

Chapter Fifteen

∽≈∾

Before I could dwell on this any further, I happened to glance at my watch. With a start I realised it was almost seven forty-five. I grabbed my helmet and rushed out. As I was locking my door, Gandhi's door opened and he popped out. He approached me determinedly.

'Oh no, no, no. Not now,' I said and ran.

As always, he blocked me on the staircase. One arm on the wall and the other on the banister, he looked at me mulishly.

'Mr Gandhi, this is really not a good time,' I said.

'Fine,' he said, thrusting a sheet of paper in my face.

'What's this?'

'Society notice.'

'Notice?'

'There is a general body meeting on Sunday and the society is going to vote on an isoo.'

'So? I'm not a member. I just rent.'

'Oh I think you will wont to be there for this meeting.'

Something in his expression made me stop. 'Oh? What issue are you debating?' I asked cautiously.

'Whether to allow single girls to live in the society or note.'

'What? That's ridiculous.'

'The women of the society don't think so. They feel it's baid influence on our children.'

I swallowed. 'So . . . so it's decided?'

Gandhi hesitated, then moved closer and said conspiratorially, 'I'm not supposed to say this but an informal vote had already been carried out and the society is evenly divided on the isoo.'

I couldn't conceal my dismay. 'There has to be a way out of this!' I cried.

Gandhi inhaled. 'There is. Note everyone has voted. There is still one vote remaining.'

I seized his arm. 'Who is it? Maybe I can talk to him. Or her.'

'Me.'

I stared at him stupidly. 'You?'

He nodded.

I looked at him in puzzlement. 'So . . . what is the problem? You can veto, can't you?'

He edged away, holding up his arms. 'I don't know. After all I haiv to live here.'

'Please, Mr Gandhi, you have to help me. You have to do something,' I pleaded.

'Well,' he began with a great show of reluctance. 'I suppose we could work something out.'

'What?' I said, although I already had an idea.

He beckoned me closer.

'I can hear perfectly fine from here.'

He moved to put his arm around my shoulders. His hand slipped off and started fondling my bra strap. I was contemplating breaking his arm when, fortunately, Mrs Gandhi materialised from behind him, shouting, 'Ae Hiten, what are you doing?'

He backed off, raising his arms protectively.

'Sorry, but I haiv to live here,' he said and ran.

Crap! As if everything else wasn't enough, now I had to look for another apartment. And in six days!

On my way to Ego, I stopped at a public booth and called Ani.

'Hello?' I said cautiously. 'I'm calling from Mars Mall. Can I talk to you sir?'

'Katie? Is that you?'

'Is it okay to talk?'

'Yeah, they're gone. For now.'

'How are you?'

'It's been horrible. They went through my phone records, my bank statements, everything. They wanted to know who my friends are, who Sweety's friends were, who her enemies were, if she was having an affair, if I was having an affair, if she had a will, if she had insurance . . .'

'So, they've established,' I couldn't bring myself to say murder, 'foul play?'

'Not yet. But I think the DCP is fairly certain that's what it is.'

Damn Chodu and his gut instinct.

'Do you,' I began diffidently, 'do you want to meet someplace?'

Say yes, I pleaded silently. In my mind I was already making excuses to Em and Lizzy. Period pain, I'd say. You can never argue with period pain.

'I better not,' he said. 'There's a shady character parked outside.'

I swallowed my disappointment. 'You don't think they're having you shadowed?'

'I wouldn't put it past them.'

'Don't worry,' I said soothingly, 'they won't have anything on us. I swapped my number with the commissioner's wife's in the phone company's billing records and I've switched off my phone. So, according to billing records, it is the commissioner's wife's number, and they'll have to tread carefully.'

The congratulations I'd expected didn't come. Instead, Ani exploded. 'That's insane! If you had to exchange your number with someone else, why didn't you just do it with Sweety's?' *Now why hadn't I thought of that?*

Ego, Em's nightclub, is situated on Juhu beach. It is as close to the sea as construction limits allow, which means it is pretty darn close. It is terribly exclusive and entry is only through membership, which itself is restricted and only given after a careful screening process.

The ground floor is the general club area, where performances are held. The first floor comprises several private saloons for members who wish to entertain away from the public eye. I have my own theory about those saloons, though.

I pulled up outside the club and handed my RE to a valet. Running my fingers through my hair I sashayed down to Louis who watched me approach in alarm.

Louis is a tall, dark and hefty Mauritian. He is not the brightest spark around but he adores Em. He also dislikes me with equal passion as he thinks I'm bad for Em's business. His dislike stems from the fact that once, not so long ago, I got very drunk and insisted on dancing on a table. Em took it sportingly enough—it was she, after all, who had dared me to do so—but Louis was mortified. It wasn't that he thought I'd sullied the posh club with my behaviour, but that I'd given away for free something Ego charged a bomb for. When you come to Ego you pay for your entertainment, is his motto.

'Hey Louis,' I greeted him pleasantly. 'How's tricks?'

'Zey were fine. Until now,' he said, adding under his breath, '*Maintenant je ne sais pas.*'

I gave him my bitch look. '*J'ai ça ecouté.*'

He looked at me in alarm.

I love doing this to him. I throw French words around just to spook him out. What makes it fun is that he gets taken in so easily. He can never be sure whether I actually understand or am just bluffing when I nod knowledgeably and say *D'accord.*

'Mam'zelle waits for you. Ze rest of your party is already here,' he said hastily. '*Après moi.*'

'*D'accord.*'

There it was again. The scared look. This was getting too easy. I would have to think of something else.

Louis led me inside, and in spite of the numerous times I have been there, I found myself appreciating again the sleek and minimalistic interiors. In terms of design, Ego was like any other seafront nightclub. It had a seating area, a standing area next to the bar, a performing stage and an outside deck extending right into the sea.

The club was relatively quiet. Soft music played in the background, the air was clean and the lights had not yet been lowered to near blindingly dark levels. But then it was early yet. The place would start rocking only after eleven.

Elly and Em sat on the far edge of the deck, sipping their drinks and talking animatedly. It was more shrieking than talking, though. From the little snatches of conversation that I heard, mainly awed gasps and disbelieving exclamations, I gathered they'd already caught up on the lost years and had moved onto Urvashi.

'Our dancing queen arrives!' Em chuckled as soon as she saw me.

'Aren't you out of costume?' Elly joked.

And they both dissolved into raucous laughter.

'Not as much as you were in the summer holidays of 1994!' I retorted, referring to the one time in high school we had all decided to go swimming. Elly had on a really old costume. She didn't realise just how old till she dived into the water. And emerged minus her top. In full view of everybody.

My quip prompted another round of helpless laughter. Although, Elly did screw up her face as if trying to figure out why she was participating in the merriment.

Going by the empty glasses on the table, they had both had two cocktails each and were fairly buzzed already. Louis took one look at the table and his face fell. I could tell what was going on in his mind—'Zis is going to be one of zose nights.' To add to his miseries, Em drained her glass, her third, and ordered another.

'I'm in a bit of a jam,' I said, flopping down on the sofa. 'Sweety's dead.'

'What?' Elly said drunkenly. 'No, Urvashi's dead.'

'*Sweety's dead?*' Em cried.

'Who's Sweety?' Elly asked.

The few people that were there were starting to look up and our way.

'Shhh!' I hissed. To Elly I said, 'My boy . . . ex-boyfriend's wife.'

Elly's eyes bulged incredulously and then narrowed suspiciously. She looked to Em for confirmation.

Em nodded and asked me urgently, "ow?' I shot her a warning look. She dropped her accent. 'What happened?'

So I told her about my visit to Rosie's and what transpired there, ending with, 'Chodu suspects she was murdered.'

Em frowned. 'But I don't understand. Why are you in a jam? Unless . . .' Her mind added up the parts and arrived at the sum. She clapped her mouth and looked at me in horror. 'No!'

'What? Of course not!' I said.

She looked at me pityingly. 'Oh honey! You're in denial.'

'How could you even think that I . . .?' I said.

'Not you. Him,' she clarified. 'He looks like he would do something like that. Don't tell me you helped him! Don't tell me he talked you into it!'

'Stop right there!' I ordered her.

Feeling quite like Linus Caldwell in a Danny Ocean–Rutsy Ryanesque conversation, Elly wailed, 'What are you talking about? What's going on?'

'Sweety was Ani's wife, and in such cases usually the prime suspects are spouses. If it turns out that she was indeed murdered, the police will, like, literally rip open his life for possible motives.

Then it is only a matter of time before they stumble upon our affair and we are toast,' I said gloomily.

'The bastard!' Em said acerbically. 'It's not enough that he messed with your mind. He has to take you down along with him.' She drained her glass and snapped her fingers for more. After a moment she added more sympathetically, 'Will you be okay honey?'

'I don't know. I've managed to buy some time but then I . . .' I shrugged.

'Then what?' Em asked anxiously.

'Then nothing. Hopefully they would have found the actual killer before then.'

'You mean Ani?' Elly tried tentatively.

'NO!' What was this? A virus?

'I'm sorry,' Elly said piteously. 'I've been out of this for so long I don't know what you guys are talking about.'

I threw up my hands. 'Can we talk about something else?'

'Yes, let's,' Em said, pulling a face. 'Let's talk about Urvashi.'

'That's an upper,' I said.

'Just shows how much Aniruddh depresses me,' she said.

Just then Louis caught her eye and beckoned. Em excused herself, leaving Elly and me alone. I was desperate for a smoke but I didn't want to risk Em catching me. The last thing I wanted was a lecture on smoking.

'I looked for you later at the studio,' Elly said after Em had left. 'I thought we could have had lunch.'

'I thought you said you were busy.'

'I was. But then that DCP came, wanting to talk to the crew. He went in to talk to Sameer and then Sameer came out and announced that he was too upset to continue so we packed up early.'

'Actually I wanted to ask you about that. Why would he want to talk to Sameer?'

She shrugged. 'Who knows?'

'Did Sameer have a reason to kill Urvashi?'

'Didn't everybody? God, there were times I could have killed her myself,' she said with feeling.

'So did you?'

It took her a moment to realise I was joking and she made a face. 'About Sameer Khan, though, I don't know. You see, Sameer was one of two people besides Kaustav who actually liked her.'

'What are you talking about? I thought he hated her. I read about it in *Screen*.'

'He did go out of his way to project that, didn't he? I mean, who does that in our industry?'

'What are you getting at?'

'Remember Sumit Manwani?'

Sumit Manwani was a guy in college who happened to have a giant-sized crush on me. Unfortunately, he was so ugly, he was called Bakasur. And that was one of the kinder names. He was so ugly even I was forced to decline his attentions. And I was so desperate I'd even briefly dated a guy who looked like a cross between Mick Jagger and Prince. Regrettably, the spurned lover didn't react well to my gentle-but-repeated turndowns and reciprocated by spreading malicious rumours about me. Just how vicious, I learnt only later when strange guys started turning up at my doorstep offering me money for sex.

'How can I forget him? He made me the college slut,' I said with a shudder. Even though it had happened all those years ago, the memory of it still haunted me. 'Are you saying Sameer had a crush on Urvashi? That his saying he didn't like her was a way to get her attention?'

'That's the feeling I got.'

'Anyway, who was the other? You said Sameer was one of two people to actually like her.'

'Why, Mrs Kapoor, of course.'

'That's strange. In spite of what Urvashi was doing to Kaustav's marriage?'

'Hey, her son's happy, she's happy. Maybe she accepted the fact that Urvashi was her son's choice.'

'Like Stephanie with Brooke.'

'You're still watching that rubbish?'

'Elly, do you think someone from *Ransom* killed Urvashi?'

'Could be,' she said helpfully.

'Could it be Bhanu Khanna?'

Elly choked on her drink. 'Bhanu Khanna! He'd be the last person I would peg as the murderer.'

'Why? He had motive.'

'You mean, like, him being Vidisha's brother an' all?'

Now it was my turn to choke. 'He's Vidisha's brother?!'

Elly was taken aback. 'You didn't know?'

'No! I was talking about him being upset with Urvashi for interfering in *Ransom* and ruining his career.'

'Oh please! That's just hogwash. Bhanu is, like, so totally incompetent. He doesn't know the first thing about directing. He's in Blazar only because he's Vidisha's brother. He messed up *Ransom* and had he got his way, the film would have been a complete dibba. I have to bite my tongue to say it, but Urvashi actually saved the project.'

Interesting. Then why were Neena and Chandan going out of their way to pin the blame on him?

'Still, he could've been upset with her high-handedness. Hurt ego and all that, you know,' I asked. 'Plus he *is* Vidisha's brother.'

She thought about that. Finally, she shook her head. 'Nah! I can't picture him in the role of a killer. Too much of a wuss. You'd be better off pinning your suspicions on that cokehead, Desiree.'

'Oh?'

'Look at it from her angle. She's been a two-bit item girl all her career. And then she seduces Bhanu and lands the role of second lead in *Ransom*. Imagine her chagrin when the meaty role is snipped down to, like, two scenes, thanks to Urvashi. She is pushing thirty, you know, and *Ransom* was her last chance.'

'Could she have done it?'

'She's not too bright but she's capable of it. She's wild. And she's got guts. Especially when she's high.'

And yet the murder must have been committed by someone bright enough to make sure there were no clues left. Or could it be that Desiree killed Urvashi and was lucky enough not to leave any clues? She certainly knew about Urvashi's whereabouts. So did sissy, incompetent Bhanu Khanna. Did they both kill her together?

Elly continued, 'I don't know if this helps, but I just remembered something about Desiree. The day before we wrapped up the Pune schedule—'

'The 16th?'

'Yes, the 16th. Something happened that upset Urvashi. I remember she stormed onto the set and claimed that someone had been inside her Green Room and rifled through her stuff. She started screaming abuses at everybody. She told them to confess or there would be hell to pay. As if anyone would, when faced with . . . that. When no one stepped forward she turned to me and threatened me. She told me to find out who'd done it or she'd get me fired.'

'Why? Was something missing from the Green Room?'

Elly shrugged. 'It doesn't matter whether anything was stolen. Urvashi's Green Room is supposed to be off-limits to everybody. The very fact that someone dared to go in was enough to set off the queen bee.'

'So who do you think did it?'

'I know who did it. Desiree.'

'Desiree!'

She nodded. 'After Urvashi threatened me I asked around. Like I had a choice. And one of her make-up girls, in confidence, told me that she had seen Desiree sneak into Urvashi's Green Room. According to her, she was in there for about five minutes.'

'So what did you do?'

'I didn't know what to do about it. I could hardly afford to tell Urvashi 'cos then there would certainly have been a showdown with one or both of them storming off the sets. But, as luck would have it, I didn't have to say anything—when I saw Urvashi next, she seemed to have forgotten all about it.'

'So what do you think Desiree was doing in Urvashi's Green Room?'

'Who knows? Maybe she was just checking out Urvashi's wardrobe so she could tell her dress master to make her a better costume. Normally heroines do such petty things to upstage each other. And in Desiree's case it was also revenge for snipping her role.'

'So she didn't steal anything? Then why was Urvashi screaming? How did she know anyone had been in her room?'

'I never thought about it like that. Perhaps she did something while she was in there . . . maybe pinched something. Now that you mention it, the make-up girl did say Desiree looked excited . . . her body was tense and her hands were clenched and she had a particular look in her eye. Like a gleam . . . like . . . like she was bursting . . . I don't know how to explain it.'

'What about Baweja? And Neena Pundir?' I asked.

'Let's not even go there.'

'Oh?'

She grimaced. 'They couldn't stand each other. Of course they were cordial in front of others but I could always feel this tension, especially in Neena. Like, she actually, physically hated her . . . you know what I mean?'

'Is it because of Kaustav? She certainly appears to be smitten by him.'

She seemed unsure. 'By that logic most of the women in Blazar—and some of the men—should be under the scanner.'

I asked Elly about Mayuri and she shrugged. 'I heard about her. I heard they were friends but I never saw her around.'

'Why would Urvashi be friends with a small-time choreographer?' I asked, puzzled.

Elly snorted. 'Who will she be friends with? Katrina? Please! They wouldn't touch each other with a barge pole.'

Em came then, trilling, 'By the way, I've asked someone to join us later. Just for a little while. It's important. I hope you don't mind.'

'Is it Noel?' Noel was Em's boyfriend.

'Idiot. If it were him I would have said Noel.'

'Point.' Then I looked at her suspiciously. 'You're not trying to fix me up with someone, are you?'

'Well . . .'

''Cos if you are, bring it on,' I threw my arms wide open, knocking over my glass which went clattering, spilling the remains of my drink on the table.

'Oh shoot!' I looked around for serviettes to mop up the mess. There weren't any. I reached into my bag for some tissues. As I was taking the packet out, Gandhi's society notice fell out as well.

Em bent down and picked it up. 'Kay, what's this?'

'Oh that.' I told them about the society vote on Sunday. 'I don't know what I'm going to do. How will I find a flat so fast?' I said glumly in the end. I absently picked up Em's glass and took a sip. And immediately spat it out. 'Jeez, Em. What are you drinking, club soda?'

'I do have to work,' she said pointedly. 'Anyway, I wouldn't worry too much. They can't throw you out without notice.'

'And if they do, you could come and camp out with one of us for some time,' Elly offered.

'Yes I could, couldn't I?' I said, looking at Em hopefully. It had only just now occurred to me that this might be one way out of the whole Sweety mess. Even if Chodu pieced the whole thing together, he could hardly arrest me if he couldn't find me, could he?

But Em didn't extend the invitation. When I stared at her pointedly, she averted her eyes. 'Or you could sleep with Gandhi. That pervert is just angling for a lay. Why don't you give him what he wants and finish it off?'

Yikes! Sleep with Gandhi. This day was getting better and better. 'You can't be serious!' I yelped.

She sighed. 'Of course not.'

'What's going on?' I asked her. 'This is the third time you've blown me off in as many days!'

She had the good grace to look ashamed.

'It's Deshpande!' I exclaimed.

Em looked at me, aghast. 'What?'

'There. I can see him,' I said, gesturing towards the entrance.

He saw us too, and the next thing I knew, he was snaking his way forward towards us. He wore a dazzling white linen shirt tucked inside blue jeans. His hair looked lustrous and he was freshly shaved. He looked kinda . . . sexy.

I thought about last night when he had said my hair looked nice, loose and swinging free. I saw the whole thing in my mind. My hair is piled up on my head, Deshpande reaches up and removes the clip from my hair and the tresses tumble down to my waist in a lustrous, hypnosis-inducing symphony. Like Denise Richards' hair in that *Friends* episode. *What was I doing? He was the enemy!*

I don't know what came over me. I can only attribute what I did next to a feeling of intense loneliness coupled with excess booze. 'I'm going to kiss him,' I said suddenly.

Em looked appalled while Elly looked encouraging.

'You're not serious!' Em said.

'Why not?' I argued. 'We're both single. And available. Besides, you were trying to fix me up with someone. Why not him?'

'You don't even like him!'

Ignoring her, I mused, 'Maybe we'll have hot sex. Maybe I'll even move in with him.'

Elly nodded enthusiastically. 'Good idea.'

'Shut up!' Em said fiercely.

'Why?' Elly said plaintively. 'He's cute. If she's not gonna, I'm gonna.'

'What about . . . Ani?' Em said.

'What about him?' I said dismissively just as Deshpande reached us.

'Hello ladies,' he said pleasantly.

I slammed my glass down on the table, lurched to my feet and, before he knew what hit him, planted a full wet one on his lips. Never have I seen him look so shocked. His eyes opened wide and he froze in mid-action. Then his arms shot out in reflex and he grabbed my waist to steady us both.

'And now, I'm going home,' I said, staggering to the door.

Chapter Sixteen

❧

All night I was tormented by strange dreams. In one, I crept up behind an unsuspecting Sweety, gripping a dagger in my hand. And then slowly, deliberately, I raised my arm and plunged the blade into her back. In another, the MO was the same, but Ani was with me. In yet another, Ani was with me but the weapon was a gun. Each time I woke up sweating and gasping for breath. The dreams were so vivid that each time, in that brief moment between sleep and wakefulness, I wondered if indeed I hadn't killer her.

I finally woke up at ten, hung over and dehydrated. At once, memories of last night washed over me. I sat up in bed, cringing with shame. Had I really kissed Deshpande? I rocked back and forth, head buried in my hands, moaning in mortification. After a while, I figured all that whingeing was just a waste of energy. What was done was done. Meanwhile, I had work to do.

I jumped out of bed and drank a whole bottle of water. I threw on my clothes hurriedly, my mood magically lifted by the fact that my jeans were slightly looser in the seat area. Of course, it was a different, larger pair, but still . . . *Yippee! Smoking may kill tomorrow. It pays off today.*

I downed a hasty breakfast of boiled eggs and toast and it did much to alleviate the hangover. Then, feeling almost alive, I left.

While walking out the door, I happened to glance at the newspaper. The headline read: Sameer Khan Signs Multi-million Dollar Hollywood Project. I grabbed the newspaper and slammed the door shut behind me.

I made good time and was in Khandala, at Serenity Villa, in two-and-a-half hours. The property where Urvashi was supposed to be holed up was apparently situated next to a popular Goan-style pub-cum-eatery, Khandala Heights. Hardly conducive to isolation, I thought.

But when I entered, I saw why the place had been chosen. The property was about half an acre, with one side ending in a cliff. On the other three sides it was bordered by a thick, tall hedge, effectively cutting off view from the outside. In the middle of this stood a pretty little villa, complete with a kidney-shaped swimming pool in the rear, abutting the cliff.

The cottage itself comprised a living room, a kitchen and two bedrooms. It was fully equipped with all modern amenities. Like the property on Hermit Hill, the kitchen was stacked with enough supplies to last a person a month. But other than a couple of glasses, no dishes had been used and no supplies consumed. The bedrooms, while evidently prepared for someone's arrival, didn't seem to have been used, considering the peculiar musty smell about them. All in all, the cottage showed no signs that anyone had lived there recently.

The living room had a door leading out to the rear and to the swimming pool. I wandered out and noted that the swimming pool, too, looked like it had recently been cleaned.

While photographing the property, I wondered what Urvashi had found so objectionable. Because, to me, it looked like everything I had imagined my retirement home to be. Of course, that picture also came with a hunky husband and two cats. But then I'm a commoner and Urvashi is ... was a star. Still, it was only a question of a few days. Why did she leave? Unless. Unless she had been forced to.

At that moment, I heard the low growl of an automobile engine. A door slammed. Who could it be? The owner? The police? Alarmed, I shoved the camera in my bag and looked around for a place to hide. There was nothing. No cover anywhere! Panicked, I dived into the hedge. As soon as I did, the stupidity of my actions occurred to me. I had done nothing wrong. Okay, maybe a little. But trespassing was hardly a crime to warrant such desperate hide-and-cover tactics. Moreover, my bike was parked out front. Whoever it was would know that someone was around.

On cue, a voice called out, 'Coomaar! Where are you?'

Shit! What was he doing here?

'Coomaar! I know you're here!'

Now even if I wanted to, I couldn't come out. It was just too embarrassing. Down on my haunches, I shifted my weight a little, grinding a couple of old cigarette stubs lying around deeper into the ground. An uncomfortable, prickling sensation started on my hands. And at the back of my neck. And on my face. Soon, my skin started to burn. Dear god! Poison ivy! The inside of the hedge was bichchoo booti! With an ear-splitting yell, I flung my bag away and jumped out of the hedge. Even as Deshpande stared in shock, I streaked to the pool and jumped in, clothes and all.

'Poison ivy,' I said, scratching wildly. God, my skin felt like it was on fire!

Deshpande stared uncomprehendingly. 'What were you doing there? Taking a short cut to the shack next door?'

'I . . . I . . .'

Deshpande bit back a smile. 'You weren't hiding from me, were you?'

'Of course not!' I answered crossly. 'I just thought I saw something there.'

'What?' Deshpande asked, walking up to the hedge. 'Oh, by the way, you do know that jumping into water makes it worse, don't you?'

'Omigod! Omigod! Omigod!' I yelled, scrambling out of the pool. 'What should I do?'

'What? I don't see anything,' Deshpande complained, poking the hedge with a stick.

'Would you stop that! God, I'm dying here.'

'Unless you meant this,' he said, reaching carefully into the hedge and retrieving a half-full quarter bottle of Smirnoff. He held the bottle by the neck, carefully uncapped it and sniffed experimentally. 'Shame on you, Coomaar. Early in the morning! And lying about it too.'

'Deshpande!'

He came towards me and dumped the contents of the bottle onto my hands.

'What are you doing?' I yelled.

'This will serve you better than ingesting it. Now, rub this on all the affected areas. The way to treat poison ivy is to first cleanse the affected area by rubbing alcohol and then take a shower.'

'Oh,' I said, chastened, and did as directed.

Deshpande packed the empty bottle away in a clear plastic bag. 'Now, let's go and get you some calamine lotion.'

'What about the shower?'

'I think you've had that already,' he said, guffawing.

I considered punching his face for a second. 'It's not funny!' I exclaimed instead.

'Depends on which side of the hedge you're standing.'

I really should've punched his face.

Deshpande turned and walked back inside. I retrieved my bag and followed, leaving a trail of water behind.

We emerged from the house out front and Deshpande promptly

got into his Jeep Cherokee. He chucked the plastic bag with the empty bottle into the glove compartment.

'What about me?'

'No way are you getting into my car like that. You know how bad wet upholstery smells?'

'So I just wait here. Is that the plan?'

Deshpande pretended to think for a while. 'Yeah.'

After Deshpande had left, it occurred to me that it was rather unwise of me to trust him. Considering our history, I'd be safer trusting a rabbit to deliver carrots. On the flip side, he had been a perfect gentleman and not mentioned last night's kiss.

I sat down on the porch and reached into my pocket for my cigarettes. My hands encountered a soggy mass. And something else. My emergency cellphone. Shit! The phone was probably history. Ah well, it was a useless piece of crap anyway. I removed the SIM from the waterlogged phone and placed it in my pocket.

While waiting for Deshpande to return, I went over the case. Well, there was no clue here. Maybe Hermit Hill would yield something. I didn't know what, but something was nagging away at my brain. Like there was something at Hermit Hill which had fleetingly registered in my brain as significant but then I had forgotten about it. The thought had been so transient that I couldn't even remember what it was.

I couldn't concentrate with my skin itching like that. The good news was that I didn't notice the discomfort from my wet clothes. Or the fact that I smelled like a brewery. Still, I wished he would hurry. My skin was starting to feel raw from the scratching.

To distract myself, I read the newspaper I'd brought along. According to the cover story, Sameer Khan had signed the long-in-abeyance Hollywood deal yesterday. *How can that be*, I thought. Sameer Khan was bonded to Blazar Films for their next two films. It had to be mere speculation. But a closer inspection of the article revealed that the Hollywood studio head, Adam Goldberg, had confirmed the news. Interesting. Had Khan finally managed to persuade Kaustav? More importantly, what had made Kaustav change his mind?

I was reading my horoscope when Deshpande arrived. He chucked the bottle of calamine at me. 'Here you go!'

I grabbed the bottle, unscrewed it, poured out a generous measure of the lotion and slathered it lavishly all over my hands, neck and face. The cooling lotion on my skin felt so good that I purred and gasped. 'Oh! Ahhh! That feels good. Oh, so good,' I moaned.

Deshpande looked around sheepishly. 'Must you make sounds like that?' he hissed. Then, added suspiciously, 'First you come to my house in the middle of the night, then you kiss me last night and now you make sounds like that . . . are you coming onto me?'

'Yes, that's exactly what I'm thinking of, when I'm in excruciating pain,' I said sarcastically and turned away with a flounce. And then I caught my reflection in the window pane. Yikes! I looked like a mime artiste.

After about ten minutes, the lotion was dry enough for me to be able to put my helmet on. We bade each other goodbye and headed to our respective vehicles. Now that my skin was starting to cool down, I felt up to taking a trip to Hermit Hill. True, I looked like a freak show, but I'd rather brave astonished stares than burning skin. Besides no one could see anything under the helmet and the Gucci shades.

This time around, I didn't bother to trek up Hermit Hill; instead, I drove right up to the cottage. As before I did a cursory examination of the place. I even valiantly made a trip to the basement, irrationally hoping that Urvashi's corpse wouldn't still be there to greet me. It wasn't, but evidence of police activity remained. The spot where the body had been found had been circled in chalk and the walls had been dusted for fingerprints.

I went up to the first floor. I walked into the bedroom and from there, into the bathroom. Both had been shorn of their belongings. Like the basement, the two rooms had been dusted for fingerprints. As I was backing out of the bedroom, I saw something black peeping out from under the bed. I reached for it and saw it was a black satin pillowcase. Thanking Chodu's team for their carelessness, I put it in my bag.

Before going to the village, Indapur, I carried out another examination of the grounds, just in case I had missed something earlier. This time around I found several beedi stubs, paan-stained bits of paper and candy wrappers, obviously left behind by curious visitors.

I stood on the east edge of the property for a moment, gazing at Indapur in the distance and wondering how I'd go about my task there. I mean, I could hardly go up and ask random strangers if they'd gone to Hermit Hill on the night of the 19th. And then I remembered my dear friend Honey Tuteja and decided to pay him a visit. Maybe he had heard something.

I started my bike and got a move on. As I descended the driveway and turned right at the gate, that certain elusive something that was niggling at me smacked me right in the face. There, at the bottom of the hill, right on the wide mud shoulder where I'd parked my bike the last time around, was a set of tyre tracks, skid marks to be exact. Shards of broken red and white plastic lay strewn about. Was it relevant or just a random collision? After all, it was a blind curve.

I looked up and saw a shiny SUV approach. Was it . . .? No way! How did Deshpande know where I was? How was he doing this?

I kicked the RE into life and beat a hasty exit.

I parked my bike outside Tuteja's office and walked in. Only then did I remove my helmet and sunglasses.

One look at me and Tuteja jumped out of his chair. 'Katieji! What happened?'

'I had a little accident with my face.'

'I noticed last time also. But, that white paint doesn't improve it,' he said seriously.

I gave him my flaming-eyeball Sauron look.

Tuteja gulped. 'We were talking about you,' he said hastily.

I looked at him keenly. 'Who's we?'

'You know, us villagers.'

'What about me?'

'Well, not exactly you. We were talking about . . .' he lowered his voice conspiratorially, '. . . Urvashi. Have they found the killer?'

'No, they're still investigating. Actually that's what I . . .'

'It was a terrorist attack, wasn't it?'

Who was he, George Bush?

'Why would terrorists want to kill her?' I asked.

And what was wrong with me? Why was I encouraging him?

'To make statement.'

'What kind of statement?'

Was I insane? Why couldn't I stop talking about terrorists?

He thought it over, finally offering helpfully, 'Or it could be the underworld.'

'Why?'

I was hopeless.

Tuteja continued, 'They keep giving extortion threats. They must have given to her also. Yas, it must be underworld,' he said nodding. 'Or it could . . .'

'Mr Tuteja,' I interjected hastily.

'O ji call me Hunnee.'

Right. 'You said the villagers were talking about Urvashi. Did anyone see anything . . . or anyone out of the ordinary on the night of September 19th?'

'How do you mean ji?'

'Well, for starters, did anyone happen to go there that night?'

He shook his head sorrowfully. 'O ji, that night was visarjan night.'

'No, it wasn't. Visarjan got over some twenty days ago.'

Hunnee nodded patiently. 'Yas, but in their village they keep Ganpati for twenty-eight days.'

'But for visarjan they would have gone to the lake, right? Maybe some people took a shortcut through Hermit Hill?'

He shook his head. 'You're not allowed to do visarjan in the lake. Some environmental reason. They had gone to the river in the neighbouring village. It is over ten kilometres away.'

Tuteja told me that the muhurat for the visarjan was at one in the morning. The ten-kilometre ride to the river, with accompanying fanfare, usually took about three hours. Accordingly, the villagers had departed at around ten.

Blast! 'Anything else?'

'Well,' he said, looking into the distance and scratching his chin thoughtfully, 'Yashwant Rane mentioned he had seen Abu Salem in the village earlier that night. And Nagesh Patil saw Dawood Ibrahim earlier that day. Young Raju says he saw a huge man, dressed in black, floating down the hill. But old woman Shantabai says they all don't know anything, that it was the katey-haathwala rakshas.'

Could it be young Raju's cache of toys at Hermit Hill? Was it possible that some boys from the village had thought that playing a game of cops and robbers was a better employment of their time than the visarjan?

'Young Raju was at Hermit Hill?' I said, excited.

He rubbed his chin thoughtfully. 'Hmm, what you are saying is kract. I must tell his parents he was playing hookey.'

'Is it,' I began, trying to control my impatience, 'possible to talk to the villagers?'

'Sure ji, why not?' Tuteja said, getting up.

'Er, you don't have to come along,' I said, alarmed. 'If you can just tell me who to talk to . . .'

'It is batter if I come along.'

Better for whom? I could already hear my RE groaning.

I walked over to my RE and started it. While Tuteja locked his office, my mind worked feverishly to figure out a way to dissuade Tuteja from coming along.

Tuteja turned around, primped his hair and skipped over to the RE. 'Lat us go.'

'Umm . . . Mr . . . Honey,' I began, grimacing, 'it may be better if you took along your scooty 'cos I'm not sure that I'll be coming back this way.'

'Oh daunt worry ji. I will take lifat on way back.'

'Okay . . . but who's that calling out your name?'

As Tuteja turned to look, I kicked my bike into gear and took off.

'Wait!' he yelled.

'Oops! Sorry my brakes don't work. Follow me on your scooty!' I threw over my shoulder guiltily. I didn't know why I was feeling guilty, though. After all, I was only looking out for him. It was true, about my brakes. My mechanic had told me just last week that my brakes needed replacing. The good news was, he said, since he couldn't repair my brakes, he'd made my horn louder as a stopgap measure.

I jogged along the bumpy track, admiring the countryside. There were farms on either side of the track sporting bountiful, healthy-looking crops. I was thinking that some farmers were going to be very rich men when, out of nowhere, a herd of cows came sauntering out onto the track.

I stopped and waited for them to pass but the cows decided they liked it there and made no move to get off the track. In response to my impatient honking, the cows looked up in mild surprise and went back to ruminating.

I had to figure out a way to break up the bovine party, so I parked my bike and approached the cows. When I figured I was well within safe distance (of the bike, not cows) I clapped my hands and shouted shoo! The cows apparently thought it was my way of making conversation and responded with polite moos. And stayed stubbornly put.

The next thing to try would've been to pat them on their rumps but I dared not go any closer. I know that's silly because cows are supposed to be harmless, but I didn't want to risk my safety on hearsay. Besides, there were a couple of bulls with mean looking horns.

And then I had an idea. I hopped over to my bike and took out the box of pencil bombs I'd received in lieu of change the day before yesterday. I lit one fuse and threw the whole box in their midst. With a loud *phat*! one exploded, then another and another. The cows behaved as expected—they panicked and ran helter-skelter into the farm, trampling the very crop I had just been admiring. Oh, well, farming doesn't pay all that much anyway.

Suddenly I heard a startled shout. As I looked, a young farmer wearing a blood-red shirt came running out of a hut. He was waving his arms furiously, trying to contain the herd. Seriously. A red shirt? In front of raging cows?

He saw me. Even from the distance I could see his face turn purple. I got on my bike and fled.

Indapur was a village, but even so, it was difficult finding the sarpanch. Or more accurately, it was difficult finding someone who could tell me where I could find him. The moment they saw me, they stared, and then melted away nervously. I'd forgotten all about the lotion!

Finally, a bunch of snotty kids led by a scrawny boy obliged me.

By sending me off in the wrong direction. Apparently they thought a woman on a motorbike was a hoot—and that they were being rather selfish in enjoying the spectacle by themselves. The rest of their village needed to watch as well. So they sent me through the village fair, through a rough, bumpy kuchcha road teeming with livestock and just as many people. The kids followed on foot, with the scrawny boy screaming and shouting and generally calling everyone's attention, pointing to me and then gesturing breasts with his hands, proudly claiming credit for the astonishing discovery.

Several young men even threw themselves in my way, just to rattle me, I suppose. That was a little foolhardy of them considering the state of my brakes. And hey, even at fifteen kilometres per hour being run over by a bike is no party.

After a while, the youths got bored but the kids continued to give chase. And then, behind me, I heard someone shout out the name Raju. I spun the bike around, slammed on the brakes, and waited for the children to catch up.

Chapter Seventeen

A s soon as I removed my helmet, the kids came to an abrupt halt several feet from me. Their earlier noisy chatter gave way to deathly silence and they eyed me in a mixture of wonder and fear.

Finally curiosity won and a round-eyed girl asked, 'Are you the white-faced witch? Is it true that you eat small children?'

'What? Of course not! Where did you get that idea?'

'Aghori Baba said so last year. He said that a white-faced witch would come to the village and that if we didn't behave, she would cut us up into small pieces and eat us.'

'It's not true.' After a tiny pause I asked her, 'Do you know who Raju is?'

Her eyes got rounder. 'Why? Do you want to eat him?'

'No, I just want to ask him if he went to Hermit Hill on visarjan night.'

The scrawny boy's neck whipped up and he hastily looked around. A fat boy of about nine said to him fearfully, 'See, I told you. The witch exists! She knows about Hermit Hill.'

'Shut up! Shut up! She doesn't know anything!' shouted the scrawny one. Again that fearful look over his shoulders.

I bet he was the local bully. He looked like a bully.

'Are you Raju?' I asked him. He glared at me, not giving me an answer. I turned to the fat one. 'Did you boys light a fire on Hermit Hill?'

Finally the fat one broke. 'He's Raju! He's the one you want.'

'Shut up!' the thin one shouted. But I was gratified to note that his voice held a tiny quiver.

'Hey Raju, tell me the truth. You didn't see anyone floating down the hill, did you?'

Again the fat one moaned, 'She's a witch. She knows!'

'You know what? Your Aghori Baba was right. I do eat small children. But, if you tell me, I might spare you.'

No answer.

'Boy, am I hungry!' I looked around and said to the fat boy, 'You. Come here. You look juicy. I think I'll start with you.'

The fat one yelled, 'We were just playing. We didn't see anyone floating down the hill.'

He haltingly told me the entire story about how he and Raju didn't want to go for the visarjan because it was boring, so they'd snuck away. Since the elders were all away, they decided to go to Hermit Hill and play cops and robbers. While there, they were alerted by a screech of brakes and saw a big black car round the bend and ram into another car, a white car, parked below Hermit Hill. Through the light filtering in from Pavana Dam, they saw the driver of the black car get out and inspect the damage. The light was too dim to make out if it was a man or a woman, but the driver then went back to his car. After a minute or so, he again came back to the white car, although why, they couldn't see. Then he drove away in the black car. Almost immediately they were alerted by another sound, this time to their left, and saw a shadowy figure run down the hill. The person arrived at the white car, looked around for the culprit, paced up and down a bit, and finally drove away.

So my theory about the SUV tyre imprints at Hermit Hill being significant was wrong. Unless it was the same person at a different time and in a different car. But, on the flipside, the skid marks and the shards of broken plastic below Hermit Hill were indeed significant.

'What else?' I asked.

Raju spoke for the first time. 'The white car was a Honda Accord.'

'And how would you know what an Accord looks like?'

'Why not? Because we are poor villagers? My father owns one in black.'

'All right, Richie Rich. What about the black car?'

'I haven't seen one like it before. I think it was foreign.'

'Anything else?' I prompted him.

He shook his head. I had a feeling he was telling the truth, but I eyeballed him anyway. He met my look squarely.

And then I happened to glance around and saw someone familiar in the shadows behind one of the nearby huts. It couldn't be! I peered harder. Yup! It was Deshpande all right! Our eyes met. What was that? Was he laughing?

Absolutely livid, I snarled at the two boys, 'You're both lying! You saw more.'

'No!' the fat one squealed.

I thrust my head forward, schooled my features into my best grimace, snapped my teeth shut and growled menacingly. My shenanigans had the desired effect and the children ran away howling. They hid behind a hut and peeped out cautiously. I waited for about thirty seconds for Deshpande to come out. He didn't.

'Oh, for god's sake!' I bawled. 'Will you come out already?'

Still doubled over with laughter, Deshpande appeared. He straightened, threw up his hands and mimicked the frightened fat boy. 'Please, please, white-faced witch, don't eat me.'

'Very funny.'

'Babe!' he said, wiping away tears. 'How do you do these things?'

I had an urge to turn those tears of merriment into ones of misery. 'With great ease, apparently,' I groused.

'Apparently. You may be many things but one thing you can't be accused of is being a bore.'

'I try real hard to keep things entertaining. How did you find me anyway?' I asked suspiciously.

'It wasn't difficult. I just followed the trail of destruction.'

Very droll. 'Why are you following me?'

'I'm not. We just happen to go to the same places at the same time.'

'Uh-huh.'

'How about telling me what the boys told you?'

'Why would I do that?'

'In the spirit of cooperation,' he pointed out. 'I got you the all-access pass into Blazar, didn't I?'

'Okay, but they were just talking some nonsense about seeing a rakshas,' I lied.

'Try again,' he encouraged me.

'Fine,' I said and shared my recently acquired knowledge, taking care to fudge a few details. Like the make of the white car.

'A white Honda Civic, eh?' he said thoughtfully.

He then requested a ride to his car which was parked a short distance away. Once perched in his majestic chariot, Deshpande drove on ahead, leaving me trailing and eating dust in his wake. Cute.

On the way back, I decided to make a quick stopover at the forensic lab in Kalina. Vinay Pandit, the assistant director, biology/serology division, was universally hailed as a genius. It was rumoured that he was so good, DNA sequences practically cracked open as soon as he laid eyes on a sample.

Pandit was about my age but looked younger. But that was more to do with the perpetually bewildered expression on his face rather than the quality of his skin, although his skin wasn't bad either— nice and smooth.

'Katie, it's good to see you,' he said, enveloping me in a bear hug.

'It's good to see you too,' I said and meant it.

'What happened to your face?'

'It's a long story,' I said, waving my hand dismissively.

'Ooo-kay. Heard the news?'

'News?'

'Guess who's getting divorced?' he asked.

I felt a thrill of wholly unholy pleasure then. There was only one person he could be talking about, the only man we had in common. Jai Saxena. The guy I'd been madly in love with for two years. The guy who within a week post our break-up had been spotted happily gallivanting around town sporting a brand new girlfriend. A girlfriend who was taller, slimmer and prettier than me. He was a good-looking dude and amazingly sexy, and there were always girls panting after him, so finding one to oblige him, even the model-like Vandita, hadn't been a problem. It was bad enough that he hadn't even waited the customary month decency demands post break-up to pick up another girlfriend, but he'd gone one step further and married her. And now it was over?

'No!' I exclaimed, my eyes shining. 'What happened? Come on, tell me all. Every tiny, dirty detail.'

'Now Katie . . .' he began cautiously.

'Did he beat her up? Did Vands cite domestic violence?'

Pandit looked affronted. 'Of course not! Jai is not physically violent.'

No, I agreed, he didn't resort to that kind of violence. He just punished by holding himself back.

'He's a choot!' I said. 'He's a fucking, childish prick . . .'

'Katie!' Pandit exclaimed in panic.

'. . . who thinks he's god's fucking gift to women . . .'

He darted forward, clamped a hand on my mouth and hissed, 'People are looking!'

I took in a few gulps of air to calm down.

'Okay now?' Pandit asked.

I nodded. He removed his hand from my mouth.

'I'm sorry,' I muttered, contrite. 'It's just that he gets my goat.'

Before I got worked up again, Pandit swiftly cut me off. 'So what brings you here?'

I fished out the pillowcase I had picked up from the cottage at Hermit Hill and handed it to him. Beyond an appreciative, 'Black satin,' he didn't react at all. But then I routinely deposited items of lingerie and linen for analysis. After all, the presence of alien DNA is admissible in courts as evidence of adultery.

I asked him to get whatever he could from the pillowcase.

'Whose is it?'

Knowing his penchant for quick-fire get-rich schemes (his genius is matched equally by his avarice), I hesitated. 'Urvashi.'

A cunning look appeared on his face. He promised to have the job done soon. I wondered what he meant by that. The tests, or the sale of Urvashi's effluents on eBay.

Back home, I showered and changed. Only then did I notice angry red welts all over my skin. Like someone else I had seen recently. Feeling sorry for myself, I slathered some more calamine generously all over my body.

And then the coin dropped. That entire story about prawns was pure fabrication! Chandan Baweja had been touched by poison ivy. And not accidentally either. For one, the toxic plant grew on the inside of the hedge. Then there was the vodka. And now that I thought about it, the cigarette butts I'd ground underfoot had been brown. It looked like he'd been crouched behind the hedges, and for some time. Whom had he been hiding from? And why? If I looked at it logically, it had to be when Urvashi was in there already—after he'd dropped her off. And if that were the case, Neena was lying about them both being at Firangi Paani that night.

I was jolted out of my thoughts by a loud rap on the door.

'Who is it?'

'Aniruddh. Open up!' he said urgently.

Was he mad? I rushed to the door and flung it open. Ani stood at the doorstep, looking worried. He wasn't alone. There was a shady looking guy with him. He was short and fat, with small beady eyes and stubby legs. He was perspiring profusely and no wonder. In the September heat, he was wearing a faux leather jacket that barely contained his paunch.

'Shut the door,' Ani said, stepping in with his companion.

'Ani . . .'

He stared at me. 'Oh my god! What happened to you?'

'Poison ivy,' I said shortly. 'Ani, what are you doing here? I thought we agreed . . .'

'We're in a bit of a jam,' Ani said worriedly.

'So you brought along a friend to share in it?'

'He's not a friend. He's a fucking PI,' he bit out.

'Hey, wait a goddamn . . .' I started to object to his derisive tone when the short, fat man thrust out a meaty hand. 'Pankaj Chawla.'

I looked at his pudgy hand and pointedly transferred my gaze to his face. He shrugged, withdrew his hand and mopped his forehead with a soggy hanky. I cut my eyes to Ani.

'You want the good news or the bad news first?' he asked.

'Neither. I would like to know what's going on. Who's he? What's he doing here?'

He drew me aside and whispered, 'The post-mortem report on Sweety came back. It was as Chodankar suspected. Sweety was poisoned.'

'Poisoned! But how?'

'I don't know. I'm just telling you what the DCP told me. Accused me of, actually. He told me that the death occurred at around three in the afternoon. Strychnine poisoning, he said.'

'Are you sure she was *poisoned* poisoned? I mean, it could have been food poisoning, right? Or an accident. She could have taken it herself by mistake. Some photographers die by accidental cyanide poisoning,' I blabbed, clutching at straws. Then I sighed. 'So how was she poisoned?'

'The DCP also said her stomach contained remnants of rajma, rice and Coke. The poison could have been in anything.' His eyes held an unspoken suspicion in them.

'Surely you don't think that I . . .?'

'You were there at the beauty parlour,' he said aggressively.

'I'd just walked in!'

'That's what you say. Besides, who else would want to kill her?'

'How do I know? You had a pretty good motive yourself,' I said with equal astringency.

'Why would I kill her?'

'Well, I didn't have any reason to kill her either. I've moved on, you see.'

'You've what?'

'You heard me.'

'With who?'

'Whom. And it's none of your business.'

'Ahem!' Chawla cleared his throat. 'Could you stick to the point? I'm in a bit of a hurry.'

It was only then that we realised that as our aggravation had risen, so had our voices.

'In a minute!' Ani and I bawled at him.

'Fine,' I said, lowering my voice once again. 'Think. Who would have wanted to kill her?'

Ani shook his head glumly. 'The police are talking to the people present at the time at the beauty parlour, but it's quite clear I'm their main suspect. I'm in deep shit.' He said it in a vaguely accusatory tone. Like it was my fault he was the husband and therefore the natural suspect.

'*We* are in deep shit,' I reminded him.

'You've covered your ass pretty well,' he said bitterly.

'I like that! In case you've forgotten, by exchanging numbers with Beena Malhar, I've saved your ass as well.'

'Fine! *We're* in deep shit,' he said and conceded grudgingly, 'the good news is that Chodankar hasn't cottoned on yet.'

I sensed the 'but' coming. My heart sinking, I asked, 'But?'

'It doesn't matter because Pankaj Chawla here knows about us and is blackmailing us. He thinks we did it!'

'He? But how does he know?' Involuntarily my eyes flew to the Danny de Vito-esque Chawla who was busy playing with his mobile phone and I studied him more carefully. I have to admit, he didn't exactly look like a blackmailer. He looked kinda harmless. Then again, so did an electrical socket.

'Now, and behold the ironies of life, Chawla here was the dick Sweety had hired to tail me.'

So he was the one who took those pictures! The rat!

'But how does he know about Sweety's murder? And how did he connect the two?'

'Apparently he was at the police station when crime reporters were being briefed. He recognised Sweety's picture and deduced that we had to have done it. And now he wants half a million.'

'*Five lakhs!*'

'Why do you think I said we're in a bit of a jam?'

That was a euphemism. It was a downright pickle. Drawing a deep breath I asked, 'Okay tell me everything. Where did Sweety go, when did she come back, where and with whom did she have lunch? Everything.'

'She'd been at her parents' country house near Mumbai. She came back yesterday morning just as I was about to leave for office. She told me that she was upset after talking to you, but then she changed her mind about leaving me, and was willing to work at our marriage. She said she knew that she was also to blame for our marriage being on the rocks. And I kept thinking, why is she being so nice? I found out soon enough. You see, she had banged up my Beemer pretty bad.

'As soon as she told me I rushed outside. And I couldn't believe it. Banged up, my ass. She had fucking wrecked it. The front of the car had almost caved in. I wanted to throttle her. She said it wasn't her fault. She wanted to explain. But I was so mad I could've killed her . . .

'Ah!' Chawla said triumphantly.

Ani ignored him and whispered, 'Anyway, I calmed down and told her we'd talk in the evening and I went to work. During my lunch break I took the car to the workshop. They said it would cost two lakhs. Can you believe it? Anyway, that's when you called. That's all I know.'

'Hah!' Chawla sniggered.

'Look, if you have something to say, say it already,' Ani snarled.

'Yeah, I want five lakhs.'

'You and half of Mumbai. You're not getting it,' Ani said.

'This is non-negotiable.'

'Who's negotiating?'

He blinked, 'Oh? I thought you were trying to negotiate. You know, I say five lakhs, you say zero, and we arrive at the final figure.'

'Yeah, well, I'm not,' Ani said.

'Ani,' I quickly interjected, 'let's not be rash.'

'That's exactly what we'll be doing if we give in to his demands. It'll never stop.'

'But . . .'

'Er . . . I thought she was a PI?' Chawla said to Ani.

Ani rolled his eyes. I gritted my teeth. Really, did they have to stick so closely to stereotype and bond over a dig about women?

'I am!' I tried to snap, but it came out all defensive. 'You know what, go to the police. Tell them your story. We have nothing to hide. We didn't do anything. They'll believe us.'

'You sure about that?' He turned to Ani. 'How will you explain that call you made to me, asking me to keep your house under surveillance? And report to you the moment Sweety returned?'

'What call?' Ani said, startled.

'Ani!' I exclaimed, aghast.

'Don't act so innocent. As if you didn't know,' Chawla said reproachfully to me. He reached into his pocket and took out a single sheet of paper and a mini tape. 'Playing innocent is not going to get you two anywhere. I have all the records here. I always record all conversations. First call, 20th September, around six a.m., five fifty-one to be precise. You called me, refused to tell me your name . . .'

'That's a lie!' Ani said. He looked at me beseechingly. 'Kay, you have to believe me.'

'Ani, just let him finish first,' I said.

Chawla continued, 'You called me and gave me your address. You asked me to keep your house under surveillance. You were especially interested in the movements of a woman called Sweety. You were willing to pay well. As per your promise I got the advance money by seven a.m. So I went down to your apartment and made some enquiries. I was told that it looked like your wife was out of town. Your second call came at ten a.m., 20th September. You called and asked for a progress report. I gave it you. You then told me to continue the surveillance.

'Fortunately for me and unfortunately for you, I turned out to be the guy your wife had hired to keep tabs on you. I must admit I was curious. First the wife and then the husband. I knew there was some hanky-panky going on. I started suspecting you, but you were clever. Yes, you played it smart all right, setting it up so that when you finally did her in, it would seem like someone else, like some third person had been following her. You even distorted your voice on the phone and made it all high and thin. But it won't work. When I tell the police about you two, I'm sure they will have no difficulty in putting two and two together. And then you'll wish you'd paid me double the amount.'

My head was reeling. Some of my anxiety must have reflected on my face because in a trice Ani was beside me, begging me not to believe the lying bastard.

'But deep down you know it's true,' Chawla suggested sneakily. 'It makes sense.'

Ani looked at him in exasperation and led me inside into the bedroom. 'Kay,' he said, 'you have to believe me. I didn't do any of that stuff. I have no idea what he is talking about.'

'I know,' I said slowly.

'You do?' He looked as though he couldn't quite believe it.

I nodded. 'I just remembered. At ten a.m. on 20th September, you were with me.'

Chapter Eighteen

❧❧

Relief washed over Ani's face.

Suddenly we heard the bolts on the front door turning.

I looked at Ani in alarm. 'He's leaving! Stop him!'

We both rushed out and caught Chawla just as he was opening the front door. Ani threw his weight against Chawla who went crashing into the door. I admit that wasn't the way I wanted the door shut but it would do. Chawla put his hands out, palms flat on the door, and propelled himself back. The force of it sent Ani sprawling. Since Ani had his arms around him, Chawla also staggered. In a flash he recovered and had the door open again.

I looked around for a weapon. My frantic eyes skittered this way and that and finally rested on the lamp that Ani had given me, the one that emitted the ghoulish green light. In one fluid movement, I grabbed the lamp, rushed towards Chawla and thwacked him on the head.

His head jerked back, his eyes rolled and his knees buckled. He sank to the ground, out cold. Ani, still on the floor, watched, speechless and open mouthed. 'Oh my god, you've killed him.'

'Of course not. He's just unconscious.' Nevertheless, I felt his pulse. It throbbed healthily. 'Quick! Get me something to tie him with!'

Ani unfroze and rushed into the bedroom. Within moments he was back, carrying a silk scarf.

'What, you don't want to hurt his wrists?' I said nastily.

'I couldn't find anything else,' he said sheepishly.

I snatched it from him and tied Chawla's wrists behind his back. I used a fisherman's knot, hoping claims about its infallibility were true. After I had secured his wrists, I thrust a balled-up napkin into his mouth, just to be safe. Then we sat back and surveyed the scene in silence.

'Okay, now what?' Ani asked after a while.

'Now we figure out some stuff.'

'Actually, I meant him. What are we going to do about him?' he said, gesturing towards Chawla who was already moaning and showing signs of revival.

'We can't risk him going to the police. We'll have to keep him somewhere secure. Just for a little while. Till we find out some things.'

'It has to be here then.'

'No, it bloody well does not! Why can't we keep him at your place?'

'In case you hadn't got it the first time around, the police has a free run of my place.'

'Yes, well, I'm being threatened with eviction.'

'Fine,' Ani said reluctantly. 'I'll try to figure out something at our hardware supplier's warehouse. But we can't keep him indefinitely.'

'No,' I agreed. 'Let's hope they find out who killed Sweety by then.'

'What if they don't?'

'They just have to. And if they don't, we'll have to do it ourselves.'

'How?'

'Well, we find out who would want to kill her and then figure out if they had opportunity.' I looked around for my phone, only to remember that it was ruined. I rummaged through the pockets of the jeans I'd discarded earlier. The SIM card wasn't there. Crap! It must have fallen out in Indapur. I came back, grabbed Ani's phone and dialled directory services. I got Rosie's number from them and called her. As soon as she answered I said, 'Rosie, did Sweety eat or drink anything at the parlour?'

'What do you think Rosie's is? A barber shop?' She gasped. 'I didn't say dat. I meant hairdresser.'

'Did she or didn't she eat anything?'

'Of course she did. We served her Coke, like we do to all our clients. De police already took the bottle and her glass for testing.'

'Another thing. Was there anyone else in the room besides Sweety and you and your trainees? Maybe another facial in progress?'

'Again, what do you think Rosie's—?' she began indignantly.

'—Yeah, yeah, yeah, exclusive rooms for clients, I know. Was there?'

'No,' she said huffily.

'What is she saying?' Ani hissed.

I held up a restraining hand. 'But someone could have sneaked in?'

'I suppose.' She lowered her voice and said excitedly, all vexation gone for the moment, 'Dere's a regular client, Ghazal, who lives down at JVPD. Dina thinks she did it.'

'How does Dina know? Wasn't she with you?'

'What did she see?' Ani whispered again.

Exasperated, I put the phone on speaker.

'Yes, yes, dhikra. Dis was just before Sweety Nair came in. Dina said she was talking wid Ghazal at de reception while Ghazal was waiting for her turn. Den Ghazal said she wanted to go to de toilet and Dina said she would come too. But when dey were going to the toilet, Ghazal suddenly said to Dina, "You go on. I'll join you. I just want to speak to Maheen." Later, Dina met Maheen and asked her what Ghazal wanted to say to her that was so important, and Maheen looked surprised and said, "But she never spoke to me!"'

'Aha,' I said. 'And did anyone see Ghazal going into Sweety's room?'

'After we'd finished Sweety Nair's facial, Nancy was at de reception. Dat's when she saw her. She saw someone coming out of Sweety's room and walking away quickly. She only saw her back but she thinks it looked like Ghazal.'

'Then that must be it! That woman, Ghazal, must've killed her,' Ani said eagerly, once I'd hung up.

'Sorry to be a killjoy, but not necessarily,' I said. 'Those women would've convinced themselves they'd seen Yeti if he were a suspect. And anyway, why would Ghazal want to kill Sweety?'

Ani shrugged helplessly. 'I can't think of *anyone* who would want to kill her. She was on good terms with everybody.'

'Oh, come on. No one is such a paragon. What about family? Maybe her siblings killed her for money.'

'Nun-uh. She's an only child.'

'How about the other woman you were dicking around with?'

'Nun-uh. She's in America.'

'And you know this because?' I asked bitingly.

He didn't respond. He didn't have to. His averted eyes were answer enough. The fact that he was still in touch with her didn't surprise me. What amazed me, however, was the calm with which I digested the fact. Maybe I was getting over him.

Chawla regained consciousness and, after a dazed look around, made his displeasure known by energetic wriggling and desperate gurgling sounds.

'Okay,' I said slowly, 'it could have been an accident. A mistake. Maybe the killer wanted to kill you and got her by mistake.'

'Me?' he yelped. 'In a beauty parlour?'

'Maybe the poison was in the food at home.' He turned a shade of green. 'Oh, relax. If you're not dead already, you're not gonna die now.'

'But who'd want to kill me?'

'Could it be your partner?'

'David? Why? It's not as though he gains anything by my death.'

'In my opinion, half the company is worth killing for.'

'But my shares go to Sweety. And after her, to my sister. And to her children after that.'

I tried to picture the amiable David as a lean, mean killing machine, and failed.

'What about your sister? Could she have . . .?' He looked at me as though I'd gone mad. 'The tape!' I exclaimed hastily.

Ani frowned. 'What tape?'

'The one he was threatening us with. Look in his trouser pockets,' I commanded Ani.

Chawla was surprisingly docile as his pockets were searched. And in the next few moments we knew why. When we played the tape, there was nothing on it! We both glanced at Chawla and exchanged looks, the same thought running through our minds. The tape had been a bluff, but maybe he could tell us more. The question was, could we risk it?

I approached him. 'Okay, I'm going to remove the gag.'

Furious nod.

'But you've got to promise not to scream.'

Another furious nod.

I reached for the gag and removed it slowly.

'You took your bloody time doing that,' he said angrily.

I moved to stuff his face again.

'Okay, okay, fine,' he said grouchily. 'I won't say anything.'

'That's better,' I said.

'What are you going to do with me?' he asked, suddenly frightened. 'You're ... you're not going to kill me, are you?'

I shrugged. 'A fat, lying, blackmailing vulture like you?'

He licked his lips. 'What if I could help?'

Ani and I looked at him impassively. It was his idea to help. I thought it only fair to let him take the initiative. He did. By holding up his bound wrists and looking at us hopefully.

'You've got to be kidding,' I said.

'Okay, but if I tell you what I know will you let me go?' he asked.

'We'll think about it,' I said.

He told us everything he knew. Which was pretty much what he'd told us already with a few more details thrown in.

'It was at five fifty-one a.m. on 20th morning when I received your—'

'It wasn't me!' Ani bawled.

'—this call. You ... dammit, this guy called me from ...' he reached awkwardly into his pocket with his bound hands and took out a sheet of paper, '... from er ... a local number, which is a PCO in Juhu by the way, and gave me an address ...'

Ani gasped suddenly.

'Now what did I say?' Chawla complained.

'The person who called asking for Sweety! Remember, when I came over on the 20th, I asked you if you had called earlier, asking for Sweety?' Ani said.

'I didn't, okay?' I shouted. 'And you said it wasn't my voice anyway.'

'But it was a woman. And when I asked her who was calling, she hung up. Why would a strange woman call on the landline at five in the morning?'

'So what are you saying? This woman and Chawla's guy are connected?'

'Or the same person. What if it isn't a man at all trying to distort his voice by making it high and thin?'

'Or a man distorting his voice on both occasions,' I argued. 'There's only one way to know if they're connected. By tallying the phone numbers from which you both received those calls.' I turned to Chawla. 'Go on.'

'This guy, or girl, asked me to watch the place. He was especially interested in Sweety Nair. I said, "All that is fine but I need to know who I'm talking to." So this guy says, "Twenty grand." I said, "That's fine with me, twenty grand. When do I see you?" So this guys says, "What time do you reach your office?" And I said, "Normally I go at ten but for twenty grand I can be there in half an hour." And this guy says, "Fine, give me the address and I'll be there." By the time I reached my office, the money was already there, shoved under the door. So I went to your building; I asked around and was told that it appeared Sweety was out of town. Then I caught your bai as she was coming out of your neighbour's house. And she also said she hadn't seen Sweety since yesterday. I told all this to the guy when he called next at ten.'

'And this call came from a PCO too?' I asked.

'Yeah. When I gave him the info, he said, "Good work. Now I want you to keep a watch on the house and report to me immediately when the woman comes back." During the day I kept watch on your house and he kept calling at regular intervals. Finally your wife came back yesterday and I was able to tell him,' he finished and again held up his hands.

'Then what happened?' I asked Chawla.

'Nothing. He told me that the job was over.'

'What did you do next?'

'What was I going to do? My fee had been paid in full, so I packed up and went home,' he said without hesitation.

I found that hard to believe. '*Really?*'

'Why do you think he's lying?' Ani asked.

'If I had received such an unusual assignment, I wouldn't tamely pack up and go home. I would stick around to see what happened next, if only to satisfy my curiosity. It's a PI thing.'

'No, it's a woman thing,' Chawla assured me. 'Me, I don't get paid to satisfy my curiosity. I'm a busy man you know.'

'I'm sure.'

'Hey, you don't have to be so mean.'

'Just put it down to the woman thing,' I said. 'One more thing. Did all the calls come from PCOs?'

He looked shifty. 'Yes.'

Without a word I snatched the paper in his hands and scanned through it. The lying bastard! There were a total of sixteen numbers listed on the page. While most calls were from different local numbers, one number, with an Australian code, cropped up seven times. A couple of the calls were made during the day but five were made at various times during the night of the 20th.

'What, now that it appears we are clean you thought you'll blackmail this person next?' I said.

'Oh well,' he said resignedly. 'I tried.'

'Did you at least call the number?' I asked him.

'Do I look like I'm rolling in money? That's an Australian number.' He turned to Ani and said, 'Didn't you go to Australia sometime ago?'

'So you assumed it belonged to me?' Ani said, simultaneously dialling the number. 'It's switched off.'

Next, Ani and I had a hushed conference where we decided that it was sufficiently late in the night, and therefore safe, to move Chawla to the warehouse.

'You have no intention of letting me go, do you?' Chawla accused as we tried to hustle him out of the apartment.

'Just how stupid do we look?' I asked and gagged him again.

I opened the door and peered out. There was nobody on the landing, but the elevator sported an 'out of order' signboard. I opened the door wider and stepped out, gesturing for Ani to follow me. We started down the stairs with both of us holding Chawla by an arm each.

We reached the second floor without incident, but just as we were about to descend to the first floor, I heard a sound. A scraping of feet. I looked at Ani for confirmation. It couldn't be someone on the . . .? A solid footstep next. Yep, it was someone on the stairs. We rushed back up.

We had barely made it into my apartment when the doorbell rang. Ani and I looked at each other in panic. Had we been seen?

'Who . . . who is it?' I asked querulously.

'Deshpande.'

'Take him into the bedroom,' I hissed at Ani. I stole a quick glance in the mirror and ran my hand through my hair. The bell rang again. 'Just a minute,' I yelled, applying some lip gloss. Ani's eyes met mine in the mirror. His expression was sardonic.

I opened the door a crack. 'Don't you believe in calling before coming?'

'Unlike you, I do believe in those niceties. And I did call. But I can't seem to get through. Unavailable.'

'Uh . . . well, I lost my phone,' I invented. 'What is it?'

'It's not so bad anymore,' he said, gesturing towards my face.

'Yes, well,' I said and didn't move.

Bang. Something crashed to the floor. Deshpande looked at me enquiringly. I looked back.

He held out a brown paper packet. 'Apply this and it will all be gone by morning.'

'Thanks,' I said, grabbing the packet.

He looked at me oddly. 'Can I come in? I have some information.'

'Um . . . Now's not a good time.'

Thud. Thud. Thud.

'You got somebody here?' he said craning his neck to look in.

'Somebody? No, no, no. It's the cat,' I said.

'Cat? '

'Yeah. I'm cat-sitting for my neighbour, Miss Poonawala,' I said brightly.

'Then why can't I come in?'

There was a sharp rap on the bedroom wall from the other side and Miss Poonawala called out, 'Kasthuri! What's all that banging?'

'It's nothing Miss P. It's just the cat,' I shrilled, stepping outside and shutting the door behind me.

And before Deshpande could ask why I was cat-sitting for Miss Poonawala when she was at home, I said, 'Listen, the problem is that the society doesn't like guys visiting my apartment, especially so late at night. They've already put in a motion to evict me. The voting's on Sunday and there's a chance, a tiny one, that I may be allowed to stay. I don't want to jeopardise that.'

I could see that he wasn't buying it. But it was damn decent of him not to argue the point. After he left, I stepped back in and hurried into my bedroom where Ani was trying to restrain Chawla. Chawla's hands might have been tied, but he was putting the rest of his body to good use, slamming against the wall and crashing into things and generally creating a ruckus.

'Help me!' Ani said desperately as soon as he saw me.

I helped Ani restrain our boisterous prisoner. Then I strolled downstairs to check if the coast was clear. As usual, Shyam was missing from his post. But, unfortunately, that night of all nights, he had decided to be conscientious and had locked the gates.

I hung around in the hope that he had gone for a quickie and would be back soon. When, after fifteen minutes, he still hadn't arrived, I went out back to his little hovel. He wasn't there either. I decided to make another inspection after an hour.

Back in my apartment, the events of the day caught up with me and I felt my eyes drooping. Ani and Chawla were already spread out in the living room, asleep. To keep myself busy I applied the ointment Deshpande had given me. I was done in ten minutes though, and it seemed too much of an effort to try and stay awake.

I went into my bedroom, lay down on my bed and shut my eyes. Just for a little while, I told myself. I was just nodding off when I felt lips pressed against mine. A tongue darted out and flicked across my lips. My eyes flew open in surprise and I saw Ani's face, looming over mine. Before I could react, his tongue forced my mouth open and probed wetly inside, a manoeuvre guaranteed to get me going. But tonight his mouth felt fleshy and disgusting.

I mumbled something in protest and turned over to my side. Ani sidled in beside me and pushed his body against mine. His aroused body. Oh god, no, not now, I prayed. I shut my eyes tight hoping he'd lay off. He didn't. His arm stole around me and he nipped at my ear lobe. I shivered and felt goose bumps sprout all over my body. Ani took this to be a positive sign and started massaging my breast. He turned me over, flat on my back once again. He brushed aside my mumbled protest and climbed over me.

Finally, I couldn't bear it anymore. I put my hands squarely on his chest. 'Ani, I'm tired,' I said firmly. He stopped as if shot and I felt a wave of remorse. Without another word he rolled off, turned on his side and went to sleep. I felt horribly guilty. What was wrong with me? Since when had Ani's touch become repulsive? *Since you met Kaustav*, a little voice in my head whispered. Disconcertingly, the face that popped up along with the voice was Deshpande's. I determinedly pushed the image out of my head.

Sometime during the night I must've fallen asleep. Next thing I knew, sunlight was streaming in through the windows. I woke up with a start and looked around groggily. Next to me, Ani was still fast asleep, his mouth open and a spot of dried drool caked at the corner of his lips. I lumbered off sleepily towards the loo. A little

252 / Smita Jain

distance away, in the living room, Chawla was also stretched out, dead to the world. For a moment I couldn't quite recollect who he was and what he was doing in my apartment.

'Crap! Crap! Crap!' I yelled, as it all came back to me.

Ani's eyes flickered and he muttered something. Then he turned over and went right back to sleep. I prodded him viciously, and he, after a little resistance, awoke.

'Did you have to poke me so hard?' he complained straight off. He looked around, realised it was morning and echoed my dismay. 'Shit! We're screwed.'

He started scrambling around, picking up his things.

'What are you doing?' I asked as he poked his head inside my closet.

'Leaving.' He recovered a pair of his briefs and slammed the closet door shut, causing Chawla to wake up.

'Oh no, you're not! You're not leaving me here with this . . . this Chawla,' I said, momentarily lost for appropriately derogatory names that I had not already used.

'I'm sure Chodu will be getting my whereabouts checked. How will I explain why I didn't go to work? What will I tell him about where I was at night?'

'But we have work to do,' I argued. 'We have to find Sweety's killer. We have to find out who's been calling Chawla. We can't fob off Chodu forever with the wrong number. Sooner or later he's going to catch on to us.'

'There's only one option then. We'll have to leave him here alone,' Ani said.

'Uh-uh? And how do we ensure he doesn't create a racket?'

'Let's strap him to your bed,' Ani suggested.

Ugh! I'd probably have to burn my sheets afterwards. Along with the mattress. But it didn't seem like we had any other choice.

'How do I go to the loo?' Chawla objected.

Dammit! We hadn't thought this through. Wait! There was another way out of this mess. 'What's Chawla's car like?' I asked Ani.

'Car? Why?'

'Just tell me,' I said impatiently.

'Beat up. Ramshackle. Dilapidated.'

For fuck's sake! We were fighting against time and he was impressing me with his vocabulary?

'What make? Colour?'

'Oh. Right. A white Zen.'

'Registration number?'

'Dunno. Why don't you check? It's parked outside, by the gate.'

'You came in his car?' I asked Ani.

'Yeah. I didn't want to take out my car in case the police had someone following me.'

I nodded in approval and left. I ran outside, sparing a glance for Shyam who looked weary as though he'd had a taxing round of night duty.

Chawla's white Zen was parked outside the building just as Ani had said. Armed with the registration number, I walked across the road to the public telephone booth and squeezed myself in. I dialled Prado's landline number. As soon as he answered, I said, disguising my voice, 'Can I speak to someone in charge of the Sweety Nair murder case?'

'You can speak to me,' Prado said. 'I'm ACP Prakash Dogra.'

'Sir, I live in the neighbourhood and I just thought I'd mention that for the past few days there's been a shady man hanging around here. He is short and fat and wears a leather jacket. He comes in a white Maruti Zen and then just sits around in his car all day, watching the Nair residence. Or at least he used to, till two days back.'

'Did you get the number?' Prado asked, his voice high-pitched with excitement.

I gave him Chawla's car registration number.

'Okay. What's your name?'

'Sir, I'd rather not say. I don't want to get involved.'

'But how do we know it isn't a hoax?'

'Why don't you wait till there's a bomb blast to figure that out?' I said and hung up.

I went back home and said gleefully to Ani, 'Both of us can leave.'

Ani stared at me. 'What about him?'

'Let him also leave.' I told him what I had done, ending with a triumphant, 'Let him go to the police now.'

Chapter Nineteen

Both men looked at me in admiration—Ani, openly awed and Chawla, grudgingly appreciative.

'I have another proposition,' Chawla offered tentatively. 'I can go along with you and help you find out who killed Sweety.'

'I thought you might feel that way,' I said triumphantly.

After Ani had left, I dressed hurriedly. While getting ready I flicked on the telly. One of the news channels was running a story on Urvashi's murder case. The reporter had found out about the publicity stunt and was interviewing Omkar, who was making the most of his two minutes of fame. He was relating the story with such feeling, it sounded like a radio drama. 'As per the plan, I was to go there the next morning. Alas, when I reached Serenity Villa, she was nowhere to be found. I looked around everywhere, but she was gone. I asked myself, where can she be? Has she gone somewhere on her own?' Not to be outdone in the drama department, the channel was playing strident background music comprising the sound of a gong being hit after every sentence. It was increasingly hit with more force, and was positively deafening when he said dramatically, 'Or has something happened to her?'

I opened the door cautiously. Knowing Gandhi, he would be listening for the sound of my door scraping open. I peered out. No

Gandhi. Still, I sent Chawla out first just to be sure, and left the apartment only when I heard the sound of an owl hooting, which was the signal we had agreed on.

I personally thought appointing animal sounds as signals was quite cheesy and only happened in commando movies when 'all communication off' had been signalled. I wanted him to cry out, 'Chakoo, chhuri ki dhaar banwa lo', which was more of an everyday kind of sound, but Chawla protested quite vehemently. He said it made him feel silly. Instead, he suggested an owl hoot, and turned out to be surprisingly proficient at it.

Down below, Chawla wanted to move his car somewhere out of sight. Which was a good idea. So I bribed Shyam into letting us park Chawla's Zen inside the building in one of the empty slots at the back. It would be safe there for the time being. The police had no reason to come poking around my apartment. Yet.

Chawla wanted to know where we were going. I told him I had to drop in at Blazar first, and then go to the forensic lab.

'Blazar, eh?' he asked intrigued. 'You involved in the Urvashi case?'

'Hmmm,' I answered noncommittally.

'So who do you think did it?'

I gave him a look, kicked the RE into life and waited for him to hop on.

'You know, I can probably help you with that case as well.' Yeah, right. And probably put the bite on some fat fish in the process.

On the way to Blazar, he shouted, 'You've got penis envy.'

'What? Why would I want a penis? Other than to facilitate pissing anywhere.' Which, I had to admit, was a compelling reason in itself.

'Penis envy does not mean actually wanting a penis. It means you wanted to be a boy. In my opinion, girls who drive bikes suffer from penis envy.'

I grunted in response.

'So what's your problem?' he asked next.

'Excuse me?'

'I said, what's your problem?' he shouted in my ear, nearly deafening me.

'I heard what you said. I thought we'd established it was penis envy.'

'No, I'm talking about your love life. I mean, first, he's married. Then he's cheating on you. It's not that you can't get anyone else. You're not bad looking, good looking even.'

'Gee, thanks.'

'So why'd you hook up with him?'

'I have bad taste in men.'

'I can tell.' Then, 'In my opinion, a lot of women have bad taste in men. No, I take that back. All women have bad taste in men.'

'Yeah? Who should they go for? You?'

He laughed a short barking laugh. 'Not a chance. Been there, done that and seen entirely too much to go down that road again.'

I was startled—*Chawla had been with a woman? Women?*

While walking towards the Blazar corporate office, we passed the parking lot, as usual. And then I saw it. I had probably seen it before, but hadn't really noticed. In front of the space labelled Ms Neena Pundir was parked a white Honda Accord. With a badly dented fender and hood.

I grabbed Chawla's arm in excitement. 'The Accord!'

He looked genuinely puzzled. 'Which one?'

I looked at him in confusion. 'What do you mean which one?'

Even as I said it, I realised, to my dismay, that there were six Accords. All of them were dented and four of them were white. And another white Accord had a headlight missing.

'I take it, the white Honda Accord is significant in some way?' Chawla said.

Significant! I should think so, after the Indapur boys' testimony. But, even as I thought about it, I realised my excitement was premature. If Neena had indeed been the murderer, she would have repaired the damage to the car. Unless she'd been confident that no one had seen her. Or perhaps she hadn't expected Urvashi's body to be discovered so soon.

We walked inside and I asked for Baweja at the reception. The receptionist told us he was busy and we settled down to wait. I saw Chawla eye me, and I quickly picked up a magazine, hoping this would discourage him from starting with his psychoanalysis again.

No such luck.

'You know I have a theory,' Chawla said.

'Uh-uh?'

'I think you have abandonment issues.'

I rolled my eyes behind my magazine.

'No, really,' he said insistently. 'I see a pattern here. I mean look at Jai. Look at Vishal.'

I was so surprised that I nearly dropped the magazine. He laughed. 'I've checked up on you.' He took one look at my mutinous expression and clarified hastily, 'When I was working for Sweety. You see, people who've experienced feelings of deep loss or abandonment have a phobia about commitment. I think that's why you deliberately go for men who are unavailable or unsuitable in some way.'

I hated to admit it, but he was right about the last part. Which made me consider, was he right about the other stuff as well? Did I suffer from penis envy? Was I commitment-phobic? Did I harbour feelings of abandonment? I didn't think so, although there was this one time when my father had lost me in a fair in Aligarh. I was pretty young then, but I still remember feeling scared and helpless. That somehow I'd done something to anger Papa and he'd knowingly left me behind. But that hardly qualified as 'abandonment', did it?

'So do you?'

'Jeez Chawla, would you drop it? It's not as though I went after Ani knowing he was married.'

'But you stuck with him even after you found out. Or, maybe it is childhood abuse,' he said thoughtfully, rubbing his chin.

Thankfully, before he could expatiate on his 'childhood abuse' theory, the receptionist said Baweja was free and buzzed us in.

'Kay-rie!' he slurred expansively.

'Chandan,' I returned the greeting and wondered how to proceed. I knew that getting him to admit to being at Serenity Villa after he'd dropped Urvashi off was going to be difficult. My best bet was to entrap him by asking a seemingly harmless question. But how? And then I looked at his face and had an idea.

'You're looking good,' I said. 'The welts on your face are nearly gone!'

He grimaced. 'Yeah, thank god!'

'But that's how it is with poison ivy. It takes about a week or so to subside.'

He shrugged. 'And thash not a momt' too soon.'

'So where did you get touched by poison ivy?'

A moment of acute clarity flitted across his eyes and his body stiffened. And then, almost instantly, he was his former relaxed self. He waved dismissively as though through alcohol induced amnesia. 'It washn't posion ivy. Wash prawnsh.'

I would have been fooled had I not looked closely at his eyes. They narrowed and sharpened in focus. The drunkenness was a façade. Oh, he had been drinking, but I suspected that he was so used to alcohol now, he was probably able to hold it well.

'Oh, drop it. It was at Serenity Villa, wasn't it?' I asked.

He shrugged. 'Coul' be.'

'What were you doing inside the hedge, Chandan?'

'Inside?' he said as though puzzled, 'I wasn' inside.'

'Poison ivy was growing only on the inside of the hedge. You couldn't have accidentally touched it by brushing past the hedge.'

'Ah!' he said, 'I rem'ber now. My lighter fell down and rolled into the hedge. I went to pick it up.'

'You must smoke pretty fast. You take out your lighter to light a cigarette, it rolls into the hedge and by the time you go to pick it up, the cigarette's finished! No, make that three! You see, I found several brown cigarette stubs in the hedge.'

'Maybe they were there b'fore.'

'Nuh-uh. Brown cigarettes aren't so common. I also found a bottle of alcohol there.'

'So? There's a pub nex'door. Someone could've chucked it.'

'So the cigarette stubs, the bottle, neither of those belong to you? Let's see if the police buy it. Especially when I tell them the pub owner next door saw your car there late that night when he went to empty out the trash,' I lied, just in case he got it into his head to say he was there earlier in the day. 'Don't be surprised if they come to you with a swab. They'll probably run DNA tests on the stubs and the bottle. Come on Chawla.'

Chawla and I had almost made it to the door when Baweja said, 'Wait!'

We turned around. Almost at once Chandan dropped his drunken act. His eyes shot towards Chawla.

'Don't worry about him. He's just a colleague,' I explained.

On cue, Chawla fished out his business card and thrust it at Baweja. 'Pankaj Chawla, PI. Anything you need you come to me. Guaranteed full satisfaction or your money back, minus expenses. Only the fee will be refunded, you understand?'

'Oh, for god's sake!' I said.

Chawla looked injured. 'What? He might need a PI sometime,' he said and added quickly, 'A man.'

I ignored him and turned to Baweja. 'Fine. I was in the hedge.

But it's not what you think. I was only trying to find out who Urvashi was meeting there.'

'Urvashi was meeting someone there?'

'Remember I told you about the phone call she received in the car earlier that day? I had a feeling that was John D'Costa. And that she was meeting him there on the sly.'

'John D'Costa, the head of CTE Films?'

He nodded. 'Urvashi had been unhappy with Blazar for a while; she thought they weren't giving her good roles anymore. She'd been getting offers for more lucrative and challenging assignments by other producers which, because of her . . . relationship . . . with Kaustav she wasn't accepting.'

'John D'Costa was one of the producers to offer her a film?' I asked.

He nodded and continued. 'I'd heard rumours that she'd been meeting him and I thought she might have asked him to come to Serenity Villa. So I pretended to drive away, parked the car a little distance away from Serenity Villa, came back and hid behind the hedge.'

So had Abdulla been actually telling the truth about negotiating dates with Urvashi on behalf of a client? Was he working for John D'Costa?

'Then what happened?'

He shrugged. 'I don't know. I waited for a long time but nothing happened. So I came back.'

'So you didn't see Vidisha having it out with Urvashi?'

'So it's true Vidisha was there?'

I ignored the question. 'What time did you leave?'

He shrugged. 'Maybe around ten? I didn't look at my watch.'

'You didn't, by any chance, follow her to Hermit Hill?'

'No,' he said looking straight into my eyes.

'Sure?'

'Sure.'

'If it were that innocent, why did you and Neena lie about being in Firangi Paani on the 17th?'

'That's because by the 19th it had become clear something was wrong. So we just . . .'

'Covered your tracks.' I stayed silent for a while, mulling it over. 'What if I told you the call on Urvashi's phone just before Khandala came from Blazar? What's more, it came from your direct line.'

He looked baffled, but had no suggestions about how that could have happened.

'What car do you drive?'

'A Triumph.' He looked at my raised eyebrows and said dryly, 'It's second hand. I bought it off Kaustav.'

'What colour?'

'Black.'

Could that be the imported black car that had collided with the white Honda Accord? If the publicity stunt story was correct though, Baweja would have been in an Accent. I made a note to check into this anyway.

As I was leaving Chandan's office, I bumped into Neena at the door. She looked somewhat discomfited and I had the feeling that she had been listening in at the door. However, as soon as she saw me, her face creased into a smile that did not quite reach her eyes.

'Katie,' she said with forced geniality. 'I was just coming to talk to Chandan.'

'In a minute,' I said, stepping outside and shutting the door. 'I wanted to ask you something.'

'Oh?' she ventured cautiously. Like Baweja's before her, her eyes dwelt on Chawla enquiringly and I found myself explaining his presence again.

Chawla, irrepressible as always, handed her his card. 'Pankaj Chawla, PI. Guaranteed full satisfaction—'

'—I was just wondering why you lied about being with Chandan in Firangi Paani on 17th night?' I cut in with a glare at Chawla. 'Chandan says he was at Serenity Villa till late that night.'

Her mask of cordiality slipped momentarily, but then she collected herself admirably. 'So Chandan's told you about that. Well, that answers your question about the conversation you overheard between us on the 19th. You were right. We were talking about Urvashi. And our plan to have Chandan stakeout Urvashi after he had settled her in. He must have also told you why we did it?'

I looked at her expressionlessly.

She shrugged. 'I was merely doing it for Kau . . . Blazar. Chandan told me he suspected Urvashi had been talking to John D'Costa. Now, Blazar owns . . . owned all her dates for the next three years, so why would she be talking to John D'Costa? Unless she was planning to shaft some Blazar project. Where did she get off thinking she could do that? I . . . We were merely trying to prevent that from happening. But first we needed to know exactly what was going on. That's why Chandan hung around.'

'So what happened?'

'What do you mean what happened?'

'What did Chandan see?'

'He didn't see anything. At least that's what he told me.'

'Oh, but he told me something else. He said he saw Vidisha there,' I bluffed.

Shock, confusion, anger—a variety of emotions reflected on her face. 'That's news to me,' she said tight-lipped.

I looked at her, trying to make up my mind about whether she was lying. I couldn't figure out either way. 'Neena, why didn't you tell me earlier about Urvashi receiving a call just before Khandala?'

She shrugged. 'I guess I forgot.'

Right. 'Who do you think called Urvashi on her cell just before Khandala? Just before she switched off her mobile?'

'Chandan must have told you he thought it was John D'Costa.'

'What if I told you the call came from Blazar? From Chandan's direct number?'

'It did?' Again, that veneer of surprise that didn't quite hold.

'It wouldn't have been Vidisha, now, would it?' I said sneakily.

Her eyes narrowed. 'How would I know? It could've been anybody. Anybody could have popped into his office and used the phone. It's not as though we keep our offices locked around here.'

'You drive a white Honda Accord, don't you?' I asked.

She frowned and looked at me searchingly, as though trying to figure out where I was going with that line of questioning. 'Yes,' she said guardedly. 'What about it?'

'A white Honda Accord was seen at Hermit Hill on the night of the 19th. There are witnesses who saw a person dressed in black run down the hill, get into a white Honda Accord and drive off. This was right around the time of the murder.'

'Well, it wasn't me or my car. Both of us were parked here till I went home. You can check the time with security. Are you sure it wasn't some other Accord? It's a fairly common car. There are at least seven in Blazar itself. We got a corporate deal and a lot of us opted for them.'

'That's reasonable. Except, according to the witnesses, the Accord was involved in a collision with another car. Your car's hood looks pretty beaten up, too.' I stopped and waited for her to react.

She stared back expressionlessly. 'Here's the thing about driving in Mumbai. Cars get dented. Did anyone get the number on the car? Either car?'

She stared at me but it wasn't an aggressive stare. It was an apprehensive one. I evaded the question. 'You know what I think? I think you and Chandan are lying. I think you knew about Hermit Hill. Chandan waited at Serenity Villa and then followed Urvashi to Hermit Hill on the 17th.'

Beads of sweat fought their way through her moisture-proof compact and the sub-zero temperature levels in Blazar. She fished out a tissue from her bag and dabbed her upper lip. 'So you're saying we killed her? Together? Why? And why would we wait till the 19th? And why would we not get the car repaired?'

I looked at her resentfully. I was the one who was doing the questioning, not her. And those were the questions I wanted answers to.

She gasped, as though she'd just remembered something.

'What?' I said.

'It's probably nothing, but I just remembered. On the 17th, when Urvashi's mother was told about the publicity plan, she was very upset. She came down to Blazar to meet Kaustav. Kaustav had a million things to do. Last thing he wanted was to soothe an irate mother. So he asked me to show Geeta into Chandan's office.'

'So what you're saying is . . .'

'All I'm saying is this was around five. And now, if there's nothing else . . .' She turned smartly on her heels and walked away, chucking the tissue into a nearby bin as she did so.

'Actually there is one more thing,' I called out to Neena. 'When did you last speak with Chandan on 17th night?'

'Around ten. I remember because I received the call when I was entering the edit suite for a last-minute check on a promo we were cutting. I had to punch in my card. That's when I saw the time. He said that he hadn't seen anything and was coming back.'

Their stories matched, but I was convinced the two of them were lying. The question was, why?

After Neena left, I quickly hopped across to the bin, picked up the discarded tissue and placed it in a zip-lock pouch. Next, I borrowed Chawla's phone and dialled Geeta's home number. The maid answered the phone and said that Geeta wasn't home.

'What's the problem?' Chawla asked.

'Geeta isn't home.'

'So call her on her cell.'

I hesitated. 'I don't know. These kinds of questions are better asked in person. To gauge if they're lying, you know.'

'So? Even in person these people were running circles around you anyway.'

Good point. I dialled Geeta's cell number.

'Ms Geeta, is it true that you were in Chandan Baweja's room on the 17th at around five p.m.?' I asked her.

I could hear the surprise in her voice. 'As a matter of fact I was. I was upset about the publicity plan and wanted to talk to Kaustav. But he was busy and asked me to wait. Neena suggested that I wait in Chandan's room. She practically herded me in there. Why?'

'Did you call Urvashi from there?'

'No. Why?'

'Urvashi got a call on her cell at around that time and the records show that the call came from Chandan Baweja's direct line.'

'Well, I didn't call her. I bet that b . . . witch Neena did.'

'Perhaps,' I said. 'What time did Urvashi call you from Serenity Villa that night?'

Geeta thought for a bit. 'I guess it must've been just before ten. I know because *Dance Dance* was on that night and Uru was the guest judge on the show. I was waiting for the previous programme to end.'

If that was correct, Vidisha and Urvashi had had it out by ten p.m. By his own admission, Baweja was there till ten or so. That meant he would have seen the whole thing.

'Another thing. Urvashi has a friend called Mayuri?'

'If by friend, you mean parasite, then yes. She was only interested in getting a break into Blazar and stuck to Uru like a leech. And Uru was such a kind girl, she let her tag along. I warned her repeatedly about Mayuri but she wouldn't listen. Besides, what would my baby and a two-bit dancer have in common?' she said and disconnected in a huff.

Chapter Twenty

Next, I decided to get the matter of Vidisha's alibi out of the way. As we were waiting for Vidisha outside her office, Chawla said, 'You know, what we were talking about earlier?'

'About what?'

'Abuse. You see, girls who've been abused as children usually go for abusive men even when they grow up. Their self-esteem is so low they believe they don't deserve to be happy. And so they go for abusive men again and again. Men who will reinforce their low opinion of themselves.'

Jai was definitely in that category. Was Vishal? His discovering he was gay while we were together had dented my self-esteem somewhat. I somehow felt I was responsible for turning him gay. Em's light-hearted jest at the time, 'You take men who are on the brink and push them over' hadn't helped. Was Chawla right, I thought in alarm. Was I abused as a child? I didn't think so. Could the one time my father had thrashed me be classified as abuse? Could it be that I had been abused as a child and didn't know it?

What was wrong with me? Why was I listening to him?

'Will you stop with this pop psychology shit already?' I complained.

'I was just trying to help you,' he said in an injured tone.

'You wanna help me? Then shut up and let me think,' I hissed.

'About what?' Chawla asked.

'About how I'm going to get a sample of Vidisha's DNA.'

'Why?'

'I've given a pillow case from Hermit Hill for forensic testing. If there's alien DNA on it, I'll need another sample for comparison.'

From the corner of my eye I saw Vidisha's office door open and disgorge a visitor. Bhanu. I called out to him.

He stopped and turned. His face broke into a huge smile. 'Katie!'

'Hey. You have a minute?'

'You're kidding! For you, always.'

'I wanted to show you something,' I said, fishing for the pieced together map in my bag.

'Me too. I wrote the first scene. Check this out. Fade in. Exterior, sarson fields, day. It is just short of harvest season in Hoshiarpur, Punjab. The fields are resplendent with magnificent mustard, wheat and sugarcane crops ready to be harvested. Nice, eh?'

'Yes, just like in *Diya Jale Jaan Jale*,' I muttered. What was with Blazar and mustard fields?

'What was that? Anyway, through the fields sounds of boys playing football can be heard. Camera moves forward, cutting through a sarson field and comes upon a small clearing which has been converted into a football ground. A group of young boys are playing ball in the field.

'A young sardar boy runs up with the ball. The opposing side runs alongside and closes in. His own team is cheering him on, giving him directions. A young boy of about thirteen or fourteen, Babloo, standing nearby claps and cheers. Anyway, the young sardar is within striking distance of the net. And thwhack! He hits it into the net.

'Both the young sardar boy and Babloo erupt, "Goal!" They cheer and do a little bhangra. Suddenly they realise, no one else is cheering. Their team looks downcast and the opposing team is grinning. And then they realise he's done a self-goal! When the young sardar learns what has happened, instead of being upset, he gets aggressive. He says, "Oye toh kabhi kabhi aisa ho jaata hai!"

'This naturally upsets his team and they run to attack him. The young sardar and Babloo run. They run helter-skelter. Hold it, did we say sardar boy? Well, not quite.

'Cut. Camera on the back of the young sardar, running. And then the sardar boy removes his turban and a cascade of long, shiny hair is let loose. He turns to face the camera and we see the sardar is a young girl—Chandni.'

Big surprise. I was going for Anjali, the heroine's name in *Tu Hi Re*, *Ek Main Aur Ek Tu* and *Chhupa Lo Dil Mein*. Chandni, the heroine's name in *Diya Jale Jaan Jale*, *Tum Pukaar Lo* and, more recently *Ransom*, would have been my next choice.

Bhanu nudged me. 'That is you. Or, rather your character,' he said with a wink. He addressed Chawla. 'We're making a movie on Katie's character. Well, not exactly her character. More like a Katie meets Kajol in *Pyar To Hona Hi Tha*.' Then, turning to me, he asked, 'What do you think?'

'I . . . I . . .' Words failed me.

'Mind-blowing!' Chawla declared.

'That's what I thought!' Bhanu said, looking pleased.

'*Mind-blowing?*' I muttered wrathfully. 'Speaking of which, I have something mind-blowing too.' I took out the road map, unfolded it and handed it to him. 'Look familiar?'

He turned white. 'I . . . I don't think I've seen it before.'

'Really? Then why did you and Desiree tear it up and throw it away the other day?'

He started trembling. His hands shook so much that he dropped the map. The paper fluttered a little and fell on the floor. It landed with the handwritten message facing up. Bhanu seized the lifeline and said quickly, 'It looks like a note I wrote to Desiree. What about it?'

'Are you telling me you had no idea of the map?'

His Adam's apple bobbed up and down nervously. 'No, I didn't notice it till you showed it to me just now.'

'Then how did the map come to be there?'

He swallowed a couple of times. 'I . . . I . . . it must have been there already. I remember writing the note on the first piece of paper I found lying around.'

'Then why did you tear it up?'

'Are you crazy? What if someone got hold of it and showed it to my wife?'

So that's how he wanted to play it? I let it be for the time being. 'Where were you on the night of 19th September?'

'Why? You can't think that I . . .?'

'Then you won't have a problem answering the question.'

He swallowed. 'I was home.'

'Anyone else there, besides you?'

'My wife,' he said quickly. A little too quickly.

'Another thing. What car do you drive?'

He looked frightened again. 'A Honda Accord. Why?'

'What colour?'

'It's white. It's not here. It's in the workshop.'

'Why, what happened?'

He looked shifty. 'Nothing. Regular service.'

'Then you wouldn't mind giving me the name of the garage?'

He looked positively terrified. Nevertheless, he gave me the name, adding, 'Why, what's going on?'

'It appears Urvashi's murderer arrived at Hermit Hill in a white Honda Accord. On the way out, he or she also had a little accident with the car. So all we need to do is look for an Accord with a little bit of body damage.'

At that moment, Vidisha's door opened once more and she stepped out. So, leaving Bhanu to stew in his own juices, I walked up to her.

'Well, well, well, if it isn't the adulteress,' she drawled.

I groaned inwardly. Not again. My face burning with embarrassment, I shot Chawla a look from under my lashes. He was looking keenly interested. Oh god! I would never hear the end of it now.

'I didn't . . . I mean I haven't . . . it's not like that,' I finally said lamely.

Chawla looked like he wanted to say something. 'Don't,' I said warningly and flashed him my Voldemort look. He gulped and retreated.

Vidisha raised her eyebrows. Whatever, she seemed to say. She tapped her sneaker-clad foot impatiently. 'Well? You asked to see me?'

'Ah . . . um . . .' I hedged momentarily, at a loss for words. 'I wanted to ask you a few questions about the night of 19th September,' I said brightly.

She rolled her eyes. 'Again?'

'Actually some fresh evidence has come to light.'

'And it all points to the jilted wife,' she said scornfully. 'It always does. The "jilted" wife tops almost everyone's list of prime suspects.'

In some cases, however, the dice fell the other way. In some cases it was the 'jilted' wife that ended up dead. Involuntarily, almost guiltily, my eyes flew to Chawla. I was sure it was what he was thinking as well. To my surprise, I found him staring at Vidisha. A steady, unblinking look, as though he'd seen a vision.

When there was no response from me, she said, 'Fine. Come into my office,' and strode back inside.

We followed her in and found her standing behind her desk, shuffling some papers. 'And what is this new evidence?' she said without looking up.

'Well, there are witnesses who saw a person arrive at Hermit Hill in a car, a white Honda Accord. It's likely this was the murderer. This person went in and finished his or her business. Then when this person was on his or her way out, another car drove up and rammed into the parked Accord.'

'But that just proves I'm innocent. I don't have an Accord.'

Damn! But there was something niggling away in the dim recesses of my mind. Something someone had said about the accident? A phrase carelessly thrown in? Something relevant mentioned in passing?

'Aw, disappointed?' she smirked.

'Not really. You don't have to own one to drive one. Blazar's lot is full of Accords. Your brother has one. So all we have to do is look for one which also happens to be dented. Or has had recent bodywork done.'

She pinned me with a long stare and abruptly sat down. 'Well, as I told you earlier, I was home that night.'

I was thrown. What made her change her mind? Did something I say set off alarm bells in her head? The mention of her brother perhaps? I snuck a look at Chawla for validation. He was still staring fixedly at Vidisha. What the fuck was he doing? What was so incredible about her? Truth be told, he was starting to creep me out. I had seen exactly such a look on a serial killer's face in *Law and Order SVU*.

I wasn't the only one getting creeped out. As if drawn against their will, Vidisha's eyes cut to Chawla and then she looked away hastily.

'From what I've gathered you were with Mrs Kapoor for a while after dinner. Thereafter, she assumed you were home, in your room. She didn't see you. No one seems to have actually seen you.'

She shot Chawla another glance and looked away. 'That's strange. Because Kaustav did see me. Twice. Once at around nine before going into my room—I wanted to talk to him and so I went to his room-slash-study. I saw him again at about eleven when he came out of the study to fetch something. Some water, I think.'

That was certainly changing her tune! 'Just two days ago you'd told me something else.'

'I did? I don't recall.'

'You did! You pointed to two different ends of the house and indicated that you hadn't seen him! You went out of your way to point out that your bedroom and Kaustav's room were at opposite ends of the house.'

'I was upset, okay?' she said sulkily.

I tried to figure out if she was lying. She certainly looked shifty.

'What did you two talk about?'

'This and that,' she said evasively.

'This and that?' I repeated questioningly.

'For god's sake, what does a married couple talk about? We chit-chatted about some problems at work.' Chawla's unblinking stare finally got to her and she cried, 'Who *is* he? Why is he staring at me?'

Before I could respond, Chawla walked up to her and started stroking her hair lovingly. 'I'm sorry,' he said. 'It's just that you have such beautiful hair. I just had to touch it.'

Vidisha stiffened and then relaxed. 'I don't believe this. Are you here for that role of a psycho?' She turned to me and asked, 'Is he an actor or something?'

Under the pretext of caressing her hair Chawla deftly plucked out a strand.

'Ow!' she cried, swatting at him with her arms. 'Get him out of here!'

She reached for the intercom, muttering angrily.

'Don't call security!' I implored her. 'He's harmless. You're right. He's an actor. He was auditioning . . . *I'm taking him away!*'

I grabbed Chawla and tried to drag him away. He resisted. 'Enough!' I snarled in his ear. He just grinned at me. The bastard was enjoying playing the hair fetishist!

'Were you trying to get us thrown out? Because there are easier ways to do that,' I hissed at him outside Vidisha's office.

He held up the strand of Vidisha's hair. 'It got the job done, didn't it? Without her getting suspicious. By the way, what was that about a movie role? Do you think I could audition for it? Come on, where's your sense of humour?'

I grabbed the hair and ziplocked it. 'You call that . . . that preposterous act funny?'

'It wasn't preposterous!' he said indignantly. 'It was good. And you know it was good. I saw you. You had fully bought into it. I could almost see the thoughts running through your head. "Oh god! What if he is a serial killer? What if he is a serial killer and not a detective at all? After all, what do I know about him other than what he's told me?" Come on, admit it. I had you fooled.'

'So did not!' I denied hotly, my face burning with embarrassment.

As we were leaving, I snuck a look at the parking lot. Chandan's Triumph sat there proudly, all shiny and gleaming. I was disappointed, although I didn't know why. Even if it had indeed been the Triumph that had run into the Accord, it just proved Baweja couldn't have been the murderer. Regardless of the fact that Baweja could have had it fixed, the murderer was in the Accord and not in the car that collided with it.

A Merc pulled in. It stopped beside us and the rear window rolled down. My heart beat faster when I saw who the occupant was.

'Katie,' Kaustav said with a smile. I nearly spontaneously combusted at the sight of the tiny grooves that appeared at the corners of his mouth.

'Hey,' I said shyly.

Only then did I notice that he wasn't alone. I hastened to wipe the goofy smile off my face, but it was too late. Meher Kapoor had seen the adoring expression on my face and was looking at me with a mocking smile. Kaustav got out of the car and instructed the chauffeur to drive on ahead. Meher Kapoor looked like she wanted to hang around and listen to our conversation but she didn't argue.

'Katie, what's going on?' he asked worried. 'Why is this thing still dragging on? I thought the police had their guy?'

'They do?'

He nodded. 'ACP Dogra spoke to me. Said something about Urvashi having spoken to a shady character called Abdulla. Asked me if I knew who he was. He gave me the impression that they were actively pursuing that line.'

'That's one of the lines,' I agreed, 'but there's a problem. You see, Abdulla was out of the country when Urvashi was murdered.'

'So they think I did it?'

'What?'

'The DCP came and took a swab.'

I felt a shiver of alarm. 'He did?'

'Yes. He also took my fingerprints.'

Okay, okay, don't panic. 'It's probably nothing. They must be getting samples from everybody. Besides, knowing Chodu, he was just looking for an excuse to invade your mouth.'

His eyes widened as the implication of that sank in. 'Now that I think about it, he did unduly feel up my cheeks. And hands,' he joked feebly. 'Anyway, what are you doing here?'

'Oh, I was just talking to Vidisha.'

'About what?' he asked.

'You know, about what she was doing on the 19th. There are witnesses who saw someone in a white Honda Accord near Hermit Hill that night.'

His eyes widened a fraction. 'Oh, but we don't have a Honda Accord.'

'I know!' I bellowed and quickly apologised when he looked taken aback.

'No problem. And what did Vidisha say?'

'She said she was home. That she saw you twice. Once at nine and then at eleven.'

'Of course! How could I forget? That's right, she did,' he said casually. Too casually. Was he trying to protect her?

'Why didn't you say so earlier?'

'I guess I forgot. Anyway, I'm glad I caught you. I was going to call you.'

'Oh?'

'What are you doing tonight?'

'Tonight? Nothing much. Why?'

'How about some dinner then? You like seafood?'

'Love it.'

'Great. And then how about popping in at one of my friends'? He's having a few close friends over for dinner. One among them is an English curator who specialises in Renaissance art. The moment he said that, I immediately thought of you. I knew you'd want to meet him.'

Fuck. 'Er . . . It sounds great.'

'Great. I'll pick you up at eight-thirty?'

I agreed. With a salute he turned and walked off.

'Shit! Shit! Shit!'

'Who was that?' Chawla asked.

'That was Kaustav Kapoor. The owner of Blazar Films.'

He looked awed. 'Really!' Then, 'You have no idea about Renaissance art, do you?'

'Shut up!'

'So why didn't you say no?'

'Why don't you mind your own business?'

He shook his head and muttered something that sounded like, 'Classic case of low self-esteem.'

I rounded on him aggressively. 'What was that?'

'Nothing. I just said, it's good to blow off steam.'

We walked the rest of the distance in silence. 'Now what?' Chawla asked when we were outside

'Now I need to buy a prepaid SIM card. Which reminds me, I need to find out who that Australian SIM belongs to. And then I have to do a little digging on Baweja and Neena Pundir and find out why they're lying. But first, I need to make a stop at the forensic lab.'

Chawla nodded. 'By the way, I can probably help with Baweja and Neena Pundir. I know this really connected film PR guy.'

I looked at him suspiciously. He backed off laughing. 'I promise I'll tell you everything. I won't try to use the information in any way.'

A little later, when I presented myself at the forensics lab with Neena's and Vidisha's samples, Pandit boomed excitedly, 'Guess what I found on the pillowcase?'

Why was he looking like that? Bursting with excitement, like he'd discovered something of great importance? This looked bad.

A moment later, my fears were confirmed when he said, 'Semen.'

Chapter Twenty-one

❧❧

'Semen,' I repeated in a daze.

'Semen.'

Fearfully, I asked, 'Whose is it?' *Here it comes. It's . . .* Wait, did he say . . .? 'Did you say *not Kaustav's?*'

Pandit looked chagrined. 'Yeah.'

I felt a rush of relief—to be perfectly honest, I hadn't been completely convinced that Kaustav had not known about Hermit Hill. Maybe even visited her there. 'That was fast,' I said.

'Yeah, his was the first sample Rajesh Chodankar brought.'

Ergo, the swab. 'You . . . you told Chodankar about the pillowcase?' I choked.

He was taken aback. 'Wasn't I supposed to? Hell, it's a murder case. I had to tell him. Besides you didn't tell me it was top secret.'

'So what did he say?'

'Nothing to me. But I heard him say to Dogra that it appeared their original theory about an intruder may be right. That a man broke in and raped and killed her. But they were way off and I told them so. Her body didn't show any signs of forced intercourse. It was consensual sex.'

'What did Chodu say when you told him that?'

'Well, he wasn't happy for sure.'

By now I felt light-hearted enough to say flippantly, 'Of course. And not only because he'd have to go door-to-door with a plastic cup.'

He gave me a look. 'You do know that you don't actually need semen samples to compare DNA?'

'That was a joke, Vinay.'

Before getting a SIM, I needed to pick up the relevant identification documents from my office. On the way, I cruised past Versova police station and decided to stop there first. Prado was on the phone talking agitatedly. 'What does the doctor say? . . . Fine keep me posted.' He replaced the receiver. Almost immediately it rang again.

'Hey Prado,' I greeted him.

He held up his hand and picked up the phone. 'Bola . . . did anyone see anything? . . . Besides that . . . I know it was crowded . . . okay keep digging.' He replaced the receiver and turned to me enquiringly.

'I need a favour. I need to find out about a SIM. I've been getting these crank calls and . . .'

'Not now,' he said, uncharacteristically cutting me short. 'There's been a terrible accident. A man was stabbed in a crowded marketplace.'

'So? These things happen everyday,' I said plaintively. 'I'm being harassed. Maybe even stalked!'

'You didn't just say that!'

I didn't blame him. I couldn't believe I'd just said that. 'Is he okay? What happened?' I asked sheepishly.

'It's pretty bad but he'll live,' Prado said gloomily.

'Gee, talk about me being callous.'

'No, you don't understand. He was our main suspect in another case.'

That indeed was a bummer. I made appropriate soothing noises.

'Anyway,' Prado said, shaking off the funk. 'What was the number you wanted checked?'

I gave him the Australian number.

'Fine,' he said jotting down the number. 'I'll give you a call later.'

'About that, I'll call you. I lost my phone,' I said.

His phone rang again. So he nodded and waved me away. I hesitated. I also wanted the investigation report on the Urvashi case. And the Sweety case. But he was clearly very busy so I decided to leave it for later.

When I pulled up in front of my office, Rajeshwari was conducting a flirtatious conversation over the parapet with the paanwala below. As soon as she saw me she raced away, presumably to hide evidence of whatever mischief she'd been up to. Or to warn Zara to hide evidence of whatever mischief she'd been up to. It turned out to be the latter.

'Katie,' she said as soon as she saw me. 'I've had the most disturbing revelation.'

'Not now Zara,' I said, unlocking the door to my office. 'I'm in a bit of a rush.'

She followed me into my office.

'You're wasting your time, Zara. I don't have booze here.'

She waved dismissively. 'I heard you're working on the Urvashi case?' she asked, sounding uncharacteristically sober.

I started rummaging about in my filing cabinet for my PAN card and tax returns. 'How do you know?'

'One hears things,' she said, making a gesture of vagueness. 'I just wanted to tell you, yesterday Baba Vimalanand visited me. He asked about you. Said he had some helpful information for you.'

Baba Vimalanand was an Aghori and a self-proclaimed enlightened soul. He was also Zara's guru. Upon her urging, I'd visited him once, and during that short meeting he'd flashed me, saying I was to have sex with him as rinbadhana, some squaring-off of karmic sexual debts.

I found the relevant documents and stuffed them into my bag. I opened my desk drawer and looked for the little envelope which contained my passport-size photographs. I found the envelope, opened it and glanced at the photos. Yikes! Eyes opened wide in startled confusion, lips puckered in a pout, hollow cheeks and a sallow complexion, I looked like a convicted serial sexual offender.

'Don't you want to know what it was?' Zara repeated.

'What?'

'Baba Vimalanand's information,' Zara explained patiently. 'He said and I quote, "A man, just alone, also a fly, just alone, in the huge living room."'

Great. Now he was reciting haiku. 'You might tell him it's the wrong metre.'

'He also said that you had accumulated a large karmic debt and that if you didn't start paying it off you'd be born a creepy-crawly in your next life. He said there was a way that you could pay it off in one shot.'

'By having sex with a creepy-crawly in this lifetime?' Her jaw dropped open. 'Thanks, but I'll take my chances.'

After Zara left, I took out the Yellow Pages and thumbed through the book till I arrived at the page listing authorised Honda service centres. The list was huge and would take me the whole day were I to attempt it alone. I set it aside for the moment.

I grabbed the landline and called Dikshit to ask him if there had been any development.

'God, where have you been?' he said.

'My phone had a slight accident. What's up?'

'Listen, about that guy Deshpande? I think you'd better stay away from him. He's bad news.'

'Oh?'

'First of all, I can't trace anything on him beyond the last five years. There are no birth records, no school records, no bank statements, no income tax records, no property ownership, nothing beyond five years back. It's like he came into this world a grown man and a multi-millionaire.'

'So I was right about him being Satan's progeny.'

'What?'

'Uh, nothing. What else did you find?'

'He has all these businesses going, real estate, security, all seemingly legit. But the inflow of money exceeds invoiced amounts . . . not by a lot . . . only marginally per invoice but it all adds up to quite a bit. And when I looked into their financial statements I traced them back to several holding companies which, in turn, are held by other holding companies and so on. All the money is being transferred to offshore accounts.'

'Money laundering.'

'That's not all. When I looked at the other shareholders, you'll never guess the names I found.' He inhaled sharply. 'Dude, I think he may be a bhai.'

Big surprise. 'Uh-huh.'

'That's it?' he asked, astonished. 'Uh-huh?'

'I suspected as much. Did you find any solid evidence of it?'

A pause. 'Well, nothing direct or actionable.'

Again, no surprise. 'Any connection to Blazar?'

'He does their security. Also, the balance sheet of one of his companies, the media one, shows several investments in films. *Ransom* is one of them.'

'Okay. Anything on Abdulla?'

'Where's the time? I've got three people working on Deshpande alone,' he complained.

'Okay, get on it ASAP.'

I stopped at the nearest telecom shop and bought a cheap, second-hand phone and a prepaid SIM card. Then I called my contact in the phone company and had her activate it immediately. To celebrate my new-found communication facility I called Ani.

'Hello?' Chodu's unmistakable baritone wafted over the line.

Shit! What was he doing with Ani's phone? My mind raced. If I disconnected without speaking that would surely alert Chodu. My best bet was to pretend it was a sales call.

'Good afternoon sir. I'm calling from Best Bank. We're offering personal loans at very reasonable rates of twenty-one per cent. Are you interested?'

'Tozhi aichi!' Chodu cursed and disconnected.

Heaving a sigh of relief, I called Dikshit and Chawla and gave them my new number. I put on my helmet, fired up my RE and headed home; it was close by, and there was leftover biryani in the fridge beckoning me.

As I entered the apartment gates, I was surprised to see Miss Poonawala emerge from Shyam's cabin. She frantically gestured for me to stop.

'Thank god I caught you,' she panted when I pulled over. 'Why's your phone switched off?'

'I lost it. What's up, Miss P?' I asked, surprised.

'Don't go in,' she said.

As I stared at her, she explained in a rush, 'A DCP Rajesh Chodankar was here looking for you. He said dat you were wanted for questioning in a murder. Kept asking questions about dat girl, Sweety, you had a fight wid. You know, your boyfriend's wife. He left strict instructions dat he was to be contacted da moment you showed up. What did you do, Kasthuri?'

Shit! Shit! Shit! That was fast! I had expected him to take at least a week to piece everything together.

'Fine, I'll just pick up some stuff and leave,' I said, jumping off the RE.

She grabbed my hand. 'You don't understand. Dat Gandhi has been lying in wait for you. Even now he must be already calling da police. If he hasn't already. Don't look now, but he's at his window.'

Of course I immediately swivelled around. Sure enough the lecherous bastard was there at his window. I thought I saw a cordless telephone in his hands.

'Shit! As if the society vote wasn't enough,' I complained bitterly.

'What vote?'

'The society meeting on Sunday?' I asked in surprise. 'To decide whether to allow single women to rent apartments here?'

'What are you talking about? Dere's no such vote.'

The rat! He'd made up the entire thing to blackmail me into sleeping with him!

'Here,' Miss Poonawala said, thrusting a plastic bag into my hands.

'What's this?' I asked peering inside.

'Just khakhras and theplas to see you through for de next few days. And some pickle.'

Was she serious? What did she think this was, the 1950s? Hadn't she heard of hotels and restaurants? But still, she had gone through so much trouble for me. I felt a lump in my throat the size of an apple. My eyes misted over.

'Thank you, Miss P,' I managed to choke.

'It's nothing,' she said bashfully, but I could see she was pleased by my reaction. 'Just be careful. I'm looking forward to continuing our tea ritual.'

'Miss P, I don't . . .'

She waved her hand dismissively. 'Go!'

I didn't need further urging and kicked the RE into gear and shot off. Luckily I had all my documents with me in my satchel. While riding, my mind wandered towards Miss Poonawala. Who would have thought that the tightwad would do what she had done. When this was all over, I would treat her to the finest Lopchu India had to offer. Well, maybe not Lopchu, since it cost upwards of seven hundred bucks a kilo. Maybe a fine Makaibari?

It was only then that I realised I had instinctively ridden towards Ego. I stalled the bike in the parking lot and sat thinking. Should I go in? Em had been blowing me over time and again and had generally been behaving like a total bitch. On the other hand, did I have a choice?

I was sitting there, munching on khakhras and mulling over my options when she called out to me from the window of her pad. Because of the ungodly hours involved, the manager of Ego is allotted a flat on the second floor.

'Are you planneeng to just seet zere?'

How humiliating to be caught out like that. I flushed. 'No!'

'Zen what are you doeeng outside?'

'Force of habit. Don't worry, I'm leaving.' I jumped off the bike, put on my helmet and kick-started the bike.

'Don't be stupeed Kay. Caam on een,' Em said.

'Not if you insist on speaking like that. Besides, I don't want to inconvenience you,' I said.

'You're not inconveniencing me,' she assured me. I sat on my bike, engine idling, unable to make up my mind.

'Come on!' she called.

With a great show of reluctance, I switched off the engine, parked the bike and started walking towards the entrance. Louis, who had been watching the drama from the door, followed me in, casting hateful looks my way. Em was down by the time I got inside. We sat in the club area on the ground floor while Louis sidled in behind the cash desk by the door. He quickly became absorbed in the account books, but I knew his ears were firmly cocked in our direction.

Meanwhile, Em kept shooting speculative looks my way. I guess she wanted to break the ice and was looking for any signs of thaw in my demeanour. I decided not to help her out.

'Have you been smoking?' she finally said.

Er. 'I . . . well maybe just a puff.'

She sniffed around my face and clothes. 'Oh Kay, how could you? And after all that hard work you put in to quit.'

'Look, it's my life. Besides, it's not as though by not smoking you're gonna live, like forever. You'll still die, only in good health. Which means, good health is merely the slowest possible rate at which one can die. So why not smoke?'

She stared me. 'That can't have made sense even to you.'

'Yeah, well, there's lots of things that don't make sense to me right now,' I said pointedly.

'I don't know why you're so upset,' she exclaimed in irritation. 'I said I'll explain everything soon!'

'Since when have we started keeping stuff from each other Em? No matter how bad, we've told each other everything. We swore on our first bras we'd be best friends forever. So what changed?'

'You developed a big mouth,' she muttered under her breath.

I gasped. I was so outraged that I could only stutter. 'I never . . . I can't . . .' I jumped up and rushed to the door. Simultaneously, Louis slid out from behind the desk and opened the door obligingly, unable to, or not bothering to, conceal a triumphant expression.

Em followed me and laid a hand on my arm just as I reached the door. 'Stop, Kay, for god's sake, stop. You're behaving very childishly.'

'Oh yeah? Then you should be glad to be rid of me.'

'Please Kay, sit down. What's the matter with you? I said I'll tell you everything soon. Why are you giving me so much grief over this?

'Is it a new boyfriend?'

'Did I say it was a boyfriend?' she sighed.

'Is he married?'

'Did you hear me at all?'

'Then what?'

'It *is* someone new. A new owner,' she said, exasperated.

I looked at her uncomprehendingly. 'A new owner?'

'Ego's been sold. It's been acquired by someone else. That's what I've been busy with. It was very hush-hush, but now that it's done, I can talk about it. So you see, it's not about you. Not everything is.' She patted my knee reassuringly, but I knew she meant it bitchily.

I guess I deserved that. 'So who's the new owner?'

She shrugged. 'I don't know. Never met him. He conducted the whole thing through his rep.'

'So . . . what does it mean for you?' I asked anxiously.

'The new management is keeping me on. For now.'

'For now? What does that mean?'

'Come on, let's go up to my flat. We'll talk there.'

My phone rang as soon as we entered the elevator. Shit, Prado! I let it ring.

'Aren't you going to answer that?' Em asked.

'It's not important.'

'So what brought you by?' she asked chattily.

'Nothing. I just needed a place to camp out for a few days,' I said casually.

'DCP onto you already?'

I nodded.

'No problem,' she said, equally casually.

As soon as we entered her apartment, Em announced that she was beat and wanted to take a nap so she could be fresh for the evening.

I dumped my satchel in the guest room and decided to get some lunch. On the way to the kitchen, I stopped over at Em's room to ask her if she wanted something. 'I'm just going to grab something to eat . . . Em!'

Em was standing in the middle of the room, clutching her

mouth. She shot me a look and rushed into the loo. I ran in after her and found her retching into the WC.

'My god, Em! Are you all right?'

She yanked a length of the toilet roll, wiped her mouth and nodded. 'Acid reflux. Drank too much last night.'

She brushed past me and went back into the room. I turned and followed.

'You sure you're all right? Want something? Alka Seltzer? Eno?'

She shook her head. 'I'll be fine.'

On an impulse I asked her, 'Em, what do you think of the way I look? Really, really think.'

'The way you look?'

'Yeah, face, body, you know. Is my nose too big? My hips too big? My tits too small?'

'It's all fine,' she replied, puzzled.

'Really?' I pressed her.

'Really. You look great.' Then, intuiting that I needed more reassurance, she elaborated, 'You have this perfectly oval face and these high cheekbones and these big brown eyes. And your body . . . it's just the kind that drives men crazy.'

'It is?'

'Mais oui. I would kill for a body like yours.'

Now it was my turn to stare at her. This was a revelation. 'Really?'

'Really. I mean look at me,' she said disparagingly. 'I'm a clotheshorse.'

She isn't. But that is the great thing about her. She is totally oblivious of her smashing looks and not in a fake-modest kind of way either. She knows she is good looking but doesn't think her looks are anything special.

'You, on the other hand, are tall and curvaceous, like Beyonce; what's not to like?'

I would've preferred Nicole Kidman, but Beyonce wasn't bad either. I wondered if that wasn't a backhanded way of calling me fat, and just as soon discarded the idea. Em can be bitchy like best friends sometimes are, but she's not an actress. No way could she fake such sincerity.

'Anyway, why the sudden insecurity over your appearance?'

'I don't know ... it's just ...'

'It's Tejas, isn't it?'

'What? No.'

'Then why did you kiss him? What was that all about?'

'Just drunken stupidity,' I said dismissively.

Her eyes searched mine. 'Sure? You're not holding a torch for him, are you?'

I looked at her as though she'd lost her marbles. 'Please. Why are you so concerned anyway?'

'I don't how to say this. It's just that he's ... I ... he ...'

'He's bad news? I know.' She stared at me till I felt myself go all hot under the collar. 'Just stop, okay? It's not ... It's Kaustav,' I blurted.

Her concern turned into dismay. 'Oh, Kay.'

'It's not what you think. It's just a date.'

'Explain.'

I sighed. 'He's taking me to dinner to a friend's place. He's ... the friend is having a guest from the art world over, and Kaustav thinks I'll be interested.' At her astounded look, I said. 'It's a long story. You know I've been working on the Urvashi case—so naturally I've been meeting him. And during one of those meetings I may have casually mentioned that I'm ...' I let my voice trail away.

'What?'

'That I'm interested in art.'

'Since when?'

'So I lied! If I remember correctly you were more excited about my meeting him than I was.'

'Yeah, that's when I thought of him as a producer, not your potential boyfriend! *Another married boyfriend.*'

'So what? It'll be a fling. What's wrong with that? Maybe it's just what I need after Ani.'

I opened and shut the drawers of her bureau in agitation. I noticed a colourful square packet in one of them. 'What's this?' I said.

'Just a temporary Botox type thingie.'

'Goodie. I'm taking it.'

'Sure. If you're going to do it, you might as well look good. And now, if you don't mind, I'd like some sleep. I do have to work tonight.'

Leaving Em to rest, I made my way to the kitchen where I found some leftover pizza. After an unsatisfactory meal of the chewy pie, I opened the face pack and eyed the viscous liquid inside. Dubiously I rubbed a little between my fingers. It felt . . . adhesive. I read the label once again wondering if it wasn't Fevicol. Nope, it seemed okay. Throwing caution to the winds, I applied it all over my face, hoping when the time came to take it off, my skin wouldn't peel right off with it.

While waiting for it to dry, I fetched several sheets of paper and decided to spend some time updating the information I'd received so far. I wondered if I should risk a smoke. I decided I could, if I opened the windows out wide. Even though Em wouldn't be up for another two hours, it couldn't hurt to be careful.

I lit a cigarette and started writing.

September 17:

Urvashi leaves Hotel Princeton at four p.m. in a Hyundai Accent. A little distance away, Chandan Baweja meets her and takes over the wheel. They drive out to Khandala. Just before Khandala (five and five-thirty) Urvashi checks in with Kaustav and then receives a strange (blackmail?) call. They both reach Serenity Villa at around six where Baweja purportedly settles her in and departs for Bombay. It is now established that he lied about this and, in fact, stayed on till quite late.

Questions:

Who called Urvashi between five and five-thirty p.m.? Was it Neena? Vidisha?

What time did Chandan Baweja actually get back? Did he see Vidisha having it out with Urvashi? Did he hear her subsequent telephonic conversations?

Where were the others—Vidisha, Neena, Kaustav, Bhanu Khanna, Desiree, Meher Kapoor, Deshpande—on 17th evening?

September 18:

Omkar, a junior artiste, goes down to Serenity Villa to act out the role of the kidnapper. He finds Urvashi gone. No signs of struggle or suggestions of foul play. He reports back to Blazar where everyone goes into a tizzy. During the day, Deshpande's people make several trips to Pune but come back empty-handed. Urvashi's property in Pune is also thoroughly checked out. That evening Kaustav hires me.

Questions:

Was Urvashi already at Hermit Hill (good probability)? Went of her own volition? Taken there by somebody? If taken by somebody, why did the killer wait till 19th night to kill her?

What about the others—Chandan Baweja, Neena, Vidisha, Bhanu Khanna, Desiree, Meher Kapoor, Kaustav?

September 19:

I go down to Blazar. I speak to Neena who tells me that Urvashi might have taken off on her own. The Falguni episode takes place, where I see Chandan Baweja for the first time. He has red welts on his face which he attributes to an allergy. Later, Chandan tells me he has a feeling something bad has happened to Urvashi. I am interrupted by Deshpande, but before that I manage to overhear Neena and Baweja talking. They seem worried about Chandan having messed up something that could land them both in trouble. My name is also mentioned in the conversation.

I check with Dikshit and find out that Urvashi's cellphone and credit cards have not been used since the evening of the 17th.

Geeta goes along with the story of Urvashi's disappearance.

September 20 onwards:

Spoke to Baweja, Neena, Vidisha, Kaustav, Meher Kapoor and Bhanu about their alibis.

Yet to speak with Desiree for hers.

Action points:

1. Check everyone's whereabouts from September 17th onwards.
2. Verify Vidisha's story for the 17th. Did she or didn't she go down to Serenity Villa?
3. Check Neena's alibi with her roommate. Bhanu's with his wife.
4. Speak with Desiree. And Bhanu Khanna? How did they get the map? Desiree going into Urvashi's Green Room— significant? Is that how she got the map?
5. Urvashi having spoken to Mayuri. Significant?
6. Who is Abdulla?
7. What about the Indapur boys' story? Who is the person dressed in black?
8. Whose tyre tracks were on the ground next to Urvashi's Merc?
9. Who does Hermit Hill belong to?
10. Whose semen is on the pillowcase?
11. What is Deshpande's role in all this?

Next, I fetched my Urvashi file. I took out my older notes, the pictures I'd taken of Hermit Hill and Serenity Villa and spread everything around me. I studied the paperwork and even lingered over the pictures. I don't know why but my gut was telling me there was a clue in those pictures. Something significant. Something I'd overlooked. But the pictures remained annoyingly coy.

At that point, my skin started to feel like it was being stretched wide and tight with toothpicks. I went to wash my face. Thankfully, the substance came off with only minor derma-buse. I was drying my face when my cellphone beeped a message. It was Dikshit asking me to check my mail.

I walked across to Em's computer and logged in. Dikshit had sent me information about Abdulla, including his bank statements and a list of phone calls he'd made during the last week. He had also thoughtfully appended a photograph. I had one look at the man in the picture and sat back in shock. I recognised him and his Rastafarian hair—it was the guy who'd delivered Deshpande's message to me.

Chapter Twenty-two

Ⓘ messaged Deshpande, asking him to meet me at Em's ASAP.
Then I went over the information carefully, highlighting one
important bit of data. I was taking a printout of Dikshit's mail
when the latch on the door rattled softly: I'd asked Deshpande to
be quiet so as not to disturb Em.

'What's up?' he said as soon as I opened the door. Then, 'What's
with your face?'

'Why?'

'Nothing. It's . . . well you're looking . . . younger.'

'Thanks,' I said, pleased.

'It's a compliment,' he insisted.

I stared at him. 'I know. I could tell.'

'Then you might try smiling,' he groused.

'I *am* smiling!'

'On the inside doesn't count.'

'What's wrong with you? Can't you tell when a person's smiling?'

I turned and peered at my reflection in the mirror on the wall.
I smiled. Nothing. I strained every muscle in my face till the veins
in my neck popped. Nothing. Yikes! I was stuck with a Manmohan-
Singh-after-the-Bombay-terror-attacks face for goodness knew how
long! Damn the face pack!

'Never mind.'

He shrugged. 'What did you want to see me about?'

He was looking wary so I figured he knew something was up. I suspected he knew that his connection to Abdulla would come up sooner or later and had probably already rehearsed his story. He hadn't survived five years in the big, bad jungle of the Bombay underworld without having his wits about him. My best chance was to lull him into complacency before going in for the kill.

I waved my hand casually. 'Oh, I just wanted to talk to you.'

He raised his eyebrows speculatively.

'I'd really appreciate it if you joined me for a cup of tea.'

His lips widened into a lopsided smile. 'Sure, babe.'

And he bounded into the room.

'Sit,' I said and gestured towards the living room. 'I'll make the tea.'

I went into the kitchen and opened the cabinets.

'What type of tea do you want? The separate, brewed kind or the dhaba variety?' I called out. It was a redundant question, though, as the only tea around was jasmine.

'Jasmine's fine,' he called back.

I filled the kettle with water and turned it on. While the water was heating, I took two mugs off their hooks and reached for the sugar jar.

'Sugar?' I called out.

'Yes,' he whispered in my ear.

Surprised, I dropped the steel jar with a clatter and turned around. Deshpande was standing right behind me with only a foot's distance between our bodies.

'Wha . . . what are you doing?' I stammered.

'What you want me to,' he said and took a step closer.

I was horrified. Did he think I had invited him to . . .? Did he think I was that desperate? Or that easy? I pressed back against the kitchen slab. He leaned forward. I bent my upper body as way back as I could, with the slab digging into the small of my back. If I moved backwards any more my spine would snap.

'You know, I've been thinking about this since that kiss you planted on me,' he said huskily. His breath fanned my face and the sensation wasn't unpleasant. My stomach did a curious flip-flop.

Then I shot out my arm and pressed him back. 'That was a drunken mistake!'

'I'm sure we can remedy that. There must be some alcohol around.'

'What's wrong with you? Did you . . . do you think I invited you for this?'

'Didn't you?'

'NO!'

'Don't worry, I'm not saying no. I'm game,' he said.

'I said, no!' I hissed and was rewarded with a hoot of laughter. I stared at him in mortification. He had been playing with me!

'That . . . that was funny,' he gasped.

'Oh, it's funny, is it? Tell you something else that's funny?' I brushed past him and went into the living room. I picked up the paper with Abdulla's mug shot on it and thrust it in his face.

'That's Abdulla. What about him?'

I had to hand it to him. The puzzled look on his face seemed almost genuine.

'Apparently Urvashi called him from Serenity Villa. Mind telling me why?'

'Did you try asking *him*?'

'No. He disappeared *after* delivering *your* note to me at Talyarkhan Cottage.'

He looked at me helplessly. 'I don't know how I can help you. Abdulla is a small-time broker who sometimes does assignments for me. As to why Urvashi called him, I have no idea.'

'You mean he didn't tell you when he called you right afterwards?' I thrust another printed paper in his face. The one with an item of data highlighted.

He hesitated but I don't think it came as a complete shock to him. 'Okay, fine, I'll tell you. Abdulla was negotiating with Urvashi on my behalf for dates for another project. A non-Blazar project. We were making headway but it was slow. Urvashi would regularly express her keenness but wouldn't actually sign a contract. Her dates were committed to Blazar and she was afraid to cross Kaustav, I suppose. Then I got this call from Abdulla, saying Urvashi was ready to sign. I don't know what made her change her mind.'

Maybe the showdown with Vidisha did get to her. 'You knew she was at Serenity Villa, didn't you? You went down there.'

'I did. Abdulla was out of the country so I went down there instead. But I swear I don't know how she got to Hermit Hill. All I know is, between her call to Abdulla and my going to Serenity Villa, something happened to change her mind. When I reached Serenity Villa, she was gone. Perhaps her second conversation with Kapoor had something to do with it.'

'How do you know she spoke with him again?'

'Do you think only you have access to information?'

I looked at him encouragingly. 'Try again.'

'What do you mean?' he said, surprised.

'If it was all so straightforward, why didn't you want her found?'

This time his hesitation was genuine. 'Okay, fine, I'll tell you,' he said for the second time. 'If you must know, it wasn't dates we were negotiating with Urvashi. Actually Abdulla was soliciting some information. Sensitive financial information about Blazar.'

'Why?'

'Why, because I suspected there's a lot of . . . how do I say it, a lot of their cash flow is suspect.'

'In part contributed by you, no doubt?'

He stared at me expressionlessly. 'And lots of others.'

'Why were you soliciting this information? In a way they are your partners, aren't they?' I said, although I already had an idea. That information was going into one of the several dossiers in his flat. Just friendly business practices.

'Why not? Information is power. Anyway, as I said, Urvashi disappeared before giving me the info. And I didn't want her found because I wanted to find her first. To find her and persuade her to give me the info before anyone else . . . most likely Kapoor, got to her and persuaded her not to.'

I looked at him sceptically.

'Dammit, why would I want to kill her?' he exclaimed irritably. 'In fact, there's a good chance she may have been killed because of me.'

'Excuse me?'

'Think about it. What if she had been killed to stop her from giving me the information?'

'Who would do that?'

'I don't know, but the person she spoke to after she spoke with Abdulla would be my first guess.'

I stared at him. 'No.'

He shrugged. 'If I were you I'd float the idea in any case and see what comes up. Think about it. What if she told him she'd spoken with Abdulla?'

'No, you're insane. Kaustav would never kill anyone. If anything, his call must have reassured her. That's probably why she changed her mind. How do I know you're not saying this to deflect suspicion from you?'

'You don't.'

I stopped. 'Oh, that's helpful. That really narrows down the field. And then there are the others . . . there's Neena and Chandan and Vidisha and . . . all of them had greater motivation.'

'Like what?'

I threw up my hands in agitation. 'I don't know. I don't know enough about them yet.'

'Maybe I can help?'

I exhaled. 'Okay. Begin with Baweja.'

'From what I've been able to find out, it's all pretty routine. He started his career as an actor. There was the usual period when he struggled, during which time he may not have got any offers to be the lead actor, but he made good contacts. My source says that he was always genial and had a way with people. Anyway, the acting thing didn't pan out.'

'Shocking.'

'Yes, after acting in a couple of indifferent movies in inconsequential roles, he stumbled into PR. His first job was with a television production company where he also met his wife, Jaya Mattoo.'

'*He's married?*'

'Used to be, at any rate. But check this out. About five-six years ago, she disappeared. No one ever saw her again.'

'What do you mean disappeared? She left him?'

'I don't know. Don't think so. If she left him why would no one have ever seen or heard of her again? It's like she was here one day and the next day she was gone.'

'Maybe she died?'

'Well, there were rumours about a hit-and-run accident. But if she did die, no body was found.'

'You're not making any sense. How can a person just disappear?'

'You move cities and start over.'

'It's not that easy. There are millions of things to think about: documents, bank accounts. You need to change your identity.'

'Just how difficult is it to do that?'

Not very, I had to admit. 'But it's still extreme.'

He agreed. 'People do desperate things when they are desperate.'

'She was desperate?'

'There are indications that there was domestic violence. Jaya would often have bruises on her body. When people asked her about them, she made the usual excuses that all abuse victims make—she fell down the stairs, she hit her head on a lamp post, you know the stuff.'

So, the otherwise affable PR guy was a wife basher. Who would have thought.

'Why didn't she just leave him? Or, at the very least, report him?'

'Fear, I suppose. And shame. Why do most women, educated, elite women even suffer it in silence?'

'And Neena Pundir?'

'As far as I know, she belongs to Dehra Dun and came to Mumbai about eight years ago after her graduation. Here she did a short course in mass communication and joined a film production house as a trainee. Then, about five years ago, she joined Blazar.'

'So she must be quite loyal to them.'

'To Blazar?' he said, puzzled. 'I suppose so. Why?'

I decided to tell him my theory about Baweja and Neena conspiring to do away with Urvashi. 'I don't know why, but they are working together. I know there's a connection.'

'They are not romantically involved, if that's what you're thinking.'

I stared at him. 'The thought hadn't even crossed my mind.'

'As well it shouldn't, seeing as how Neena is gay.'

I choked. *Neena was a lesbian?*

He looked surprised. 'I thought you knew!' he said. 'I thought that was why you said it hadn't crossed your mind!'

I looked at him suspiciously to see if he was yanking my chain, but he looked sincere enough. But what about her gazing at Kaustav doe-eyed? What was that all about? Was that all an act? Why? And then a thought entered my brain. What if it was to hide the real thing? What if she was really interested in *me*? What if hostility was her way of showing attraction? And at once I saw a mental picture of her grabbing the back of my head and smacking my lips in a lesbo kiss. To my surprise, I didn't find the thought all that revolting.

'Imagining her with a woman?' Deshpande asked.

I blushed. 'The thought didn't cross my mind because I thought she was sweet on . . .' I blustered, to cover my confusion.

'Kapoor? She is,' he said. Oh, he was maddening.

'But how can that be?' I whined. 'Is she bi?'

He rubbed his chin thoughtfully. 'I don't think so. Not anymore, she isn't. Of course she used to be married, briefly. But that didn't work out.'

'Again, shocking.'

It looked like he knew more but, for whatever reason, was holding his tongue.

'Go on.'

'Your turn,' he said.

'Okay, fine. Remember how I said it was a Honda Civic that was seen at Hermit Hill? It wasn't. It was a white Honda Accord.'

He kept looking at me expectantly as though waiting for me to continue.

'What? That's it,' I said.

He shook his head and sighed exaggeratedly. 'Then that's it for me, too. Say, what are you doing here?' he asked me after a moment

'Camping out for a few days till it's safe to go back.' I could've bitten my tongue the moment I said it. I saw Deshpande's eyebrows rise and hastened to explain. 'Remember I told you I was having a problem with the society?'

'Yeah, what was that all about? I wanted to ask you then but you so obviously wanted me gone.'

I reddened. 'Well, they're throwing me out.' I lied and told him about Gandhi's society vote.

'Anything I can do to help?'

'Can you gratify a dirty old man's sexual fantasies? According to Marie, he's doing it just to get me into bed.'

Deshpande looked appalled. 'Sorry, I don't do old men.'

After Deshpande left, I considered the merits of venturing out to Mayuri's place, but discarded the idea. With Chodu and his police force out looking for me, it was too risky to leave Ego. Of course, it was just as risky to go out on a date, but I was willing to hazard it for two reasons. One, I wanted to go. And two, it was unlikely that the police would spot me behind the near-black tints of Kaustav's Merc.

I glanced at my watch and saw that it was only six-fifteen. Far too early to start getting ready for my date. With nothing else to do till eight, I decided I might as well read up on Renaissance art; hopefully, I wouldn't make a complete fool of myself at dinner. I made myself a cup of coffee, plonked down in front of Em's computer and Googled 'Renaissance art'. I clicked on the Wikipedia listing and started reading. I learned that the Renaissance was a cultural movement that began in Italy in the fourteenth century and swept across all of Europe, influencing not only art, but all intellectual pursuits. For a while I was absorbed, but then it became too much and my Michelangelos started mixing with the da Vincis, and Giottos with Raphaels. Oh, screw it, I thought. At least, I now knew enough to throw around jargon like perspective, depth and light and appear passably knowledgeable on the subject.

Pankaj Chawla called just then and asked if I could meet him some place. It was almost seven p.m. so I asked him if it could wait. He insisted that it couldn't. 'It's about Baweja and Pundir,' he said.

'Then don't bother. I know pretty much everything myself.'

He was taken aback. 'Oh. So you know about their connection then?'

'There's a connection?'

'Meet me and I'll tell you.'

'Why can't you tell me on the phone?'

'Because I have to show you something.'

'But I can't step out. It's too risky. Chodu is onto me.' And I told him about my fugitive status and how I had to camp out at Ego.

'Tell you what, there's a small joint behind the Tulip Star. It's called Saarthi. You can just walk across and it's not likely that you'll meet anyone you know there.' He sounded beside himself with excitement so I reluctantly agreed.

Saarthi, I figured, was an Udupi joint. As I approached it, I realised, to my dismay, that it was, in fact, an extremely shady hooch joint. The kind where people order by the bottle, not peg. And even though it was fairly early, the place was almost full.

I stood at the entrance and scanned the crowd till my eyes rested on Chawla. A palpable hush fell on the only-male crowd and they all followed my progress to Chawla's table in awed silence.

Chawla saw me and flashed a huge smile. He already had a quarter bottle of rum in front of him. 'Just in time,' he said.

'Jeez Chawla, did you have to drag me to this place? Couldn't you have done this later, after our meeting?' I complained.

'Yes, but then I would have to pay. Besides I have an appointment later on. Of course, if you're uncomfortable, we can always walk across to the Marriott,' he said slyly.

'I'm fine,' I conceded grudgingly.

The crowd, already boring of the novelty, went back to their conversations and the noise level gradually picked up once again.

'See, I knew you'd see the merits of this place.'

'Yeah, yeah, what did you want to tell me?'

'All in good time. Order first.'

'Fine, I'll have a small Jack with Coke,' I told the hovering waiter. He stared at me uncomprehendingly.

'What?' I snapped.

'I don't think they have Jack,' Chawla said.

'Fine, get me a small of whatever whisky you've got. And soda.'

Still, he stared at me.

'What's wrong now?'

'Try a quarter bottle,' Chawla said and turned and repeated the same to the waiter. The waiter's face broke into a huge smile and he scurried away to do Chawla's bidding.

I drew out a cigarette and lit it. Another hush fell upon the room. I looked around and saw that everyone was staring at me, unabashed and unblinking.

'What are you looking at, madarchods?' I yelled at them. They reddened and looked away; some into their glasses as though they suddenly found the liquid there fascinating; some at their companions as though carrying on a conversation that had never been interrupted.

'For this, you'd better have something really good,' I threatened Chawla.

He nodded enthusiastically, gulped his drink down and reached for his portfolio bag. 'You know, after Ishraq . . . the connected filmi friend . . . told me about Chandan Baweja, I got curious about his missing wife and decided to dig a little more.'

'Why, you thought he'd killed his wife too?'

He gave me a look. 'Very funny. Anyway, I took a trip down to a cyber cafe and searched news archives for information on Jaya Mattoo.'

While he sifted through his papers, the waiter placed before me on the table a quarter bottle of some whisky called Jani Wokker, a tea glass usually found at dhabas, a decanter of flattish soda and some ice which still bore grains from the packing sack. He opened the bottle with a flourish and retreated.

I sniffed the whisky experimentally. Strong fumes hit the top of my skull, almost knocking me unconscious. I poured a small measure of it into the tea glass and added the soda. I ditched the dodgy looking ice and took a wary sip. Pure, liquid fire sloshed down my throat, taking away a sizeable part of my larynx along with it. I choked, gasped and sputtered. My eyes watered.

Meanwhile, Chawla found the document he was looking for and slapped it down on the table.

I glanced at it. 'What is it? It seems to be a missing person's notice,' I rasped, my throat feeling raw.

'Read it.'

'Jaya Mattoo. Missing: Since 16 May 2003 . . . blah blah blah. I told you, I already know about her disappearance.'

'Read the entire thing,' he commanded.

'Fine.' I stubbed out my cigarette and peered closer. 'Anyone with any information on her please contact Neena Mattoo cell number . . .'

He placed a business card next to the printout. 'Check the two numbers.'

And then the coin cropped. 'Oh my god! Pundir was Neena's married name. Neena is related to Jaya! Neena and Chandan Baweja are related!'

Chapter Twenty-three

~~~

The two numbers were identical. Like many people in the film community, Neena Pundir née Mattoo had retained the same cell number through the years.

What did this mean? So Baweja and Neena were related. But I was sure they couldn't stand each other. There was that look of dislike on Baweja's face that I'd seen when I'd first entered his office with Neena. And Neena barely tolerated him. Of course, it could all be a put-on job. Somehow, though, I didn't think they were acting. After all, Neena was probably Jaya's sister or cousin, and as such would hardly have been indulgent of her relative's repeated bashing at the hands of the husband. And yet, they were covering up for each other. I resolved to do a little more research on my own.

'Can I keep this?' I said.

'Sure. I've made a copy.'

I paid the bill and stuffed the bottle of whisky into my bag. There was no point in wasting alcohol, no matter now noxious it was.

When I returned to Ego, Em was up. But she was hardly about. She was propped up in her bed, looking peaky. I dumped my bag on a chair and offered to make her a cup of tea. She shuddered and declined. 'Tea makes me sick.'

What was with all the nausea?

'It makes me acidic if I drink tea on an empty stomach,' she explained.

I tched-tched. 'You really have to do something about your late nights. They've thrown your system out of gear.'

'And how!' She flung back the covers and stepped out.

'Whoa! Where do you think you're going?'

'To get dressed. The club will open soon.'

'Did you even hear me?'

'So, I'll pop an Alka Seltzer. Jeez Kay,' she said when I looked obstinate, 'it's acidity, not a terminal disease.'

I was halfway to the guest room when I remembered I'd left my bag in her room and retraced my steps. The door to Em's room was closed. I knocked, waited a few seconds and knocked again. No reply. Figuring she was in the loo, I turned to go when I heard muffled sounds coming from the room. Was Em . . .? I listened. The sounds were being repeated. Yup! There was no mistaking it. Em was barfing. Again.

I turned the knob and entered. The door to the bathroom was open and I rushed in. Em was bent over the toilet seat, retching. She saw me gaping at her, wiped her mouth on the back of her hand and smiled weakly. 'I guess you know now.'

So this was what she'd been hiding! And also why she'd had only club soda the other night. 'Are you . . .?'

She nodded. 'I guess that's a relief, huh? This will go away in nine months. Acidity's a lifelong problem.'

I ignored her feeble attempt at a joke. 'Does Noel know?'

She didn't answer me.

'My god, Em, you haven't told him? Why?'

Silence.

'You think he'll want nothing to do with it?'

Wretched silence.

'Is it because you haven't decided what to do with it?

Miserable silence.

I tried another tack. I put my arm around her shoulders and said, 'Look Em, you have to tell him. I'm sure you two will be able to work it out. He loves you.'

'I haven't told him because I don't know if the baby's his!' she cried and burst into tears.

'WHAT?'

'See, that's why I didn't tell you. I knew you'd be all judgemental and say, "My god, Em, how many guys have you been sleeping with,"' she said amidst sobs.

Hardly. I was in no position to be judgemental. I'd actually been going in for, 'in this day and age, how stupid does one have to be to get knocked up?' But I held my tongue and hugged her tighter. 'Oh Em, sweety!'

That, of course, gave her licence to dissolve into great heaving sobs. 'Don't tell anyone. Please. Promise me, you won't tell.'

'But . . .'

She clutched me tighter. '*Promise!*'

'Okay, okay, I promise.'

After a while she calmed down. 'I guess I better get dressed,' she said with a wan smile.

I nodded and got up to go. 'I'd better do the same.'

And then I remembered—I had nothing to wear! All my clothes were at home. What's more, Kaustav was supposed to pick me up from my place. 'Shit! Shit! Shit!'

'What happened?'

'I have nothing to wear!' I wailed.

'Excusez moi, mais you do,' she said, triumphantly. 'I forgot to tell you. I'd gone to meet Ayesha the other day. I picked up something for you.'

Em's cousin, Ayesha, is the editor of a magazine called *Trés Chic*.

Being the leading fashion magazine, *Trés Chic* regularly received samples of clothes, cosmetics, shoes, bags and belts from designers and manufacturers who wanted to be featured in the magazine. Some stuff, especially designer clothes, were grudgingly returned to the boutiques after a photo shoot, but most of it was usually whacked by the staff. Anything left over was stuffed into the storeroom. That's when Em and I usually entered the picture, humbly, for leftovers.

Em went to her wardrobe and rummaged about. A moment later she proudly held up a hideous, frilly, black-and-grey dress.

'You had a whole room to choose from and you chose this . . . this Isha-Koppikar-in-aaj-ki-raat abomination?' I said, dismayed.

'They didn't have anything else in your size. And it's not all that bad,' she said defensively.

'If you're Priyanka Chopra!'

I took out my phone and started dialling. 'Kaustav was supposed to pick me up from my apartment. I forgot to tell him . . . hello? Kaustav. There's been a change in plans. Can you pick me up from Ego? I'm . . .'

'Actually I was going to call you. Something's come up and I won't be able to keep our date. I'm terribly sorry.'

'That's all right,' I said, with a curious sense of relief. But that was just because I wouldn't have to wear that hideous dress, I told myself. Annoyed was what I felt, considering I'd spent the better part of the evening reading up on Renaissance art. *That* turned out to be a waste of time.

'I'll try and drop in later at Ego, if that's okay?'

I mumbled yes.

'And if I can't, I promise I'll make it up to you.'

'Okay.' I hung up and said, 'That was Kaustav. He won't be able to make it tonight.'

Em nodded sympathetically. 'Tell you what, why don't you come to the club with me? I could use your help.'

I declined, saying I had work to catch up on. 'I may drop in a little later,' I added.

I sat in front of Em's computer once again and entered 'Jaya Mattoo' in the search engine. I was about to hit go when I stopped. I added +Baweja+Neena and pressed enter.

The first listing read: '. . . husband alleges that he has witnesses who saw a car run over Jaya Mattoo at the Indian Oil crossing in Andheri West on the night of 16 May 2003.'

I clicked on cached and scrolled down the page till I saw the terms Mattoo and Baweja highlighted. I started reading. After I'd read the story, I noticed a link on the page that said 'similar pages'. I clicked on that. There was a lot of material on Jaya Mattoo and most of it made for very interesting reading. An hour, three coffees and four cigarettes later, I sat back cross-eyed and exhausted but quite a lot wiser about Jaya Mattoo's disappearance.

Apparently, on 16 May 2003, Jaya Mattoo and a couple of colleagues had stepped into TGIF after work. After a couple of drinks, they decided to head to their respective homes. It was around two in the morning and there were no auto-rickshaws around, so they decided to walk a bit till they found one. They walked till the Indian Oil crossing, where Jaya Mattoo turned right, towards Four Bungalows. Her two colleagues continued straight as they lived in Santa Cruz and Bandra respectively.

That was the last time Jaya Mattoo was seen. Now, people in media routinely work late so her absence from home at night went unnoticed. But when she still hadn't returned the next morning, Chandan Baweja and Neena Pundir got anxious. They spoke to her colleagues who assured them that they had left her at the Indian Oil crossing. Worried, Baweja and Neena went to the police station to register a missing person's complaint. But the police didn't take the case seriously. In his press interview, ACP Ravi Menon defended their inaction saying it was required that a person be missing for at least seventy-two hours before the police could register a complaint. Moreover, he said, they felt there was a possibility that Jaya Mattoo had taken off on her own. This theory was based on the testimony of Jaya's colleagues, who both mentioned that she had seemed depressed in the pub. The colleagues also mentioned their suspicions that Jaya was being physically abused by her husband.

Tiredly, I clicked on another newspaper report; this one was an interview with Neena. Complaining about police apathy, Neena said Chandan and she weren't convinced that Jaya had taken off on her own, and had started doing some digging on their own. During their investigations, they'd talked to the pavement dwellers at the Indian Oil crossing, who all reported seeing a woman matching Jaya Mattoo's description being run over by a foreign car. According to them, the driver and her companion had picked up the bleeding victim, put her in the car and driven off in the direction of Versova.

Next, Neena and Baweja made the rounds of all the hospitals, figuring that the driver had taken Jaya to one, but to no avail. So they came back and spoke to the pavement dwellers again for more details of the accident. All the pavement dwellers were vague on the make of the car, with one exception. One man remembered the car and the number vividly. He had even made a note of it. Neena said, at their exhorting, the police investigated the information, but refused to act on it. The reason, they cited, was that the witness was a notorious drunk and a drug addict, and therefore unreliable.

I scanned the rest of the interview. All this was very interesting, but I couldn't see how this was linked with Urvashi's murder. And then I spotted it. The report said that the number belonged to a black Merc, registered in the name of some small-time starlet, Urvashi.

Bingo.

This was enough to establish that Neena Pundir and Chandan

Baweja had a motive for a bout of vigilante justice, but I was puzzled about several things. One, what had happened to Jaya Mattoo? Was her body ever found? Two, with such acrimony going around, how did they all survive at Blazar together? And three, shouldn't this also have been obvious to Chodu as well?

After this, I was too restless to sit by myself and decided to go down to the club. I went back to my room and studied my appearance in the mirror. My clothes were crumpled and my hair matted. I decided I looked like a train wreck.

There was nothing much I could do about my clothes, but at least I could ensure that I smelled better. I stripped off my clothes and stepped into the shower. The water was nice and hot and I let it wash over me for a minute. Then I turned off the shower and vigorously soaped myself. While rinsing off the soap, I aimed the water jet between my legs and a familiar tingling sensation shot through my loins. I considered abusing the shower head but then guiltily turned off the jet. If Jennifer Aniston could champion three-minute showers in the west, I, living in a developing country, could do without hydro-eroticism.

I dressed in the same clothes, and applied some kajal and lip gloss. I fluffed up my hair and went down to the club. Em spotted me and came over. As she walked across, my eyes kept slipping down to her tummy.

'For 'aiven's sake, eet won't show for anozer three months,' she said impatiently.

'I know. It's just that I've known you since we were kids. And now you're going to be a mommy. It's all very . . .' I stopped, stuck for the right word.

'Tail me about eet,' she said sourly.

'So whose is it?' I asked her casually.

A middle-aged man, apparently a regular, walked past us.

"Ey, Mr Patel, 'OW ARE YOU?' Em greeted him rather

aggressively. Mr Patel looked startled, muttered a hasty hi and scampered away.

'Em?'

'Looks like Louis ees 'aving some trouble. You'll be all right?' she said, and practically ran from there.

Fine, so she didn't want to tell me. Like I cared.

I was wandering around when I spotted Deshpande sitting in a private booth with . . . no, it couldn't be! Smeer Khan. In the flesh. Without wasting another second, I made a beeline for the booth. They were engaged in a serious discussion and didn't see me approach.

I was about to greet them gaily when I overheard Smeer Khan say, 'Smeer told you man, he can't tell you that. He'll be in deep shit.'

'You'll be in deeper shit if you don't. *This is a murder investigation!*'

I swerved towards the neighbouring booth and slid next to a lone, middle-aged, uncle-type guy nursing a drink.

'Hi,' I said with a friendly smile. 'Mind if sit?'

At first, the reaction to my greeting was a startled look. A few furtive glances later, he made up his mind and sidled closer. He sat there rigidly, bolstering his confidence and mapping his next move. This should have sent alarm bells screaming in my head, but I was too busy listening in on the conversation next door.

'That has nothing to do with Smeer,' Khan said.

The uncle's hand shot out and came to rest next to my thigh.

'How can you be so sure?' Deshpande said. 'Look, whether you're involved or not, you're going to be questioned. Everybody's going to be questioned.'

The hand climbed up my thigh. I absently swatted at it. The hand's progress was checked, but only momentarily. It fell back, regrouped and advanced again.

'Nuh-uh. The police have nothing on him.'

'Besides the fact that Hermit Hill belongs to you?'

I gasped. Pieces started falling into place. The only two things that didn't make sense were Urvashi's distress over Kaustav's ambivalence about his divorce and Sanj's interlude with Smeer. Unless Smeer was bi. I waited to hear more.

The uncle looked pleased. 'You like that?' he slurred.

'Once they find out, they'll come to you for fingerprints and then . . . oh god, they've done that already, haven't they?' Deshpande said.

'So what if they have? They took everyone's fingerprints.' *So it was routine*, I thought in relief.

'And even if Smeer's prints are all over the place, it does not prove anything. Smeer hasn't been there in weeks. Besides he has an alibi for the night of the 19th, the night this . . . thing took place,' Khan said after a moment's silence.

'You like that, do you?' the uncle slurred once more, and emboldened by the lack of protest from my side, plunged his hand between my legs.

I yanked his hand off, but because I was trying to listen in, refrained from issuing a vocal reprimand. Perhaps thinking I was just being coy, he tried his luck again, latching onto my boobs this time. Annoyed, I glanced around and caught Louis's eye. He was doubled over with laughter and showed no inclination of coming to my rescue. I grabbed the hand once more and held on to it to stop it from wandering. This time I coupled it with a warning, 'Listen, uncle, you do that once more and I'll yank your arm off.'

Unfortunately, in all this, I missed what Smeer said next. When I tuned in again, Deshpande was saying, 'Try again. It's not so much that Louis saw you till late that night as much as he assumed you were there. It was a busy night and he lost track of you.'

'That doesn't mean . . .' Smeer started to say.

'I checked with the valet,' Deshpande interjected. 'Your car clocked out at ten.'

Silence.

'Mind telling me where you were?'

'Smeer can't.'

'Can't or won't? If you're worried about the implications for your career or otherwise, let me tell you, if you're in jail, your career is pretty much finished anyway.'

'Look, man, twy and understand. Smeer was with ... with somebody.'

'Then you won't mind giving me her name?'

'Look man, dwop it. It's complicated.'

My hand went slack, and the uncle, taking advantage, removed his hand from my grip. He grabbed my boob and gave it a painful squeeze.

'Ow! Ow! Ow!'

This alerted the duo next door and Deshpande's head popped up over the partition, above me. Smeer's head followed. They took in the situation and, after the initial shock, Deshpande's lips started twitching.

Why, god, why did he always have to be around whenever I was making an ass of myself?

Inwardly cringing with mortification, I mustered all the dignity I could, stood up and adjusted my clothes.

Deshpande, like always, was dressed in snug-but-comfortable jeans and a tee with a shirt thrown over it. He looked and smelled minty fresh, sending low intensity tremors inside my stomach. *What are you doing? He's dangerous!* But that realisation only served to heighten his attraction. Odd. I didn't think I went for bad boys.

Smeer's eyes screwed up in concentration as he tried to remember where we'd met. 'The dancer! You're the dancer fwom the *Wansom* shoot! What are you doing here?'

Deshpande looked interested. As did the inebriated uncle.

'I'm not!' I said. 'I mean, I'm not a dancer.' The hand made a tentative move again. I slapped it away and wagged a finger at the uncle. 'Don't even think about it,' I admonished him and scuttled out of the booth.

'So, what, you're stalking Smeer now?' Smeer asked.

'You're stalking Sameer?' Deshpande sounded more outraged than Khan.

'I am not!'

'She *is* stalking Smeer. She cwashed the *Wansom* shoot also,' Khan told him.

Deshpande shook his head reprovingly. 'Not done, Coomaar.'

'Quit fooling around, Deshpande.'

'I'm afraid I'm going to need more details,' he said. The bastard was enjoying himself vastly.

'Wait,' Khan said, 'Smeer'll have her wemoved.' He looked up, caught Louis's eye and gestured for him to come and take me away.

Louis materialised. Of course, he did. Now that he had an excuse to get rid of me.

I ate crow and said to Deshpande, 'Look, I just wanted to talk to Smeer Khan and, with his security, it was impossible to get close to him. And then Angel thought I was a dancer. And I thought here was a good opportunity to get close to Smeer. So . . .' I shrugged and stopped.

Louis cleared his throat. 'You called for me?' he said. He looked at Smeer and then Deshpande.

I could see Deshpande was having difficulty controlling his laughter. Nevertheless, he took pity on me. His lips twitching, he said, 'No Louis. Everything's fine.'

'No, it's not,' Khan protested.

'I'll handle it,' Deshpande said to the both of them.

Louis looked disappointed, but retreated. Khan, too, subsided, muttering angrily to himself.

Deshpande said, 'Sam, this is Katie Kumar. She's a private investigator. Not a stalker. Or dancer.'

Khan looked from Deshpande to me, trying to make up his mind. Finally, he said, 'Weally? Smeer *thought* she was too fat.'

'Is she?' Deshpande mused, running an appraising eye over me. 'I don't think so. Voluptuous maybe, not fat.' He looked to Khan for confirmation.

This was Khan's cue to run an eye over me. 'In bed, maybe. She's too fat to be a dancer. You should have seen her in that bikini.'

Deshpande looked intrigued. I cleared my throat noisily. Both men looked at me enquiringly.

'If you've finished dissecting me anatomically can we talk?' I said.

'Waiiit. Let me imagine you in the gold bikini.'

'It was *red!*'

'Not in here, it isn't,' he quipped, tapping his forehead.

'Smeer, if you don't mind, can I ask you something?' I said peaceably, ignoring Deshpande.

'About what?' Khan asked.

'About Hermit Hill. I couldn't help but overhear your conversation,' I said, studiously avoiding Deshpande's sardonic gaze. 'I understand the property belongs to you? Any idea how Urvashi got there?'

'Oh, man, don't be such a buzz-kill, man!' he said, dismayed.

'Come on man, she's a friend. Help her out. She deserves a break,' Deshpande said.

'Fine,' he said. 'Smeer has no idea how Urvashi got there. He hasn't been there in weeks. He hardly goes there anyway. And in case you are wondering, he didn't kill her. He had no reason to.'

'But Smeer, Hermit Hill wasn't broken into,' I pointed out. 'How do you explain that?'

He professed helplessness. 'He can't.'

'Is it because she had a key?' What I was going to say next was tricky, since it was pure conjecture. I licked my lips. 'She did, didn't she? She's had it for a while. You gave it to her. I was told that you pretended to hate her, that in fact you had feelings for her, and this façade of dislike was just a way of getting Urvashi's attention. And it worked. Urvashi reciprocated your feelings and you two were seeing each other on the sly. You continued the pretence though, to throw Kaustav off track.'

Ignoring Smeer's protests ('That's widiculous!'), I continued. 'When the publicity stunt was planned, even though it was supposed to be a secret, word leaked out. Everyone on the set knew something was afoot. And when Urvashi disappeared from Serenity Villa, you figured she must have gone to Hermit Hill. Or maybe she planned it with you in advance. I don't know how, but you knew. Maybe she made a call to you from somewhere. Anyway, you went to Hermit Hill.'

'You can't believe her!' Smeer said to Deshpande.

Deshpande hesitated. 'Actually it doesn't make sense. If Urvashi reciprocated Sameer's feelings, why was she so upset about Kaustav not leaving Vidisha?'

'That puzzles me too. And the only thing I can think of is that for her it was just a fling. That she actually loved Kaustav and wanted to marry him. Wanted to be Mrs Kaustav Kapoor at any rate.'

'You can't believe her!' Smeer repeated plaintively to Deshpande.

But before Deshpande could speak, I said, 'You don't have to believe me. There's evidence. When I first went there, I noticed another set of tyre tracks next to Urvashi's Merc. I have a picture which I'm bound to hand over to the police, or they'll take my licence. I'm sure they can compare the picture with the tyres of your Porsche,' I lied.

'They can't pwove they're fwom Smeer's car,' Smeer scoffed.

'They don't have to.' And then I went for the jugular. 'Also, at Hermit Hill, I found a pillowcase. A black satin pillowcase. The forensic lab found semen on it. And it isn't Kaustav's.'

Silence. Moisture glistened on Smeer's upper lip. 'Okay fine, Smeer admits he went to Hermit Hill. But that was on the 18th. You've got to believe him. He didn't kill Urvashi,' Smeer said.

'I didn't say you did,' I said. 'You couldn't have. You were with Sanj on 19th night.'

Chapter Twenty-four

'Who's Sanj?' Deshpande asked.

'He's a transvestite,' I said.

Deshpande stared at me. 'A transvestite.' He looked at Smeer and asked, 'Is it true?'

'Leave it, bro,' Khan said. *He would.*

Just then Rene, one of the hostesses at Ego, walked past. 'Wene, babe,' Khan said. 'Come here. You're ignoring Smeer shamefully.'

Rene made a face. 'Now you remember Rene. What about the other night? You didn't look at me once!'

'Babe, Smeer was preoccupied. Trouble at work.'

'Trouble at work,' she repeated and flounced off.

'Attitude from escorts; what has the world come to?' Smeer said in wonder.

Deshpande changed the subject. 'By the way, did you know Sameer Khan has recently signed a Hollywood project?'

'I read about it. It was on the 20th, wasn't it? Congratulations,' I said. 'I believe you've been trying for a really long time.'

Before Khan could say anything Deshpande butted in. 'Yes, how did that happen? How did you convince Kapoor to release you?'

'Smeer just reasoned with him,' Khan said.

'Hmmm . . . must be some persuasion you used.'

Deshpande had said it innocently enough. So, why had Khan's eyes suddenly narrowed? Become watchful? Or was I reading too much into it?

'Speaking of which,' Khan said, draining his glass, 'Smeer's gotta go study the script.'

Deshpande stood up with Khan. 'I'll walk with you outside,' he said. To me he said, 'Don't go anywhere. I'll be back. I want to talk to you.'

'Katie wouldn't dweam of it.'

A tiny smile escaped his lips.

I decided to have a smoke in the garden outside. I chose a shadowy spot, took out a ciggie and lit it. I was halfway through the cigarette when the door slid open and two women spilled out. One of them, I saw, was Vidisha Kapoor. Vidisha said something to the other one and they both giggled. And then, before my very eyes, they locked lips!

They seemed not to have noticed that anyone else was about. Not that it would have made that much of a difference. They were clearly drunk out of their wits.

Soon, they were fully at it. There was a lot of slurping, coupled with some heavy-duty petting. Vidisha's hand had travelled up the other girl's skirt. She must have liked what Vidisha was doing there because she was moaning her head off. I wondered if they would do it right there. What 'it' was I couldn't imagine. Oral sex? Sadly, I never got a chance to find out. The two women decided that they had possibly gone as far as PDA norms allowed. Giggling drunkenly, they lurched back inside.

I wondered what it meant. Was Vidisha gay or was that just drunken tomfoolery? Did Deshpande mean Vidisha when he made that cryptic remark about Neena Pundir being sweet on Kapoor? And was Baweja referring to this when he warned me not to believe anything Neena Pundir said as she was partisan?

I suddenly remembered Vidisha standing close to me and fiddling with my hair the night I'd gone to the Kapoor residence. Omigod! While I'd been busy picturing scenarios with Neena, Vidisha had been the one hitting on me! I must have made some kind of a noise because from somewhere to my right, I heard a man say, 'Tell me about it. You should have seen them on Saturday.'

Saturday!

I squinted in the dark. About ten feet away from me stood Mr Patel, the man Em had greeted earlier. Like me, he had come out for a smoke.

I strode up to him. 'Did you say Saturday?'

He nodded.

'You saw her? The taller one?'

'Er . . . yes . . .'

'On this Saturday? The 19th?'

He licked his lips. 'Yes. At least I think it was Saturday. Or maybe it was Friday . . . I come here pretty often so I forget . . .'

'Yeah, yeah. Think. Was it was Friday or Saturday?'

He thought. 'Yes I'm sure it was Saturday. I know because Vinyl Vanitha was on that night.'

I nodded at him and left. On the way inside, I asked Louis, 'Which day was Vinyl Vanitha on?'

'Friday and Saturday.'

Blast.

Vidisha and her companion must have been making out at the door, because as soon as I opened it, they tumbled out. Vidisha fixed her unfocussed eyes on me. 'Oh, you're here,' she said in some confusion.

'Why wouldn't I be?' I said.

'But I thought . . . You didn't . . .?' Then who was . . .?' And then she got a peculiar look in her eye suggestive of some cruel irony. She started laughing raucously, cackling actually. That, coupled with the copious amounts of alcohol she'd had, caused her to stumble. I grabbed her shoulders to steady her.

'What are you talking about?'

She gazed at me, unseeing. 'Talking about?' Her face brightened. 'Ah, yes.' She leaned closer and beckoned me to do the same. Right. Like I was going to risk her giving me a big smooch. 'I'm drunk,' she giggled. 'You think I look drunk?'

'You're fine,' I said shortly. 'Now why were you surprised to see me?'

'I thought you were a bitch,' she said, conspiratorially. 'I thought you were out to get my husb . . . hub . . . sand.'

I gritted my teeth. 'You said something like, "then who was . . .?" Who were you talking about?'

'You?' she said hopefully.

'Come on Vee,' her companion staggered up to us and pouted.

'Gotta go,' Vidisha said with a beatific smile. 'Call me. We must have lunch.'

She tottered away, leaving me behind with my doubts. All her disjointed half-sentences led me to think she was talking about Kaustav and another woman. Tonight. Was that why he'd cancelled on me? Because of another woman?

The club was packed and the night was well underway. Exotic Esther was grinding sensually around a pole. People were in high spirits as they either celebrated something, or simply unwound after a hard day's work. All in all it was a gay atmosphere. And I felt like shit.

My self-esteem at an all-time low, I swung to the bar and spent the next half hour productively, chasing beer with tequila. Then I stumbled to the elevator. The second floor was dark and as I alighted from the lift, someone grabbed me. Before my brain even processed the thought, *Thief! Rapist!*, he took me in his arms and planted the sweetest, gentlest kiss on my lips. *Kaustav!*

'She was wrong. You came!' I murmured.

He mumbled something that sounded like, 'Of course, I said I would,' and pulled me closer. My hands went around his neck and nuzzled the nape of his neck. *His hair seems longer*, I thought hazily, as his tongue parted my lips. I clung to him and kissed him back with equal passion. I whimpered and a tiny moan escaped me.

We lurched into the living room. Next thing I knew, I was lying down on the carpet and he was on top of me. For a while, the only sounds to be heard were the rustle of clothes as we feverishly undressed each other, and our heavy breathing. His fingers fumbled with the hook of my bra. He bit back a curse and moved to switch on the lamp.

Rather hazily, I thought that the man on top of me, looking at me with eyes full of desire, didn't look like Kaustav at all. In fact, he looked like . . . like Deshpande! And he was naked! Seeing the confusion in my eyes, he stopped. He stared at me and I stared at him. Then he slowly, deliberately, lowered his mouth. His tongue flicked my lips questioningly as if to ask if he could go ahead. And I realised, it didn't feel bad at all. It actually felt quite good.

I decided to go with the flow. He killed the lamp. He ran his fingers through my hair and grabbed my head. He kissed me insistently, only breaking off when one of us threatened to pass out for lack of air. I could feel his erection pressing against my legs and felt an answering rush of moistness.

His hand cupped my breast while he nuzzled my nipple with his mouth. He teased me until I could stand it no more. I whimpered in protest but he crushed it with a kiss. I thrust my breasts into his face. With a low laugh he relented and took the throbbing nipple into his mouth.

His other hand went down, between my legs, and found the sensitive spot. His fingers set up a rhythmic massage till I was ready to explode. He stopped and I heard something tear. There was a brief lull and then he was back. Still kissing me, he removed his hand and snuck it under my hips. I let out a groan as he entered me with one quick, efficient thrust. And then, suddenly, we were going at it, like primeval animals, till we both burst into a shuddering climax.

Something awoke me the next morning. Was that the doorbell? For a moment I lay still, wrapped in a warm post-coital glow, trying to take in my surroundings. All was quiet outside and going by the quality of light pouring in, it was relatively early. I glanced up at the wall clock. *The clock was gone!* Oh no, it wasn't. It was just on a different wall. Why was it there? Nothing looked familiar and I felt a mild sense of panic.

I glanced around me. Why was I looking up at the underside of a coffee table? I frowned in confusion. Was I on the floor? Covered by a duvet? And I was naked! My eyes narrowed and then widened as dim recollections surfaced. I felt dread seep into my body. No, it couldn't be!

I jackknifed up, wrapped the duvet around me and ran to Em's room. She was stretched out on the bed, fast asleep. *Dear god, had she seen me when she came in? How much had she seen?* Then the doorbell rang again shrilly. The suddenness of the sound made my racing heart go still with shock for a moment. I padded across to the door. I opened it and gaped in surprise.

Chodu stood leaning against the wall. 'Isn't it about time you and I had a chat?' he said.

I stared at him in dismay. But the bright side was that his arrival drove all memories of 'the nasty' with Deshpande out of my mind.

'You've been very bad,' he chided me in a tone one usually employs with five-year-olds.

I licked my suddenly dry lips. 'I can explain.'

He nodded and detached himself from the wall. 'Tell your story walking. We're going for a ride.'

Yeah right. Like I didn't know what that meant. I might as well jump off a cliff. 'Now wait just a minute. I'm not going anywhere with you! Do you have a warrant?'

He looked aghast. 'Why do I need a warrant to take you to a hospital?'

'If you're going to arrest me, I demand . . . a hospital?'

He nodded. 'A hospital.'

'You're not taking me to jail?'

'Who said anything about jail?'

I looked at him suspiciously. Was he lying? Why would he say he was taking me to a hospital though? Unless! Unless, it was a *mental* hospital. Oh, so that was what was going on. He didn't get a warrant for my arrest so was doing the next best thing. He was getting me committed. After all, there were more places than one to lock people up. And with my recent history, he could easily do it too.

'What kind of hospital?'

'Lilavati.'

'Why Lilavati?'

'You'll find out soon enough.'

Why was he looking at me like that? Did Lilavati have a mental ward? Shit, why couldn't I have paid more attention the two times I'd visited people there?

'Fine. But let me tell you, you'll never get any doctor to agree. I've got certificates testifying to my progress . . . towards complete normalcy.' I added the bit about normalcy, just in case he thought I was talking about progress towards insanity.

'I won't even bother trying to understand what you're talking about,' he said.

I nodded resignedly. 'Fine, let me get dressed. But I want to call Dr Sharma first.' Dr Vanita Sharma was my therapist.

'You can call whomever you want later.'

Moments later, I stepped outside and shut the door behind me. On the way down, I asked him, 'How did you find out where I was anyway?'

The elevator stopped and we emerged on the ground floor.

There, dressed in his usual jeans and a tee and leaning against his Merc, stood Deshpande. I stared at him dumbstruck. *Should I be mortified? Should I be angry?* For god's sake, how was I supposed to react? I looked into his eyes for some kind of clue, but he looked completely nonchalant. I was assailed by uncertainties. Had it happened? Or was it just a dream? And then, 'You! You told him!' I raged.

'Yes. Should I not have?' he asked, puzzled.

'What do you think, you moron?'

To his credit he did look genuinely dismayed. 'I didn't know you were hiding from him. You said you were having problems with your society!'

I wasn't about to be pacified so easily and poured hot coal over him with my eyes. My fiery response had the desired effect and he hastily bit back whatever he was going to say next, even opting to follow us to Lilavati in his car, in spite of Chodu's invitation to join us in his Jeep.

'Why are we going to Lilavati?' I asked Chodu once we were on our way.

'To see a patient who happens to be a suspect in one of our cases,' he said, offering me a cigarette.

I accepted it gratefully. 'Why me?' I asked, surprised.

'You'll know,' Chodu said after a brief hesitation. Curiouser and curiouser.

'By the way, you do know Deshpande is in up to his neck in this Urvashi thing?'

He nodded.

'He knew Urvashi was at Serenity Villa. He even went down there on the 17th.'

'Yes.'

'Because I just figured with you cosying up to him, you might not know the full picture. That he might even be our murderer?'

'He's not. He has an alibi for the 19th.'

'Oh, one of his floosies?'

He gave me a look but didn't elaborate.

Why was he protecting Deshpande? 'Omigod! It's you. You two are having an affair. You were with him!'

'*What?*'

'Wow, sleeping with the enemy,' I said.

'Don't be ridiculous! Stop it.'

'No, really, tell me.'

'I said, stop it,' he repeated in a voice that brooked no argument.

At Lilavati, he asked me to wait a little distance away while Deshpande and he spoke to the receptionist. I was starting to feel a little uneasy. I've never been a great fan of hospitals and the pervasive smell of formaldehyde or whatever antiseptic they use makes me queasy. On top of that, all this cloak-and-dagger stuff was really starting to give me a sinking feeling in the pit of my stomach.

A couple of minutes later, after the formalities had been completed, they came back and escorted me into the already crowded elevator.

'Fifteen,' Chodu told the elevator operator.

It was a long ride to the fifteenth floor, made longer by the frequent interruptions as the elevator stopped at almost all the floors on the way. Throughout the ride, both men studiously avoided my eyes. By the time we emerged onto the fifteenth floor and walked over to room number 1514, my uneasiness had given way to full-blown dread.

I walked in and saw a man lying on the bed, looking as pale and lifeless as the sheets he was lying on. My eyes travelled to his face and stopped in shock. For what seemed like the longest time, but was only a second or so I'm sure, everything went blank. Sounds faded away to barely audible levels. The sterile white of the hospital grew darker and darker. I barely registered Ani's face and then all noise stopped and everything went black.

Chapter Twenty-five

~∂∘≈~

When I came to, I was lying in Deshpande's arms in the hospital corridor. He was sponging my face with what looked like a tender expression on his face. I struggled momentarily with my confusion. Then it all came back and I sat up straight.

'Ani!'

Deshpande put his hand on my arm. 'You've had a great shock.'

I brushed his arm aside. 'What's fucking wrong with you? Ani's lying there ... all ... and you ...' My breath caught on a sob.

I stood up suddenly and at once another wave of blackness hit me. I held the wall for support and finally sat down, holding my head in my hands. Tears started streaming down my face. I felt, rather than saw, Chodu and Deshpande exchange glances.

Someone put his hand on my shoulder. I looked up.

'He's going to be all right,' Deshpande said. 'He's lost a lot of blood but he will be okay.'

Things started falling in place. Chodu's remarks about visiting a suspect in hospital, Prado's conversations on the phone, his concern for a suspect in a case. It was Ani he had been talking about.

'What happened?' I asked dully, wiping my tears.

Chodu looked at me for a moment. 'He was stabbed in the back—his kidney was injured. Someone found him in an alley and called us. By the time we found him, he'd lost a dangerous amount of blood.'

'He was mugged?'

Chodu shook his head. 'Nothing seems missing.'

'What does Ani say?'

'We haven't spoken to him. He hasn't recovered consciousness yet.'

'But who would want to kill Ani? And why?' I cried.

'That's what we want you to tell us,' Chodu said.

I looked at him in confusion. 'Me? Why? Oh, wait a minute. You don't think I did it?'

I looked at Chodu and from him to Deshpande. Neither answered me.

'But why would I want to kill him?' I said, panic-stricken.

'Why not? It fits. You were having an affair with him, weren't you?'

My eyes shot to Deshpande's, silently accusing.

'He didn't tell us,' Chodu said.

'That's right,' Deshpande said defensively. 'I didn't even know about the Sweety Nair homicide, let alone its connection to you. I know now, of course.'

'Then how . . .?'

'After Sweety Nair's death, we were going through Aniruddh Nair's personal details. Solanki was looking into the phone records. There was one number that kept cropping up. When she dialled the number it was switched off. But the company records showed that the number belonged to the commissioner's wife. So, naturally she was a bit cautious. And then I got exasperated and decided to find out what was going on. Imagine my surprise when I dialled the number from my cellphone and my phone book threw up your name! Apparently there was a glitch in the phone company's database because of which the error happened.'

I decided not to enlighten him about the true cause of the glitch. Although, I could have. As it was, I was staring at a homicide charge. A little database fraud added to it would hardly make that much of a difference.

'We went down to your society to talk to you. You weren't there, so we spoke to some of your neighbours. Two of them confirmed that you and Ani were having an affair. They also said they witnessed a fight between you and a woman who matched Sweety Nair's description.' He paused and fixed a pair of penetrating eyes on me. 'So what happened? Sweety Nair found out about you two so you both decided to do away with her? And then later you and Aniruddh Nair had a falling out? Maybe he got jittery and wanted to come forward and confess? So you decided to kill him? Is that what happened?'

I have to admit that for a moment I did think of fibbing my way out of the situation, but decided to gamble on the truth. I told Chodu everything: how I'd met Ani, my fight with Sweety, how she vanished with Ani's BMW for a few days. 'She returned on the 21st, in the morning, just as Ani was about to leave for work. At least, that's what he told me after Sweety was . . . after she was . . . Apparently she told him that she had gone to her parents' place outside Bombay.'

'Mumbai,' Chodu corrected automatically.

'. . . She told him she wanted to try and work things out, and he agreed. He also told me that she had banged up his Beemer pretty badly.'

I told them about Chawla, about his alleged mystery caller and how he'd tried to blackmail us.

'So you think the mystery caller had some kind of a vendetta against the Nairs?' Chodu asked after I'd finished.

'*Alleged* caller. After all, we only have Chawla's word that there was indeed someone who asked him to tail Sweety. Maybe *he* attacked Ani,' I said.

'Him? Nah! He's seems like a small-time blackmailer. I can't picture him as the killer,' Chodu said.

'A small-time blackmailer, no; but an honest, upright citizen, in a heartbeat!' I said, outraged.

'When that citizen has a history like yours, yes,' Chodu said. 'Chawla ... Chawla, where have I heard the name again?' he mused aloud.

He reached for a file, flipped it open and leafed through the pages. 'Here it is. A call came in on 22nd morning from an anonymous caller. The caller said a suspicious-looking person was seen hanging around the vicinity of the Nair residence. She gave a description of a man and that of his car, as well as the car registration number which was traced to a Pankaj Chawla.'

'See?' I said.

'Chawla could've been hanging around to keep tabs on Sweety Nair. After all, that's what his client had asked him to do,' Chodu argued.

I was suddenly tired of all this. 'I'd like to see Ani now,' I said and without waiting for a response, went in.

He looked so young, and helpless, lying there like a little boy. I felt a surge of love. I sat by his side for the longest time, telling him how much I loved him, recounting all the good times we'd had, and that we would have again when he was all better. I knew he was unconscious but I didn't care. I knew he could hear me.

I only stood up when the doctor came in for an examination.

'Is ... will he be all right?' I asked.

The doctor nodded. 'He's lost a lot of blood and one of his kidneys is completely useless, but he'll survive.'

Visiting hours were over, the accompanying nurse said, so I left the room. Deshpande was waiting for me outside. Of Chodu, there was no sign.

'Chodankar had to go away,' Deshpande said. 'Another homicide.' Then he added on a more solicitous note, 'Are you okay?'

I nodded. 'Visiting hours are over. I think I'll head home,' I said.

He jumped to his feet. 'I'll drop you.'

'You don't have to drop me. I'll just catch a rick,' I said somewhat belatedly when we were already inside his car.

'It's all right. I don't have anything particular to do.'

'Good—since you've already done so much.'

Deshpande's neck snapped up and he looked at me sharply. 'What's that supposed to mean? If you're still carping on about my telling Chodankar . . .'

'Let's just drop it, okay?'

'Fine with me.'

We both lapsed into an uncomfortable silence. My preoccupation with Ani had wiped all thoughts of the previous night's events from my mind, but it all came flooding back now. Had it been a dream or had it actually happened? I stole glances at Deshpande from time to time, but his body language didn't betray anything.

Presently we arrived at Ego. Deshpande stopped the car, engaged the hand brake and turned around to face me squarely.

'Why don't you just come out and say it,' he said quietly. 'You know you're dying to.'

'I . . . well, it's just that . . . I had the strangest dream last night,' I said in conciliatory tones. 'I mean I think it was dream but . . .'

'So much fretting over a dream?'

'That's just it. The damndest thing is it felt real . . . like it was actually happening.'

He smiled enigmatically.

'What? Why are you smiling like that?'

'Like what?' he asked innocently.

'In that oily fashion. Like you know what I'm going to say.'

'I do. You're going to tell me we made wonderful love.'

'How did you . . .?'

He shrugged. 'That's what women usually say to me. When they begin telling me about "strange dreams" that they've had,' he said.

'Really?'

'Really. But do go on,' he said. 'Was it as good for you?'

'Never mind,' I snapped at him.

I got out of the car and slammed the door shut. Deshpande responded by laughing and pulling away with a screech. Later, I remembered his remark and wondered what he'd meant by 'as good for you'. But by then it was too late.

On entering Em's apartment, the first thing I saw was the living room carpet and images of my alleged love-making with Deshpande flashed before my eyes. I looked away angrily. Em emerged from her room just then. As soon as she saw me she flew at me and gathered me in a hug. 'Oh honey, I heard. I'm so sorry.'

She hadn't seen me last night, I decided. Or had she indeed seen me but her concern outweighed her outrage for the time being? Which reminded me, 'Who told you?' I asked, surprised.

She waved her hands dismissively. 'It doesn't matter. The important thing is how you're holding up.'

I walked into the guest room and started gathering my stuff. 'I'm fine.'

'What are you doing?' Em asked from the doorway.

'Packing. The problem with Chodu is gone so there's really no need for me to impose on you any further,' I said.

She reacted to my brusqueness by wringing her hands agitatedly. 'Who said anything about imposing? Honey, you have to stay. Your parents are away too. You need me at this time.'

Wordlessly, I slung my satchel over my shoulder and walked out.

'It's Tejas.'

I stopped by the door. For some absurd reason my heart started hammering against my chest. I took in a couple of deep breaths and turned around. 'What about him?' I asked carefully.

'He's my boyfriend,' she said.

If I was honest with myself, it wasn't really such a shock—somewhere deep down I'd known.

How else would she have known I was working on the Urvashi case if she wasn't the one at Deshpande's the night I'd impulsively decided to visit him? How else could he know about Em's latest fetish for jasmine tea? I hadn't actually said that the only flavour available was jasmine. And then another dreadful thought entered my brain. Till now I had only been worried about censure over my shameless behaviour. The fact that Deshpnade was her boyfriend lent a whole new complexion to the episode. I stole a look at her but nothing in her demeanour suggested that she had seen anything untoward. But how could that be? Unless she stumbled straight into her room. It was possible to miss us in the dark. The other explanation was that Deshpande had left soon after our 'alleged love-making'.

'I'm sorry I didn't tell you—but I knew you'd give me grief! I would have reacted the same way, if you'd told me you were dating a guy I hated.'

True. Em and I had a pact never to date a guy the other one didn't like. We'd said that it was like a betrayal. And in Deshpande's case, considering how he'd sabotaged my divorce case, it actually was. How was she to know things had changed since then? No wonder she'd been appalled when I'd kissed him. Agreed, it had been a drunken stunt on my part, but still, she must have felt like Lynette when Gabrielle had kissed Tom Scavo in *Desperate Housewives*.

'How did it happen?'

'I met him during the negotiations. I mean I'd met him earlier but I really, really got to know him during the negotiations. He was the new buyer's representative. He's the real reason I've been so secretive.'

I licked my lips. 'So is he the . . . is it . . .?'

'I don't know,' she said miserably. 'Oh Kay, I didn't want to keep secrets from you. You're my oldest friend, my best friend, and it was killing me. But I just didn't know how to tell you.'

So, what, Deshpande was screwing us both? It *could* have been a drunken mistake on his part. Like it had been with me. But even as I thought about it, I knew I didn't believe it. How he must be laughing at us. Gloating over his coup. *How cool am I. See how I screwed them both. And neither knows a thing!* There was a ringing in my ear. *I'm going to faint again. This is too much. This day is too much. I can't handle it.*

I heard Em sobbing dimly. 'I'm sorry. I'm so sorry.'

I pulled myself together. 'It's all right,' I said, robot-like. 'I'm not mad.'

She was so surprised she forgot to sob. 'You're not?'

I shook my head. 'I forgot to tell you, but things have changed. I don't *hate*-hate Deshpande anymore. It's just minor dislike now.'

Even she had to smile at that.

Another thought struck me. 'He was with you on 19th night?'

'Yes, why?'

'It's nothing.' After a beat, I asked, 'Do you love him?'

'I don't know. I think so.'

At this point I felt another pang. He obviously didn't feel the same way, if he was callous enough to sleep with her best friend. But no way was I going to tell her. Some things are better left unsaid and it wasn't as though I was planning on repeating the exercise.

'So now that it's sorted out, will you stay?' she asked.

'I'd better not. What with the big new romance and the baby, last thing you need is a kabab mein haddi.

Em protested good-naturedly, but I could see she wouldn't be too devastated if I left.

I met Gandhi on the landing outside my apartment. He was

waiting for the elevator which I'd just vacated. He opened his mouth to speak.

'Not now, Mr Gandhi,' I said warningly.

Once home, I watered my plants and switched back to my original SIM card. Immediately it rang, startling me. I jumped and almost dropped it. It was Deshpande. I put the phone on silent and set it aside. I hadn't eaten anything since morning and figured that I ought to break my fast, but the thought of food caused major upheavals in my stomach. I looked over at the sofa: I could do with a short nap. I had too many things to sort out in my head though, so instead, I made myself a cup of tea and chain smoked.

I thought about what Em had told me about her and Deshpande. At once, a snapshot of Em and Deshpande, happily smiling and holding a baby, flashed in my brain. Immediately on the heels of this portrait of happy domesticity came another snapshot. This time it was Em and Deshpande hogging centre-stage while I stood in one corner, holding the baby like a nanny.

Em looked happy in both snapshots. I supposed that I should be happy for her. Then why did I feel ... a sense of loss? And betrayal? Although, whom I felt betrayed by was unclear. I vowed to be happy for Em even if it killed me.

My eyes kept straying to the sofa and again I resisted its lure. I thought about Ani. I wondered, lethargically, almost academically, about how I really felt about him. Of course, I felt terrible about what had happened to him. And yes, I did feel affection for him. That was only natural. But did I love him? I concluded that I supposed I did.

I wondered if I wasn't having another breakdown. *Don't be melodramatic*, I admonished myself for succumbing to self-pity. Nevertheless, I knew I should be calling Dr Sharma. Just as a precautionary measure. But I was reluctant to do so. And who wouldn't be, with all the Prozac-induced nausea and vomiting to look forward to? I decided to let Shirley make the call for me and picked up the *Mid-Day*. She wrote: Events over which you have no control unfold fast and furious, like pieces of a giant jigsaw puzzle. And even though nothing makes sense right now, remember, there are no coincidences. Everything has a meaning. Meanwhile, don't resist and just go with the flow.

I went into the bedroom, lay down on my bed and promptly fell asleep.

The doorbell woke me. I glanced at my watch and saw that it was three p.m. I had been asleep for two hours! *Should I answer it?* The thought of getting out of bed made me laugh. The doorbell rang again. Twice, thrice, in rapid succession. *Ting-tong, ting-tong, ting-tong,* I chimed, laughing silently, hysterically. *Go away!* I screamed silently.

'Coomaar?' Deshpande called out.

Right. That decided it. No way was I going to answer it.

'Coomaar, you there?'

Ting-tong, ting-tong, ting-tong, ting-tong, ting-tong.

I pressed a pillow over my ears.

TING-TONG, TING-TONG, TING-TONG, TING-TONG, TING-TONG, TING-TONG, TING-TONG, TING-TONG, TING-TONG.

Oh, for fuck's sake. I jumped out of bed and padded across to the door and yanked it open. 'WHAT?'

'Why aren't you answering your phone or your door?' he asked impatiently.

I looked at him in shock. No apology, not a trace of guilt on his face. Instead, indignation and aggression. Like *he* was the injured party. Amazing.

Without waiting for my answer, he said, 'Okay, the shit has hit the ceiling. The homicide Chodankar . . .'

A clatter of footsteps on the staircase—Prado, nattily dressed in flat-front trousers and a crisp shirt, followed by a grim looking Chodu. Deshpande muttered an expletive that sounded like behenchod. I looked at him in surprise. I'd never heard him curse.

'What's going on?' I asked. I looked from Deshpande to Chodu to Prado, feeling more bewildered by the moment.

'Kasthuri Kumar, you are under arrest for the attempted murder of Aniruddh Nair, and the murder of Sweety Nair and Pankaj Chawla,' Chodu announced.

Chapter Twenty-six

～∂∾

My first thought was he was yanking my chain. 'Stop fooling around Chodu. I'm not in the mood.'

'I'm not fooling around. Handcuff her,' Chodu directed Prado.

I can't even begin to describe what went through my mind at the moment. *Chawla was dead?* Was he saying what I thought he was saying? That I was the suspect? I just stared at him dumbly, too shocked to speak.

'She didn't do it,' Deshpande said.

'How do you know?' Chodu said cuttingly. 'Who else would stand to gain from his death? After all, he was blackmailing her.' To me he said, 'So what happened? He didn't want to wait any longer for his money? Upped his demand? Things got a little heated, one thing led to another and before you knew it he was dead. Isn't that what happens, you said?'

Prado responded by launching into me. He grabbed my wrists, turned me around and flattened me against the wall so hard I banged my nose.

'Ow!' I cried.

'Sorry,' Prado said, easing the pressure. He snapped a pair of handcuffs around my wrists, then he systematically, if a little invasively, patted me down, lingering over my breasts and between my thighs. Okay, this was taking the Hollywood tough cop act too far.

'Prado!' I cried.

'Is that really necessary?' Chodu asked in exasperation.

'Just making sure she isn't packing a concealed weapon,' Prado said somewhat sheepishly.

Between my legs I could buy, but, '*On my breasts?*'

'They *are* the concealed weapons,' Prado quipped weakly.

'If they are, they're of a small calibre. Hardly assault weapons,' Chodu chuckled, and then, perhaps remembering what he was there for, 'Mind telling me where you were last night? Say between nine and eleven?' Chodu asked.

'Killing people with my miniature weapons?' I said.

'True,' Deshpande said unexpectedly. 'And I was the casualty. She was with me last night.'

I felt as though someone had slapped me. My neck snapped up and my eyes flew to his face. It was expressionless. Prado didn't know what hit him. His face crumpled. Chodu sensed the charged atmosphere and looked at us speculatively.

He sighed. 'I knew it was a long shot. But given your medical history lately . . . Anyway, I had to eliminate the possibility.'

I avoided Prado's wounded gaze. '*By giving me a heart attack?*'

'Don't be melodramatic,' he said. He turned to a chagrined Prado, who was freeing me from my handcuffs. 'Sorry, buddy, another time. I told you it wasn't going to happen.' To me he said, 'Dogra here was looking forward to having you in custody and spending some quality time with you. He prepared a cell especially for you. He even put in flowers.'

Prado coloured. 'I didn't.'

'Did too. I smelt roses,' Chodu said.

'That's because I had it cleaned with a rose-perfumed cleaner.'

'Oh, okay. But he did put in a TV,' Chodu said.

I changed the subject. 'How did he ... I mean how was he killed?'

Chodu said that he had been shot by a .32 calibre at close range. His body was found on Juhu Beach, on a lonely stretch near Aurus. Prima facie, the doctor estimated the time of death at sometime between nine and eleven p.m. And the cause of death was a single bullet wound to the heart. 'It looks like Chawla was going to meet someone, someone he considered dangerous—he was carrying a licensed gun. He never had a chance to draw it though.'

'Oh my god! I met Chawla yesterday evening at around seven-thirty. He said that he had an appointment with someone later on,' I said.

'Did he say with whom?' Chodu asked sharply.

I shook my head regretfully. 'I figured it was with some film personality. Someone who could throw some light on the entire Jaya Matoo-Neena-Baweja-Urvashi angle. He was researching something for me.'

'You hired the guy who was blackmailing you to help you?' Deshpande asked.

'He offered to help! Free! What was I going to say? No?'

'What is this Jaya Matto-Neena-Baweja-Urvashi thing you were talking about?'

I sighed. 'This is going to take a while. You might as well come in.' Like I had a choice. But his arrival had cured me of my melancholy and got me into functioning mode again. Who said crises only induced depression?

Chodu and Deshpande walked in, but Prado listlessly declared that he was going back to the station to catch up on some work and left. As soon as they stepped in, Deshpande made a beeline for the fridge.

'I'm going to have a beer.'

'It's the middle of the afternoon!'

'Ideal time for a beer,' Deshpande affirmed.

'I'll have one too,' Chodu added.

'You're working!' I said.

'I said one, didn't I?' Chodu said.

'There's no beer,' Deshpande said from somewhere inside the fridge.

'I'll send Dogra to get us some,' Chodu said and hollered, 'Dogra!'

'Have a heart,' I said. I was feeling really bad for Prado.

'First she breaks his heart and now she wants me to have one,' Chodu said.

He held out his hand. Deshpande gave him a quelling look and took out some money from his wallet.

I grabbed the money. 'I'll get it,' I said impulsively.

I ran out and caught Prado just as he was getting into his Jeep.

'Prado!' I said. 'I just wanted to say . . .'

He held up his hand. 'It was a long shot anyway. It's just that I thought that if I could spend some time with you alone, I could make you like me.'

'I do like you,' I insisted.

'You know what I mean,' he said reproachfully. 'But I'm a realist. I know what I'm up against. There's no way I can compete with him.'

'It isn't like that. There's nothing going on between us.' The moment I said it I could've bitten my tongue. Was I crazy? Why was I denying it and giving him the impression that he had a chance?

Prado fixed a pair of hopeful eyes on me for a moment. Then he shook his head. 'The tension between you two . . .'

Tension? *Tension?*

He sighed. 'I know what I saw,' he smiled wanly. 'Don't worry, I'll get over it.'

I exhaled in relief.

Prado looked like he wanted to say more, but then he changed his mind. 'Be careful,' he said and drove away.

As soon as I re-entered my apartment, Chodu asked, 'Where's the beer?'

I blinked. 'Oh. I forgot.'

Deshpande muttered an expletive. He grabbed the money from my hands and stormed out.

While he was gone, I fetched and arranged my notes. I wondered where and how I should begin. I considered going by individuals, but then figured it would get confusing. In the end I decided to go as events unfolded.

Meanwhile Deshpande came back with the beer and went about uncorking the bottles. He silently offered me one.

'Oh, what the hell,' I said and grabbed it. 'Do you have any cigarettes?' I asked Chodu.

Chodu fished out his packet, took one stick for himself and offered me the pack. We both fired up our cigarettes and I started explaining the sequence of events from when Kaustav hired me to find Urvashi. By the time I got to my visit to Serenity Villa, the first round of beers and cigarettes had ended and another began.

I told him about what I'd found in the hedge.

'We. We found,' Deshpande interjected.

I described my visit to Indapur and the interviews with the boys there. 'From what the boys told me it appears the murderer came in a white Honda Accord, parked it below and walked up. Apparently, while the murderer was returning to the white Honda Accord, a black car, probably an imported one, rounded the sharp curve and banged into the Accord.'

Chodu exploded. 'And when were you going to tell me this?'

'Gee, I don't know. In prison maybe? With you on a manhunt out for me, I could hardly call you. Anyway, now that you know you might want to start calling Honda service stations and figuring out which Accord from Blazar came in for some bodywork post the 19th.'

I told them about my suspicion that Baweja hadn't left immediately after dropping Urvashi off at Serenity Villa and if that were the case, Neena was covering up for him. Later, Baweja himself admitted that he had indeed waited for some John D'Costa to show up and had left at about ten that night.

'But I think he saw something. Perhaps Vidisha, having it out with Urvashi? But if that was the case, why were Baweja and Neena lying about it? Anyway, it was enough to get me thinking about digging deeper. In the process I stumbled on the connection between Neena and Baweja. Deshpande will tell you that I'd asked him about it.'

Deshpande nodded.

'And then you'll never guess what I learnt,' I said, in a voice high-pitched with excitement.

'That Neena Pundir and Jaya Mattoo were sisters?' Deshpande said blandly.

Oh.

'It's better than that.' I turned to Chodu.

I searched for and found the article on the Jaya Mattoo case and the missing person's notice and slapped them down side-by-side on the table. Both men leaned forward to have a look.

Chodu scanned the articles. Then he looked up, puzzled. 'But I don't understand. What did happen?'

'Why don't we ask Ravi Menon?' I said.

He nodded and dialled Menon's number on his cellphone. He put the phone on speaker and set it down on the table.

Menon answered on the sixth ring and after the pleasantries were out of the way, I asked him, 'Do you remember the Jaya Mattoo case?'

'Like it happened yesterday.'

'So, did Urvashi mow down Jaya Mattoo or not?'

Pause. 'I don't know. Contrary to what everyone thought at the time, we did investigate. We checked out Urvashi's car but there was no damage on it. We spoke to the main witness but he was a drunk and a drug addict. Besides Jaya's body hadn't been found. So . . .'

'But Baweja and Neena were convinced that it happened?'

'Yeah. After speaking with the pavement dwellers, they apparently made the rounds of all the hospitals in the city, just in case Jaya Mattoo was injured. And when they couldn't find her, they concluded that she had died.'

'That's quite a stretch!' I said.

'That's exactly what I said. I told them that the police couldn't accept that theory because her body had not been recovered. But Baweja and Neena felt that the driver, Urvashi, and her accomplice had gotten rid of the body. They felt that the body had been dumped in a construction site a little ahead on JP Road, towards Four Bungalows. The foundation was being laid for a new building there.'

'That's quite a leap. Why did they think that?' Chodu asked.

'Apparently they talked to the labourers there as well. According to them, when Jaya's body failed to turn up, they investigated all along the road from the Indian Oil signal up till Versova, looking for possible dumping grounds. They hit pay dirt at the construction site as some labourers remembered seeing a couple, a man and a woman, late one night some weeks before. The couple dragged something from a car, something heavy, and flung it into the pit.'

'And was that what happened?' Deshpande said.

'I don't know. We never did find out. By the time Baweja and Neena figured it out, many weeks had passed. The foundation work at the site was almost finished. Even if I believed them, we couldn't have gotten a warrant to dig it up.'

'Let me guess,' Deshpande said, his voice dripping sarcasm. 'Not enough evidence.'

'There's no need for sarcasm. Baweja and Neena were so insistent, I went down to the site as well. But none of the labourers could identify Urvashi and her companion with certainty, or say with any confidence that it was indeed a body that was flung into the pit. What was I going to do?'

'Surely, based on the pavement dwellers' testimony and the labourers', there was enough circumstantial evidence to get a warrant?'

'You would think so. But then when I went to get the pavement witnesses' statements in order to get a warrant, they had disappeared.'

'Intriguing,' I said.

'Tell me about it. I figured that the builder, staring at losses running into millions, possibly joined hands with the driver. And he, along with Urvashi presumably, bribed the witnesses into disappearing. Of course, from then on, there hadn't been any accident in the first place so Jaya Mattoo could not have been buried in the pit.'

Two minutes after Ravi Menon had hung up, Chodu's phone rang. He spoke into it briefly. Then he turned to me and said, 'You asked Dogra to check out an Australian number?'

'Yes.' I said. 'It's the number from which Chawla said he received those calls.'

'He said to tell you the SIM was bought two years ago by a Vidisha Kapoor.'

Chapter Twenty-seven

〜✵〜

Omigod! That was huge! When I looked around, I saw that the men were similarly impressed by the information. Then we all spoke simultaneously.

'Of course! She was there at the beauty parlour also!' I said.

'Vidisha Kapoor as in Kaustav's wife? Blazar Films? But why would she want Sweety Nair dead? I'm assuming that that's why she hired Chawla to track her?' Chodu said.

'What is Blazar? Jamaat-ud-Daawa? Sweety Nair is killed by Vidisha and Urvashi by Vidisha or Baweja and Neena?' Deshpande said.

'Don't forget Bhanu Khanna and Desiree,' I said.

Chodu looked ready to tear his hair out. 'Now, how did they come into the picture?'

I took out the map of the route from Serenity Villa to Hermit Hill. 'I saw Bhanu Khanna and Desiree arguing about something. It was on the 21st, the day you had come to question the *Ransom* unit. Bhanu looked kind of worried. Then I saw him take this piece of paper from Desiree and tear it up. Later I went and picked up the pieces and this is what it was.'

'So they knew about Hermit Hill?' Chodu said.

'Bhanu Khanna denies it. Claims it was the note written on the other side that he was getting rid of. But it's safe to assume they did.'

Chodu flipped over the piece of paper. His eyebrows rose as he read the message. 'And did they have motive?'

'That's debatable,' I said. 'One report suggests that Urvashi ruined *Ransom* because of her excessive interference and Khanna blamed her for killing his career. Another report suggests that they were actually on good terms and that Urvashi helped save the project. But he's also Vidisha's brother. So he might have motive from that side. As far as Desiree's concerned, Urvashi apparently chopped her role to two scenes or something like that,' I said.

'It's all too much,' Chodu groused.

'Yeah? Check this out. Bhanu Khanna owns a white Honda Accord which, when I spoke to him yesterday, was in the service garage.' I gave him the name of the garage.

'And we haven't even talked about poor Chawla yet,' Deshpande said.

'He was shot, right? So all you have to do is establish motive and then do a ballistics match,' I said.

'There are only thirty thousand or so licensed .32s out there. So, that should be fairly simple,' Deshpande said.

'You have a better idea?' I said.

'I suppose his murder is tied to all these other murders. So that should narrow down the field,' Chodu said.

'Not necessarily.'

'But you just said he had an appointment with some film personality. Someone who was going to give him information on the Baweja-Pundir-Mattoo axis of evil.'

'I said I *thought* that that was the case. But I can't be sure. Knowing him, it could be anybody in the whole wide world. God knows who all he was blackmailing and for what.'

Chodu asked me to come down to the morgue to identify

Chawla's body. 'Of course, he has his driver's licence with him, but still.'

I agreed and told him I'd follow him on my bike. Chodu departed, leaving Deshpande and me alone.

'Where does that leave us?' I asked, more from a desire to fill the sudden silence than a need to know.

'Exactly where we were before?' Deshpande said.

There were certain undercurrents in his tone which made me suspect that he wasn't just talking about the case.

'Okay, so now I'm going to draw a fresh action plan. First I'm going to call up the hospital and check up on Ani. Hopefully he'll be up and can help us. I have to ask him about Vidisha as well. Then I'm going to have a talk with Desiree and Bhanu Khanna. And then . . .' *Omigod, omigod, someone stop me. I'm blabbing.*

'Coomaar.'

'And . . . and . . . oh, then I'll check out Chawla's office and go through his stuff. Maybe there's a clue there that . . .'

'Coomaar.'

'. . . can help. I mean there's got to be something in his documents. A phone number, a bill . . .'

Suddenly I was all done. I stopped talking and stared at him.

'Are we going to talk about it?' he asked.

I feigned innocence. 'Talk about what?'

'You know what. It really happened.'

'No, it didn't. Like you said, it was a dream. Just a dream.'

'Is that how you want to play it?'

Of course not! 'Yes. And if you know what's good for you, you will, too. I swear to god, if you tell Em . . .'

'Relax. There's no need to read me the riot act. I'm not stupid.'

'No, not stupid. A cad.'

'Hey! Can I help it if you're so goddamn attractive? Besides, it's not as though it's serious between Marie and me. It was always supposed to be a fling.'

'What's that supposed to mean?'

'Just that. It was supposed to be a no-strings-attached affair.'

Not that, stupid. The bit about me being so goddamn attractive. But, of course I didn't say it.

'You might have wanted to tell her that!'

'I did. And she agreed.'

'Well then, things have changed. She's in love with you!'

Deshpande looked dismayed. 'Oh shit! I didn't mean for this to happen. How did this happen? She said she had a boyfriend!'

'Sort it out between yourselves. I'm not involved,' I said irrevocably.

He stared at me for a minute or so, but I refused to give him anything to go on. Finally, he got up to go, his face blank. 'By the way,' he said casually, 'did you know that Blazar is in financial straits? They've had a string of flops recently and it's showing in their accounts books?'

I stared at him. 'What does that mean?'

'They can't afford another flop, which *Ransom* was shaping up to be. Not only will a flop ruin them financially, it will do irreparable damage to their reputation. As it is, Blazar Films is slowly losing their top-draw status. *Ransom* looks to be the final nail in the coffin and I suspect they know that. Better to kill the project. At least that way they can collect on their insurance.'

I licked my lips. Was he saying what I thought he was saying?

He was. 'What better way to kill a film than to kill the lead heroine?' he said. 'You have legit reasons to collect on the insurance. You can't complete a project if your heroine's dead.'

'You do know that that makes you a strong suspect yourself?'

'Don't waste your time on me.'

'Because you have an alibi?'

'Because if I had done it, you'd never find anything on me.'

You'd never find anything on me? 'What kind of gangster talk is that?'

He shrugged and left.

At the morgue, Chodu accompanied me inside. The doctor on call led us to a particular bed and unceremoniously uncovered the shroud. I shuddered and recoiled. Only when I saw Chawla's lifeless form did reality hit me. I felt my eyes welling up. Notwithstanding his pop psychology, or perhaps because of it, I was really starting to like the guy.

I looked at Chodu and nodded. 'It's him.'

Chodu gestured to the doctor and he covered the corpse once again.

'He looked so peaceful, like he was sleeping,' I said huskily.

He looked taken aback. 'You're feeling bad for *him*? The guy who was blackmailing you?'

'He wasn't all bad. It's complicated.'

'I'll say.'

'By the way,' I asked casually, once we were outside, 'did the test results on the glass and Coke from Rosie's come back?'

'Yeah. They're clean. So was the rajma and rice from the Nair residence.'

'So where was the poison?'

'In the Coke,' he said.

'But you just said the Coke was clean,' I said, irritated.

'Yes, the one at Rosie's. You see, she had a sizeable amount of Coke in her stomach which led us to suspect that she'd had more than one glass. Perhaps she had one at home? So we tested the Coke bottle at the Nair residence. That, too, was clean. But there were two glasses, drying by the sink. Unfortunately, they had been washed.'

'So what's your theory now?'

'Strychnine takes anywhere from twenty to sixty minutes to kill. And we know she was definitely at Rosie's at three p.m. So we're checking out all the visitors to the Nair residence between two and three p.m. on the 21st.'

'How do you know the poison was administered to her at home? Someone at the beauty parlour could have slipped some in her glass and then switched glasses before she was discovered.'

He agreed that it was possible.

After Chodu left, I considered what to do. Whom to talk to. Although the case against Vidisha was growing stronger by the minute, there was also an argument to be made for talking with Neena, Baweja, Bhanu Khanna *and* Desiree.

And Kaustav Kapoor. *The person she spoke to right after she spoke with Abdulla . . . If I were you I'd float the idea and see what comes up.* Deshpande's words kept coming back to remind me of the one interview I was putting off.

I bit the bullet and kickstarted the RE. On the way to Blazar, I happened to go past Kaustav's residence. A quick glance at my watch told me it was just past four p.m. It was unlikely that Kasutav was home. I decided to stop there anyway, just in case.

The Face wasn't around, so, in his absence, Asha answered the doorbell. As soon as she opened the peephole in the gate I asked her if Kaustav was home. She said no.

'Is your memsaab home?'

She shook her head. I was about to go when a voice called out mockingly from behind me, 'Well, well, well, look who's here!'

Dismayed, I turned around and saw Meher Kapoor alighting from the Lexus. 'Looking for my son?'

'It's okay. I'll catch him at Blazar.'

She waved her hand dismissively. 'Come in. Actually I wanted to talk to you, too.'

She looks worried, I thought.

'So, Vidisha told me you have a new theory?' she said once we were seated in the living room.

'Oh?' I said non-commitally and waited for her to continue.

'According to her, your theory is that the murderer arrived at

Hermit Hill in a white Honda Accord? That he or she killed Urvashi and drove off? And that he or she also had an accident?'

'Yes.'

She nodded. 'And the person in the Accord was Abdulla?'

'What makes you say that?'

'Well, it couldn't have been Vidisha. She's asthmatic so she couldn't have walked up the hill.'

Of course. Asha, the maid, had said she was going out to get an inhaler for Vidisha. 'Why didn't she tell me?'

'Perhaps she forgot? Or didn't think it was relevant?'

Really? Her life and liberty hung in the balance and she forgot? But then, one tends to forget such things if a loved one is in the hot seat. Especially for something you have done. Perhaps there was merit in my theory that the mention of Bhanu Khanna had sent off alarm bells in her head.

Meher Kapoor shrugged. 'It happens. Besides, I thought Abdulla was your man? DCP Chodankar said Urvashi spoke to a shady man named Abdulla on 17th night. He thinks Urvashi may have told him where she was and that he followed her to Serenity Villa and from there to Hermit Hill.'

I shook my head. 'He was out of the country when she was killed.'

'So he had an accomplice.'

I shook my head again. 'He had no reason to kill her. We know that Urvashi was going to give him sensitive financial information about Blazar. So why would he kill her?'

'Perhaps because he didn't get the information he wanted? Or maybe it wasn't about information at all? Perhaps it was extortion?'

'Maybe it wasn't Abdulla at all.'

She sat back. 'You're obviously getting at something. What is it?'

I hesitated. How could I tell her that her son was what 'I was getting at'?

'Urvashi called Kaustav after she spoke with Abdulla,' I began delicately. 'The police suspect that she may have told him about Abdulla.'

'So?'

I stared at her. Surely she wasn't that dense?

'Oh, I see,' she said after a moment. 'That explains the swab, of course.'

Aah. So that's what she was worried about. Interesting. Why would the swab worry her unless she had reason to believe Kaustav had gone to Hermit Hill?

'You think he killed her to stop her from giving the information to Abdulla. See now, that would make sense if there *was* any sensitive information. All our financials are above board. That's what I meant when I said Abdulla may not have received the information he wanted. There's no murky data to be had.'

That was a matter of opinion.

'I also heard that Blazar was afraid *Ransom* was turning out to be a flop—a flop that the company can't afford, financially or otherwise. That Urvashi may have been killed to collect on insurance.'

'I assure you, if we wanted to collect insurance, there are other— easier—ways to do so. We don't need to kill off our heroines for it,' she said dryly. 'We are also covered for losses suffered because of delays in completing a project. So all we have to do is go slow on a project and collect a tidy sum on cost overrun.'

Damn! So much for floating the idea.

Once outside Kaustav's house, I decided to call the hospital and check on Ani's status. I was told that he had regained consciousness and was in fact asking for me. I decided to make a stopover at Lilavati.

When I peeped into Ani's room, I found him not only conscious, but in fine fettle. A pert, young nurse was by his bedside, preparing an injection, and Ani was flirting with her.

'And how are we feeling now?' she asked him.

'Depends. Will you undo your buttons for me?'

'I'll tell you what I will do,' she said. 'If you promise to behave, I'll be gentle with you.'

'Come on, one button?' he begged the nurse. 'Ow! Ow! Ow!' he howled, as she plunged the needle into his vein with sadistic carelessness.

I bit back a smile.

He saw me then and called out to me. 'Katie! Now don't be upset . . .'

'I'm not,' I assured him.

'Really? Because it was just harmless fun.'

I shrugged. 'Whatever.'

He looked at me probingly. 'You've changed,' he complained.

He wanted me to be jealous, now?

'You said you loved me!' he said accusingly. 'Didn't you mean it?'

I hesitated. Did I still love him? Taking advantage of my silence, he took my hands in his, and gazing straight into my eyes, said earnestly, 'I love you. And I want to be with you. I promise I'll try my best to make you happy. I know I haven't exactly been a model human being in the past, but I've changed. What happened these past few days has made me think, really think about what's important in life. I know it sounds like a cliché and maybe it is. But it's different, you know, when it happens to you.' And then he went and ruined the perfect, if a little mawkish speech, by adding, 'Just you and me baby, what do you say?'

'I'll think about it,' I said and changed the subject. 'Any idea who did this to you?'

'No,' he said sulkily.

I bit back my impatience. 'Come on, Ani. Don't be a child. The person is still out there. He may still try to kill you.'

'I said I don't know! I had stepped out for lunch. I was walking back to my office when someone bumped into me. Hard. I turned around to complain but he was lost in the crowd. It hurt like mad but I didn't realise I had been stabbed and kept walking. Somewhere near my office I started feeling dizzy. That's all I remember.'

'Did you know Chawla's been murdered, too?' I said quietly.

The enormity of the implication hit him and I saw terror reflected on his face. 'Are you saying the same person is behind all . . . this? Is there . . . a serial killer out there?' he said haltingly.

'Hardly. But you have to agree—first Sweety, then you and then Chawla. There seems to be a method to the madness. Which makes me think that it has something to do with that mysterious person calling Chawla and asking him to track down Sweety.'

'Even if you're right, why try to kill me? And then Chawla?'

'I don't know.'

'So what do we do now?' he said, relenting a little.

'It's back to the drawing board for me. I suggest you go to some place safe for the time being.'

He nodded. 'I can go to Sweety's parents' place near Mumbai. Just in case you have the urge to see me, it's a small village between Khandala and Pune. I don't remember its name. But I can tell you how to reach it.

'Take the Mumbai–Pune Expressway. Get off it at Khandala. Drive towards Amby Valley. Take the right turn ten kilometres after Amby Valley. You'll pass Pavana Lake on your right and a picturesque hill property on your left. Drive on straight till you reach—'

'—Indapur,' I said.

Of course! That was the connection.

Chapter Twenty-eight

Ani started. 'Yes, I think that's right. How did you know?'
'I should've known sooner,' I said in the manner of a lament.
'You telling me about Sweety banging up your car, that she had
gone to her country house near Bombay, the boys in Indapur
telling me about a late night bang-up between an imported black
car and a white Honda Accord. I should have put it all together
sooner.' And I would have if all the information had been given to
me at once instead of in a piecemeal fashion. I now remembered
the elusive something that had been nagging at me while I was
talking to Vidisha Kapoor at Blazar yesterday.

It was a little far-fetched, but could it be, that by the strangest
quirk of fate, it had been Sweety in the imported black car? It was
easy to mistake midnight blue for black at night. Had she been
killed because she saw Urvashi's murderer? And Ani, because the
murderer was afraid Sweety might've told someone?

But why Chawla? By his own admission he'd never seen his
mystery client. Was it possible that there were multiple murderers
out there after all? And that Chawla's murder was unrelated to the
other ones?

I pecked Ani on the forehead. 'Got to go. Thanks a ton. '
'Glad I could help,' he said, mystified.

I raced out of the room, dialling Chodu's number as I did so. There was no response. I checked my watch. It was six p.m. I was about to call Vidisha when I thought the better of it. I called the Blazar board line and asked the receptionist if Vidisha was in. She replied in the positive, adding that Vidisha was in a meeting.

Vidisha was still in a meeting when I reached Blazar, so I decided to talk to Neena Pundir and Baweja first.

I swept into Neena's room, grim-faced and purposeful.

She half-rose in her seat angrily. 'How dare you!'

'Don't get your knickers in a knot, Neena Pundir. Or should I say Mattoo?'

She stiffened. We both eyeballed each other.

'I want to talk to you and Chandan both,' I said.

She nodded, picked up the intercom and dialled Baweja, all without taking her eyes off me. 'Can you come to my room? . . . Yes, now.'

She replaced the handset and joined her hands together under her chin. She studied me thoughtfully and in silence. On any other day, this steady and relentless scrutiny would have had me squirming. Today, I returned her gaze, unflinching. It's remarkable what a confidence-booster it is to know more than your opponent.

The signature track from *The Good, the Bad and the Ugly* started playing in my head and had almost reached a crescendo when she spoke.

'How did you find out?'

'It's a long story.'

Baweja walked in then. Slowly, and deliberately, I took my eyes off Neena and fixed them on him. 'Have a seat,' I said.

Baweja looked at Neena in confusion.

'She wants to talk to us about Jaya,' Neena said expressionlessly.

They must have figured it would come out at some time, feared it at any rate, because it didn't seem to be as big a shock to them as I'd expected. He nodded and raked a trembling hand through his hair.

'I have a theory,' I said. 'You both loved Jaya Mattoo. When she was run over, you tried to get justice the legal way but failed, so you decided to take matters into your own hands. Here you had an unexpected ally. There was another person who had a score to settle with Urvashi. Vidisha. So you all teamed up and came up with a plan to kill her. How am I doing so far?'

They exchanged glances. Here it comes, I thought. *How did you know? We can explain. It wasn't like that.*

'Why would we kill Urvashi?' Neena asked.

I peered at them owlishly. 'What do you mean? Didn't she run over Jaya?'

'It wasn't like that. The papers got several facts wrong. For one, only one person actually saw the whole thing happen. The rest of them were sleeping and only woke up after the accident. They only saw a woman who looked like Urvashi kneeling beside Jaya. She was hysterical and the pavement dwellers naturally thought she was the one who'd done it. Plus they saw a black Merc, which matched the car Urvashi had at the time.

'The man who actually saw it happen, the one who made a note of the registration number, said he saw Urvashi emerge from the driver's side of the car. So he also assumed she was the one driving,' Neena said.

'So?'

'Urvashi's Merc is a European model. It's a left-hand drive.'

It took me a while to process this, but when I did, *Omigod!*

'It took us the longest time to figure it out. Because when he said the driver's side, we assumed he'd seen it was a left-hand drive. By the time we worked out that maybe, just maybe, he hadn't seen a left-hand drive, he had disappeared.'

I leaned forward. 'Then?'

'I was driving by the Indian Oil signal last week when I saw him again. After all these years, he was back. Naturally, I slammed on the brakes. It was only when I asked some pointed questions that he said he saw Urvashi emerge from the door on the right,' Neena said.

'So, who was the driver?'

Neena and Baweja again exchanged glances. Then she inhaled sharply. 'We don't know. The witness didn't recognise him.'

'But he must have provided some sort of a description?' I persisted.

Baweja opened his mouth to speak and I thought I saw Neena shoot him a warning look. 'You know what eyewitness accounts are like. Plus of course it's been so many years now; his memory is cloudy. We can't figure it out,' she said.

Oh, for fuck's sake. What would it take to get anything worthwhile and honest out of her? 'Or maybe, you're lying. How do I know you didn't just concoct this whole story about the witness getting his facts mixed up? You know this looks bad for you. Maybe the witness didn't reappear. Or, if he did, maybe he just confirmed Urvashi was the driver?'

Baweja started to squirm. Just a little. But Neena didn't bat an eye. 'There's only one way to find out. You'll have to talk to him.'

Nix that. Chances were Neena had successfully planted the idea firmly in his head that it wasn't Urvashi who was driving that night. There's another phrase for 'pointed questions' and it's called 'power of suggestion'. Witnesses' memories dull with time. Combine that with leading questions and you can get them to say whatever you want.

'Are you sure?' I asked pointedly. 'Because if you're holding something back, this would be the time to come clean. I mean, you *are* up shit creek.'

'How? Based on a white Honda Accord seen at the scene? I told you, it wasn't mine. It's easy to make mistakes, especially at night. *I should know.*'

'And then there's your alibi.'

'What about it? I told you I was home.'

'Yes, but it is entirely predicated on receiving a couple of phone calls—'

'—Which,' she cut in, 'only I could've answered as my flatmate was cooling her heels in a lock-up.'

'You said she was at a party!'

'She was. But then there was a police raid and she ended up in jail.'

She wouldn't lie about something like that. Damn. Not that I thought she'd done it, but it would've been nice to rattle her a little. Get her to admit she and Vidisha were in it together.

'Now about the night of the 17th,' I said to Chandan.

'What about it?'

'Why were you really there?'

'I told you. I suspected she was meeting John D'Costa.'

'Oh come now, is that really how you want to play it?'

'I don't know what you're talking about,' Baweja said.

'That phone call you claim Urvashi received—which you say got you thinking about John D'Costa, the one that came from your extension—Geeta says she didn't make that call. You made that call didn't you, Neena?'

'Fine,' Neena said. 'I made that call.'

'*You* did?' Chandan said. 'Why? And why didn't you tell me?'

'I only did it to rattle her. It was no big deal,' she said sulkily.

'So who came to Serenity Villa?' I asked Baweja.

'I said I didn't—'

My phone rang then. It was Chodu.

'Hey, Chodu, wassup?'

'You tell me. You called me.'

'Um . . . I'm in a meeting . . .'

'Okay, but now that I've called, let me tell you, I had Dogra check on those Honda service stations. Guess what? Bhanu Khanna's car came in with a cracked windscreen and some minor damage to the bonnet.'

'And what does he say?'

'That a coconut fell on it.'

'You believe him?'

'It's possible. But check this out. He says he was home and his wife corroborates his story. But the driver says he took the wife to a bridge party that night.'

'It has to be him then.'

Chodu agreed, saying, 'Looks like it. Because other than that, there's no record at any authorised Honda service station of any Accord from Blazar coming in for body work.'

He hung up, and I was about to do the same when I had an idea. I kept the phone glued to my ear. 'Uh-uh . . . uh-uh . . . really? You don't say!' Then I turned to Baweja. 'That was Chodu. And he just had an extremely interesting conversation with one of the regular customers at Khandala Heights. This customer said that he was out, smoking, when he saw a woman emerge from the villa. She got into a car and drove off. Then he heard screaming and shouting from Serenity Villa, following which another woman came storming out, luggage and all, got into a black Merc and drove off. After a while, another guy came out. He couldn't be sure in the dark, but he gave a pretty accurate description of the guy's build.' I paused and looked at Baweja meaningfully. 'You know what this means, right? The woman in the Merc had to be Urvashi. And that means you were there when she had that row.'

Dear god, I was telling more lies than a pair of falsies! I only hoped they were within ballpark range or else I would be laughed right out of the room. I looked at them anxiously. Their exchanging glances and looking down was my first indication that I was onto something.

Baweja started to say something but his cellphone rang. He looked at the display, started and shot a surprised look at Neena. 'I have to take this,' he said and left the room.

'I can fill you in,' Neena volunteered, to my dismay. I bet the bitch had engineered his exit. I was willing to wager my discount Diesel jeans it was she who'd called him. I couldn't see her cellphone anywhere.

'You're right, he did see something, heard rather. We can't be sure because they stayed inside. They seemed to be arguing about something. Chandan was in the hedge and really far away and their voices were muffled so he couldn't hear anything specific.'

'Then what happened?'

'We assume the other woman left because, a while later, he heard Urvashi talking on the phone with, presumably, her mother. She was hysterical; she kept ranting about the row and screaming "I'm gonna screw him. This time I'm really gonna do it." She made a couple more calls, during which she ranted some more. Then silence. At that point, Chandan ventured out and peeped inside. It was empty and the front door was open. He ran out, but by then Urvashi was already putting her stuff into the car. Then she got in and drove off. His car was parked further down the road and by the time he ran to his car, she was gone.'

'He didn't try and find her?' I asked, incredulous.

Neena shifted. 'Well, he did cruise around for a while but couldn't see any signs of her. So he came back.'

I decided to try another tack. 'What about Sweety Nair? Where does she fit in?'

Sadly, I didn't get the reaction I wanted.

'Who's she?' There was genuine puzzlement in her voice.

'Never mind. Who was the other woman at Serenity Villa?'

Neena shrugged. 'He was too far away to make out anything.'

I stared at her for a beat. 'Are you protecting Vidisha?' I asked.

She met my gaze, unflinching. 'I am fond of her. But not to the extent of risking a jail sentence,' she said dryly.

'When you say you're fond of her, you mean . . .?' I saw her eyes narrow and added hastily, 'I wouldn't even be asking you if it wasn't material to the case, you understand?'

'How is it material?'

'It establishes motive or lack thereof on your part. And Vidisha's.'

'I thought my motive was my sister's death.'

'Yes, yes it is. But there could also be another motive considering you appeared so in love with Kaustav.'

She averted her eyes.

'You certainly went out of your way to project that, didn't you? Behaving all proprietorial and gazing at him gooey-eyed. And preventing Vidisha from meeting her own husband, what was that all about?'

'If you must know, it wasn't Kaustav I was proprietorial about,' she said, 'it was Vidisha. I wasn't jealous of her! I was jealous of him! And that whole act was to throw people off track.'

'Off track what? Is something going on between Vidisha and you?'

She hesitated. 'Yes. At least there was.'

'So Vidisha and you are . . .?'

'No. She loves Kaustav. She made that very clear yesterday.'

'I don't understand. Then what was she doing with you?'

She sighed. 'Kaustav hurt her and she was looking for kindness. Some love. Companionship. Someone who'd make her feel good about herself. Some . . .'

'Yeah, yeah, yeah, I get the picture.'

'Anyway, I was around and she turned to me for comfort. One thing led to another and we ended up fooling around. That was it. She was only looking to alleviate her loneliness. I just got the wrong message.'

I asked Neena if Kaustav was around. She told me that he was. 'He should be by the poolside. They're shooting an action scene there.'

On the way out, I made a quick stopover at the loo on the ground floor. A quick, light application of liquid rose lipstick and a thin line of kohl on my lower eyelids later, I studied my appearance in the mirror. The fresh-faced-yet-luminous look was the one I was aiming for. Fresh-faced I got, but the luminous look happened only if I opened my eyes wide. Like I was in a perpetual state of wonder. Determined to have this look when I met Kaustav, I was practising my optic moves when Vidisha swept in.

She looked amused. 'Still trying to seduce my husband?'

More embarrassed by the pity in her voice than the fact that I'd been caught making faces in the mirror, I stuttered. 'Well . . . I . . .' Shit! That's not how I wanted my interview with Vidisha to begin.

But she had already lost interest and made to enter a cubicle. 'Just a moment. I wanted to talk to you,' I said.

'About what?' she asked nonchalantly.

'Urvashi.'

'Urvashi,' she repeated.

'And Sweety Nair. And Aniruddh Nair.'

'Who're they?' she said, amused.

'Sweety's the woman who was murdered in the beauty parlour.'

'Oh yes, I remember reading about her. I made a note about using the situation in one of our films. What about her?'

'Why were you tracking her down?'

'Why was I what?' The surprise in her voice seemed genuine.

'You say you don't know Sweety Nair. And yet you called a private investigator and asked him to keep tabs on her? Incidentally, it was the same PI who was with me the other day. The guy you thought was auditioning for the role of a psycho. And who, by the way, has also been murdered.'

She leaned closer and peered directly into the pupils of my eyes. 'Are you on drugs?'

'Some of the calls came from an Australian number—' I took out my notes and rattled off the number. 'If I'm not mistaken, this number belongs to you?'

'It does not!'

'And yet records show that you purchased the SIM two years ago.'

'I did . . .?' she said and stopped. 'When two years ago?'

I thought she was beginning to look frightened. 'January 2007.'

'I think I know what you're talking about. We were shooting *Champions* in Australia and needed local SIM cards. I had bought several in my name.'

'Why is it still active?'

She shrugged. 'We keep going to Australia. There's no point in buying them again and again.'

'You have these SIM cards with you?'

'No, they're all kept here, in office.'

'Are you saying anyone can have access to the SIM?' I could feel the beginnings of dismay.

She nodded. 'By signing for it.'

'Can you tell me who was the last person to sign for it?'

'Sure. I'll call the admin guy.'

We walked out of the loo. At reception, Vidisha dialled the admin guy's number, and from the one-sided conversation, I figured that no one in the recent past had signed for it.

'He's gone to check the stock room,' she said.

I nodded.

'Yes, Satam,' she said into the phone after a minute. She listened and then said, 'But how is that possible?'

She replaced the phone and turned to me in a daze. 'It's not there. He can't explain it, but it's gone,' she said, confirming my fears.

Chapter Twenty-nine

O f course this didn't mean that she wasn't lying. She had the motive and the opportunity.

'What's going to happen now?' she asked, frightened. She licked her lips. 'Will they . . . are they thinking . . .?'

'I don't know. But if I were you, I'd think of some foolproof alibis for the 17th and the 19th,' I said and turned to go.

'Wait!' she said.

I stopped.

She started breathing heavily. 'I did go down to Serenity Villa on the 17th. On the 16th, I saw Kaustav and Urvashi talking. After that Kaustav was very upset. I wanted to talk to him then, but something or the other kept coming up. Then, later, when we came back to Mumbai, I asked him about it. He admitted that Urvashi was threatening to ruin him if he didn't marry her. Obviously that made my blood boil and I went down to Serenity Villa and had it out with her. I warned her to keep away from my husband . . .'

'Or what?'

Her breath became laboured. 'Look, I did make threats. But that was in the heat of the moment. I swear I left after that. I didn't kill her.'

'Do you own a .32 calibre gun?'

She suddenly looked afraid. 'A gun? Why?'

'Do you?'

'No. But I think . . .' And she started gasping.

'Are you all right?' I asked in mild panic.

She pointed to her bag. 'My . . . my inhaler,' she gasped.

'Hold on,' I said and rummaged through her bag. I found the inhaler and handed it to her. A few puffs of the inhaler and the colour returned to her face.

'Why didn't you tell me yesterday you were asthmatic? You must have realised that it would help your cause.'

She frowned. 'I didn't? I don't know why I didn't.'

I stared, puzzled. 'Are you protecting somebody? Is it your brother?'

'Bhaiyya? Why would he . . .? Don't believe all the rumours you hear. Bhaiyya had no reason to harm Urvashi.'

As soon as I stepped out of the corporate office, I whipped out my cellphone and dialled Chodu.

'Hello, Chodu? Can you do me a little favour? Can you check if a Yula Menezes was in jail on 19th night?'

'Sure,' he said. 'As soon as I get all the jails on the hotline.'

'Juhu jail,' I corrected myself. 'Remember that raid on a rave party on the 19th? Apparently she was at that party.'

'Just let me make a note. Yula Menezes, you said? . . . Wait, what's that?' I heard him confer with someone and some rustling of paper. 'Solanki here says that Yula Menezes was indeed hauled in during the raid. She was in the lock-up from ten p.m. till the next morning.'

'Okay,' I said. 'Another thing. I was just talking to Vidisha. She says she doesn't know anything about the Australian SIM card. She bought it two years ago for local communication during a shoot. Apparently it is part of a common pool and anyone could have taken it. But check this out, when I asked her if she owned a .32 . . .'

'YOU WHAT?' he yelled.

'What? It was a reasonable question . . .'

'I was getting a search warrant for their premises and now you've gone and alerted them.'

Oops! 'But how did you . . .?'

'What, you think only you can piece together stuff? You don't think it occurred to us that Chawla ending up dead when he was tracking Sweety makes a case for the killer being the same person? I had applied for a warrant to search the Kapoor premises as soon as I left your house. Long before *you* figured it out. And now you've ruined my case!'

I gulped. 'But you still have a case. If the gun turns up in the house, fine. If it doesn't, you'll know she's gotten rid of it.'

'Why, did she admit she had a gun?'

'Not in so many words—she was interrupted by an asthma attack. Now why would she have an attack just then? I think—'

He cut me off with some profanities which weren't altogether unjustified. Then there was a loud *thwack* after which the line went dead. That was ten thousand bucks of taxpayers' money dashed against the wall. Ah well, compared to the millions of rupees regularly siphoned off, ten thousand was peanuts.

'Scene. Interior. Blazar Corporate Office. Night. Katie storms out of the Blazar office.'

I stopped and turned. Bhanu Khanna and Desiree were stepping out of the reception. They came towards me. 'Katie, meet Desiree. Desiree, this is Katie Kumar.'

'Oh, so you are *the* Katie Kumar!' Desiree said, wide-eyed.

I looked at her inquisitively.

'I was just telling them about you,' Bhanu said.

'Them?' I said.

'Yeah, the team. We were having a pre-production meeting.'

'Oh. So you're going ahead with the film?'

'Of course. Why wouldn't we?'

Desiree grabbed my hand and pumped it enthusiastically. 'It is such an honour to meet you. Bhanu was just narrating the script and it's so totally rocking. I'm so excited about the role.'

I was in shock. 'You're ... excited ... about ... *you're* playing the part?' I faltered. I guess, somewhere I knew I wouldn't be playing the part—but I'd hoped.

'Of course,' Bhanu said. 'Why, did you have someone else in mind? You didn't think *you* would . . .?'

I responded with what I hoped was a disdainful—albeit shrill— laugh. 'Where did you get that idea? I ... uh ... it's just that it's so soon.'

'Why? The script's ready.'

'Already?' Let's see, how long had it been since he'd narrated the first scene? Two days? Three?

Bhanu nodded. 'In fact, I've practically written the whole screenplay since we spoke last. Want to hear it? Scene—'

'—Maybe lat—'

'—Exterior. Goa docks. Foggy night.'

Foggy night in Goa? Really?

'Agent 402 holds up a disc and says to someone next to him, "Here's the disc. It has all the information. Let's go." The figure pulls out a gun and points it at 402, who looks up, surprised. He says, "You?" The figure shoots him. Agent 402 is hit in the stomach but his reflexes kick in and he rolls to the ground as the other bullet goes sailing overhead. He rolls into an underbrush and runs away. Cut—'

'Bhanu—'

'Next scene. Exterior. Nearby, a little ahead. Night. Chandni and Babloo emerge from the fog and look around as if lost. They are walking around with their luggage.'

Now how did Chandni and Babloo end up wandering along sandy beaches, on foggy nights, in Goa, when just a little while ago they were playing football in the gently undulating mustard fields of Punjab? Unless he'd explained it earlier and I'd simply tuned out. I thought not.

Desiree cut in excitedly, 'The revelation will be something else. The fog parts to reveal this kickass figure in silhouette. As she walks ahead in slowmo, a little bit of light falls on her. That's when we see her for the first time. She is tall and slim, with long hair streaming down her back. She is wearing a pair of denim shorts, a halter top and thigh-high boots, like . . . like . . .'

'Aishwarya Rai in *Dhoom*,' I said helpfully.

'Exactly!' she said.

'Dez,' Bhanu said patiently, 'I thought we discussed that. That doesn't go with Chandni's character.'

'Then how is she wearing a short skirt in the song later?' she demanded peevishly.

'It's a song! Anything goes,' he said.

'Well I won't be styled like a gaon ki gori,' Desiree declared sulkily. To me she complained, 'Do you know what he has in mind? Short kurtas and big billowing salwars in loud colours.'

'Yuck! Rani Mukherjee in *Bunty Aur Babli*,' I blurted out.

'See?' she said triumphantly.

Cornered, Bhanu said defensively, 'It spawned a whole new fashion!'

'True.' *Why was I getting involved? What did it matter what the styling was? It wasn't as though I was going to be wearing any of it on screen!*

I tried once more to interrupt. 'Bhanu . . .'

He rubbed his hands enthusiastically. 'Anyway, it looks like they've been lost for some time, 'cos Babloo says defensively, "Bus yahin kahin hai." Chandni curses Babloo and says, "That's what you've been saying for the last one hour." Suddenly 402 appears from the fog and approaches them. "Let's ask him," Chandni says. But the man brushes past her and is gone before Chandni can ask him for directions. As he brushes past her, Agent 402 slips a CD into Chandni's bag and manages to say "Happy birthday" and runs away. Happy birthday, as will be revealed later, is the password to a file on the CD. Of course, Chandni and Babloo don't know that yet. So Babloo calls out, "To you too." Cut.'

'Bhanu . . .'

'Wait. It gets better. Next scene. Exterior. Still further down the road. Foggy night. Chandni and Babloo are walking past a telephone booth when the phone rings. Babloo says, "Wow we've hardly been in Goa for two hours and people have already started calling us." Chandni looks around, and seeing nobody, answers the phone. As soon as she does that, she is shot at. Bewildered Chandni and Babloo look around when another shot sings past them. They duck . . .'

'Speaking of which, you two have been doing some fair bit of ducking yourselves,' I cut in determinedly and reached in my bag for the road map.

I held it up for Desiree to see. She took one look at it and blanched.

'No, I've never . . .'

'I told you . . .' Bhanu began.

'Nuhn,' I said warningly. 'Dez?'

He reddened. 'Anyway,' he said hurriedly. 'I had nothing to do with it. It was Desiree. She got hold of it. I was merely telling her to get rid of it before—'

'I like that!' Dez said, arms akimbo. 'Suddenly it's all me? You were pretty kicked about the map as well.'

I looked at Bhanu. 'Get rid of it before what? The police found out about it?'

He remained silent.

'How did you get it?' I asked Desiree.

'Fine, I'll tell you. I think it was on the 15th, no the 16th. We ran out of cigarettes.'

'We?'

'Bhanu and I.'

'But we knew that Urvashi always keeps a supply. I said to Bhanu, "How about me raiding Urvashi's Green Room and pinching some of hers?"'

'Seems rather drastic. Why not send someone to buy a packet?' I said. *Unless* . . . 'Urvashi didn't stock cigarettes! It was coke!' I looked at them questioningly.

They both piped up simultaneously.

'We don't do coke.'

'It wasn't like that.'

'Doesn't matter anyway. Go on,' I said.

Bhanu continued, 'Knowing Urvashi, I figured there would be hell to pay if she found out. I had a bad feeling about it and warned Dez not to do anything stupid. But she went ahead and did it anyway. Of course, Urvashi found out about it and threw a royal tantrum.'

'You were only too happy to share in the spoils till then,' she said sarcastically.

Bhanu ignored her. 'Later when I confronted her, she showed me the map.'

'When I was looking for the . . . cigarettes . . . I found this sketch. I somehow knew it was important. I quickly made a copy of the map on the other side of a note Bhanu had given me and replaced the original,' she said.

'Why did you think it was important?' I asked.

'Everyone at *Ransom* knew something major was being planned. For the last few days the entire set was . . . was abuzz with some kind of invisible energy . . . you know, like when you feel something is about to happen. You don't have anything to back it up but you just feel it? Something like that. We all knew it was a publicity stunt involving Urvashi but what it was, we had no idea. I figured the map had something to do with it.'

'So you put two and two together and figured that Hermit Hill and not Serenity Villa was where she was going to be holed up.'

Bhanu shook his head. 'Not until later. We only figured it out when the news about her disappearance broke.'

'So why did you make a copy?' I asked Desiree.

'I don't know what I was thinking. Or, if I was thinking at all. Maybe I thought I could tell the whole unit. I thought I could use the map to play a prank on her. I don't know. I just instinctively copied it.'

'A prank like what? Show up there?' I said.

'No!' she denied. A little too quickly.

'Uh-huh?' I said, sceptically.

'Where were you both on the night of the 19th?'

'Wait a minute! You can't be . . .' Bhanu said.

'I have nothing to hide,' Desiree declared. 'I was home with my family. We were celebrating my brother's birthday. '

'As was I. You can check with my wife, Pragya,' Bhanu added hastily.

'Oh but how would she know? She was at a bridge party, wasn't she?' I said.

They both exchanged glances. Then Desiree said, 'Okay, he wasn't home. He was with me. He picked me up from my brother's party. Then we were together.'

'At her place. Not driving to Hermit Hill,' Bhanu added hastily.

I decided that I wasn't going to get anything more from them so I headed towards the poolside. As Neena had said, there was a shoot in progress.

Scene. Exterior. Film set. Night. A shoot is in progress. There are massive lights mounted on stands, light cutters and reflectors, mazes of wires running all over the place and the steady chug-chug of a generator parked nearby. People mill about busily.

Cut to Kaustav as he sits in one corner, going over some papers with a hefty guy in a Pathan suit. The guy in the Pathan suit listens carefully and then walks across to the far side of the pool. He picks up his mike and ... *Stop it! Stop talking like Bhanu Khanna.*

Kaustav saw me approach and shot to his feet. He grabbed my hands. 'Katie,' he said warmly.

I proffered my cheek for some air kissing. 'You're directing?'

He grimaced. 'No choice. If I want to see it completed and released on time. As you know, it's a lot of money.' He gestured towards the empty chair next to his, inviting me to sit.

I slid in. 'About that. I heard a curious thing today. Is it true that Blazar is in financial straits?'

He was lowering himself into the director's chair and the fluidity of his movement was broken for a split second. 'Is that the line the police are pursuing?' he asked at last.

'It's one of the avenues they are investigating. They think that Blazar was nervous *Ransom* might be a flop, which would have meant a loss of reputation, of money. And then there's the insurance angle,' I added reluctantly.

His body went rigid and his hands balled into fists by his side. 'Are you saying that Urvashi was killed for insurance?'

'Hey, don't shoot the messenger,' I protested jokingly.

He seemed not to have heard me. He raked his hands through his hair. 'This is crazy! Vidisha could never kill anyone. She could never do something as cold-blooded as that for money.'

My head snapped up in surprise. 'Vidisha?'

'Well, yeah. Vidisha owns Blazar. The bulk of it anyway.'

'Since when?'

'Since about five years ago. Blazar was in trouble and Vidisha's father helped us out. In return he got the bulk of our shares. When he died, Vidisha and Bhanu inherited everything. Vidisha got the Blazar stock.'

'I met your mother earlier. Why didn't she mention it?'

He shrugged.

'So Vidisha stood to gain a lot . . .?'

'I simply cannot believe she would do such a thing. For money or any other reason. Besides, she couldn't have done it. She was home.'

The pathan-suited man spoke into the mike, cutting short our conversation. From what I gathered, they were filming an underwater action scene. I settled down to watch. Smeer Khan in swimming briefs was always worth a dekho. I couldn't recall him ever having donned a pair on screen. Right then, though, he was modestly covered in a bathrobe.

'That man talking on the mike is the action director, Afzal Mohammed,' Kaustav explained.

'You are in the pool, you are in the middle of your lap, stroking away energetically when you feel another presence around.' Mohammed stopped, lowered the mike and tensed dramatically. He crouched down and looked from left to right. 'Who's there? Who's there? You quickly stop and look around but there is nothing. You shake your head in confusion and continue your lap. After a few metres you again feel something. This time you also detect a movement from the corner of your eye. You again stop.' He repeated his vivid performance. 'Again there's nothing. You are about to resume your lap when someone tugs at your legs from under water. You thrash, you struggle, but the guy is too strong. You go down, still thrashing wildly. Got that, Ahmed?'

Ahmed? I did a double take then. That man wasn't Smeer Khan at all—it was Smeer's double! And at once I berated myself for being so stupid. Of course, that was Smeer's stunt double. It was too risky to use the real McCoy—they'd only get him for close-ups.

'Okay, let's rehearse,' Afzal said, clapping his hands.

Ahmed shrugged off his robe and stood at the edge of the pool. The skimpy briefs that he wore showed off his marvellously toned body to perfection. They also left little to the imagination, especially where his genitalia were concerned. I gasped.

Kaustav looked at me, saw what I was looking at, and drawled, amused. 'Oh, come on. You know that isn't real. It's enhanced.'

I'll say. Judging by the bulge, he had to be at least eight inches. *When flaccid!* At once my mind was flooded with pictures of the 1980s Tata Ok advert where a man in the shower looks down somewhere off screen and says, 'Sach much kaafi bada hai.'

'It's not that,' I stuttered. 'It's the tattoo on his groin.'

At the point where the upper thigh meets the pelvis was a tattoo of a snake wrapped around a dagger. Just like Sanj had said.

Chapter Thirty

❧

My mind was in a whirl. What did this mean? Was the man to whom Sanj had given a blowjob on the 19th Ahmed, Smeer Khan's double? Then where was Smeer Khan? And why was he being so cagey about his whereabouts on the night of the 19th?

Kaustav looked at Ahmed and turned to me. 'What about it?'

'It's ... uh ... you see, Smeer Khan told me he was with someone on the night of the 19th. I just happen to know that friend and h ... the friend told me that Smeer had a tattoo on his groin. That means it was Ahmed! And then at Ego, the hostess also said that Smeer had neglected her all night on the 19th. Now I know why. It wasn't Smeer there either! And Ahmed couldn't afford to get close to the hostess lest she notice the difference.' I paused for a moment to catch my breath. 'I'm not making too much sense, am I?'

His mouth quirked up amusedly. 'Am I to understand that Smeer Khan was not where he said he was?'

'Basically. Which leads us to the question, where was he? And why set up such an elaborate charade?' While the action unit rehearsed the fight sequence, I said to Kaustav ultra casually, 'That reminds me, do you have Smeer Khan's number?'

'Actually, no. Neena deals with the stars.'

'Will you excuse me for a moment?'

'Of course. But don't take too long.'

'I won't.' I rapidly walked a little distance away and, much as I was loath to, called Deshpande.

'Well, well, well, guess who wants to talk now?' he drawled.

I ignored the jibe. 'What's Smeer Khan's number?'

Silence. Then, 'my God, you *are* stalking him.'

'Don't be stupid. I need to ask him something.'

'What?'

'That's between him and me.'

'So is his number.'

'Fine. Have it your way. I don't care.'

'You don't?'

'I don't. Because he'll call me.'

'Will he?'

'Yes, because you'll tell him something for me—that I know what he did on the 19th,' I said and disconnected. After a few minutes Kaustav came up behind me.

'Everything okay?' he said.

'Yeah. Just when it seemed like everything was sewn up, an angle opened up and blew the case wide open again. So . . .' I shrugged.

All of a sudden, Kaustav froze. 'Is that a . . .? Oh my god! Bomb!' he cried

I started. 'What? Where?'

He pointed a shaky finger at my bike and pulled me down onto the ground. I followed his finger to a tiny beacon-like red light that was flashing on and off on the bike's underside.

'Don't be ridiculous. There's got to be another explanation,' I said, getting up and striding across. I bent down and examined the underside of the RE. Was that a . . .? Yes, there was no doubt about it, I thought, absolutely livid and also a little humiliated.

I detached the small object from the bike and walked across to where Kaustav lay prostrate on the ground.

'Are you crazy? Throw that ... that ... thing away!'

'It's not a bomb,' I said with some disgust. *What a wuss.*

'Good news, you don't have a killer on your heels. Bad news, I think you have a stalker,' he joked, when I told him it was a tracking device and he knew that his life was no longer in danger of being cruelly snuffed out.

I gave him a sore look.

'Sorry about flipping out like that,' he said sheepishly. 'It's just that with so many bombs going off ... and you have to admit Blazar is a high-profile target.'

Well, when he put it like that, it did kind of make sense. Besides, he didn't have the benefit of police training to know the difference.

'You've got to report this to the police.'

'Never mind,' I said tightly. 'I know who did it.'

'You do?'

I nodded. 'I'll deal with him later.'

He looked at my set face and refrained from asking any more questions. Instead he said, 'Tell you what. Let me take you out to dinner. You look like you can use a break.'

'Oh, but I thought you were shooting?'

'So, we'll pack up.' He grinned suddenly. 'Perks of being the boss. Besides I owe you a dinner anyway.'

'Okay,' I said.

'Good. I've made reservations.'

Only then did I notice he'd changed as well. He had been that sure I'd say yes. For some reason that made me feel a little resentful.

He smiled and offered me the crook of his arm. After a moment's hesitation, I slipped my hand through it. He did look yummy.

Dressed in a maroon silk shirt, slim black pants and moccasins, he looked the epitome of casual elegance. A bit dandyish, but yummy, like Antonio Banderas in *The Legend of Zorro*.

He led me to his waiting car. Zuari Mal, code name The Face, greeted us by holding the rear door open. His face was as expressionless as before. I sank into the luxurious upholstery and took in the rich, heady smell of expensive leather. Kaustav walked around and slid in from the other side.

'I hope you like sashimi,' Kasutav said conversationally.

I don't. I hate it. I hate the thought of eating raw fish and would only do so at peril of death. Or to cure acute asthma, which was peril of death anyway. I felt fresh resentment bubbling inside me. I tried to give him the benefit of the doubt. It was obvious he thought he was being thoughtful and indulgent. And, considering women practically threw themselves at him all the time, it wasn't his fault he was so cocksure.

Still, he might've asked instead of presuming, a voice in my head perversely whispered. I wondered how to put him in his place and still retain my allure. But femme fatale I wasn't, and rudeness only made me look bitchy.

'I'm vegetarian,' I blurted. Shit! Shit! I'd told him I liked seafood.

His brow creased in consternation. 'Really? I thought you said you liked seafood.'

'Today,' I said at the same time. 'I'm vegetarian on . . .' Shit, what was the day today?

'Oh well, they have sushi as well,' he said.

His brow furrowed in confusion when I only offered a tepid smile in return. I was aware that I was coming off as churlish. Didn't I always fantasise about being treated in style? Like being-flown-to-Italy-for-a-pizza style?

I vowed to be more amenable. I turned to him and smiled brilliantly. That allayed his concern, I think, because he moved closer. His scent, a heady lime 'n' lemony thing, crept up my nostrils and made me giddy. He reached out for my hand and casually laced his fingers through mine. His thumb caressed the palm of my hand, sending mild shock waves through my body. He smiled at me. His dimples are really quite something, I thought hypnotised.

Presently we arrived at the restaurant, Ken-Taro. I had never been there. It was the kind of restaurant where everyone, the maitre d', the waiters, all knew their patrons personally, including their families, business interests, likes, dislikes and hobbies. They certainly knew Kaustav.

The maitre d', a cadaverous Japanese man named Kikuchi, deferentially ushered us to a discreet corner table in a private section away from the main restaurant. He seated us and inconspicuously vanished. Literally. It was like he was there one moment and the next moment he had disappeared. Vaporised.

'Much better for talking,' Kaustav said.

'Ah . . . ummm.'

'What would you like to drink?'

I think I'm already quite drunk, thank you very much. 'Sake?'

He smiled in approval. 'Excellent choice.'

I didn't see him make any moves, slight or overt, but Kikuchi, along with a waiter, magically appeared. Kikuchi held up a bottle of sake while the waiter placed tiny ceramic glasses on the table. Kikuchi poured the rice wine and placed the bottle in an insulated container on the table.

'Cheers,' Kikuchi said, rather occidentally.

We both picked up our glasses and said cheers. The warm rice wine exploded in my mouth in a variety of sensations—stinging, sour, sweet—all of them good. It was so good that I was tempted to quickly finish off the rest. I would have too, but for the fact that it would only have prompted another stopover from Kikuchi.

'So, what do you think?' Kaustav asked.

It's a pretentious restaurant and looks hideously expensive. And that's precisely why it's been chosen. To impress me. 'It's a very nice restaurant.'

'I meant the sake.'

'Oh, the sake! Mmm, it's very good.'

'It is, isn't it? Shall we order?'

'If you want to. I can wait.'

He shot out his hand and started stroking my wrist, near where the pulse is, with his thumb. Goosebumps erupted all over my body and I shivered slightly. I hastily gulped down the wine. 'Tell me about yourself.'

He raised his eyebrows. 'Me? There's nothing much to tell, really. It's all very normal, very staid. You'll soon be bored.'

'Come on, you don't seriously expect me to believe that!'

'You think my life is exciting?'

'Isn't it?'

'Only people outside the industry think it's glamorous. Let me assure you most of it is grit, drudgery, working under inhospitable conditions.'

'So you don't shoot in exotic locales?'

'We do.'

'And you don't consort with glamorous actors and actresses?'

He laughed. 'I see your point. Now you.'

'But I already told you.'

'Not your story. Tell me about you. Who is Katie? What does she like? How does she spend her time? Tell me about the case.'

'My god, you sound like Bhanu Khanna.'

'I do?'

'Katie, I'm working on the character, her quirks, etc. and I would really love some inputs from you,' I said, mimicking Khanna. 'He hasn't put you up to this, has he?'

He laughed. 'How did you guess!'

He was joking, but I was assailed by doubts. Was this why he'd asked me to dinner? So he could pump me for info? I knew that I was being paranoid, but after my disastrous track record with men, who could blame me? Plus, there was Vidisha's jibe about me being blown over for another woman.

'Katie, I'm kidding. Forget it. Let's talk about something else,' he said, lifting my hand and pressing it against his lips. His eyes were warm and liquid, like molten chocolate.

Over the next couple of hours, he chipped away at my defences. He wined and dined me in style. Bottle after bottle of sake and mountains of food mysteriously found their way to our table. He recounted hilarious filmi anecdotes. He finger-fed me the food. He insisted I do the same, sucking on my fingers when I finally did. He aroused the most unbearably erotic sensations in the pit of my stomach.

Heady with physical and sensory gratification, I thought I had to be the worst paranoic to doubt him. Worse, to believe the drunken rantings of a petulant wife. Soon to be ex-wife. He had been nothing if not solicitous. Of course there was no other woman.

Having put my fears to rest, I had no reservations about agreeing when he suggested we go back to his pad for a nightcap. Outside the restaurant, Kaustav dismissed Zuari Mal, saying he would drive us himself. I had my qualms about that, considering the amount we'd drunk, but resisted voicing them out aloud. I've learnt from experience that if you tell a drunk man he's too drunk to drive, more often than not, he'll insist even more on doing it. Then you'll not only have a drunk man behind the wheel, but a drunk driver with something to prove.

Still, I might have risked it had I known his 'pad' was a cosy log cabin in a plush twenty-acre hillside property in Lonavala, a hundred kilometres away. Thankfully, I had no cause to regret my decision and we reached unscathed.

He told me that the property had been passed onto him by his maternal grandfather, Sir Jamshed Desai. 'He used to host hunting parties for his British friends,' Kaustav told me.

I looked outside at the bald mountains silhouetted against the midnight blue sky and giggled. 'What did they hunt? Squirrels?'

Kaustav gave me look. 'The mountains *used* to have lush forests. My mother will tell you they hunted a variety of wildlife—birds, panthers, deer. Especially deer.'

'Of course,' I said chastened.

We made love frenetically. Unfortunately his performance didn't stand up to the foundation he'd laid. Oh, he was good: his hands and mouth teased, nipped, aroused, doused and aroused again till I begged him for release. But for me, the thing that played major spoilsport was his constant need for validation: 'Yeah, baby, you like that?' 'Tell me, you like it.' I'm not a big fan of talking during sex. But hey, different strokes for different folks. At first my umms and aahs sufficed, but later, his demands for a more articulate response grew insistent. At one point, when I was oh-so-close, he suddenly paused and asked, 'Yeah, baby, you like that? Tell me, you like it.' My orgasm receded immediately.

I bit my tongue to stop myself from snapping, 'Let's just get it over with.' But I also knew his ego would never allow him to leave his partner unsatisfied. And I couldn't bear the thought of working myself up all over again. So I just faked it. Immediately, I felt an answering shudder as he climaxed.

Exhausted, we lay back in bed. I would've killed for a cigarette but that wasn't an option. So we talked. I told him all about me. He did the same. Later we slept in each other's arms.

I woke up the next morning feeling vaguely grumpy. And then I saw Kaustav sleeping beside me. I thought about last night.

Although it was frustrating, it wasn't his fault the sex was bad. It happens. I was old enough to know that. Even with Ani, it hadn't been good in the beginning. But over time he'd learnt to please me. Maybe it would be the same with Kaustav.

Still, logic is one thing and acting on it quite another and I couldn't resist kicking him in the shin when he tried to cuddle.

'Ow!' he said sleepily and rolled over.

I immediately felt stupid and, to make up for my childish sulk, snuggled closer to him.

'What time is it?' he mumbled.

'Go back to sleep. It's only seven,' I whispered.

His eyes flew open. 'Seven! I have to go!'

'Go?' I said in dismay. 'Oh but I thought . . .'

'You shameless hussy,' he teased. 'I thought you'd had enough last night.'

Riiigghhht. 'I didn't mean that. I mean, can't you stay?'

'I'd better not. It'll take two hours to reach at this time and there's a morning shoot,' he said.

He got up and headed for the bathroom. Presently, I heard the water running in the shower. I spent a few minutes savouring the early morning quiet.

A message beeped. I reached for my phone lying on the bedside table, but the display screen was dark. It must have been Kaustav's phone. Automatically, my eyes skittered to the chair against the wall. His clothes lay on the seat, neatly folded, just as he'd placed them last night.

The desire to check his phone was strong, but I resisted the urge. *It must be a work related message.* I lay back on the bed, trying to think of other things. *But what if it isn't? You've been cuckolded once before.* My eyes kept going back to his clothes. *I just had to know.* Before I could talk myself out if it, I scampered over and fumbled in the breast pocket of his shirt. I took out his iPhone and slid it open. Sure enough, there was a new message—Kadam asking Kaustav for some clarification on an expense voucher. But there was another message, just below Kadam's one-liner, from someone called MuuMuu. I touched the screen on the ludicrous name and an entire conversation opened.

Kaustav: Good? You were fantastic last night.

MuuMuu: If u think dat was fantastic, then what i have in mind for tonight will blow you away.

Kaustav: Do tell.

MuuMuu: Hw abt i greet u coverd in nothing but whipped cream.

MuuMuu: And high heels. u like?

Kaustav: Like? I've a hard-on like you wouldn't believe.

MuuMuu: hw about a li'l head?

Kaustav: Depends. Spit or swallow?

MuuMuu: swallow.

Kaustav: I'm cumming.

MuuMuu: lol. btw, u no where to cum.

The conversation ran from 1.09 p.m. to 1.34 p.m. yesterday. I pressed call and waited for the line to connect.

'He*n*llon,' A familiar nasal voice greeted me. Mayuri! I disconnected the phone.

The bastard! Vidisha was right. He had ditched me for Mayuri the night before last.

My eye fell on the dresser at the far side of the room. There was an array of jars on it. Creams, lotions, perfumes, hair styling products; my lip curled in distaste. *What a woman.*

The water stopped running in the shower. I hastily moved to replace the phone. As I was fumbling with his clothes, my hands encountered something solid in the pocket of his trousers. Suddenly my phone rang, startling me. I dropped Kaustav's phone with a clatter. It bounced on the hard floor and slipped under the bed. I went down on all fours and tried to reach for it but it had slid in too deep. Meanwhile, my phone continued to ring stridently.

Muttering curses, I looked around for something to reach under the bed with. My eyes spotted a clothes hanger. I grabbed it and tried to sweep the phone out with it. After a few vain stabbing attempts, my hands shaking in nervous haste, the hanger encountered something solid just as the water started running again in the bathroom.

Exhaling in relief, I carefully tugged with the hanger and was surprised when the hanger pushed out not one, but two objects. One was Kaustav's phone and the other was a small box.

I replaced the phone in Kaustav's pocket and shook the box. It rattled with a cacophony of sharp metallic sounds. My phone rang again. I walked over to the bedside and scooped it up, glancing at the display as I did so. 'Deshpande, this had better be . . .' I started to say.

'Coomaar, where are you?'

'My, my, you don't know? What happened to your homing device? Did it stop beaming?'

Silence. 'I don't know what you're talking about.'

'You know those little thingies you attach to an object so you'll know where the object is at any given point of time? Like the one you attached to my RE?'

'I repeat, I don't know what you're talking about. Anyway, where are you?'

I was about to retort smartly, but something about the urgency of his tone stopped me. 'I'm not at home.'

'I got that much. Where? I need to talk to you.'

'Uh . . . now is not a good time.'

I sensed him go still. 'You're with someone?'

'So what if I am?' I said petulantly, only later remembering that maybe I should have sounded just a little bit blasé.

Obviously, the snub bounced off him like water off a duck's back. Not that I'd hoped to 'show him' or anything.

'Anyway, I spoke to Sameer Khan. He told me everything. You were right. It wasn't him on all those occasions on the 19th. It was Ahmed. Because, at the time, between nine and eleven p.m. to be precise, Sameer Khan was busy trying to sneak into Kapoor's house to steal his contract with Blazar. This whole charade with Ahmed was engineered by him so if any suspicion fell on him about the missing contract, he could claim he was elsewhere,' he said.

'Obviously he was successful because he's signed the Hollywood project,' I said.

'Trust you to latch onto the one irrelevant thing,' he said caustically.

Dread enveloped me. 'You mean . . .'

'If Sameer Khan was in Kapoor's study, where was Kapoor?'

Chapter Thirty-one

'That's ridiculous! Kaustav could have gone down to the hall. Or to the kitchen. He could have been anywhere else in the house.'

'That's exactly what I said,' Deshpande said. 'But Sameer told me the whole story. He said he was desperate to get out of his contract with Blazar. The Hollywood company was putting pressure on him and he knew he had to get hold of his contract somehow. On the 19th, he went to the Kapoor residence, determined to get in. While he was parked outside, contemplating what to do, he got lucky. He saw Kapoor get up from his chair and switch off the light in his study. A couple of minutes later, Kapoor walked out of the main gate and got into a white Honda Accord that was parked outside. This was around nine.'

'But they don't have a white Honda Accord,' I said stupidly.

'So it was an office car.'

'But Vidisha said she saw him! Twice. She even spoke to him once,' I objected.

'That must've been some feat, with her tongue rammed down another woman's throat five kilometres away. She was at Ego that night, getting hot and heavy with some gal. Naturally, she wasn't wild about it getting out, and that's why she didn't tell us earlier.'

'That *was* on Saturday? 'Cos I spoke to a guy, a Mr Patel, who had seen her but he couldn't be sure which day it was.'

'Chodankar checked it. Patel and he reconstructed the events of the day. It was Saturday.' Deshpande said.

'Then what happened?'

'Sameer knew he had his chance then. After Kaustav drove away, he gave it five minutes and then snuck in past the sleeping guard. But he knew he couldn't get into the house through the main door. While he was wondering how to get in, he noticed a ladder lying just below Kaustav's window. He propped up the ladder and entered Kaustav's room. But then another problem cropped up. While he was looking for his contract, someone had removed the ladder. Sameer was trapped.'

'So how did he leave?'

'How do you think? By the main door. But he spent a long time in Kaustav's room, waiting till things were quiet enough before he could risk leaving. Even then he almost didn't make it. Just as he was at the main door the maid came out of the kitchen. At the last minute Sameer ducked into the nearest room. Otherwise he would've been toast.'

I remembered that Kaustav had asked me out to dinner after I'd told him my theory about Sameer Khan's switcheroo. He obviously knew that Sameer's contract was missing, and he might have guessed when Sameer took it. Was that why he'd asked me out to dinner? Because if I'd spoken with Sameer, his alibi would be blown?

I sat down heavily on the bed. The box slipped from my lifeless hands onto my lap. *Okay, don't panic! There's got to be a reasonable explanation.*

I lowered my voice. 'But it doesn't make sense. Why would he kill Urvashi? He loved her. Agreed, the philandering bastard is hardly the prototype for the ideal boyfriend . . .' I said, my voice rising with each syllable.

'Why are you shouting?'

I lowered my voice again. 'Sorry. But he had nothing to gain by her death. Not even insurance. The company belongs to Vidisha.'

'What if he could kill two birds with one stone? Get rid of Urvashi and frame Vidisha for her murder? As her husband, he would have the power of attorney and practical ownership of Blazar.'

I shifted restlessly on the bed. The movement caused the box to slide to the floor. It cracked open and some jewellery fell out. 'Hold on,' I said. I leaned down and picked up the box. And then I saw it. Winking at me in the morning sun was a diamond solitaire ring with the Bulgari logo on it.

'Oh my god! *Oh god!*' I moaned.

'What?'

'I think I just found Urvashi's missing jewellery.'

'Where?'

'In Kaustav's cabin. On his Lonavala property. What am I going to do?'

'You're there with Kaustav? You have to get out! Coomaar, listen to me. Sameer Khan told us that while looking for his contract, he came across a gun in Kaustav's desk drawer. He couldn't say what millimetre it was, but it wasn't there when Chodankar went with a search warrant.'

My eyes shot to Kaustav's clothes once more. Was that a gun in his pocket?

I heard the bathroom door being unlocked and Kaustav emerged with a towel wrapped around his waist. I hastily hung up on Deshpande and chucked the phone onto the bedside table.

'Did the phone ring?' he asked.

My legs felt weak. 'Phone? Nuh-uh,' I said.

'Really? I thought I heard a ring.' His eyes skidded to the chair where his clothes now lay in a heap.

Shit! I should've folded them carefully. 'I . . . uh . . . was looking for my bra.'

'Uh-uh. This bra?' he said and picked up the offending garment from right under my nose.

I grabbed it. 'This bra.'

He gave me an odd look and walked over to the chair. 'You know what, I changed my mind. Let's spend the day here.'

He casually reached for his trousers and pulled them on. The shirt came on next. He felt his breast pocket and took out his cellphone. He glanced at it and put it back. I went into action then—I wasn't going to wait around for him to shoot me. I hastily pulled on my bra and singlet. I rummaged about and found my jeans under the blanket.

'What are you doing?' he said.

'I just remembered. I've got to go,' I said, pulling on my jeans.

'Rather sudden, isn't it?'

He took out his phone again. He squinted at the display and looked at me speculatively.

He held up the phone. 'It wouldn't have anything to do with this?'

Shit! In my haste I'd forgotten to return to the main screen—the MuuMuu conversation was still open.

I feigned ignorance. 'What's that?'

'You don't know?'

I shook my head. 'Nope. Not a clue. I have to go because I have to do something.'

'Something to do with Sameer Khan?' he said.

My eyes flew to his face. 'How do you know?'

'You told me last night,' he said, giving me a strange look. 'Katie, what's going on?'

'Nothing! I just have to leave!'

He came forward and hugged me. 'But honey, don't you know, you can't leave?'

My heart started pounding. In one fluid move, I twisted around in his grasp and pounded on his bare foot with my heel, just like Sandra Bullock had demonstrated in *Miss Congeniality*. He yelped with pain.

'What do you mean I can't leave?' I said. Taking advantage of his slackened grip, I wriggled out of his arms. I scooped up my shoes, ran out and bolted the door from outside. Shit! Shit! Shit! I'd left my phone inside.

While Kaustav hopped around, muttering profanities inside, I stood leaning against the door, trying to calm my breathing.

'Katie! I only meant there's no transport.'

Oh.

He banged on the door. 'What's going on?' I didn't answer. 'Katie, I know you're there. Answer me.'

'How about you answer me first? Why did you kill Urvashi?' I said.

'I did WHAT?'

'You heard me. And poor Sweety and Aniruddh? And Chawla?'

'Katie, listen to me. I didn't kill anybody. I've never even heard of these people.'

'That's good. But I'm not buying. Where were you on the 19th? And don't say in your study because I know you weren't!'

I could almost hear the wheels of his mind turning frantically. 'I, well, I was with someone, okay? Come on, let me out now. I'll explain everything, I promise.'

'Uh-uh. I'm not buying. Why did you really bring me here? To stop me from going to the police? What are you going to do to me?'

'Don't be ridiculous, Katie. You're being paranoid.'

'Really? You were busy last night. And yet, as soon as I told you about Ahmed and Smeer you decided to take me out? Why? Unless it was to stop me from talking to Smeer? You were afraid it would blow your alibi. You knew Smeer had stolen his contract from your study that night.'

'No! I mean, I always suspected Sameer had stolen his contract. Someone called from the Hollywood company on the 20th and told me Sameer had signed the contract with them. As soon as that happened, I looked for his contract with us, and it was gone. When

I asked Zuari Mal if he'd seen anyone come into the house, he said he saw Bhagwan Ram. Everyone dismissed it as one of his drunken ravings but I had my doubts. Sameer Khan was shooting for *Taaron ki Baraat* that night.' His voice sounded hollow, like he was in the bathroom.

'So?'

'*Taaron ki Baraat* is a mythological drama where Sameer Khan is playing the role of Lord Ram. And I thought, what if he'd come straight from the shoot? Still in his costume?' Why was his voice sounding strange? First it kind of wafted off, like he was far away, and then stronger, like he was close to me. 'It would have made for a good disguise just in case anyone saw him,' he said, from somewhere to my side.

I whipped around. There he was, in the flesh. I bolted, even as he called out, 'Katie!'

I ran out of the house as if my life depended upon it. At first I stayed on the gravelled pathway. But then it occurred to me that this was unwise. I was a sitting duck, just in case he got it into his mind to do a bit of target practice. I veered off the pathway and started zigzagging through the property. The area was thick with prickly shrubs but I dived into them regardless of the thorns. Soon, I was cut and bleeding, but I was too petrified to stop.

I heard the crash of the thick brush behind me and a few muttered curses, as Kaustav gave chase. Suddenly I couldn't hear it anymore and I stopped to catch my breath. I looked around fearfully. Where was he? Just then a twig snapped somewhere to my left.

I started backing away, trying to be quiet. Suddenly he grabbed me from behind. With an ear-splitting yell, I elbowed him in the ribs and kicked him in the shin. With a pained *Oof!* he released me. I waited long enough to see him stagger backwards and then took off once again.

'Katie! What's wrong with you?' he shouted.

'You killed Urvashi. Admit it.'

'I did not!'

'I found her missing jewellery in a box under your bed.'

'What are you talking about?'

I stopped and changed directions. I was going downhill, but then I decided to climb uphill, just to throw him off a bit. I treaded carefully, making as little noise as I could. Fortunately, the post-monsoon heat hadn't seared the vegetation yet and there were few dry leaves.

I was successful in my subterfuge and Kaustav's voice grew fainter as the distance between us increased. Presently, I came upon a small plateau-like clearing. I stopped there to rest awhile, and also to figure out my next course of action. I sat on the edge of the plateau and looked out. It was a clear day and I could see for quite a distance. There, beyond a smaller hill out front was a little grey-blue stream with a small settlement around it. At an estimate, the settlement was at least ten kilometres away. I wondered if I could trek it there and call for help. *Like I had a choice.*

I'd go there but in just a little while, I promised myself. I lay back tiredly and tried to think, to solve the puzzle. I knew I had all the pieces. But frustratingly, things just didn't make sense. There were too many inconsistencies.

I don't know how long I lay there. I must have drifted off at some point. I woke up suddenly and sat up. The sun had risen higher up in the sky and shone down on the stream, making it sparkle. All was calm. A fly buzzed overhead.

For no reason, Baba Vimalanand's haiku went off in my brain. *A man, just alone, also a fly just alone, in the huge drawing room.*

And then more insistently. *A man, just alone, also a fly just alone, in the huge drawing room. A man, just alone, also a fly just alone, in the huge drawing room. A man, just alone, also a fly just alone, in the huge drawing room.*

Of course! That was it.

Awash with adrenalin, I stood up and dusted the seat of my pants. Then, I practically ran all the way down to the cabin. I was so intent upon my mission that I missed the white car parked on the pathway, a little distance from the cabin. I burst into the cabin and ran straight for my phone still lying on the bedside table. I dialled Chodu's number.

As soon as it connected, I shouted, 'I know who did it.'

'Katie! Are you all right? We're on our way there.'

'Did you hear me? I said I know . . .'

I heard the door slam shut behind me and the bolts fall into place. Too late. I remembered the white car on the pathway. 'The white Accord!'

'Emberra actually, but close,' a familiar husky voice said from behind me. I turned around in dismay. Meher Kapoor. And she had a .32 pointed at me. 'Drop the phone.'

One doesn't argue with a .32. I killed the line.

'Kaustav's going to be here any time,' I said.

'Oh please! I sent him back. When I arrived, I found him in quite a state. He said you'd taken off yelling something about him killing Urvashi and three other people. He also said you kept blabbing about Sameer Khan and Ahmed, and them blowing his alibi. So I told him I'd handle it. Tell me, how did you figure it out?'

'It was many things, but a haiku mainly.'

'Oh? Do explain.'

'*A man, just alone, also a fly just alone, in the huge drawing room.* That was the haiku which got me thinking. You see, Sameer Khan said that he sneaked into your house, into Kaustav's study on the 19th. While that shook Kaustav's alibi, it also shook yours. Because, just as Sameer was leaving, your maid came out of the kitchen and he had to duck into a room next to the main door. That's your room. So how come he didn't get caught?'

'Go on.'

'You gave yourself away on two other occasions. The first time we met you were defending Vidisha. You were at pains to point out that only a burglar could have done it. What was it you said? Yeah, "Her room was ransacked, her suitcases rummaged through, her jewellery was missing." How did you know?'

'The DCP told us. He showed us the pictures.'

'He didn't. He couldn't have. He had to photograph the crime scene as it was.'

'So?'

'You know I kept getting the feeling there was a clue in the pictures I took of Hermit Hill. I just couldn't figure out what it was. I got it just now. You see, when I photographed Hermit Hill, Urvashi's suitcase was open. But I had dropped the lid on the suitcase much before Chodankar arrived on the scene. So how could he have photographed it open? How could you have known about it being rummaged through, unless you were the one who did it?'

'Coincidence. Or I could just have assumed it. It's one of the things one assumes when there's a burglary in question.'

'And the second time around. When I came over to your house you said that Vidisha couldn't have climbed up Hermit Hill as she's asthmatic. I asked you why Vidisha didn't tell me herself. The reason she didn't, was because she saw no reason to. I never mentioned anything about the murderer parking below Hermit Hill and walking up the steep hill. So how did you know?'

'Impressive. Unfortunately, you won't live to tell anyone. Lucky, isn't it, that I dropped by today? And to think I was just coming to tell you to lay off my son.' At the unspoken question in my eyes, she said, 'Oh yes, he told me last night he was bringing you here.'

'Why did you do it? To protect your family?'

'My son. I couldn't care less about Vidisha. Urvashi was insisting that Kaustav marry her. Kaustav didn't want to. As if he'd want to marry the slut. But she had something on him. My son had a minor . . . accident, shall we say, some years ago.'

'Jaya Mattoo! Neena wasn't lying. Urvashi wasn't the driver. It was Kaustav!' I blurted.

'Oh, so you know about that?'

'Naturally. I did research everyone's backgrounds for motivation.'

She inclined her head. 'Anyway, Urvashi was threatening to tell the police if my son didn't marry her. Somebody had to stop her. So I went to Hermit Hill to reason with her and also give her assurances. Believe me, I wasn't planning on killing her. But she'd made up her mind and was in no mood to listen. So I had no option but to go back up, sneak up on her and kill her.'

'How did you know about Hermit Hill?'

'Why, Kaustav told me. And Vidisha. You see, there are too many leaks in the company. And Kaustav didn't trust anybody not to prattle to the media about the publicity stunt. So he hatched this scheme along with Urvashi whereby, after Chandan Baweja left Serenity Villa, she would too. He asked her to suggest some place where she could hole up. She mentioned Hermit Hill and that's how she came to be there.'

She had her back to the window whereas I had a clear view of the outside from where I was standing. My gaze was fixed on Meher Kapoor but from the corner of my eye I saw a Cherokee glide up noiselessly. A moment later, Deshpande got out.

'What about Sweety Nair?' I yelled before Deshpande banged the door shut and alerted her. He got the message and left the door open, motioning to someone inside to keep quiet.

Fortunately, Meher Kapoor thought my sudden outburst was one of outrage. 'Piggy on the railway,' she said, in a bored kind of way. Noting the look of confusion on my face, she explained, 'You know the nursery rhyme: Piggy on the railway, picking up stones. Down came an engine, and broke piggy's bones. "Ah," said the Piggy, "that's not fair", "Oh", said the engine driver, "I don't care". She was simply in the way.'

I chanced a glance behind her. Chodu had alighted from the car, as had Kaustav. I saw Kaustav motioning towards the back of the cabin. The other two nodded in understanding and hot-stepped it to the rear.

Desperate to keep her talking, I said, 'It was her, wasn't it, in the BMW you had a bang-up with?'

She nodded. 'I had to kill her because she could place me, my car at any rate, at Hermit Hill on the 19th. Luckily for me, she, very considerately, left her name and contact details on my windscreen.'

'So, it was you who called her husband early on 20th morning?'

'Of course I had been trying to contact her since the night before but there was no answer. And after I spoke with the husband, I couldn't risk calling again. So I did a little voice distortion and hired Chawla. He found her for me. Then I fixed a meeting with her on the pretence of discussing the damages to both our cars. She hadn't read the papers and didn't suspect a thing. She let me in and even offered me a soft drink. Then all I had to do was distract her and slip a little something into her glass. It was that simple.'

'Then why Aniruddh Nair? Was he a piggy too?'

She shrugged. 'Just a little extra insurance. Sweety told me she'd told her husband about the accident. I didn't know just how much. I couldn't take the risk. I already knew where they lived. So I just followed him from there to his office. I got my opportunity when he stepped into the crowded street. Then it was as simple as stepping in behind him, a quick stab and stepping off the street. Poor guy, I saw him turn around and look behind him in bewilderment. He didn't even know what happened. And then Chawla.'

'That's what I don't understand. Why him? He never even saw you!'

Where the fuck were they? I was running out of things to say.

'Oh but he did. In Blazar that day, with you. And he started blackmailing me. Apparently, after I'd told him the assignment was over, he hung around the Nair residence. He saw me enter the Nair residence. He told me he didn't think too much of it at the time because Sweety Nair was alive when I left. She even saw me out. But later, when he saw me in Blazar, he put two and two together. Anyway, now it's all over.'

Just then, Deshpande and Chodu burst into the room. 'Drop it!'

She hesitated and then her gaze returned to me. For a moment, one long horrible moment, I thought she was going to shoot me.

And then Kaustav stepped in behind them. 'It's over, Mom.'

With a curt nod, she dropped the gun to the floor. Deshpande swiftly advanced and picked up the gun, while Chodu slapped a pair of handcuffs around Meher Kapoor's wrists.

Sobbing with relief, I rushed into Deshpande's arms.

He held me. 'It's okay. You're safe now.'

'And not a moment too soon,' I said, tearfully. 'You took your own sweet time!'

He gave a low laugh. 'You're welcome.'

I looked up at Deshpande. 'Don't be too hasty in welcoming me,' I said. 'I still haven't stopped looking into your affairs.'

He smiled. 'You'll never find anything on me.'

I sighed contentedly and nestled in closer to his body. When I looked up I saw Chodu looking at us, his expression unreadable. I stepped out of Deshpande's embrace.

'I'm okay now,' I sniffed.

He took a step forward. 'Katie . . .'

That was the first time he'd called me by my name. I liked the sound of my name rolling off his lips.

'I said, I'm okay,' I said shrilly.

He stopped and nodded. Without a word, he turned and joined Chodu. Together they left, herding Meher and Kaustav out with them.